FRANK J. CAMACHO

THE MONSTERS' THEY MADE US

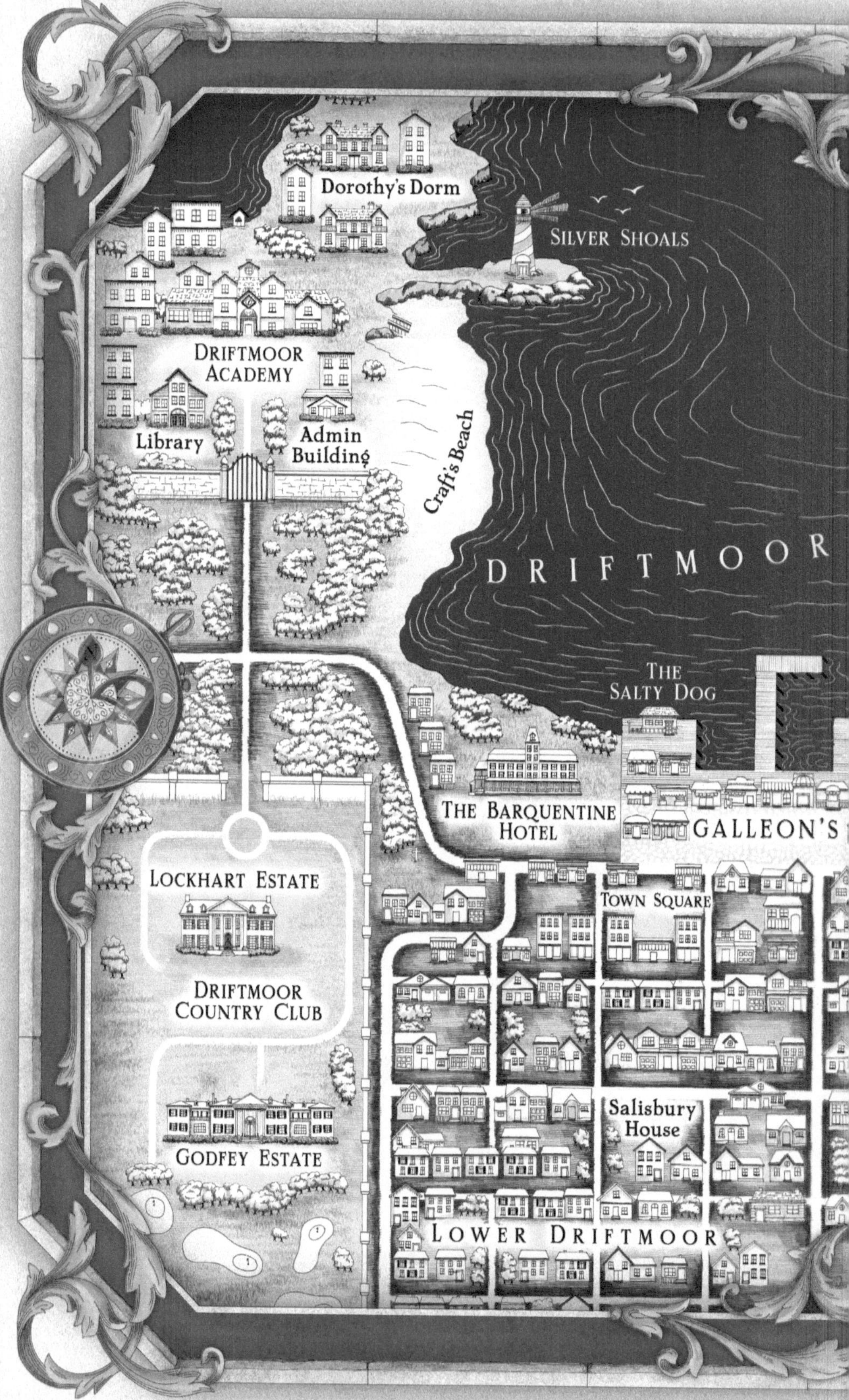

Dorothy's Dorm
SILVER SHOALS
DRIFTMOOR ACADEMY
Library
Admin Building
Craft's Beach
DRIFTMOOR
THE SALTY DOG
THE BARQUENTINE HOTEL
GALLEON'S
LOCKHART ESTATE
DRIFTMOOR COUNTRY CLUB
TOWN SQUARE
GODFEY ESTATE
Salisbury House
LOWER DRIFTMOOR
N

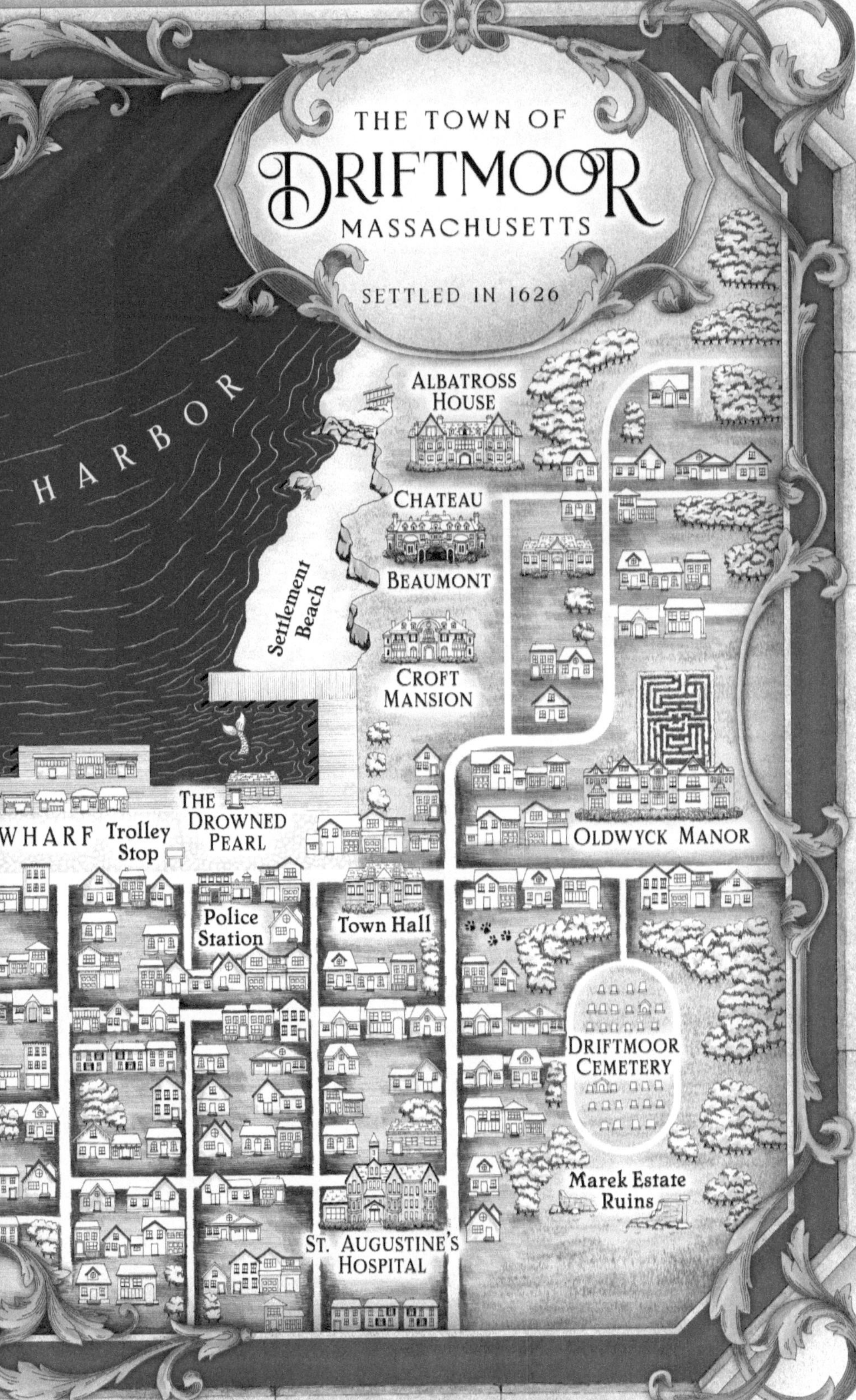

THE TOWN OF
DRIFTMOOR
MASSACHUSETTS
SETTLED IN 1626
HARBOR
ALBATROSS HOUSE
CHATEAU BEAUMONT
Settlement Beach
CROFT MANSION
THE DROWNED PEARL
WHARF
Trolley Stop
OLDWYCK MANOR
Police Station
Town Hall
DRIFTMOOR CEMETERY
Marek Estate Ruins
ST. AUGUSTINE'S HOSPITAL

The Monsters They Made Us

ISBN: 979-8-9987818-2-7 (eBook)
ISBN: 979-8-9987818-0-3 (paperback)
ISBN: 979-8-9987818-1-0 (hardback)

Library of Congress Control Number: 2025900480

Cover Design and Illustration by Tim Byrne
Map Illustration by Travis Hasenour/To the Moon and Back Design
Interior Design by Ashley Holstrom

First Edition 2025

Printed in United States of America

frankjcamacho.com

For Jason, who held me together while I created this world.

And to those who have ever felt haunted by their own story.

PART ONE

September

Summer dies slowly in Driftmoor. The sun lingers too long, as if it doesn't know it's no longer welcome. Shadows stretch before they darken. In September, everything still looks golden, until you look too closely.
—*From the diary of a Driftmoor Academy student, 1913*

CHAPTER 1

Dorothy Hale

BLOOD GUSHED FROM DOROTHY'S NOSE AS HER HEAD WHIPPED FOR-ward, then slammed against the seat. The car flipped, wrenching her from gravity and hurling her into chaos. Metal shrieked against the asphalt, each jolt rattling through her bones as shards of glass burst across her skin like fractured stars. For a moment, they might've been dazzling. Ethereal, even. But death lurked too close for beauty to matter.

For a breathless second, the tumbling ceased, and the car floated through the night, suspended between what was and what would be.

Then came the crash. Brutal. Absolute. And unforgiving.

Dorothy woke gasping, hospital air dragging her back into a life that no longer felt like hers. The accident clung to her like a nightmare, but the ache in her spirit, the pull of stitches at her shoulder, and the bruises blooming plum and ochre left no doubt that it had been real.

The pain she could endure. It was the quiet and bottomless guilt that hollowed her out and left her staring at nothing.

"You haven't touched your food again," Sister Alma said from the chair by the window.

Dorothy cast a glance at the lunch tray beside her bed. Mashed potatoes slumped next to a watery tangle of vegetables, both congealing under the fluorescent lights. Somewhere down the hall, a monitor beeped.

"I'm not hungry," she muttered, eyes fixed on the scratches where glass had been plucked from her arms. The skin was rosy and taut, but it didn't look healed. It looked unresolved, like her body had moved on while the rest of her was still dead on the side of the road for those few minutes.

The click of beads drew her attention across the room. The sun streaked Alma's hair with silver and deepened the lines around her mouth as her fingers moved over a rosary.

"How is he?" Dorothy asked, knowing the answer wouldn't make her feel any better.

Alma lowered the rosary into her lap. "He had another surgery this morning, but the doctors aren't sure." She adjusted her skirt with slow motions. "All we can do is wait and pray."

Dorothy's eyes drifted to the crucifix, its shadow distorted by the sunlight coming in through the high, grimy window. Back home, her parents never prayed. She couldn't remember ever touching a Bible, let alone stepping inside a church. God had always been a stranger in their home, a place shaped more by struggle than faith. But a few days ago, Alma had said that God brought her back to life for a reason. "You may not understand it now," she'd said, "but He does nothing without purpose."

Dorothy had nodded to hold back the bitter questions. *If there was a purpose, why had Elliot died? Why was Jack hooked up to machines? What kind of god needed a purpose like that?*

The memory passed, but its weight remained.

Dorothy inhaled shakily, then let the words she'd been holding spill.

"I know it doesn't make sense," she murmured, her fingers worrying the edge of her hospital gown. "But I can't shake it. This feeling that something's going to go wrong. That he's not going to be okay."

Alma laid her hand over Dorothy's. "I know this feels heavy, child," she said. "But give it to the Lord, little by little. Even the saints didn't surrender all at once."

Dorothy's eyes traced the constellations of age on Alma's skin, each spot a mark of time and endurance. She wondered what they'd seen, what losses, what hauntings. Would her body one day bear such proof of survival? Or would it all stop before then?

"Perhaps you could draw." Alma nodded toward the sketchbook on the nightstand. "Sometimes the soul speaks through our hands when our hearts are too tired."

Dorothy managed a faint smile. "Yeah, maybe."

Alma gently patted her arm and stood. Her shoes clicked against the linoleum as she stepped into the hall. The door stayed ajar, letting in the noise of hospital life: carts squeaking, a TV crackling with static, nurses murmuring over notes. Further down the corridor, a child coughed, thin and persistent.

Dorothy picked up her sketchbook. An ache pinched at her shoulder where stitches pulled beneath the bandages. Its corners were frayed from her carrying it around. She loved drawing birds and capturing them mid-flight, as if she could trap their freedom in graphite. But now, the blank pages waited like a void she didn't dare cross. Her fingers hovered, twitching with the urge to create, but the anxiety thrumming beneath her skin kept her frozen. Every creak of the bed, every shuffle in the hallway made her flinch. The world had shifted. And she didn't know how to meet it with lines.

Long after St. Augustine quieted, Dorothy lay awake, staring at the water-stained ceiling. The sheets were stiff, the air too still, but it wasn't the discomfort keeping her up. It was Jack. Except when she thought of him, it wasn't the beeping machines or the sterile scent of antiseptic that rose first. It was that evening at Albatross House, the cusp of summer giving way to fall. The air had carried a faint chill, like a warning. Lamps glowed in the drawing room, casting halos over frayed velvet and mahogany polished thin by time. Laughter had echoed down the halls—low, rich, effortless—a world she didn't belong in. But somehow he'd seen her anyway. And in that sprawling house full of chandeliers and ancestral portraits, Jack had made space for her. A seat beside him. A look that lingered.

A sob beyond the door snapped her back.

She sat up, swinging her legs over the bedside. Cold linoleum met her feet as she padded toward the hall. Her hospital gown grazed her knees, its loose ties swaying behind her with each step. The young nurse didn't notice her approach. She was leaning over the nurses' station with her face in a crumpled tissue.

"Are you okay?" Dorothy hugged her arms close.

The nurse turned quickly. "You scared me. You shouldn't be out of bed," she said. "Are you okay? Did you need water or something?"

"I'm fine, thanks. But I heard you crying."

The nurse gave a short laugh. "Oh, sorry. Didn't mean to wake you. It's just girlfriend troubles. She dumped me. Over dinner, if you can believe that."

Dorothy lingered in front of the counter. "I'm sorry," she said, though the words felt borrowed, like a phrase she was supposed to know how to use. She'd only seen heartbreak in movies or overheard in bathroom stalls. She'd never had a boyfriend or been held in the way other seventeen-year-olds mused about to their friends. Love had always been something that happened to other people.

The nurse blinked her tears away. "It's dumb, isn't it? Me falling apart over a breakup while you're all beaten and battered."

Dorothy didn't know what to say. Maybe she'd never been in love, but she knew the ache of being alone. She thought of her parents, thousands of miles away, trying to figure out how to afford a visit.

"It could be worse," she said. "That's what my dad always says. I don't know if he really believes it though."

He'd say it as if pain could be measured, compared, and filed into categories: bad, worse, worst. As if knowing it could be worse was supposed to make her feel better.

The nurse's lips twitched. "He's probably right." She waved Dorothy off back toward the rooms. "You should go on back to bed now. Before Alma catches you."

Dorothy offered a fleeting smile before turning away. But she didn't return to her room. Instead, she sneaked down the corridor, drawn by something she couldn't name. The hush of night clung to the wallpaper, broken only by the whir of machines and the occasional shuffle of nurses behind closed doors.

She paused near the end of the hall. A door had been left slightly open where a patient lay beneath a nest of wires and blankets. Elderly, unmoving. The monitor beside them ticked out a weak rhythm. Dorothy stood in the doorway, hands curling against her sides. Her gaze drifted to the patient's chest, rising only slightly with each breath. Something twisted low in her ribs. Not sadness. More like a presence.

She backed away before she understood why.

A few doors down, she stopped outside a room she'd visited more than once in the last three weeks. The chart read: *Jack M. Salisbury.* Her hand trembled as she eased the door open.

He lay beneath a tangle of tubes and wires, his body connected to monitors and IV lines. His wounded face held the waxy undertone of a person caught between life and death. There was no trace of that easy grin. No spark in his gaze that had made her feel seen. What lay before her wasn't Jack. It was stillness dressed as survival.

"I'm sorry," she whispered from the foot of his bed. "I'm so sorry this happened."

In the corner, the television flickered to life, static blooming across the screen. White noise seeped into her pores and hummed in her teeth. And before she could make sense of it, the screen went black.

Dorothy looked back at Jack. At first, she thought it was a trick of the light. But a shadow hovered above him, faceless, rippling, its edges flickering in the monitor's glow. Its limbs unfurled, coiling like smoke that learned to breathe. It didn't just loom; it inhaled him.

Her breath caught as something cold brushed the back of her neck. She couldn't move. Couldn't blink. It was like her bones recognized a threat her mind couldn't name. She pressed a hand to her chest. A pressure curled in her throat. Beneath the humming machines came a whispered language foreign to her tongue but fluent in her bones. It rushed in like waves as the room shrank, her fingers clawing at her temples. It wasn't the machines or the television. Her knees gave out, and she dropped hard, catching herself on trembling hands. Pain shot up her arms, but it was nothing compared to the force building in her. The scream didn't rise from her throat. It erupted from marrow and memory and shattered the air.

The overhead lights pulsed violently, casting the room in a strobe of flashes. Jack's monitor shrieked. Its green lines fractured, spiking and collapsing in erratic fits as his body jolted against the mattress. The machines glitched like they were reacting to more than just his vitals. Like they were reacting to her.

Dorothy continued screaming. The sound tore from her throat, raw and full of something older than fear. The air cracked around her, as if the room itself had recoiled. The shadow had swallowed Jack whole—only the outline of his body remained, dim beneath the flick-ering lights. It loomed over him, faceless and shifting, like it was draw-ing the life out of him.

Footsteps thundered down the hall right before the door burst open. Alma stepped in first, her rosary clenched tight, beads clinking with every breathless step. A nurse followed, her eyes scanning the chaos, heels skidding slightly on the linoleum.

Alma's face twisted. "Blessed Mary."

She dropped beside Dorothy and clutched her shoulders as Dorothy wailed. "Lord have mercy," she whispered, eyes lifted toward the ceiling.

Dorothy nails caught in Alma's tunic as the scream fractured, folding into a sob.

"I'm right here," Alma said, her voice steady, even as the machines shrieked and the shadow above Jack recoiled into the corner.

The nurse moved swiftly—a flash of silver, then a needle. Warmth bloomed through Dorothy's veins. Her body began to sag as her limbs grew heavy, and the lights steadied into a blur. Alma's prayers gradually thinned into whispers. And just before darkness claimed her, Dorothy looked up and saw Jack staring with hollow eyes.

CHAPTER 2
Lola Godfrey

LOLA SAT AT HER VANITY, WRAPPED IN A SILK ROBE THAT OFFERED little comfort against the restlessness inside her. The room glowed with curated elegance—perfume bottles catching the chandelier's soft light, velvet cushions in blush and ivory arranged just so. Her jewelry box sat open, its contents a careless profusion of pearls and gold spilling like secrets. She traced her collarbone, as if searching for proof that she was there. These treasures around her—the excess sculpted for admiration—felt meaningless. They were merely trinkets of status. Shiny distractions that never filled the space they were meant to, no matter how high she let them pile.

Beyond the window veiled in sheer curtains, the harbor reflected streaks of rose and saffron, reluctant to yield the first night of autumn. Color bled across the sky, plunging Driftmoor in that momentary limbo between light and dark.

Lola turned back to the vanity, reaching for her silver-plated hairbrush, then paused. A bracelet peeked out from beneath a jumble of necklaces and brooches. She picked it up, twirling it between her fingers. Each thread held a color. And each color held a memory. The kind made of summer-kissed tans and slumber parties that stretched till morning. The kind that didn't glitter but stayed.

A knock at the door pulled her from the thoughts.

"Miss Lola?" Miriam said.

"Yes, Miriam?" Lola's hazel eyes remained on the bracelet.

"The car is ready. Shall I tell Xavier you're coming down?"

Lola held the bracelet up in the light, half-tempted to see how it looked on her again.

"Tell him to keep the engine running. I shouldn't be long," she said.

"Very well," Miriam replied, slipping away as silently as she'd appeared.

Lola dropped the bracelet back on the vanity. She picked up her lipstick and dragged the pomegranate shade across her lips. She leaned closer, adjusting a stray lash and noticed the photograph tucked in the mirror's corner: she and her friends standing in front of the lighthouse, frozen at thirteen. That day returned in fragments. Heather's sunburnt cheeks, sorbet melting down their wrists, laughter clinging to the warmth of an endless, cruel summer. But a thick black slash cut through the center, right over Ophelia's face.

Driftmoor still carried traces of her. She lingered in the cracks of the sidewalks, in the salt-streaked air, in the rusted carousel at Galleon's Wharf. It was as if she'd never left, and yet, everything she touched had curdled in her absence.

Three years ago, Lola would've given anything to see her. She'd prayed for it during sleepless nights, rehearsed words that might mend what had broken. But in the mirror, her reflection warped with disillusionment. Ophelia's return wasn't a miracle. It was a sadistic joke, arriving when it no longer mattered.

Lola stared at the photograph again. The ache in her ribs spread, pressing against the parts she kept hidden. Ophelia's return wasn't just a nuisance or a threat to her social standing. It was worse than that. It was another mirror forcing Lola to confront the parts of herself that had never been whole without her. And she hated that. Hated how easily Ophelia could fracture the illusion of control she'd spent years building.

The town car crunched into the gravel lot at Craft's Beach. Xavier stepped out to open the rear door. Lola emerged, heels clicking against the stones, her frame wrapped in a wool coat lined with satin. Beneath it, she wore a pleated skirt the color of dried roses and a high-neck blouse fastened with a velvet ribbon. A cardigan was draped over her shoulders, not for warmth, but to soften the severity of the rest. The wind tugged at her hair and bit through the wool, but she pulled it closer, chin lifting.

Silver Shoals rose ahead, the lighthouse framed by the lavender wash of approaching twilight.

"Thank you," she said to Xavier. "If you don't hear from me in five minutes, you're allowed to leave."

He nodded before returning to the car.

She stood before the steel door, fingers curled around the handle. The Founders' Ball was hours away, and she should've been home curling her hair, perfecting her makeup, but she was here instead, minutes from possibly making a mistake.

The air hung thick with brine and the breath of rotting wood. The cast-iron steps groaned beneath her while rust flaked where her hand skimmed the rail. She could turn back and walk away from this. But no. She had to face it, even if every instinct screamed to run back home.

Through clouded portholes, the harbor flickered in glimpses, whitecaps crashing into the rocks below. At the top, the lantern room opened in a mosaic of light and shadow.

"Hello?" Her voice bounced against the walls.

The room stood littered with past gatherings: cigarette butts, broken bottles, and beach chairs cloaked in dust and cobwebs. At the center, the lantern loomed like a relic. She couldn't recall the last time the lighthouse lit up.

"Ophelia?" she called, stepping onto the balcony.

Wind caught in her hair, whipping strands into her eyes and mouth. She pushed them away and squinted toward the cliffs, where Driftmoor's mansions rose like gods. Terraces and loggias spilled along the bluffs, their towering windows aglow with candlelight.

"Boo."

Lola spun, heart lurching.

Ophelia stepped from the curve of the lighthouse, her fox-shaped face curled in a smirk. Even after all this time, Lola felt that same jolt of weaponized beauty. She looked heavenly. Lola couldn't remember a day in her life where she didn't. The gown clung in all the right places, the breeze doing half the work. It was infuriating. And breathtaking.

"You're still too easy," Ophelia said, crossing her arms.

Lola smoothed her cardigan. "That wasn't funny," she said. "But I suppose cheap thrills have always been your specialty."

"Maybe not for you."

Lola planted her heels on the grate. "Enough with the games. I came for answers. Not theatrics."

"I'm surprised you're even here." Ophelia walked up to the railing. "I honestly thought you'd ignore my call."

"Like the way you ignored mine all those years ago?"

Ophelia traced patterns along the railing. "So tell me. What'd I miss?"

Yale came to mind first, a moment Lola had once dreamed of celebrating with her best friend. Then Declan's parents' divorce, which hollowed him in ways he refused to admit to. And her brother's promotion to colonel, news their mother had dismissed because her only son was drifting further from the family. While Ophelia was gone, the world both ended and began again. She'd walked away from a life, but none of Lola's milestones felt like the right place to start.

"I'd ask where you've been, but I doubt I'd get the truth," Lola said. "You've been back for weeks and haven't said a word to Declan. Why?"

Ophelia's smirk faltered. "I have nothing to say to him."

"Please. You broke his heart. And let's not forget the money you stole from him. Or are we pretending that didn't happen?" Metal groaned underfoot as Lola stepped forward. "Don't you think you at least owe him so much as a flimsy excuse?"

The color drained from Ophelia's face. "Let me guess. He put you up to this?"

"He doesn't even know we've been in contact. If he did, trust me, he'd be far less merciful than I'm being."

A memory flared—fourteen, pounding on the Lockhart's door, her voice cracking as she begged to see Ophelia. She shoved it away before it could sink its teeth in.

"You can't just come back and pretend like you didn't just abandon us," she said.

"You want to know why I left?" Ophelia gripped the railing. "Because staying would've killed me. Driftmoor, Declan, my parents, you. Every second here made me hate myself."

There were nights when Lola whispered her own grievances to the dark because of how Driftmoor had felt more like a cage than a home. She'd suffocated beneath the demands of a scripted life and resented a future carved without her say. But that didn't mean Ophelia deserved pity. Whatever burdens she bore, whatever demons she fled, none excused the way she left.

"You think playing victim suits you?" Lola asked. "Or is this your way of covering up the fact that you knew you'd always be second best?"

Ophelia's knuckles whitened around the railing, her mouth tightening as tears filled her eyes. Lola thought she might break or that she might apologize. But instead, she lunged at her.

Her fingers tangled in Lola's hair, yanking her sideways until her spine struck the railing.

"What the hell, Ophelia!" she gasped, scrambling for balance.

Ophelia's grip tightened, eyes wide and feral.

Lola clawed at her wrists as her heels slipped on the grating. Wind howled around them. Below, the sea slammed into the rocks like an audience eager for tragedy. She was losing as the railing dug into her back—until it didn't.

Metal snapped.

Ophelia's fury shattered, replaced by shock. Lola reached for her and missed.

The lighthouse reeled away as wind screamed past her ears. She twisted midair, the sky spinning out of focus. By the time she turned her head, the fall was nearly over. The rocks rose fast as if the ocean had been waiting for her all along.

CHAPTER 3
Declan Albatross

EVERYONE ASSUMED DECLAN FLOURISHED AT EVENTS LIKE THIS. GALA dinners, fundraisers, nights heavy with names and futures. And maybe he had, once. But tonight, his smile felt thin. He moved through the Founders' Ball with practiced charm, his anxieties tucked neatly behind it. Faces lit up as he passed. He offered hellos despite the tightness in his chest, posed for photos, lingered just long enough for small talk. His green eyes swept the ballroom but never settled, always flicking, never connecting. Classmates and professors showered him with praise and good lucks, their enthusiasm almost dizzying. But not one of them noticed Lola was missing.

Marble columns veined with gold framed the Barquentine Hotel's ballroom, stretching toward the ceiling where a medallion cradled the chandelier. Cascades of crystals scattered light across the parquet floor. Conversations rose and fell, punctuated by laughter and the clink of glassware. Along the walls, mirrors caught flashes of guests: the tilt of a champagne flute, the flick of a fan, a diamond glinting at a woman's throat.

Declan kept glancing toward the entrance, expecting Lola to walk in. They were supposed to navigate this night together. Without her, everything felt off-kilter.

Movement cut through the crowd.

"Mr. Albatross!" Headmistress Mortimer waved at him, her silver-streaked hair piled high beneath a jeweled comb. She wore a gown that trailed behind her, its sleeves lined in velvet that shimmered as she moved. "You look dashing, though I expected nothing less," she said. "Will Doris be joining us? I was hoping to see her, but she never responded to my invitation."

He cleared his throat and forced a smile. "Unfortunately, she's abroad on business at the moment, but I'll make sure she hears you said hello."

Mortimer's gaze held his. "There's no need for lies with me." She touched his arm, her rings cool against his sleeve. "Your mother was unforgettable as queen, but you—you're carving your own path. Whatever tonight brings, she would be proud of the young man you've become."

Declan had the grades, the record, the recommendations. On paper, he'd done everything right. But her words still landed wrong. Pride wasn't something he aimed for. Results were. And right now, he wasn't sure what this evening would result in. Only that he wasn't in control of it.

"Thank you, Headmistress," he said, managing a nod.

"Wishing you all the luck tonight," she said. "Also, when you see Miss Godfrey, please tell her that I'd like to speak with her about the upcoming fundraiser."

She walked away toward a cluster of professors and townspeople, her presence drawing subtle nods as she passed.

He scanned the ballroom again. Chandeliers spilled over a sea of gowns and tuxedos. Familiar faces passed in waves—classmates, professors, family friends—each one present, except for Lola. She wouldn't have missed the Founders' Ball. Not when they were supposed to be crowned together. They'd campaigned as a team, practiced their waltz for hours, whispered strategies like it mattered. If she was angry, she'd make an entrance that left no one breathing. If she were sick, she'd find a way to be seen. Lola didn't disappear. And yet, in the blur of servers balancing silver trays and orchestral flourishes, she was nowhere.

"Who are you looking for?"

Declan's shoulders eased when he saw Aiden. The sharp lines of his dark suit contrasted with the softness of his features—freckled cheekbones, mussed waves, the smudge of tiredness beneath red-rimmed eyes like he hadn't slept or had been crying. Maybe it was allergies, but Declan doubted it.

"Everything okay?" he asked, eyeing him more closely.

Aiden's expression shifted. Just a flicker. But enough. "Of course. Just Heather being Heather," he said. A weak smile followed, the kind used to smooth over discomfort. "I see there's still no sign of Lola?"

"No. I tried calling her, but she didn't answer. I'm thinking of calling her brother, but I don't want to make a big deal, and it turns out she just had a wardrobe malfunction."

Aiden reached for Declan's collar. "Your bowtie's crooked," he said.

It was a simple gesture. A friend helping him look presentable, but the brush of Aiden's fingers at his neck made his chest seize. He glanced at the concentration in Aiden's brown eyes and felt the floor tilt slightly beneath him.

"There." Aiden's touch lingered before falling back to his sides. "I'm sure she'll show up. It's Lola. She has to."

"You're right," Declan murmured. A pause, then: "I'm glad you're here."

Aiden looked at him and an unspoken acknowledgement passed between them. Aiden wasn't supposed to make it to senior year. Not with everything stacked against him.

"I wouldn't have done it without you," Aiden said.

Before either of them spoke, the conversations around them began to fade into whispers, subtle and contagious, pulling the room's attention toward the entrance. Declan didn't look right away. But an unexpected force was threading into the atmosphere. He straightened instinctively, certain it was Lola, making her grand entrance at last. But the spark vanished just as fast.

Ophelia entered the ballroom as if no time had passed at all. Her dress shimmered like constellations stitched into silk. A clutch dangled from her hand, and her lips were painted a deep hue of pomegranates. Her deep blue gaze was the kind people leaned into, desperate to believe they'd been chosen by the girl everyone wanted. Declan knew that allure all too well. Just like he knew now, that looking into those eyes meant searching for someone who was never really there.

Beside him, Aiden looked at Ophelia, then back at Declan.

She didn't glance around for old friends. Didn't pause for greetings or offer explanations to once-favorite professors. She never had to. Driftmoor had always reshaped itself for Ophelia Lockhart, and tonight was no different.

Questions Declan had buried out of self-preservation resurfaced: *Why hadn't she said goodbye? Why leave like that, like he was nothing? Had any of it meant what he thought it did?* He'd spent three years unlearning the reflex to search for her in hallways, to stop glancing at shadows, hoping one might become her. But Ophelia had never been the storm he told himself she was. Storms pass. She had been the house. And he'd been trapped, wasting time in rooms she left empty, breathing stale air that still carried her perfume.

Now she stood just beyond the crowd, close enough to reach, yet light years away.

Yes, she was back. But he wanted her to hurt. To know what it felt like to be the one left behind. To haunt a love that no longer belonged to you. To live in the wreckage while the other person walked away. But more than anything, he wanted to understand why she'd left. Because no matter how many reasons he had to hate her, he still didn't know how to let her go.

CHAPTER 4

Dorothy Hale

A panic attack. That's what her doctor had called last night's episode.

Dorothy wanted to believe that. She wanted to categorize her confusion and to distill her experience into something clinical. But genuine panic was suffocating, tightening its grip until every sense heightened. She hadn't felt any of that. The scream she had let out hadn't come from fear or discomfort. It had risen from a part of her she hadn't realized ever existed. And now that it was free, she wasn't sure she could silence it.

The next day, dread swelled through St. Augustine's halls like old wallpaper—impossible to peel away. It pulsed beneath the linoleum floors that had been worn smooth by restless pacing. She heard it in the rattling gurneys and in the hushed voices of nurses. It was in the sighs of those waiting for news that would break them. Dread had entered the hospital with her, and she had no idea why.

A knock sounded at her door.

She glanced up, expecting Alma, but her stomach dropped at the sight of her father. A rumpled button-down clung to him, sleeves rolled to the elbows while his hair, once dark and parted, had faded to a soft ash at the temples. Dark circles pooled beneath the blue eyes she had hope hers would one day mirror. Hers were murkier—green-gray like swamp water, the kind her mother had always said skipped a generation. *Your grandmother had eyes like that*, she'd say. A woman Dorothy barely remembered, all mothball perfume and silence, with hands that trembled and a voice like wet paper. The kind of woman who saw too much and said too little.

The door shut with a soft click, but Dorothy's body stiffened. She didn't need to see his face to know the look that would follow. Richard Hale stood there, shoulders tight, jaw clenched, eyes scanning her the way he used to after report cards or sleeping in. His gazed dragged over her bruises, the hospital bracelet around her wrist, and his expression hardened into anger.

"A party?" he said. "What were you thinking?"

"Dad, I–I didn't mean for this to happen."

"You weren't thinking." He let out a breath. "Do you know what it's like to get that kind of call? I thought I was going to have to come here and—" He rubbed his face. "I thought I'd be identifying your body. Can you imagine that?"

She'd lived it from the other end, bracing herself in the wreckage, wondering if she'd ever see him again. But he wasn't asking. He was hurting. And he wanted someone to blame.

"Dad...I'm so sorry. I really am."

He paced. One hand raked through his hair, the other clenched at his side.

"I said this would happen," he muttered. "Told your mother a place like this wasn't built for you." He didn't look at her—just past her, to the wall, the machines, the future unspooling behind his eyes. "Those other kids, they'll bounce back. They've got nets. Names. But you? One mistake like this and it sticks. It changes things."

Each word cut deeper than the ache in her shoulder. Her throat burned. The tears hovered, but she refused to let them fall in front of him. He'd use them as proof she was too gentle for this place. Or worse, pretend he hadn't seen them at all.

"I'm not trying to control your life," he said finally. His voice softened. Not enough to be comforting, just enough to suggest he regretted how hard he'd come in. "But you need to get it together. This scholarship—this place—it's not a safety net. It is a once in a lifetime opportunity. And these people will write you off before you even get the chance to prove them wrong."

She bit the inside of her cheek. "Yeah. I understand," she said. "I'll make sure nothing like this ever happens again. Promise."

He looked at her long enough that she thought he might say something kind. His mouth opened, then closed again, as he rubbed his temples with a sigh.

"I need to check into my hotel. I'll stop by later." His fingers tapped the doorframe. "Try to get some rest."

He walked away before Dorothy could summon the courage to call him back.

But even if she had, she wasn't sure what she would've said.

Dorothy lay in bed, staring at the crucifix, as its shadow twisted in ways that didn't match the lamp's flicker. Seeing her father had sent her mind back to Seattle, to the apartment she'd once hated but now yearned for. She missed her bed with its creaky springs. She missed the clamoring pipes behind the kitchen wall and even the draft in the bathroom their landlord never fixed. But most of all, she missed the simplicity of the life she had before all this. Her eyelids grew heavy as sleep took hold. Thoughts slipped into that liminal space between waking and dream, where memory blurred and nothing held shape. She felt herself drifting, until a cold shift prickled down her arms. Her fingers twitched against the blanket, as if reaching for the night.

Then—

A shrill ringing yanked her eyes open. But something was off.

She couldn't move.

Her body was locked and pinned to the mattress as if the weight of the entire room had settled on her chest. Gravity squeezed the oxygen from her lungs in slow, deliberate increments. It felt like someone was sitting on her—watching. Her limbs refused to move, frozen beneath the pressure. When she tried to scream, only a strangled whimper escaped, muffled and broken, as if some invisible thread had sewed her lips shut. Panic clawed at the edges of her mind, but her body wouldn't answer.

That's when she saw it.

The shadow bled across the ceiling like an ink spill. It hovered there, a shapeless mass, curling like vapor. Its faceless head studied her, as if deciding who or what she was. She told herself it was just a nightmare. A medicine-induced hallucination. But all rationality crumbled when the shadow began to descend toward her.

Tears welled as its tendrils stretched outward. A chill flooded her veins. The stench hit next. Rancid, like rotting seaweed and burnt copper. Then came the sound like nails dragging across glass. She begged her body to move, but the harder she fought, the heavier she sank, like the mattress was swallowing her. The shadow loomed closer until it felt certain: she wasn't going to survive.

One breath. Then another. Her body snapped free all at once. She sucked in a breath so sharp, it sliced her throat, her fingers clawing at the sheets. She lurched upright with a scream. The shadow recoiled, twisting into itself before dissolving into the dark. The door burst open, and light flooded the room.

Alma rushed to her side. "Dorothy! You're alright!"

Dorothy pointed at the corner, sobbing. "Something was here—I saw it!"

Alma followed her gaze, brow furrowing. "I don't see anything, but perhaps it was just a nightmare. You've been through so much."

"No!" Dorothy pulled her knees up to her chest. "It was right there. I swear, I wasn't dreaming. I saw it." She inhaled deeply. "I felt it."

Alma knelt beside her and took her hands. "Hush now, child. You're safe." Whatever it was, it has no power here," she said. "Let us pray. The Lord will help calm your spirit."

Dorothy's chest heaved as she glanced at the corner. Praying had never belonged in her world. She'd never needed it. Never wanted it. But with the shadow burned into her memory, she wondered would these words protect her? Did she even deserve their comfort?

"Our Father, who art in Heaven, hallowed be Thy name..." Alma whispered.

Dorothy closed her eyes, letting Alma's voice carry her through words that felt both alien and soothing. Her heartbeat began to steady, but doubt lingered, and beneath it, a bit of relief.

A low buzzing hummed through the night, rising until it droned in the walls.

The blanket slipped from Dorothy as she strained to locate the sound. It wasn't coming from the machines or even the hallway. It felt cemented in the building's infrastructure. Her gaze drifted to the observation window. The nurse sat behind the counter, flipping through a newspaper. Quietly, Dorothy slid from bed.

Her hospital gown brushed against the linoleum as she stepped into the corridor. The overhead lights flickered in and out, but they weren't the source. Pipes clattered somewhere above, close, but not quite it. She turned a corner, and the buzzing led her to a pair of wooden doors. A tarnished plaque read: *Chapel.* Her breath fogged, though the hallway held no chill. She hesitated, pressed her palm to the door handle, and pushed.

Skeletal votive candles cast shadows that crawled across the floor. The stained-glass windows, robbed of color by the night, looked mournful—each saint trapped in darkened glass. The buzzing drew her gaze to the altar. Jack knelt at its base, draped in a hospital gown identical to hers. His lips moved erratically, while his shoulders twitched with each syllable. A swarm of flies circle him, their wings humming into a maddening, dissonant choir.

"Jack?"

His back stayed bowed, hands tight.

"Jack…is everything okay?"

His shoulders convulsed, as if strings were tugging at his spine. Mechanically, he turned.

Dorothy stumbled back. His face flickered, blistered and raw, skin sloughing away to expose red tissue beneath. His pupils were glassy, but they stared right through her.

"You should've stopped him," he rasped. "You didn't even know us. Didn't care. And still…you're the one who lived."

The back of her knees hit a pew. "That's not fair," she whispered. "I didn't know—I didn't know this would happen."

Candles sputtered one by one, plunging the chapel into darkness. Jack lurched forward, his limbs bending at inhuman angles, joints popping. Dorothy spun—shadows had already begun to unfurl from the stone walls, pooling around her feet.

"Please," she whispered, stepping back. "I didn't want this."

The flies erupted in a frenzy. His form glitched in and out of focus, as if reality couldn't decide whether to hold him.

"I see his face every time I look at you," he said. "And it makes me hate you."

His fingers were outstretched like he wasn't sure whether to touch her or crush her. Then they closed suddenly. Cold and clammy, they wrapped around her throat, not with sudden violence but like he was testing how easily she might break. The pressure tightened. Her breath hitched. Her pulse kicked against his palm.

"J…ack!"

The chapel doors burst open. Dorothy collapsed, gasping, clutching her throat as blood pooled in her mouth. A flashlight beam seared over the pews, catching her in the eyes.

"Miss? Miss, can you hear me?"

She fought against the glare, trying to focus on the security guard. "Where did he go?" she asked, looking toward the altar. But the candles burned undisturbed. There were no flies. No crawling shadows.

"Miss, there's no one else here," the guard said. "It's just us."

Footsteps echoed behind them. Alma appeared in the doorway, her gaze locking onto Dorothy. "What happened?" she asked the guard, but her attention never strayed from Dorothy.

"Not sure," he replied. "She had some kind of episode. Says she saw someone."

Alma nodded. "Thank you, Officer Gideon. I'll take it from here." He glanced at her once, uncertain before walking away. Once the doors shut, Alma took Dorothy's arm and guided her to the nearest pew.

"Jack was…but he wasn't—" Dorothy shook her head. "He blamed me for the crash. For Elliot."

Alma's hands closed around hers. "When we suffer deeply, the mind and spirit can play fiendish tricks. Our pain—it calls out in strange ways. Sometimes it wears familiar faces. Like Jack."

"But it felt so real," Dorothy murmured, gaze drifting to the altar. "I believe you," Alma said. "But real or not, those tricks cannot follow you where the Lord's peace resides. Come. Let's return to your room. You need rest, and prayer."

Dorothy nodded. Though her feet dragged as Alma helped her stand.

As they left the chapel, the candles sputtered until nothing, but darkness remained.

CHAPTER 5
Declan Albatross

Around him, the other nominees adjusted bowties, smoothed gowns, their excitement thrumming through the upstairs corridor. To them, the Founders' Ball was another performance. An evening steeped in glamour and tradition. But to Declan, the night felt like a stage without a safety net. One misstep, and he'd plummet. Every laugh rang too loud. Every voice, too bright. He kept glancing toward the end of the hall, expecting Lola to appear—windblown auburn hair, somehow still beautiful.

"Five minutes!" Parvati Clark strode past with a clipboard in hand. "Everyone, take your places. Quickly, please!"

The nominees shifted into formation, some giggling, others nudging one another as they lined up against the wall. Declan took his place and caught Aiden's eye. They didn't speak, but the look they shared said everything: *Where the hell is Lola?*

Speakers crackled from the ballroom. Headmistress Mortimer's voice rang clear.

"Welcome students, faculty, family, and esteemed guests. As many of you know, the Founders' Ball is a ceremony rooted in our town's origins. The opening waltz is more than a mere dance.

It is a remembrance. A ritual that honors the legacy left behind by those who shaped our beginnings."

No one really knew who had founded Driftmoor. The stories differed depending on who told them. Every family claimed descent from the original bloodlines, their versions embellished by generations of vanity and privilege. But all records of Driftmoor's origins had vanished over a century ago. Some said a nor'easter destroyed it. Others claimed it was never meant to be found and that the founders had their reasons for erasing themselves from history. Witchcraft. Betrayal. Or maybe they just wanted to disappear.

Parvati stopped in front of Declan, pen poised over clipboard. "Declan Albatross," she muttered, scanning her list. "You're paired with Lola, but…" Her gaze lifted, sweeping the hallway. "Where is she? We're about to start. Has anyone seen Lola Godfrey?"

"I think she's in the restroom." Declan smiled, practiced enough to disarm the deepest suspicion. "It's Lola. You know how she is."

Parvati's doubt lingered in the crease between her brows as the quartet's music drifted upward.

Mortimer continued over the speakers. "Legend holds this waltz symbolizes unity and balance. A ritual meant to ward off misfortune for our students, faculty, and our beloved town. Tradition tells us that any disruption, any misstep, is an omen. A shadow cast over the year ahead. Tonight, our nominees uphold that legacy as we look toward the future."

Declan adjusted his bowtie, but his throat constricted with pressure he couldn't swallow.

"We begin tonight with the presentation of our nominees for king and queen of the Founder's Ball," Mortimer intoned. "First to descend will be Camille Adelaide Beamount, escorted by Rowan van Winkle the third."

Hands came together. A polite smattering of claps that faded quickly.

"We're starting," Parvati whispered to Declan, tightening her grip on the clipboard.

"Next to descend, Isabelle Laurent, escorted by Aiden Claypoole Oldwyck."

Aiden caught Declan's eye while walking past with Isabelle—a look mixed with concern on his face—before they vanished down the steps.

"Declan, listen," Parvati said.

"She'll be here." He stepped into position, shoulders squared. Each second stretched, tightening the hollow in his chest. He kept his chin lifted, eyes fixed on the entrance as if there was still a chance.

"And at last," Mortimer said, "presenting Lola Milagros Godfrey, escorted by Declan Sterling Albatross."

Murmurs rippled through the crowd as Declan stepped into the spotlight. The ballroom unfolded around him like a painting. Vaulted ceilings etched with scalloped frescoes, their brushstroke gilded by the chandelier light. He began his descend, expectation pressing against his spine as hundreds of eyes followed him.

"It seems there's been a last-minute change," Mortimer said.

Whispers broke along the tables of gowns and suits. A few heads turned toward the opposite staircase, others toward Declan.

"Declan Sterling Albatross will now be escorted by Ophelia Lockhart."

Time seemed to slow as Ophelia appeared at the top of the opposite staircase, her aura an icy elegance that made the room seem dim by comparison. For a heartbeat, uncertainty crossed her face. Then she lifted her chin and begun to descend, graceful, every step deliberate. At the bottom, she offered him her hand. It trembled just enough for him to notice. He stared at it, then reached out. The moment their fingers met, feelings he wasn't ready to face, flared.

Declan's gaze swept over her. "What are you doing?"

It wasn't just a question. It was everything he hadn't dared to feel.

"Saving you from humiliation," Ophelia replied.

"But you don't even know the steps."

Just as the string quartet began, she sank into a curtsy, matching the other nominees.

"Don't underestimate me," she whispered, eyes locked with his. "Now, move."

Their hands rose in unison, but the rhythm was uneven. They weren't partners. Just echoes of who they used to be, bound by memory and absence. His hand settled at her waist. Her palm rested against his shoulder. And then the music pulled them into motion.

His gaze dropped. "Where the hell are your shoes?"

Her bare feet skimmed the floor. A faint smile tugged at her lips. "Ballet taught me how to keep going. With or without shoes."

Bowstrings stretched each note into a fragile melody. Around them, couples swept across the floor, skirts flaring like petals, tuxedo jackets carving shadows through the candlelit haze. The choreography unfolded like a duel where palms hovered shy of contact. But Declan and Ophelia fell half a beat behind. Where others glided, they resisted. Her eyes darted away during a missed pivot. His hand lingered near her waist, caught between instinct and restraint.

"Why are you here?" he asked. "Why are you helping me?"

"After all this time, that's what you want to ask me?" She spoke like Ophelia, but she sounded like someone else.

"Fine." Declan pulled her closer. "Tell me then. Where have you been for the last three years?"

"London." She pushed against him. "I needed a fresh start."

One day she was beside him, and the next her parents pulled her out of Driftmoor Academy. Rumors swirled with whispers of rehab, reformatory school, and even kidnapping. Ophelia Lockhart, a name commanding attention, had become nothing more but a mystery.

"That doesn't explain why you left the way you did."

"Does it matter?" Her eyes dropped to his lips. "I'm here now. With you."

The music crescendoed but couldn't hide the fissure between them.

"And you've been avoiding me," he said. "Why?"

Her next step faltered. "What did you expect? That we'd fall back into each other's arms like some star-crossed lovers?"

"No," he said, quieter now. "But I'd like to know if you cared about me at all. Not the idea of me. Not what I meant for your reputation or your story or your guilt. Just me."

"You probably won't believe it, but I never stopped caring," she said, then almost as if to herself, "Not about you. Not about any of you."

Her fingers tensed slightly in his, and though her posture remained poised, she missed the next turn by half a beat. His hand settled at the small of her back and her breath caught, before softening against his neck, as if the touch reminded her to keep moving.

They turned and pivoted, more from obligation than willingness. But it was enough to convince the crowd. To them, it looked like a reunion of old lovers. To him, it only amplified the questions he didn't know how to ask. Her presence confused him more than her absence ever had. And yet, beneath the resentment, part of him wanted to believe in the girl he once loved.

The quartet dwindled into a decrescendo, and scattered applause rose through the ballroom.

"There's something I need to tell you," Ophelia said. "It's about Lola."

"What about her?"

Her hand twitched at her side.

"Ophelia?"

She wasn't looking at him anymore.

Lola stormed into the ballroom, her gown catching light in a blaze of rubies. Her presence traveled through the atmosphere. He'd spent the entire night waiting for her. And now she stood before him, and her expression gave nothing away. Not anger. It was heavier and quieter.

Ophelia reeled back. "No," she said. "Impossible."

She clutched her gown. "I'm sorry. I need to go."

And she fled, leaving him alone once again.

CHAPTER 6
Lola Godfrey

HER FEET SANK INTO THE SAND, EACH STEP A COLD REMINDER THAT she should've been dead.

Behind the Barquentine Hotel, the private beach stretched wide and empty, the night heavy with stars that offered no comfort. Her heels dangled from her fingers, the straps digging crescents into her palm, but she barely felt them. From the moment she first saw Ophelia, Lola had wanted to be her friend. There was a gravity to her. And Lola, like most people in Driftmoor, had been drawn to her. But earning her friendship was never easy. It had to be earned. And Lola had earned it. Or so she thought. She'd once believed there was no distance she wouldn't travel to stay close to her. Never, not even in her darkest, most wounded thoughts, had she imagined the girl she worshipped would leave her for dead.

Ahead, Ophelia stumbled through the sand, teetering on the edge of collapse. Wind whipped her hair across her face, her gown trailing behind her.

"Enough already!" Lola shouted. "There's no outrunning this one."

Ophelia's ankle twisted, and she fell into the shallows with a splash.

"No...I saw you fall," she said, scrambling backward. "I watched you go over. You—you shouldn't be here. You can't be here."

Lola stopped and tilted her head. "At the very least, you could look at me."

"I don't understand," Ophelia sobbed. "No one could've survived that. I thought you were gone."

"And yet, you left me."

Even barefoot and mascara-streaked, Ophelia looked like the girl poets wrote about. The breeze tangled her hair into windswept perfection, and her gown clung as if styled by intention, not accident. She was everything Lola had once thought mattered: beautiful, tragic, untouchable.

"I didn't plan it. I didn't want it," Ophelia said. "It just happened. And I've been replaying it in my head all night."

Lola wanted to hate Ophelia. Needed to. Hatred was easier and preserved the bitterness. But seeing her trembling at her feet stirred a sympathy she thought she killed off a long time ago.

"You should've called my brother. Or anyone. Instead, you powdered your nose, slipped into your dress, and twirled around the dance floor with Declan like nothing happened," she said. "So, tell me Ophelia, what the hell is wrong with you?"

"I—I couldn't face your brother." Ophelia's fingers curled into the damp sand. "I only came tonight to tell Declan what happened. What I thought happened to you."

Lola arched a brow. "How thoughtful."

Ophelia's eyes pleaded. But Lola kept her gaze fixed, not out of cruelty, but because looking away would feel like surrender.

"How are you even alive?" Ophelia whispered, scanning Lola's unmarked skin.

"It doesn't matter." Lola crossed her arms. "Who'd believe you, anyway?"

"You think I want to tell anyone about this?" Ophelia pointed to the horizon where Silver Shoals loomed in the dark. "I didn't mean to hurt you. That wasn't why I went there."

Lola wanted to believe her. And for the most part, she did. Silver Shoals had always been a place wrapped in warnings. Parents told their kids to stay away. The doors were boarded up, but someone always found a way in. Still, that didn't mean she was ready to let her guard down.

"What happens now?" Ophelia asked.

"With what?"

"Us. This."

Lola's gaze dropped to the sand, then lifted. "There is no us," she said. "As far as you're concerned, tonight never happened. It'll be a blip in your memory until you grow old and die."

She didn't trust the fear in Ophelia's eyes. Fear made people unpredictable, and Ophelia had already proven she ran when things got hard.

"Just don't come near me again. And while you're at it, stay away from Declan, from Heather—from all of us. You're not welcome here anymore. Your reign ended the second you left."

Lola cast one last glance over her shoulder before sprinting up the dunes toward the Barquentine Hotel. Applause swelled with every step, the joyful clamor clashing against the turmoil inside her. At the wraparound porch, she paused. Light spilled through the tall windows.

She straightened her spine and stepped inside. Confetti drifted from rafters, catching in her hair as she stood near the edge of the ballroom. On stage beneath a spotlight, Declan and Camille stood side by side, crowns gleaming on their heads. His smile held, but it never reached his eyes. Camille, on the other hand, bathed in the attention, chin tilted toward the applause like it had been owed to her all along.

"Your new king and queen!" Headmistress Mortimer's voice rang from the speakers.

The chandeliers' brilliance had become unbearable after the dark beach. Light scattered across the marble floor in dizzying, kaleidoscopic patterns, while cheers and applause merged into a deafening symphony. Declan stood in his tuxedo, smile in place, scanning the crowd. He stopped when he saw her. The noise, the lights, the people all blurred as their eyes locked. His eyes widened. Camille leaned in, touched his arm, and whispered something in his ear that caused his attention to shift.

Lola's mouth held the right shape, but her chest caved inward, piece by piece. The crown sat crooked on Declan's head, Camille's hand laced in his, and the ballroom shimmered with approval. He looked beautiful. Not in the way he had with her when they practiced speeches, but like someone she no longer fit beside. She blinked against the sting, her clapping matching the rhythm of the words she wouldn't let herself say.

Smile. Clap. And remember, no crying.

CHAPTER 7
Aiden Oldwyck

HE COULDN'T SAY WHEN THE PICTURE DISAPPEARED. ONE DAY, IT WAS there. The next, it wasn't.

As Aiden descended into the foyer, morning light spilled through the windows, staining the black marble floor in shades of pearl and flame. His gaze drifted toward the mantel where the picture used to sit. Gilded flourishes curled like vines dipped in gold. But look closer, and figures emerged from the scrollwork of women with wild hair and hounds at their heels, flames dancing along their fingertips. Where the silver frame had once been—his five-year-old self grinning from his father's shoulders, a too-big pilot cap slipping over one eye—stood a brass urn. Flame motifs licked its surface. He'd overheard whispers once: *Ashes*, someone said. But whose?

From somewhere in the manor, opera echoed. His mother always played music in the mornings. He moved down the hallway, footsteps absorbed by Persian rugs. His Driftmoor Academy uniform clung to him—pressed slacks, dark blazer, the school's crest embroidered above his heart. He passed a mirror without meaning to look but caught a glimpse anyway. Dark waves brushed his collar. Copper-flecked eyes, too thoughtful for a seventeen-year-old, stared back.

Outside his mother's sitting room, sunlight ignited damask

wallpaper, marigold and crimson burning at the edges. Bookcases sagged with tomes and romance novels. Between two harbor-facing windows stood a glass cabinet—its mismatched teacups arranged, delicate and unloved, relics from an era that never ended.

"Mom?" Aiden's voice barely carried over the soprano's voice.

Irene reclined in her armchair, one leg crossed over the other, her heel tapping against the rug. Smoke curled from the cigarette in her hand as she studied the paintings arranged on easels. She flinched at the tap on her shoulder, then reached to lower the gramophone's volume, her rings catching the daylight as she turned the dial.

She looked up, smiling. "Good morning, button," she said. "All ready for school?" Her dark brown hair was pinned back in a loose chignon, her preferred style.

"As ready as I'll ever be." Aiden's gaze lingered on the cigarette between her fingers. It was a habit of hers he never got used to. "I thought you said smoke can damage paintings."

She stubbed it in an ashtray. "If they were acrylics, yes. But nothing in the manor has been as pedestrian as acrylics."

Oldwyck Manor, one of Driftmoor's last surviving structures from the Gilded Age, was less a home than a curated archive. Its maze garden and museum-caliber collection were the stuff of town lore. Priceless paintings adorned every room, even the old nursery, where Aiden had once slept beneath a Matisse. Irene liked to recount that his first word was *Picasso*. This was a testament, she claimed, to the brilliance of his upbringing.

"I'm assuming these are all for the auction?" He nodded toward the easels.

"Correct," she said. "It wasn't easy deciding which ones to release, but the choice, as always, had to be made."

Most were dream-soaked visions of surrealist scenes where logic dissolved. But one stood apart: a red-haired woman cloaked in shadow, rooted in a forest that seemed to breathe.

"I don't think I've seen this one before," he said. "Where is it from?"

"It's been in my bedroom since I was your age."

Her bedroom. The one room he wasn't allowed in though she had never explained why.

"It must be important then."

She studied the painting. "It was. But alas, even our most treasured things must find their way into new hands."

Aiden glanced around. The walls were a shrine to his sister Veronica, five years older and everywhere, even though she lived in Boston. Baby pictures. Graduation portraits. Field hockey trophies. Her entire childhood had been preserved behind glass in their mother's favorite room. He didn't expect to see himself. But he looked anyway, just in case there had been a change.

"Gwen mentioned what happened at the ball," Irene said.

Gwen Croft, her best friend since childhood and Heather's mother, had always kept her looped into town gossip, whether about Academy board decisions or whose summer home was being remodeled. These days, Gwen was married to a woman who wanted nothing to do with social circles, which only made Gwen more committed to staying informed for both of them.

"You don't have to talk about it," she added. "I just wanted to check in. Are you alright?"

Aiden nodded. "Yeah. We both kind of knew it was time." He hadn't planned to break up with Heather during the ball. He was going to wait a few more weeks and give it some more thought. But it just happened. Right before Ophelia had arrived. Four years together, and it wasn't heartbreak he felt. It was a lightness that settled over him, like shedding a weight he hadn't realized he was carrying.

A smile touched his mother's lips. She smoothed a wrinkle from his blazer. "Okay, button." She turned back toward the paintings. "Oh, before I forget. The matriarchy's coming for dinner on Thursday."

His hand froze on the strap of his backpack. The last time they'd all gathered was for his grandmother's funeral, last winter. A dozen women with the same russet eyes and soft-spoken voices had filled the manor. A tangle of aunts and distant cousins, bound not by blood but by a tradition older than any family tree. They moved through Oldwyck Manor like they owned the land. Whispers crept through corridors. The air smelled of herbs and ritual. That day, the manor had turned watchful and less a place of mourning than a convergence of power.

"What's the real reason for their visit?"

Irene didn't look at him. "You know I can't tell you that."

Just like always.

"They'll only be here for a few hours," she said, like it was a coffee date and not a summons from a lineage that treated him like a mistake. "While they're here, I expect you to stay in your room. Understood?"

He sighed. "Why can't I just go to Declan's? Or go to the Wharf?"

"It's safer for you at home." Her tone softened, but it wasn't new. That same explanation, worn thin by years of repetition.

"Right. Like when I wasn't allowed downstairs for Grandma's funeral."

"Aiden, that's enough. Just…let it be for now. Go on. Try to enjoy the day. Weatherman reported a sunny front for the afternoon."

Opera trailed behind him as Irene turned up the gramophone. At the doorway, he glanced back. She was lighting another cigarette, but it wasn't the absence of a lighter that caught his eye. It was the fire. Flickering at her fingertips, conjured with a thought, shaping itself to her will. He'd grown up watching this, when she thought he wasn't looking. It was effortless as a breath. Delicate as the strike of a match. And yet, no matter how often he saw it, emotions stirred inside him. Awe. Resentment. But beneath them both, longing.

Magic defined the Oldwycks, but it didn't include him.

CHAPTER 8
Dorothy Hale

HER FATHER'S FLANNEL HUNG FROM THE SPIRALED BEDPOST WHILE A towel drooped over the desk chair and a pair of jeans lay exactly where she'd left them. In the corner, her suitcase gaped open, half-unpacked, its contents folded with the care of someone who once believed in a fresh start. Three weeks ago, Driftmoor Academy had promised reinvention. A scholarship had pulled her from Seattle's rainy gloom to Massachusetts' affluent, sea-bitten cliffs. The brochure had painted a vision of stone archways, ivy-clad buildings, and a place where she might finally shed her insecurities. But morning light spilled across unfamiliar furniture and bare walls, illuminating not a promising future, but the ghost of who she'd almost been.

Her eyes drifted to the window where, the lighthouse (Silver Shoals, they called it) stood sentry over the shore. Sunlight gilded its spine, beautiful and indifferent, untouched by the dread she'd brought back from St. Augustine's. Jack surfaced—charred flesh peeling, lips curled in accusation. She blinked hard and turned to the empty bed across from hers. Amani had once sat there, legs folded, dabbing foundation on her cheeks.

"There's an off-campus party tonight if you wanna tag along," she had said.

Dorothy could still hear her voice, a subtle invitation masking a test. She had gripped the sweatshirt in her lap. "Off-campus? " she had asked. "Is that allowed?"

Amani shrugged. "It's at Albatross House. There's a strict guest list, but my friend Nijah knows the guy throwing it. It's supposed to be wicked fun."

Dorothy had never been the kind of a teenager who went to parties. The last one she remembered was at a bowling alley—cake, neon lights, someone crying in the bathroom. Crowded rooms unsettled her. Strangers brushing past, voices too loud, her awkwardness on display terrified her. And yet, a longing stirred. Not for chaos, but for the hope of belonging.

So she went. One night. One decision. And everything changed.

The crash hadn't just broken bones. It had fractured her sense of reality in places no X-ray could reach. Now she had panic attacks. Unexplained sleepwalking episodes. Alma had also mentioned she talked in her sleep. And every time she closed her eyes, Elliot was there, watching her with hatred in his bloodied gaze.

Back at Driftmoor Academy, in a dorm room frozen in time, what once seemed like it could be home felt foreign and unwelcoming. Trepidation lingered beneath her ribs, whispering questions: *Could she rebuild a life in this new version of herself? Or had the accident stolen that possibility for good?*

Dorothy stood before the mirror, tugging at the hem of her blazer. The pleated skirt and white blouse fit well enough, but the blazer with its gold buttons and embroidered crest of a stag silhouetted against a lighthouse hung stiff on her shoulders. No matter how she adjusted it, the reflection stared back like a child playing dress-up.

When she left, the wind bit at her cheeks and pressed at the gray sky. Leaves skittered across cobblestone paths, rustling against her calves.

Driftmoor Academy rose around her, all iron spires and slate rooftops, its towers hunched beneath mist. Balustrades flanked the upper walks, and arched windows punctuated the stone. Gargoyles crouched along the eaves, their gazes facing the ocean.

She clutched her wrinkled orientation map and followed paths she barely remembered as leaves shifted beneath her loafers. Voices echoed from a sunken courtyard, muffled by ivy and stone. Twice she turned the wrong way. Once toward the chapel, where bells hung silent in the belfry and another toward the library, its towering entry sealed behind iron latticework. Each misstep tightened the knot in her stomach as the campus folded in around her.

Then, beyond the trees, Eldridge Hall emerged. The stone was worn smooth in places and jagged in others, as if the building have grown tired of resisting the sea air. At the top of the wide staircase, double doors waited beneath lanterns, long dark but still shaped to suggest fire.

Inside the Atrium, sunlight spilled through the stained-glass dome, painting the flagstone in shades of copper and violet. At her feet, the Academy's stag crest shimmered, its antlers twisting toward the floor's edge. Lockers clanged open and shut. Students lounged on curved limestone benches and leaned against columns, their laughter rang out like coins on tile—sharp and expensive.

Dorothy lingered at the threshold, the collar of her blazer tight. Every step forward felt like a trespass. She wasn't part of this. Not the glances exchanged between old friends. Not the comfortable way others took up space as if the school had always belonged to them. She adjusted her grip on her map, heart thudding in her throat. Her movements felt rehearsed. As she passed a mirror flanked by ivory busts, she caught her reflection—red hair tucked back too neatly, mouth pressed into a line—and looked away before she could second guess herself.

A boy threaded through the crowd with tousled chestnut brown curls, Driftmoor uniform rumpled just enough to seem intentional.

He was all nods and shoulder taps, leaving a trail of half-laughs and smiles behind him. He was magnetic in the way people born into wealth often were. Dorothy began to turn, ready to slip past him, but his gaze cut through and locked onto hers.

"Hey," he said. "Sorry if this is forward, but—your Dorothy, right? Dorothy Hale?"

"Uh, yeah. I am. Is there something I can do for you?"

Sheepishness softened the sharp angles of his jaw. "I'm Declan. We've never met, but I heard you were at my party. At Albatross House."

The memories flooded back. Techno vibrating through a smoky, decadent room. Jack, lounging over a chaise with a joint in hand. Elliot swaying and smiling too much. The slam of a car door. Headlights. The question she should've asked: *are you sure he's okay to drive?*

Declan stepped closer. "Look, I don't know if this helps, but I've been thinking about that night. Like maybe if I'd paid better attention, if I'd checked in with who was leaving." He glanced at two girls watching their interaction. "I just wanted you to know I'm sorry."

Did he actually care? Or was this about resolving his guilt? The sincerity in his green eyes made it hard to tell.

"Thanks," she said, regardless.

He offered his hand. She hesitated but took it. When their palms met, her breath hitched.

The hallway melted into a plain of water, rushing over her skin. A roar echoed in her ears, like a frenzied ocean. She couldn't breathe and her limbs refused to move as gravity pulled her under. She ripped free, and a gasp tore from her as she stumbled back, coughing.

Declan caught her shoulders. "Hey, what was that? Are you okay? Do you have asthma?"

"No," she managed, trying to catch her breath. "I don't. That's never happened before."

How could she explain it? Someone else's last breath? The saltwater on her tongue?

He studied her, brows drawn. "Are you sure?"

"I'm fine." She forced the words out, her legs unsteady.

Declan lingered another second. "If it happens again, you should go to the infirmary just to be sure."

She pressed her back to the wall, as he disappeared into the crowd. This mirrored what she'd felt in Jack's room, when the machines shrieked and the shadow came for him. The same dread she'd felt staring at that frail patient. A warning without language. Her gaze flicked back to Declan, his figure already half swallowed by shifting bodies in uniform.

CHAPTER 9
Declan Albatross

HE TRIED NOT TO THINK ABOUT HER. BUT THE WORDS BLURRED, swallowed by the hushed voices and the rustle of turning pages. Declan sat hunched at a table in the Bellweather Athenaeum (a fancy name given to the library by the founder) pretending to care about the humanities textbook in front of him. Seeing Ophelia had reopened a wound. He'd convinced himself the pain was gone and that time had done its work. But there she was, under the ballroom's chandelier, fractured in crystal and guilt. And then this morning, walking through the dining hall as if he didn't exist. He gripped the textbook, the paper crinkling.

A slap against the table startled him.

"Define thanatology," Camille said, shoving a flashcard toward him. Her blonde hair fell in silky waves over her shoulders. Blue eyes narrowed behind delicate frames. Even in uniform, she carried herself like she'd stepped out of a fashion editorial on academic rigor.

"Thanatology," Declan muttered. "That's forensics science, right?"

Camille dragged a hand down her face. "It's the study of death and how people cope with it," she said. "Didn't you study last night?"

He smiled dryly, but his attention drifted toward the windows, where the wind chased leaves across the lawn. He had studied. But lately, everything blurred together—notes, lectures, deadlines—just one stretch of effort with no clear reward. Senior year was supposed to feel like something. Instead, it felt like coasting toward a finish line that kept moving. He was still doing the work, still checking every box, but somewhere along the way, the meaning had thinned.

"You realize Dartmouth could still rescind your acceptance?" Camille said.

"Of course." He loosened the cuffs of his shirt. The silver heirloom watch on his wrist glinted under the banker's lamp. "But they won't. An Albatross getting dropped by Dartmouth? Please. My great-grand-father donated a building to them."

The lamp cast a muted glow over Camille's stare. The mistletoe brooch on her blazer caught the light, its silver berries gleaming. "You told me Ophelia wouldn't be a distraction."

"And she isn't. Not right now, at least."

She stared at him before saying, "You're doing that thing again. The avoidance thing." She slid another flashcard toward him. "Do us both a favor. Go fetch this from the Lower Annex. Maybe the walk will shake some clarity loose."

Declan pushed back his chair. "Anything for you, your highness." He stretched until his back cracked and swept the card.

Around them, the library murmured with restrained urgency. A grandfather clock ticked beneath the portrait of a librarian. The ceilings arched high above, ribbed with dark beams and moldings that twisted into ivy and antler flourishes. Bookshelves stretched nearly to the ceiling, carved from mahogany so dark they seemed black in the shadows, while ladders glided along the rails.

Declan moved through the rows of tables, past marble busts star-ing blankly from alcoves between shelves and students hunched over textbooks or scribbling into notepads. A few glanced up, some out of habit, others with curiosity. An Albatross always drew eyes, especially after the divorce and the rumors of his mother. Driftmoor was a place where names mattered more than people. And his name was etched into this Academy.

The floor turned to stone as he reached the stairs to the Lower Annex. The light dimmed, traded for the underground repository. The ceiling got lower as he descended. It was easy to believe time had stalled down here. Easy to believe the shelves held secrets, whispering to those who bothered to listen. The overhead lights flickered as he moved down the narrow labyrinthine aisles. He scanned the rows, fingertips trailing across cracked leather bindings, exhaling ink and dust. Roman history, its gold lettering half-faded. Freud, tucked between volumes on anatomy. The books stood like sentinels, dense with knowledge he'd once feigned interest in.

Halfway in, he stopped at the sound of footsteps. He turned, but the aisle behind him remained empty.

"Anyone down here?" he called. His voice echoed, catching on the low ceiling before dissolving into silence.

The quiet pressed in, thicker than before. He moved forward, slower now, the hush of the Annex stretching. And then—just past the next aisle—he spotted a book sprawled on the center of the dusty floor, as if it had been dropped in haste. He stepped closer, brows furrowing. The leather was dull with frayed corners. At its center, was an engraving of a metallic compass-like design that reminded him of the star maps in his family's summer house. The ones his great-grandfather swore *held secrets to navigating more than the seas.*

He looked around before reaching for it. The moment his fingers touched the cover, a chill spidered his arm and sank into him. Still, he flipped it open.

Blank.

The parchment, brittle and yellowed, offered nothing. Just waterlogged pages that had stood the test of time. He turned another. And another. But still nothing.

The overhead lights flickered again as a hush flooded the aisles.

Shelves began to distort at the edges of his vision, warping like reflections beneath water. And the engraving—its lines writhed softly as if the symbol was coming to life.

Then, stillness.

The lights steadied. The faint scribbles of pens and the murmur of distant voices crept back in. But the cold stayed. He should've left the book. Tucked it in a random shelf and walked away. But something about it felt like it hadn't been lost. Like it had been waiting for him, and because of that, he couldn't bring himself to ignore it.

"What took so long?" Camille asked as Declan slid into his seat.

He handed her the slim volume she'd asked for—*The Myth of Eternal Return*, its cover pristine and barely creased. In his other, the leatherbound book remained firmly gripped, thumb tracing its spine. It was heavier than it looked, and he didn't know why he hadn't set it down yet.

"Got a little sidetracked," he muttered, finally setting it down between them. "Found this. On the floor."

Camille raised a brow. "It was just lying there?"

He gave a small nod.

"Let me see."

He hesitated, then slid it toward her.

She traced the engraving. "Looks like a compass," she said. "Or something older. Like an astrolabe, maybe." She flipped it open, eyebrows drawing together. "It's blank?"

Declan leaned in. The book had a coppery odor, like pennies left in the rain. Or blood.

"Kind of strange, right?"

Camille turned another page. "You should show Miss Alpine. If it's part of the Preserves, she'll want it logged. Could be an unused field journal or something unfiled."

He didn't want to give it up. Every instinct told him to hold on tighter, to keep it close. But with Camille watching, he agreed.

At the front desk, Miss Alpine looked up from a stack of brochures for book clubs and literary events. "Oh, if it isn't our Founders' Ball royalty!" she said. "Congratulations, you two."

Declan offered a polite smile, his face warming. "Thank you, Miss Alpine." He held out the book, reluctant. "I found this in the Lower Annex. Camille thought it might belong to the Preserves?"

Miss Alpine took it and turned it over, tracing the engraving with her thumb. "Doesn't look familiar. Interesting design, though. I'll keep it in the lost and found in case anyone comes looking."

Declan's hands hovered longer than it needed to. His fingertips tingled. A twitch pulled at his muscles. He wanted to reach over the counter, take it back, say he'd made a mistake. That it was his now. But he stood still under Camille's watchful gaze, pretending this was just another forgotten library book and not something that had already started to feel like it belonged to him.

CHAPTER 10
Lola Godfrey

LOLA SAT AT THE HEAD STUDENT COUNCIL TABLE, HER PEN CLENCHED tight. Around her, voices from the rest of the council drifted from measured debates, laughter, the occasional chair scraping the floor. The classroom itself was all shadows and age: oak-paneled walls crowded with portraits of past professors, a chalkboard stained with ghosted formulas, tall windows veiled in dust-flecked light. Her thoughts had slipped from the room entirely and back to Silver Shoals. To Ophelia. To the bloodstained cardigan beneath her bed.

The Godfrey's healing had passed through generations in warnings and metaphors. It was an inheritance cloaked in secrecy, one she was expected to guard with her life and carry to the grave. Ancestors shaped the story—this gift—into folklore, spoken as if repeating them might ward off those who would come too close.

They will smile in your face, press their hands to your heart, and call you divine. But the Godfrey's boogeyman was never the one under the bed. It was the neighbor with fresh bread. The priest with blessings. The friend who lingered in your home long after dinner. The ones who saw your blood as an opportunity for harvest. Those who believed we could heal their sickness, stall their aging, and make them a god.

"Lola?"

She snapped back.

Heather stood beside her, arms crossed, one brow arched. The rest of the council had already left. "The meeting ended five minutes ago. Where were you just now?"

Lola straightened, eyes dropping to the budget documents, already signed, though she couldn't remember when. "Here. Obviously."

"Right. You completely absorbed Rowan's riveting financial talk." She watched Lola closely. "You've been off all day. Are you sure everything's alright?"

"It's called exhaustion. Keep up," Lola said, twisting the cap back on her pen with a snap.

"You know you don't have to lie with me. Is this about the Founders' Ball?"

A humorless smile tugged at Lola's lips. "Absolutely not."

The crown had once been a title to be fought for, obsessed over, and build a high school legacy around. But after Silver Shoals, it felt like a relic in a game that suddenly felt too small.

Parvati hovered in the doorway, looking like she'd spent the last ten minutes working up the nerve to step inside.

As she approached them, Heather muttered, "I swear, if this is about that birthday party."

Lola smoothed her notebook. "Parvati. To what do we owe the honor?"

Parvati fidgeted with two envelopes. "I—um—these are for you both!" She thrust them forward. "Invitations. For my seventeenth. It's going to be on *The Argo*."

Lola accepted hers, turning the envelope over. "A yacht party. How decadent."

Heather barely glanced at hers before tossing it onto a desk. "How unfortunate. I'll be in Manhattan that weekend," she said. "Family obligations, of course."

Parvati's gaze darted between them before falling on Lola.

Lola tucked the invitation into her bag with enough delay to keep Parvati guessing. "I do love a party." She paused. "We'll see."

"You will? I mean great! Thanks!" Parvati turned so quickly she tripped over her feet.

As the door shut behind her, Heather arched a brow. "That was oddly generous of you. What's the real reason? You need to borrow the yacht for your own soirée?"

Lola smirked. "Maybe I simply enjoy watching people squirm."

The Atrium pulsed with the murmur of shifting bodies and clang of lockers. Overhead, a stained-glass dome filtered in sunlight, while the upper level wrapped around in cloisters carved with scrollwork and Latin maxims.

Heather fluffed her curls in front of her locker mirror. She appraised her reflection, then tilted her head enough to catch Lola in the corner of her eye. "Guess who I ran into between sixth and seventh period?"

Lola's pen moved across her philosophy notes, where she'd begun underlining the word *nihilism* for the third time. "The ghosts of our founders?" she said, her tone flat but edged with amusement.

"No. Little Miss Houdini herself. Ophelia."

Lola's grip tightened. Heather had been slipping Ophelia's name into every conversation, and each mention caught like a thorn beneath her skin. When news broke of Ophelia's return, they'd made a pact not to speak of her. And yet, ever since, it felt like her name came up more often than not.

"Well, did she say anything?" Lola asked, trying not to sound like she cared. "Or did she perfect the art of looking right through you?"

Heather snapped her compact shut. "She ignored me. It was almost impressive." She laughed, but there was bitterness in it. "Funny, isn't it? She's the one who vanished, but we're the ones who get brushed off."

"Right. Absolutely tragic."

Heather leaned against a locker, her gold hoops catching a sliver of light. "You know what's even more tragic? I think she believes she's the victim. And I bet you Declan does too."

Lola pressed her mouth into a thin line.

"Has she tried talking to you?" Heather asked.

Lola pulled a tube of pomegranate lipstick from her blazer pocket and began tracing it over her lips. "I don't plan on acknowledging Ophelia Lockhart ever again," she said coolly. "As far as I'm concerned, she might as well be dead."

And she had been, once—at least to everyone who believed the rumors. Until the truth became public.

Heather laughed, shaking her head. "You're scary when you're serious, you know that?"

Lola's gaze drifted to the inside of Heather's locker, where a lobster-shaped magnet held a photograph of them in front of Silver Shoals. The lighthouse seemed far less menacing than the version she'd nearly died beneath.

"Why are you still holding onto that?" she asked.

Heather traced the photo, not meeting Lola's eyes. "It's the only picture where everyone's smiling. Besides, it's not like I framed it." She eyed Lola. "Don't tell me you got rid of yours?"

Lola hadn't told anyone about her copy where she had scratched out Ophelia's face.

"No, I burned it after I realized she wasn't coming back." She shrugged. "Oops."

In the girls' bathroom, voices echoed against marble and porcelain, reverberating through the vaulted space. Dim sconces cast flickering light across the checkered floor, where water had pooled beneath a leaking faucet. The mirrors above the sinks looked like they had been around since the first graduating class.

From behind a closed stall, Heather spoke. "Maybe we should consider giving her a chance?"

Lola traced her lash line. The mirror in front of her was cracked at the corner, splitting her reflection. "Last I checked, we weren't a philanthropy for troubled teens."

She studied her reflection, adjusting a flyaway. Her summer glow had faded, the shadows under her eyes whispered exhaustion. That wouldn't do. She wouldn't give them the satisfaction of looking like someone who'd lost. Especially not to Camille Beaumont.

Heather exhaled. "I mean it."

"So do I. She doesn't deserve redemption," Lola said. "That's reserved for those capable of remorse. Not for girls who disappear when things get difficult and return only when the dust has settled."

Silence hung, broken by the drip of a faucet.

Then Heather said it quieter, almost childlike. "But...it's our Ophelia. She was our best friend. Remember all the good times we used to have together?"

Lola nearly laughed. Heather had always romanticized her, since kindergarten, when Ophelia seemed brighter than anyone else. To Heather, she wasn't just a friend. She became the girl others aspired to be, a star who lit up every room she entered. But some stars burn out, and so do friendships.

"Key word: was," Lola said, eyes locked on the mirror. She hadn't realized her fingers were trembling until she felt a warmth seeping through her shirt.

Red bloomed across her blouse. Blood.

"What the—"

Her fingers moved to the stain, heart pounding as pain lanced through her. She pulled back the blazer, revealing a rib protruding from her side. Blood dripped to the floor in thick patters, soaking into her shoes, splattering across the tile. This wasn't a wound. It was her body tearing itself open and unraveling her darkest secret.

She stumbled back, grabbing the sink, eyes squeezed shut. *This isn't real. It can't be.*

The stall creaked opened, and Heather appeared behind her. "Um. What are you doing?"

Lola's eyes snapped open. Her reflection blinked, blouse unstained, rib in place. She forced her shoulders back and lifted her chin. "I'm clearly just standing here waiting for you, aren't I?"

"Yeah, but you kind of look like you're about to pass out or something."

Lola brushed a thread from her blazer. "Just…thought I dropped my lipstick," she said. "You know how difficult it can be to find this shade."

Heather eyed her but turned toward her own reflection.

Lola's mirror-self lingered, watching her. Not the polished version she wore to survive Driftmoor Academy, but someone rawer. Someone unraveling beneath a secret too heavy for one person to carry. A stranger. Or maybe the truth surfacing.

CHAPTER 11
Aiden Oldwyck

AFTER SCHOOL, AIDEN LAY ACROSS HIS BED, GLASSES ASKEW, TOSS-ing a tennis ball up and catching it before it hit his face. Tires crunched over gravel, one after another, as the matriarchy arrived. Each car door closing landed heavy. The urge to slip downstairs and steal fragments of conversations not meant for him clawed at him. But he'd promised his mother to stay unseen. Beside him, the rotary phone rested in its cradle, the receiver propped against his pillow.

"So, why'd you call again?" Declan asked. "Miss the sound of my voice already?"

Aiden lay on his side, one arm draped across the sheets, the coiled cord stretched across him. "In your dreams," he said. "I'm just bored. We didn't talk today, Mr. King of the Ball."

He tried to sound playful. But even he heard the bitter edge. Lately, Declan's attention came in fragments, rationed out in moments that never felt enough. Their classmates gravitated toward him, and Aiden, loyal as ever, hovered outside it all.

"I don't know," Declan said. "Sounds like you just wanted to hear me talk."

Aiden pushed his glasses higher, letting the ball rest in his palm. "Sure. Let's say that."

"You can come over, you know," Declan said. Like he didn't notice the growing distance between them. Like Aiden wasn't counting the ways it hurt, measuring in glances not returned, in pauses that stretched too long.

"I would, but I can't. My family's visiting."

"By family, you mean your aunts? Aren't they your least favorite people?"

Aiden dragged a finger along the cord, winding it around his knuckles. "You can say that."

"And you're stuck there with them?"

The amusement in Declan's voice twisted beneath Aiden's skin.

"Pretty much," Aiden said. "It's complicated. You know that."

The matriarchy didn't just exclude him; they pretended he didn't exist. Their presence turned him into a tolerated inconvenience his mother excused with sighs and vague reassurances. What stung the most was the not knowing. He'd always assumed it was because he lacked the magic they carried. But even that didn't feel enough to justify the way they looked through him, like he was an echo of someone who didn't belong.

Declan laughed. "Well, that sure sounds like a party."

"A real highlight of my week." Aiden glanced at his nightstand, then added, "Hey, what are you doing tomorrow after school? Do you want to grab coffee at The Salty Dog? It's been a while since we've done that."

The pause wasn't long. But long enough.

"Tomorrow?" Declan said, probably scrambling to check his agenda. "Camille and I have to go to town hall for some dinner with Mayor van Winkle. Winners' obligation."

"Right, I forgot about that. What about after?"

"I told Lola we'd watch a movie at her place," Declan replied. "You're obviously welcome to join."

Spending time with Declan around Lola always felt like stepping into a silent competition. Aiden understood she was part of the equation—Declan's other best friend—but that didn't make it easier. When he pictured catching up, it wasn't at a Godfrey movie night with Lola holding court. It was just the two of them, like it used to be.

A longer silence.

"You okay?" Declan asked. "Is this about Heather?"

"Of course." Aiden forced a laugh. "But it's fine. You're busy. I should probably stay in anyways and focus on this philosophy exam."

"Did you need my help for that?"

"We can talk about it later."

He hung up before Declan could say anything else. The tennis ball slipped from his grip and rolled beneath his desk. Declan spoke like Declan, but the distance had grown. Quiet at first. Then constant. And it hadn't started with the Founders' Ball. It ran deeper. A shift Aiden recognized in every brush-off, every time Declan overlooked how hard he tried to keep them close.

A floorboard creaked outside his door. Aiden froze.

But there was no shadow beneath the threshold.

Stay in your room. Stay quiet. Stay unseen. Those have always been the rules.

He slipped from bed, stepped into his slippers, and crept across his bedroom. He pressed his ear to the wood. Nothing. And yet, a presence lingered. He turned the knob. The hallway was lit by candelabras from dark paneled walls. Crown moldings shimmered with dull maroon while a Persian rug stretched down the corridor, threadbare where generations of Oldwyck women had walked. An acrid scent hit his nose like charcoal and sulfur. He noticed scorch marks marring the rug, blackened edges curling. He dropped to one knee, running a finger along the seam. The fibers crumbled at his touch. A circle—no, a pattern—had been left beneath the soot, nearly erased. His gaze lifted to the wall. There were gouges. Four of them. Deep, uneven, raked through the wainscoting.

Rising, he followed the burned trail. Artwork watched him as he passed. Saints mid-martyrdom, oil portraits with eyes scraped hollow, and landscapes smeared with rot along the horizon. The burn marks twisted toward the dining room, where light pulsed beneath the doors and voices murmured just beyond the wood.

Aiden's pulse thudded. He crouched and peered into the keyhole. Suspended above the table, a man writhed in invisible restraints, his face contorted in terror.

Aiden jerked back. He clamped a hand over his mouth, nausea rising as disbelief twisted through him. He squeezed his eyes shut. But when he checked again, the man was still there. His mother Irene sat at the head of the table with a glass of wine in hand. The iron chandelier caught the smooth lines of her olive skin, glinting against the knot of hair at the nape.

"Please, Irene," the man gasped, "I've told you everything I know!"

She looked to Aunt Maeve. Silver streaks ran through her braided hair and the firm lines on her face spoke of a life fighting to stay at the top. She barely looked at Irene before nodding.

"You promised information. Yet you've delivered nothing," Maeve said. "Do you know the banshee's identity, or don't you?"

"I told you, I saw her," the man sobbed. "But now…now I can't remember her face. I swear on my children's lives."

"If her identity is obscured," Irene murmured, swirling her wine, "someone is protecting her."

Maeve's lips curled, her gaze flickering between the man and Irene. "If you have any information, tell us now," she seethed. "Who. Is. She?"

"I don't know!" he wailed. "I swear!"

Discontent murmurs rippled through the dining room. The other aunts shifted in their seats, the soft rustle of silk and lace barely rising above the crackling fire. Even beneath veils, and high collars, their burns were visible—burns along knuckles, wrists, and necks. Some were pale and smooth, like old wax seals. Others flared raw and angry, refusing to fade. Aiden had been told by Irene and his sister not to stare. But his eyes always wandered. And each time, he found himself wondering whether this was a mark of their magic or something else.

A growl rolled through the floorboards like distant thunder, but no one budged. Aiden pulled back from the keyhole, glancing toward the window. The night beyond was clear of rain and wind. He leaned in again. Inside the dining room, the man had heard it too. His head lifted, eyes scanning the corners as if the sound had come from within the walls.

Then the fireplace surged, flooding the room with searing light. Aiden squinted, the brightness warping what little he could see, shadows lurching across the wallpaper. From the fire emerged a darkness solidifying into sinewy limbs and a hulking frame. Embers and ashes swirled toward the coffered ceiling as paws stepped onto the hearth. Its eyes glowed vermillion. The beast shook, sparks dusting from its hide, before releasing a howl.

A hellhound.

Its claws clicked against the floorboards, leaving scorch marks behind. The matriarchy barely glanced at it. Muscles contracted beneath fur as it gracefully leapt over Irene and onto the table. Silverware rattled and crystal glasses toppled over, but no one seemed to care. The hound lifted its head as if to evaluate the man, who writhed, suspended like a puppet tangled strings.

"Irene," he choked out. "Please—don't do this."

She didn't look up from her wine.

His body arched, limbs pulled taut by invisible force. "I kept your secrets. I stood by you after Reginald."

The flames crackled louder, as if in response.

His voice broke into a sob. "You don't have to do this. I have a daughter. She's just a little girl—please."

Still, Irene said nothing.

His eyes darted toward the hound. "I'm begging you," he whispered. "I don't want to die like this. Who will tell my family?"

The hellhound lunged at his ankle. A strangled cry tore his throat as the magical restraints released him. Plates shattered, but the matriarchy remained still. It heaved the man, scattering silverware and toppling candles in a crash of light and metal. Scorch marks streaked the linen while the man's nails tore into the wood. Finally, it hauled him off and into the fireplace, where they both vanished, leaving nothing but embers and the smell of sulfur.

Aiden stumbled back. His foot caught a side table, knocking a vase. Footsteps sounded from the dining room. He ducked behind a curtain and pressed himself against the glass, dust filling his nose as the footsteps drew closer. Through a gap, his sister Veronica appeared inches away. He held his breath, hoping she couldn't hear the frantic pounding in his chest.

Another pair of footsteps approached. "What happened to that vase?" Maeve asked.

"I'm not sure, Aunt Maeve," Veronica replied. "But I don't see anyone here."

"That vase was hideous. Leave it. A maid will clean it tomorrow."

Aiden waited until silence settled before stepping out, legs unsteady, the hellhound's howl thrumming through him. But it wasn't the beast that frightened him. It was his mother who had been untouched by the chaos. That, more than anything, made him feel like he didn't know her at all.

CHAPTER 12
Dorothy Hale

THE NIGHTMARE ALWAYS BEGAN THE SAME: DOROTHY, TRAPPED IN THE backseat, the road unspooling beneath the tires as they sped away from Albatross House. She'd beg Elliot to slow down, but he never listened. His grip tightened around the steering wheel, knuckles straining beneath his skin. The speedometer surged to *90, 120, 150,* until the digits spiraled into the impossible, and the dashboard pulsed with warning lights.

"Elliot, please!" She would claw at the seatbelt, but it wouldn't budge.

His laughter came next, manic and joyless, as though he were reacting to a joke only he heard. It fractured, collapsing into ragged sobs that echoed inside the car. And then he swerved, missing a tree. Blood oozed from the radio, gurgled between knobs and filled the cup holders. Its scent mixed with gasoline, filled her nose, burned her throat, suffocated her. Beside her, Jack lay curled against the window, his skin pallid under the dashboard's glow. His lips parted, muttering, *we're not gonna make it.* She tried to scream their names, to pull them back from whatever edge they dangled over, but her voice morphed into an endless deafening horn. The car twisted, its tires screeching. Her stomach dropped. And then she'd wake up.

Dorothy jolted upright.

"Whoops. My bad, kids. All set!"

The trolley swayed, its underside groaning as Neil's drawl floated from the conductor's seat. Her fingers clenched her sleeve, half-expecting to see blood and glass on her palms.

Wheels clattered as she leaned against the windowpane. Riders moved across a field in graceful arcs, their horses casting shadows across the grass. Their rhythm gallops soothed her, a momentary balm against the nightmare's lingering unease.

The other students drifted in and out of conversation, absorbed in their own galaxies. Some hunched over homework with furrowed brows. Others clustered in cliques, their laughter spilling down the aisle like private currency. None of them bothered to look at her. Not directly, at least. The stiffness in their shoulders, the way they angled their knees away from her, made the message clear. She had slipped past the downturned eyes and faux polite smiles and settled into the back where the windows rattled.

The brakes screeched against the tracks as they arrived at the next destination.

"C.C. stop!" Neil shouted over the noise. "If you playin' pickleball or spendin' mommy's or daddy's money, this is you."

Students rose from their seats, dressed in track jackets with the Driftmoor crest, tennis skirts, pastel quarter zips. Duffle bags with monogrammed initials hung from shoulders. They filed off, sneakers crunching against gravel as they disappeared behind a wall of boxwoods. The hedge obscured most of it, but Dorothy glimpsed a sign:

The Driftmoor Country Club

MEMBERS ONLY

EST. 1866

Beyond it, a paved drive twisted toward a building too perfect for the real world. She could almost picture the interior: tufted armchairs gathered by a grand hearth, portraits of men with silvered temples and women draped in pearls, crystal decanters filled with aged brandy, waiting for hands older than hers.

Her fingers found the cuff of her flannel, tugging at a loose thread. It wasn't the country club. It was everything it stood for. Security. Acceptance. She turned back to the window as the door hissed shut. She didn't belong there. And maybe that was the most honest thing in her life.

"Final stop: Galleon's Wharf!" Neil called out. "Last ride back's at six sharp. Miss it, and you're hitchin' a ride with campus security!"

The briny air caught in her lungs, along with caramelized sugar. Shops lined cobblestone alleyways, cedar-shingled and painted nautical blues and whites, sunlight playing off fluttering banners. Students walked away in packs, their chatter cutting through the breeze. Some headed for a saltwater taffy shop, where its window illuminated rows of wrapped sweets. Others slipped into boutiques with names she couldn't pronounce and price tags she'd never touch. She hovered at the trolley stop, unsure of where to even start.

Neil leaned out the trolley, one arm resting on the frame. "You doin' alright there, kid?"

Dorothy smiled faintly. "Thought I'd go job hunting, but I don't know," she said. "Know of any place that might be hiring?"

He scratched his chin. "Could be tough. Tourists are just about gone. But—" He jerked his chin toward the upper quay. "Try The Salty Dog. Little café up the rise, near the shipyard overlook. Last I was in, they looked slammed. Might be lookin' for help."

She nodded, grateful for the tip. "Thanks. I'll give it a try."

"Anytime, kiddo."

She pulled her sleeves down and turned toward the boardwalk. Nearby, a sailboat rocked, its rig clinking as a soulful song spilled from a speaker, crooning with the call of gulls and the clang of a buoy.

Children darted past her, skipping rocks near the pier's edge. One leaned too far before a distracted mother yelled a warning.

A row of fishermen hunched over benches, their faces hidden beneath battered caps. One looked up. His eyes, cloudy and rheumy with age, lingered on her a second too long. Then he scattered bread-crumbs to pigeons as if she weren't there at all.

But further ahead, another fisherman worked alone at a cleaning station, his blade scraping across the belly of a fish in rhythmic pulls. He paused and looked up, his eyes locking onto hers. His bushy brows drew in, and the moment stretched.

"What you lookin' at fairy girl?" he seethed through his teeth.

She tightened her grip around herself and veered wide, as if distance could dissolve the encounter.

The café stood at the wharf's far end with moss-green shingles. Above the door, a sign hung from rusted chains, creaking like the hull of a ship. *The Salty Dog*, it read, in paint barely clinging to the grain. It creaked with every gust. Too stubborn to fall, too tired to resist.

A bell jingled as Dorothy stepped inside. Warmth rushed to meet her, rich with the scent of coffee, pumpkin spice, and cinnamon. Tables lined the fogged windows, offering views of boats and salt-worn Adirondacks. A fire crackled in a brick hearth beside a battered bookshelf, and from overhead, acoustic music played. The place was steeped in comfort. But as Dorothy stood there, nerves twisting her gut, the coffee shop seemed to close in with a loneliness that even the warmest of spaces couldn't reach.

"Order for Veronica!" called a barista with curly hair from behind the counter. He handed off a drink, apron dusted with flour and coffee stains. Noah was scrawled across his nametag in chalky letters, already smudging.

Dorothy approached, grateful to find the counter free of customers.

Still, she felt eyes behind her as bright laughter sparked by the fireplace. A group of girls in Driftmoor Academy scarves glanced her way and looked back at one another with secretive smiles.

"Hey there." Noah leaned on his elbows. "What can I get ya?"

Dorothy glanced at the menu. "How much is a regular coffee?"

"Small's a buck eight-nine." He grabbed a cup printed with a dog-and-lighthouse logo.

She hesitated. "Never mind…sorry."

The girls behind her laughed again. Too conveniently timed.

Noah's smile faltered. "You sure? It's one of the best coffees you'll ever here in New England."

She almost nodded. But instead, the words slipped out before she could stop them. "By any chance, are you guys hiring?"

He gave her a once-over, his gaze catching on the bruises along her neck before lifting back to her face. "Here? It's pretty small," he said. "If we bring anyone else on, they'll probably try to cut my hours. I'm already juggling a side gig."

"I just really need a job," she said. "My parents—my mom's drowning in bills because of some stupid thing I got myself into. I'll do whatever you need. Clean tables. Do dishes. I just can't sit back while they pay for something I did."

His face softened. "Look, I get it. Believe me, I do. But we've all got something going on, you know? Sorry."

The doorbell jingled and a gust of perfume swept in, followed by clacking heels. A girl with prominent cheekbones and curls like a beauty queen strutted in. Oversized sunglasses rested in her head despite the cloudy day, while a shopping bag swung from her elbow.

"Are you finished?" Her eyes slid over Dorothy. "I could really use a latte right now."

Dorothy stepped aside. "Sorry, yeah. Guess I am."

The girl's gaze flicked to her shoes. "Cute shoes."

"Oh, thanks, they're—"

"Oh, please. Did you think I was being serious? Nobody should be caught alive in those. A low budget thrift store has shoes in better condition."

The humiliation came first before recognition followed. It was Heather. The girl from the party at Albatross House. Dorothy remembered the way she'd looked at her that night, like she already knew too much and didn't care to hide it. Even then, she spoke with casual ferocity, each word a reminder that Dorothy didn't belong.

Noah tapped a marker against the counter. "Retro's in, you know," he said. "If you ask me, I think they're pretty badass."

Heather walked past Dorothy with a huff. "Whatever. Can I order now, please? Some of us have places to be."

Noah held up a finger as he stepped out from behind the counter and stopped in front of Dorothy. He smelled like coffee beans and pastries. "Come back Monday after school," he said. "I'll try talking to the owner to see what we can do."

"Really?" Dorothy's face lit up. "Yes, okay. Thank you. I'll be here."

Behind them, Heather tapped her fingernails against the counter. "Today, Noel."

He didn't look her way. "Coming," he said. "Monday. Don't be late."

Dorothy was unable to keep herself from smiling.

Before leaving, she looked back. Noah caught her eye and winked. It wasn't much, just a brief spark between them. But it held as if the world, had paused long enough to let her be seen. The salt air filled her lungs again and the wind curled around her like a reassurance she hadn't known she needed. Maybe it wasn't security or certainty, but it was enough to carry her forward.

CHAPTER 13
Declan Albatross

DECLAN GRINNED AT THE BATHROOM SCALE. *A POUND AND A HALF.* It should've felt like progress. But it didn't. The numbers had followed him for as long as he could remember. He still felt the playground pebbles beneath his shoes, the sudden grip of a classmate's hand around his wrist, fingers probing the bone. *God, you're so thin. Do you even eat? Does your mother feed you?*

He hadn't understood then. Only that people noticed. That his body wasn't just his, but to be evaluated, reduced, and discussed. Their laughter wasn't callous so much as invasive—air siphoned from the lungs of a child who hadn't decided who he was supposed to be. And while, he didn't think about them every day, a vigilance lingered. A subtle thread through the tapestry of his self-image, tightening whenever he caught his reflection, or a suit fit him wrong.

Downstairs, Declan passed the seahorse fountain in the foyer. Once, water had poured from its mouth in prismatic arcs, catching the sun and sprinkling rainbows across the checkered foyer floor. A wedding gift from a duke to his great-grandparents, it had been meant to honor their maritime legacy. His great-grandfather used to say seahorses guided the souls of drowned sailors to the afterlife—a belief sacred to ancient sea gods. The symbol adorned the Albatross family crest, the iron gates, even the shipping containers that funded their fortune. Now, the statue stood as a monument to neglect and everything in Albatross House seemed to mimic it.

A sound drew him toward the dining room.

The once flat blue walls, now radiated with a richness like wet paint on canvas. The leather ceiling gleamed under the chandelier's glow, lacquered to a finish that reflected the candlelight in fractals. Brocade curtains had been pulled open at last to reveal the lancet windows trimmed in oxidized copper, their panes warped ever so slightly. Beyond them, the harbor caught the last blush of sunset—a smear of rose-gold against the graying evening.

"You're just in time."

His mother emerged from the pantry, balancing a tray of hors d'oeuvres. Pink bloomed high on her cheeks, and her hair caught the light with an unnatural sheen. She wore a tea-length dress in forget-me-not blue, cinched at the waist with a navy ribbon that rustled as she walked across him.

On the table, seared steaks bled into copper-rimmed china etched with anchors and kelp twisting in filigree. Truffle fries curled like scrolls in hammered bowls he hadn't seen in years. An array of cheeses sat untouched beside cured meats arranged like petals. Grapes the color of garnets spilled from a silver dish, sweating under the room's humidity, their skins tight with ripeness.

"What's all this food for?" he asked. "Are we expecting people?"

Doris placed the tray down and sank into the chair at the head of the table. "We thought a surprise might be…refreshing," she said, folding her hands as if the evening were a performance and she its orchestrator.

"We?"

The answer came in footsteps. Declan didn't need to turn to know whose.

Theodore strolled in with a decanter of bourbon and a grin too casual to be sincere. "He doesn't write, he doesn't call, but he finds time to become king of the ball. Just like his mother."

"Dad?"

He settled across from Doris, broader in the shoulders than his son, with weathered hands and a perpetual squint carved from decades at sea. He bore none of Doris's grace, only the ease of a man who didn't care how he was remembered.

"Relax," he said. "I'm busting your balls. Sit down before your mother breaks into lecture on etiquette."

Declan obeyed, spine stiff as a board. The tension between them clung to the atmosphere like static before a storm.

"I know you've been busy." Theodore poured bourbon into a glass, ice clinking. "With school, crew. Parties. And God knows Ophelia's a handful. Her mother was the same way in high school."

"Teddy." Doris shot him a pointed look.

"What?"

"Ophelia and I broke up," Declan said, looking down at the tablecloth. "Three years ago."

Theodore's grin faltered. He studied Declan for a beat. "Hm. Must've slipped your mind to mention it."

Declan turned to his mother. "Why is he even here?"

"I invited him, of course. We thought—"

"Why? Did someone die?"

Theodore chuckled. "Your mother and I are putting the past behind us. You're almost done at Driftmoor, and we figured it was time to show up and be a family again. Like old times."

Old times. Like Sunday fishing trips, where the silence pressed heavier than the waves, each cast of the line an unspoken truce between father and son. Dinners staged for magazine spreads but always ended with his mother weeping behind a locked bathroom door. And yet, Declan didn't hate Theodore. That would require energy or passion.

Some semblance of attachment. What existed was a wound that never scarred because it never bled.

Doris peered at his empty plate. "Do you plan on eating?"

"Yes, I—"

"If you keep picking at food, you'll end up skin and bones like your father at your age."

Theodore grimaced from across the table.

"I actually gained about three pounds this month," Declan muttered.

"Pass the pepper, please," Doris said, not looking at him.

He reached for the mill. Above them, the chandelier trembled. Its crystals jingled like distant bells.

"This house." Theodore mumbled, knocking back his drink. "Always falling apart."

Doris scoffed. "I'll have you know, Albatross House is one of the most recognizable homes in all of Massachusetts."

"Yeah, it's recognizable because it's crumbling," he said. "You and your father cling to it like it's worth anything when you should've torn this place down ages ago."

Declan's fork bent under his fingers.

"There are far more hideous homes in Driftmoor," Doris said. "Like Château Beaumont. Or perhaps you prefer the Barquentine. I imagine your mistress did."

A gust swept through the dining room, and the candles sputtered. The air shifted as if the house drew a deep breath. Then came the rain. It struck the table in slow drops, pooling around plates, unaffecting the flames. Declan's cable knit sweater started to sag against him as his hair plastered against his forehead.

"Don't do this." Theodore slammed his drink to the table. Declan flinched. "Not tonight. Not when I'm actually trying here."

His parents' words clashed like swords in an endless war. But theirs weren't the only ones. The house remembered another night when their voices went past the point of no return. Where his mother's screams sliced down the tapestries in the halls. Where his father's fury rattled the heirlooms displayed like a memorial. Where doors slammed hard enough to test the centuries old foundation.

Rain fell harder. As it did the night Declan locked himself in his room, pressing a pillow to his ears, tracing cracks in the ceiling and wondering if houses could break the same way people did.

Doris jolted from her chair. "Adelaide cursed this house, and you know it!" she said. "Everything was perfectly fine until you had to go and ruin it."

Theodore's face twisted. "Oh, for God's sake. The only curse here is you and those damn voices in your head!"

Declan shut his eyes, willing it away. The rain, their argument, the past clawing back to life. Then, like a radio gone dead, the sound vanished. He opened his eyes. The chandelier hung motionless, its arms tarnished, crystals dulled beneath a film of dust. Once, it might have thrown diamonds across parquet floors and silk-clad guests. Now, it loomed over a deserted stage. The air carried mildew and mothballs, not the burn of his father's bourbon. The feast had vanished. No truffle oil, no wines, no words ricocheting off him. It was just the usual ghosts, playing house in a crumbling palace.

CHAPTER 14
Lola Godfrey

Camille won. And she hadn't even tried.

Lola's sneakers pounded into the sand as she raced the tide down Craft's Beach. The breeze tugged at her ponytail, loosening strands that whipped against her cheek. Jogging was supposed to render the shame out of her pores and clear her doubts. But every stride carved that weekend deeper: Camille's name echoing over the ballroom. Applause. The crown slipping onto her golden head. Lola had campaigned like it was war. Color-coded flyers like battle maps. Speeches written, rewritten, and rehearsed. She'd smile until her face hurt, held doors, played nice to people she'd never speak to again.

Sweat beaded along her brow. Her calves burned, but she welcomed it.

This was never about the crown. It stood for the reality that Godfreys didn't lose. Her mother drilled it into her with every trophy shelf and award, every planned affair, every family portrait in a house that worshipped success like religion. Winning wasn't the goal. It was the bare minimum. And for the first time, Lola hadn't reached it. And to make matters worse, that same night, Ophelia left her to die. The loss humiliated her, and the fall should've ended her. One had fractured her pride. The other, her body. And both happened beneath the same stars.

The tide retreated, dragging seafoam back like the world had washed its hands of her. The dunes leading back to campus rolled opposite of it. Further ahead, Driftmoor Academy's cross-country team curved around the bend in unified formation. They waved at her, but she didn't wave back. Their expressions were courteous, but the smiles weren't meant for her. They belonged to the Lola they had crafted in their minds. Clever. Immaculate. Easy to adore. If they could hand Camille the crown, they could hand someone else the future Lola had spent her entire life building for herself. She adjusted her headphones and let Declan's playlist pull her forward.

A few minutes in, her cell phone buzzed. Mid-stride, she glanced down. Mother.

She sighed, schooling her tone into practiced brightness. "Mama! How's the island? Still pretending you hate paradise?"

"Magnifico," Esmeralda replied, her accent crisp as ever. "But let's not pretend I called to talk about sunsets and mojitos."

Lola paused, adjusting her weight onto one foot as she stared at the harbor. "Oh, I don't know," she said. "I assumed it was motherly instinct. Or maybe boredom."

"Don't be so flippant," Esmeralda said. "It's not a cute look for you." "Of course. How silly of me to muster some personality."

"I heard from Gwen Croft," her mother continued. "Apparently, things didn't go as expected at the Founders' Ball."

"Oh? And here I thought you stopped caring about high school social politics the day you traded your letterman boyfriend for a hedge fund."

"You know I've never found your sarcasm charming."

"You never found anything about me charming," Lola murmured to herself.

A beat of silence. Then: "I expected more. I thought you had this under control."

The sting landed like always. Still, Lola straightened her shoulders as if Esmeralda were physically there to correct her posture.

"I did have it under control," she said. "I ran a flawless campaign. Headmistress Mortimer even said so. She called it the most organized, strategic campaign the Academy's had in over a decade."

"Then clearly, strategy isn't enough."

"I lost by a margin," Lola said, jaw tightening. "It wasn't a landslide."

Esmeralda scoffed. "There's no glory in second place. Just look at your brother. No one builds statues for the girl who almost wore the crown."

Lola didn't respond. She just kicked at a seashell debating whether she should hang up.

"You're fortunate your grades and extracurriculars are intact," Esmeralda said. "But don't mistake that for stability. A Godfrey is allowed many things, but not mediocrity. And certainly not sympathy."

Lola let the bitterness rise like bile. "Because God help me if someone sees me bleeding."

"Have you reached out to Ophelia?"

"Excuse me?"

"She's back, isn't she?" Esmeralda asked. "And from what I hear, she's making quite the impression. Reestablishing your connection wouldn't be the worst idea. I was actually thinking of inviting her and Meredith over for dinner one of these days."

Lola scoffed. "We're not fourteen anymore. That ship sailed and sunk. Or maybe you forgot," she said. "You can invite her mother. But Ophelia is not allowed in our home."

"Then remember this instead: your reputation is not a birthright. It's a performance. And you can't afford to be upstaged."

"Ophelia isn't special," Lola said, though it curdled in her throat. People still whispered about the time she crashed Mrs. Ellery's garden party and stole the microphone, gave a toast that left half the guests in tears, the other half enchanted. No apology. No consequences. Just that infuriating million-dollar smile. No matter what she did, no one ever believed the worst of a girl like Ophelia Lockhart.

Lola turned toward the water, eyes catching the ripple of sunlight stretching like melted silver. "So that's it? You want me to play nice with the girl who disappeared on me just because she's the new town spectacle?"

"Play nice or be forgotten. Your choice."

She let the silence stretch. "Speaking of performances," she said. "Will you be attending the tea this year, or should I expect another rain check written in Jesenia's handwriting?"

Esmeralda sighed. "I may not have time. I'll have her send you my itinerary. If I decide to fly in."

Lola didn't say goodbye. Just ended the call and stood still, the wind tugging at her hair. Then she continued her run. Craft's Beach narrowed ahead of her. The sand turned coarse, and the wind sharpened. Her breath steadied into even exhales, more controlled than her thoughts. A week had passed, but her body remembered the way it broke.

Her eyes lifted and there it was. Silver Shoals.

Blood hit the back of her throat first, followed by warmth that dripped down her chin and stained her neck red. Salt stung the gash at her temple and mingled with iron as it seeped into the wound. She lay twisted against the rocks, half submerged in the harbor while waves tried to pull her in. Her wrist was jutted at a crooked angle and breathing set her ribs grinding against each other.

Ophelia left me.

She remembered the shouting. The shove. The weightlessness.

Her hand fumbled to her side. It came away crimson, blood leaking from a place that didn't spare people.

The first shift came with a sound like meat being wrenched from a hook. Her muscles twitched as fibers knotted back together in erratic pulses. Ligaments recoiled and snapped into place with sickening tension. She sobbed through it because what else could she do? She couldn't stop it. Couldn't outrun it. Her entire anatomy had become hijacked by some ancient, involuntary instinct to survive. And it didn't care that it was torturing her.

Bones were next. A seismic pressure rolled through her chest as her ribs cracked apart and slammed back into alignment. Her spine arched, heels scraping rock, as her wrist reshaped. She choked on salt and blood. The gash at her temple cinched shut like a thread being yanked through flesh.

And then finally, stillness. Her cardigan clung to her, soaked and clotted with blood. She lay unmoving. Whole again but not healed. Just restored. Like a broken doll, hastily mended and returned to its shelf.

Her gaze rose to the witness that saw her break and stitch herself back together again. A sob caught in her chest. Not from the pain, but from the knowledge that she could disappear and nothing would stop. The tide would rise. The stars would burn. And when she'd walked away from this, the world wouldn't even notice.

CHAPTER 15
Dorothy Hale

Dorothy waited at the trolley stop with her arms crossed, bracing against the harbor wind. Around her, students had reunited into clusters, their laughter bright as they compared finds from the wharf. Someone passed around a sleeve of candied almonds. Another held up a scarf, initials freshly monogrammed in gold thread. Part of her wanted to drift closer, to laugh at a joke she didn't hear, to ask about the almonds. But the knot in her stomach held her still. She didn't know how to step into circles. So she waited, pretending the cold was the only thing keeping her arms crossed.

But behind them, a pub hunched beneath salt-eaten shingles, its paint blistered, and its windows smeared with the sweat and smoke. Lanterns swung, casting halos over the fishermen gathered—men shaped by tide and wind, their raincoats heavy with brine. Bottles crinkled in paper bags as they slurred murmurs and sweeping gestures. Their eyes slid over her now and then. Not long enough to be called staring, but enough to be felt.

"The sea don't take kindly to her sort hangin' about," one muttered. She stiffened. It was the same man she'd seen gutting fish earlier. "She got the look of a fairy woman, she does," he said, squinting. She hugged herself, willing her legs to remain still even as instinct begged her to move. To distract herself, she focused on the homes that leaned into one another across the street. Their stoops were adorned with pumpkins and rust-colored mums. The domestic charm didn't help. She felt no safer beneath the fluttering flags or the bustle of Galleon's Wharf. Not when drunken men ogled her from a few feet away.

She had stolen a quick glance, but not quick enough.

"What you starin' at!" the fisherman shouted, his words garbled. He stumbled sideways before catching himself on the pub's wall. But his voice traveled across the cobblestones, and a few students paused mid-conversation, whispering as they looked between him and Dorothy.

She was relieved when the trolley bell clanged down the street. Immediately, she edged closer to the curb. Not because she was in a hurry but getting on first meant a buffer between her and the fisher-men. But she didn't want to appear rushed or scared, even as her palms dampened against her jeans. The door opened with a metallic sigh. Climbing aboard, she found Neil at the front, his baseball cap tilted and a cup from The Salty Dog on the dashboard.

"Hey there, kid," he said. "Any bites on the job front?"

She paused halfway up the steps, glancing over her shoulder.

Neil followed her gaze. "Those clowns runnin' their mouths again?"

"How could you tell?"

"Let's just say a lotta old-timers 'round here get wicked superstitious."

She stepped aside as students jolted past, their chatter and footsteps a blur.

"But what does that have to do with me?" she asked. "One of them called me a weird name. A fairy woman. Do you know what that means?"

Neil scratched his chin. "Yeah, they like to spew nonsense. Say things to spook tourists. But newcomers that look—" He paused, eyes flicking toward her. "Like you? Well, they talk a little different. Like you shouldn't be here."

"What do you mean, like me?"

"They see red hair, fair skin and they start whisperin'," he said. "Just old town paranoia, that's all. Folks think women like that got one foot in this world and the other somewhere else."

She swallowed. "Like I'm some kind of ghost?"

"Just a sailors' tale. Stuff they muttah when the fog rolls in. Forget about it."

But she couldn't. Not as she slipped into a seat and hugged herself tight. Her reflection trembled in the glass, overlaid with the sky and blurred silhouettes. The trolly jerked into motion with a groan, its wheels shrieking against the tracks. She glanced out the window one last time. The fishermen hadn't moved. Their stares held her in place, even as the wharf fell away behind.

The trolley turned onto a street, the maple trees ablaze with reds, oranges, and yellows. Dorothy had never seen an East Coast autumn before. In Seattle, fall usually meant gray skies and drizzle. But here, the season burned brighter. Even after the last few weeks, its beauty softened the edges of her unease.

Lower Driftmoor unfurled in fragments. Picket fences curled inwards. Unattended lawns were cluttered with forgotten toys and overgrown flowerbeds. Moss crept up walls, and porch steps sank in the middle. Dorothy hadn't expected this part of Driftmoor. But even the prettiest towns had a rot beneath the paint.

They rounded the bend, and her breath caught. The guardrail still bore the twisted curl of metal where Elliot's car had gone through. The embankment sloped downward, and at its edge stood a wooden cross ringed with cloudy, half-melted candles. A ribbon fluttered at its based, while flowers curled inward like they no longer wanted to be seen. The air thinned, and conversations receded. In her mind, tires screeched, while Elliot's laughter rang out, and then the impact.

The seatbelt assaulting her ribcage. The last breath of innocence stolen from her lungs.

She blinked it away. And when she opened her eyes, there was a man kneeling at the memorial with his head bowed. But his edges wavered like heat rising off asphalt.

She leaned forward just as the man vanished.

No heads turned. Conversations continued. And the trolley rattled on.

Her breath hitched and returned sharp when he reappeared on the tracks with his head hung low. His grayed and translucent skin contrasted against to the autumn scenery.

Dorothy bolted upright. "Stop!"

The brakes came to a shrieking halt, sending bags tumbling as a drink hit the floor with a splash. Gasps and curses rang out as students grabbed at seats and rails, turning their bodies in confusion.

Neil snapped around, already halfway out of his seat. "Somebody yell stop? What the hell's goin' on? Everyone okay?"

"The new girl's freaking out!"

"Is she crying?"

"That's the chick from the accident, right?"

Dorothy's eyes shot to the tracks, but there was nothing there. Heat crept up her neck as she collapsed back into the seat. "I…I thought…" she murmured, but the words turned to dust.

Neil returned to his seat. The trolley shuddered to life, the wheels rattling through the floor. The colorful woods whispered past, and inside her head, the fisherman's words repeated.

Fairy woman.

Dorothy stepped out of her shoes and slid them beneath the bed, a four-poster with finials carved like spears. Cracked molding adorned the ceiling, and the striped wallpaper peeled, revealing older layers beneath, like the dorm had tried on different faces over the years and never settled. A flyer for the Driftmoor Art Club clung to the wall where she'd tacked it last week. She hovered in the center of it all, unsure what to do. She reached for a mug that wasn't there. She hadn't thought to unpack one.

There was a knock at the door. Dorothy hesitated, unsure anyone even knew where her room was, let alone wanted to visit. She peered through the peephole before opening the door.

"Headmistress Mortimer," she said.

Mortimer stood framed in the amber glow of the hallway sconces, her tan skin warm beneath the light, her suit crisp beneath a fur stole. "Good evening, Miss Hale. I hope I'm not disturbing you."

"No, not at all." Dorothy stepped aside to let her in.

Mortimer looked around. "I trust you're adjusting well," she said. "And I'm sorry to hear Miss Bradson requested a room reassignment. I wouldn't take it personally. Some students process discomfort in different ways."

When she'd returned to Driftmoor Academy, Dorothy hadn't expected Amani to be gone. She hadn't even known she'd asked for a transfer. It didn't feel personal, but not knowing carved deeper than she'd anticipated.

From the inner fold of her suit, Mortimer withdrew a wax-sealed envelope. "This is for you. An invitation to Driftmoor's annual Silent Art Auction. It's held at Oldwyck Manor and has been a cornerstone of Academy tradition."

Dorothy accepted it, the envelope heavy, the seal cool beneath her thumb. She cracked the wax, revealing an invitation penned in calligraphy:

You are cordially invited to attend
The Driftmoor Silent Art Auction
Friday, September 26th at dusk
Oldwyck Manor

Formal Attire Required

All proceeds benefit the Driftmoor Young Artists Foundation

"Why me?" she asked. "I'm not even in any art classes."

Mortimer's gaze softened. "Your professors speak highly of you. Not just academically, but in terms of your resilience. This evening is about more than paintings and sculptures. It's about becoming part of what shapes Driftmoor. And perhaps, rediscovering your creative side."

"Thanks, but I don't really think I'm an artist anymore."

"Nonsense. Once an artist, always an artist. The well may dry, but the riverbed remains." Mortimer stepped closer. "Besides, the Oldwycks have amassed a fascinating collection. I think you'll find the evening more revealing than you expect."

Dorothy's eyes dropped to the bottom of the invitation. *Formal Attire Required.*

"I don't know," she said. "I wouldn't even know what to wear. I didn't pack a dress."

"I'll arrange for Miss Pawlikowski from the theater department to assist. She'll ensure you have something suitable. Consider this not merely an invitation, Miss Hale," Mortimer tilted her head, "but a formal request. I'll expect to see you there."

With a pivot, Mortimer turned, her stole brushing the doorframe. The door clicked shut behind her, and silence settled, except for music seeping through the back wall from Dorothy's neighbor. She sat on the edge of her bed and placed the invitation on her lap. Her gaze traced the crest: two hounds, mid-howl beneath a crescent moon, their paws curled in flames. She ran her fingers along the raised parchment. Maybe this was her chance to try again. To prove, to herself, if not her peers, that she could belong. Even if just for a night.

CHAPTER 16
Declan Albatross

ALBATROSS HOUSE CREAKED AROUND HIM, ITS WOODEN BONES aching under years that refused to pass. Declan faced the bathroom mirror. His green eyes scrutinized the angles of his jaw, the slope of his cheeks, the too-slopey curve of his nose. His hands shook as he reached for the silver cufflinks on the marble counter. They slipped once. Then again.

He exhaled before finally snapping them into place. He already knew where his reflection would fail him. His shoulders sloped too inward. The collar sagged, revealing too much skin. And every imperfection—real or imagined—seemed to swell. He had spent years molding himself into the boy he thought Ophelia could love. But the more he reshaped himself, the more parts of himself he lost. And he was running out of pieces.

The pill bottle lingered on the counter. When the chemicals took hold, his skin didn't feel like it was burning. That was why he took them on days like this, when his thoughts tore through him like wildfire. He twisted the cap, shook one tablet into his palm, and swallowed. The taste was chalky, but soon the noise would fade, and breathing wouldn't hurt.

Bookshelves flanked his bedrooms walls, lined with first editions and antiques passed down from his grandfather. The furniture gleamed beneath the light, each piece placed with care, as if order might keep the ghosts at bay. A navy wool throw Aiden gifted him lay folded across the bed. In front of the bay window, a bronze telescope stood. It had once belonged to his father, before it belonged to his father. They used to stand beside it, shoulder to shoulder, breath fogging the glass as stars blinked above the estate.

"See that, Declan?" Theodore would say, pointing to a pinprick of light. "It barely looks like more than a flicker, but that's the one you follow. The sky's full of noise. But if you fix your gaze long enough, light will always guide you home."

Declan had believed that once. Before his mother stopped noticing when he entered or left a room. Before his father's voice became part of the woodwork, more memory than man.

Down the hall, he paused outside his mother's bedroom. He reached for the doorknob. Drew a breath. Stepped inside. Velvet drapes hung over the windows, deep blue threaded with silver swirls. They sagged like tired lungs. An empty vodka bottle rested on its side atop the nightstand, a smear of condensation beneath it. Doris sat by the French doors, her silhouette backlit by the gloom. Chestnut hair spilled over her, unbrushed against her nightgown.

"The waves rise," she murmured, "but they're never still. Not even for a moment." Her fingers trembled as they turned the string of pearls around her neck—a gift from Theodore when they first started dating. "Can you hear it? They're calling…Waiting."

Declan could've asked what she meant. But he'd already spent most of his teenage years trying to decode her. "Mom?"

As though waking from some distant dream, her eyes found his. "I didn't hear you come in," she said. "Going somewhere?"

"The auction's tonight." He lingered in the doorway. "I'm guessing you're not going?"

She smiled. Or attempted to. "You know I stopped going to those things." Her gaze returned to the window. "It's just not where someone like me belongs anymore."

"But what if you tried?" He looked at the family photographs lining the dresser, smiling faces caught in silver and gold frames. They all looked like strangers now.

Doris Albatross had once been surrounded by envy and admiration in equal measure. In the years before the divorce, Albatross House thrived under her reign. Over a hundred guests would gather at a time, the air alive with string quartets and laughter, champagne bubbling in fluted glassware. On nights like this, the halls buzzed with expectancy, staff moving through candlelight like dancers, each movement rehearsed.

Back then, she could muster an evening of expectations. She smiled on cue. Laughed where she was supposed to. Her lipstick never smudged, and neither did her suffering. And even when her thoughts wandered, they never showed. But after the divorce, she had changed. She knocked over drinks now. He'd seen her fade mid-conversation, and her friends—once fiercely loyal—began to drift. The cracks showed, and no amount of silk could conceal them. Lately, she spoke less to people than to the ocean, and her green eyes, once so cutting, now wandered with the weight of too many yesterdays.

Her voice was quiet again. "Tried? What would change? The sea's not interested in what we try. It takes." A beat passed. "And I'm tired of pretending otherwise."

Declan crossed to the wardrobe. The doors creaked as he opened them, the scent of cedar and fading perfume rising. Inside hung the armor she no longer claimed. He sifted through them, until his hand found her favorite dress. Emerald green, with beadwork across the bodice and a shimmer like seafoam at dusk. He held it up and brought it his face. The fabric was cold, but not unkind.

"Just try this on," he said, voice tight. "Maybe you'll feel different once you're in it. Please."

Surprise flickered in her expression and her fingers twitched. For a breath, it seemed she might reach for the dress. Then without a word, she yanked the gown and tore it down the middle. The sound split through the room as beads scattered across the rug.

Her lips moved, but her voice was barely coherent. Fractured syllables strung together, gutted of meaning. Declan stood frozen, clutching empty air, as the torn fabric slumped between them. He backed away. Each step echoed louder than it should've until he reached the hallway.

Albatross House had always been a home of contradictions: beauty tangled with decay, glamour stained with despair, comfort edged by distress. Driftmoor remembered its grandeur, the marble staircase and chandeliered halls. But within its walls, the truth endured: a mausoleum of memories, a gilded cage stripped of its luster. And Declan walked it like one of its ghosts. Not because he had died, but because the version of him that once believed she could be saved had.

CHAPTER 17
Aiden Oldwyck

AIDEN DROPPED HIS HANDS, THE BOWTIE HANGING DEFEATED AROUND his neck. This had been easier when his father was around. He rolled his shoulders, but the tension didn't leave him. It wasn't the tie. It wasn't even the thought of tiptoeing through Oldwyck Manor tonight to avoid Heather. The weight on his shoulders was about the aunts cloaked in veils, gathered like wraiths around the dining table. Their whispers beneath candlelight. A man suspended midair, his sobs swallowed by their indifference. And then the hellhound emerging from the fireplace before its jaws closed around said man as if he were nothing more than a scrap of meat.

Each night since, Aiden startled awake to claws scraping on floorboards and steps pacing outside his bedroom door. Always a dream, but the sensation lingered that someone or something was watching him.

"Need some help?"

Irene stood in the doorway, dressed in a gown that shimmered like dried blood. Her hair was pinned with precision, save for a few strands left loose.

Aiden grinned sheepishly. "Is it that awful?"

"I've seen grown men do worse." She stepped in, and her perfume followed, violets crushed with amber and a sweetness he'd never been able to place.

She reached for his collar with deft hands, her touch warm as she tightened the bow with symmetrical ease. For a moment, she stilled. Her russet eyes flickered, the mask she wore slipped just enough for him to see the woman beneath the matriarch.

"There." She smoothed the lapel of his blazer. "Now you look like someone who belongs. A dignified young man of the Oldwycks."

He searched her face for some truth or remorse, but all he found was distance.

"Mom," he said. "What…what happened to that man?"

Her hand paused mid-air. "I'm afraid I don't understand the question. What man?"

"Yes, you do," he said. "The one from Thursday. The one Aunt Maeve and the others summoned that thing for."

Her gaze dropped and lifted again. "You know nothing," she said. "And that thing has protected this family for generations."

"Protected us from what?"

He didn't mean to let it crack, but the fracture was there. The question was too big to contain. Because he didn't know what they were afraid of or what they fought behind closed doors. Only that it involved blood and magic. And the way his aunts looked at him, like he'd already failed some test he was never told existed.

"This would be easier," he said, "if you just told me the truth. Why they hate me. Why you shut me out. Anything would help. Because right now, it feels like I don't matter."

He thought she might speak. That she might unravel and reach for him the way mothers were supposed to. But all she said was, "How could you say such a thing? Of course you matter. You are the most important thing in my life. My pride and joy."

He stared at her. "I'm pretty sure that's Veronica."

Silence fell between them. It wasn't new.

At last, Irene turned to the hallway, her voice steady. "We have a long night ahead," she said. "Shall we?"

Aiden stood at the edge of his bedroom like it might be possible to stay behind, to not follow her into whatever performance tonight required. But in the end, he followed. He always did.

Conversations curled beneath the vaulted ceiling as guests wandered between velvet-draped exhibits and towering portraits. Aiden eased into the auction, exchanging nods and remarks with a smile. Tonight, among these people, he wouldn't be the son of a family who didn't want him. And that filled him with a vitality he never felt in the halls of Oldwyck Manor.

Servers moved like brushstrokes between rooms, dressed in painter's smocks, their faces transformed into surrealist canvases. Eyes melted like wax down cheeks. Mouths stretched into warped Cheshire grins. One server passed close, her third eye painted so precisely on her brow, it seemed to blink. Aiden angled his body away, pretending to study the chandelier.

Across the parlor, he spotted Heather standing beside her mother, Gwen. The two were talking with Irene, half-shadowed beneath an extravagant arrangement of orchids and oxblood dahlias. Gwen's hand rested on Heather's shoulder, a gesture Aiden knew was as possessive as it was performative. He hadn't spoken to Heather since the Founders' Ball. He hadn't even thought much about how she was doing after their breakup. Was it wrong he hadn't reached out? Or was it just the exhaustion of being human, of deciding which fractures to tend and which to let bleed?

Aiden turned away before she noticed him—only to collide with a server, whose face had been painted in the style of Picasso. Wine splashed across the boy as the tray tipped from him.

"Oh god. I'm so sorry," Aiden said, reaching instinctively. "I am so sorry about this."

A group of girls nearby stifled laugher behind manicured hands. One whispered, and the others turned toward the commotion with eyes sharp and gleaming. The server stood straight. His smock clung to his waist, red wine dripping from his collar. He pressed his lips into a line, like the night had already earned its place among the bad ones.

"It's—it's fine," he muttered, stripping off the smock and folding it over his arm.

"No, it's not. I should've been paying attention." Aiden's hands hovered, uncertain. "Wait, don't you go to Driftmoor?"

The boy glanced away. "What can I say? Not all of us are born with a trust fund."

The words stung more than Aiden let on. "Look, come with me," he said. "I have spare shirts upstairs that might fit. You can borrow one before my mother sees you and freaks."

The boy's gazed flickered toward Irene, still standing beside Gwen, her arm now looped casually at Gwen's waist. Heather was no longer with them. Irene gestured toward a sculpture, her expression animated, her smile precise. The kind she reserved for winning over donors.

"You messing with me?" the boy asked.

"Not at all. Unless you prefer looking like you got stabbed for the rest of the night."

The boy let out a breath that landed between a scoff and a sigh. "Fine. Lead the way, trust fund baby."

Aiden raised a brow. "It's Aiden."

"I know," the boy replied without looking at him.

Aiden glanced sideways. "Do I get your name? Or am I letting a stranger borrow my clothes?"

The boy hesitated, long enough for it to feel deliberate. "Guess you've earned it," he said. "You can call me Noah. No relation to the ark."

After that exchange, Aiden guided Noah through a narrow gallery. They passed a woman with no face, made of birdcage wire, and a deer sculpted from ash, its pupils pink. They slipped into a tucked-away stairwell, the walls papered in peeling brocade and lined with iron sconces.

"Wow. This is ironic," Noah said behind him.

Aiden looked over his shoulder. "What is?"

"You're sneaking me through the servant stairs. Like I'm some kind of secret."

Aiden rolled his eyes, though heat crept up the back of his neck. "There's nothing secretive about this. It's faster."

Noah's smirk carried in the dark. They emerged into the corridor outside Aiden's bedroom, where portraits of women in starched collars and pearl-drop earrings glowered from the walls. Aiden opened the door, and Noah followed.

Drapes framed the window, stitched with a faded damask pattern. Vinyl records were stacked beside a record player, sharing space with model planes and bookends shaped like lion heads. On the far wall, a glass case showcased Aiden's racquets, each one bearing a plaque with the year and tournament, their handles darkened. The room smelled of cedar and cologne, like a room meant to remember a boy trying to grow into a man someone else had imagined.

"I think we're about the same size," Aiden said, heading for the closet.

"Debatable," Noah replied. "I might have you beat in the arms department."

His fingers trailed along the bedpost. A photograph on the dresser caught his attention: a picture of Aiden with Declan, Lola, Heather and Ophelia, windswept and smiling in front of Silver Shoals. He tilted the frame. "Which one of these is the girlfriend?"

Aiden stilled. "The curly-haired one. But we're not together anymore."

"She's pretty," Noah said, setting the frame back. "How'd you screw that one up?"

Aiden pretended not to hear him. Inside the closet, brass rods and custom shelving held pressed shirts and neatly folded sweaters. He pulled a white button-down off a hanger and turned to Noah.

"Just try this on."

Their fingers brushed as Noah took it. Without hesitation, he unbuttoned his stained shirt and peeled it off, muscles flexing up his back. Droplets of wine clung to him, glistening where they hadn't dried. Aiden meant to look away, but his gaze caught on the line of his spine and the definition in his biceps.

"You okay over there?" Noah asked, adjusting the cuffs in the mirror.

"Yup. Fine," Aiden said. "It looks like it fits, right?"

A smirk crept on Noah's lips. "Think you might be right." He paused to examine his reflection. "Thanks. Guess all you trust fund babies aren't all the same."

"You'd be surprised when you don't judge people."

Noah let out a scoff. "I oughta head back before I'm fired for job abandonment."

His hand hovered on the doorknob before stepping into the hall. The door clicked behind him. Aiden stood there, the wine-stained shirt on the floor. He meant to call out, to return it, but instead, he sat on the ottoman.

This feeling wasn't new. It happened in smaller ways around Declan. During sleepovers. Summer trips to Nantucket. Mornings when the world hadn't woken, and it was just the two of them. But those were passing sparks. Moments he could rationalize and easily dismiss. This was different. This lived in him. And he didn't know what to do with it.

CHAPTER 18
Dorothy Hale

Dorothy had spent over an hour sifting through the gowns Headmistress Mortimer had delivered. Each hung in a garment bag, worlds away from anything she'd owned. Silk, gossamer, velvet. Fabrics that shimmered with lives she hadn't lived. Now, she stood before the mirror in a floor-length gown the color of candlelight. She had tamed and brushed her hair until it resembled something elegant. The dress draped over her like it had been made for a woman who wouldn't question her right to be seen. The confidence it lent her felt borrowed. Would anyone spot the seams where she didn't quite fit, the insecurities peeking through the sequins?

She reached for her coat, then her fingers twitched, as if they remembered a thought she tried to forget. The last time she'd left this dorm for a party, she'd nearly died. That thought had followed her all day. But she told herself this would be different. Not some drunken house party filled with privileged teenagers. This was an auction with adults. There would be rules. Order.

She slipped the coat on, its lining cool against her arms, and fastened the buttons with more force than necessary. Her heels clicked against the floorboards as she moved toward the staircase. From the common room, chatter and giggles drifted over the drone of a projector. But the moment she stepped inside, the noise evaporated. Her floormates lay across the couches in sweatshirts and pajamas, quilts bunched around their knees. One girl muted the film. Another looked away too fast. Amani sat with a girl who Dorothy assumed was her new roommate. The look on her face carried no malice, nor welcome. Only recognition that what had once passed for closeness had been nothing more than friendly proximity.

Dorothy lifted her chin and crossed the room. She didn't flinch or glance back to see if they watched her. She took that borrowed confidence and wore it like armor.

Outside, a black car idled at the curb. Its surface reflected the Winthrop Hall's light in wavelike distortions while a white-gloved chauffeur waited beside the rear door.

He bowed slightly as she approached, opening the door. "Good evening, Miss Hale."

Dorothy halted. "Oh thank you, but that's not really necessary."

The chauffer smiled. "Your headmistress insisted you have a smooth experience tonight."

"Guess I can't say no to that."

Her fingers dug into the seat as the car rolled forward. The cushion dipped beneath her in a way that coiled her stomach. She glanced at the seatbelt. The memory of the one from Elliot's car locking across her chest made her feel like she couldn't breathe. She pressed her knees together, palms flat against sequins. Her heartbeat thudded, too fast for the calm ride. Campus blurred past in streaks of stone and amber light. In the glass, a girl in satin stared back, but her shoulders were tight as if she hadn't left the wreck.

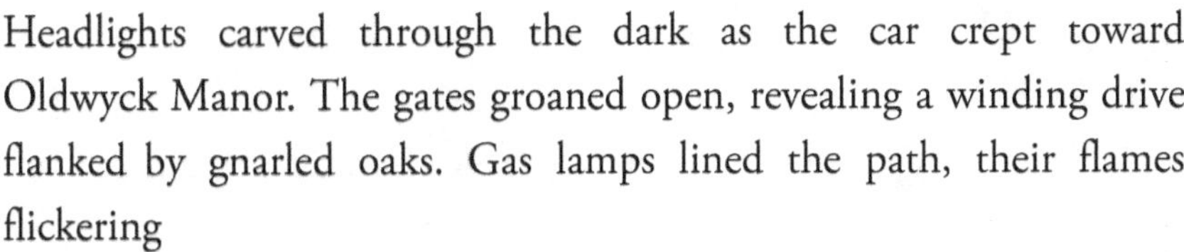

Headlights carved through the dark as the car crept toward Oldwyck Manor. The gates groaned open, revealing a winding drive flanked by gnarled oaks. Gas lamps lined the path, their flames flickering behind beveled glass. Dorothy's breath fogged the window as the manor appeared. First, turrets, slate-capped and pointed, then arched windows, aglow with candlelight behind leaded panes. A weathervane spun lazily above the central spire, shaped like a wolf.

The car slowed before a circular drive paved in granite and trimmed with bronze curbs. A limestone staircase unfurled before the manor's doors, where waiters held trays of champagne beside columns entwined with ivy. Vintage automobiles and foreign sedans gleamed beneath hanging lanterns, their lacquered surfaces winking against the rain-wet ground. Dorothy's hand hovered near the handle, her muscles clenched before she realized she was holding her breath.

The chauffeur opened the door, and it felt as though the tension from the fifteen-minute ride couldn't follow her past this point. She closed her eyes for a beat too long. The cold brushed her face like a reminder: *You're here. You made it.*

"Thank you," she murmured, adjusting the belt of her coat.

Oldwyck Manor rose in three stories of weathered red brick, veined with moss. Carvings curled above the entryway of grotesques, gargoyles, and a family crest. Inside, oak-paneled walls glowed under the iron chandelier, each twisted arm crowned with dripping candelabras. The floors beneath her were parquet, inlaid with a floral pattern that echoed the scrollwork on the banisters. The staircase split halfway to embrace a frescoed ceiling: spectral riders on horseback galloping across a scorched battlefield, their mouths frozen mid-scream, their banners burning. She felt like she had stepped into a museum designed by someone who didn't believe in death. Only the preservation of power.

"Dorothy Hale?"

Camille Beaumont approached with a sunny ease. Her rosy cheeks and glossy blonde waves gave her the sort of beauty Dorothy envied. The pale blue satin of her gown hugged her figure like it had been sculpted to her.

"Hi," Dorothy said with a nervous smile. "Camille, right?"

"Yes, it's so nice to meet you!" Camille leaned in for a light hug, her perfume crisp and sweet. "Is this your first auction?"

Dorothy nodded, already feeling self-conscious under Camille's gaze.

"You're going to love it. Irene's auctions are kind of legendary. And I heard from Headmistress Mortimer that you're an artist?"

"Kinda. I draw animals sometimes." Dorothy glanced down, brushing a hand over her waist. "Nothing serious, really."

"Well, you must be good if you're here. Ready for a tour?"

The main hall pulsed with light jazz. Silver platters floated through the crowd, balanced by servers with surrealist-painted faces. Eyes melted down cheeks, mouths spiraled into smirks, and clocks spun across foreheads. Camille guided her through it all, gesturing toward displays with a sophisticated sweep of her hand.

One portrait showed a woman in a tutu with a veil of insects. Another captured a house with spider legs, frozen mid-step across an apocalyptic skyscape. In a corner alcove, a taxidermy bird perched beneath glass, its wings replaced by paintbrushes, its beak dipped in gold.

"Most of the art is from Irene's collection," Camille explained. "Art's practically sacred to the Oldwycks. There's even a salon upstairs with panels from a Venetian ballroom. During the day, they shimmer when the light hits just right."

Before Dorothy could respond, a voice broke through the column behind them.

"Hey, look who it is."

An adorable smile tugged at Declan's lips. He wore a navy suit that skimmed his lean physique. His chestnut brown hair had been parted, though one strand fell rebelliously across his dark brows. He held a small plate stacked with hors d'oeuvres. It was more than she might've expected for someone so put together to have. She wasn't sure why she noticed it, only that it felt intentional. Like he was trying.

"Hey," she managed. "It's um, so nice to see you again." She wouldn't normally say that, but it felt like the right thing to say in this setting.

He gave Camille a quick hug, then turned to Dorothy. "This is the last place I expected to see you," he said with a grin. "Did Camille drag you against your will?"

"Ha. Ha." Camille rolled her eyes. "The headmistress invited her. Apparently Dorothy is an art prodigy."

Dorothy flushed. "Just little sketches. Nothing like this," she said. "And I honestly haven't drawn anything in forever."

"I'm sure she's being modest," Camille said.

"Bet they're better than anything I could do," Declan added. His eyes lingered in a way that made Dorothy shift. "I'd like to see them. If you ever feel like sharing."

"Sure," she said, though the idea made her want to vanish.

A girl in silver appeared beside Declan. Auburn curls framed her heart-shaped face, and her gown caught the chandelier light like frost on glass.

"There you are," Declan said. "Dorothy, this is Lola. Lola, Dorothy."

Lola extended her hand, a diamond bracelet sparkling at her wrist as she evaluated Dorothy. Dorothy hesitated and took it. Lola's grip was light yet firm.

"You're that new scholarship girl from California, aren't you?" she said.

"Washington," Dorothy corrected. "But yeah, that's me."

Lola pursed her lips. "Thought so. You've got that unpolished sincerity people find charming."

"She's trying to be charming," Declan said, as if reading Dorothy's mind. "It just doesn't always come out that way."

Lola raised an eyebrow but didn't refute it.

Camille cleared her throat. "We should keep going, Dorothy. There's an installation on women's autonomy in the conservatory that I'd love for you to see."

Lola's gaze slid to her. "Camille."

"Lola." Camille's smile gleamed like glass. Pretty, but sharp around the edges. "What happened to you at the Founders' Ball? I didn't see you on stage during the coronation."

"I had better places to be."

"Is that so?"

A crystalline chime rang out, cutting clean through the noise. The crowd turned toward the staircase where Irene Oldwyck stood, framed by candelabras and the shadow of a hound's head carved into the balustrade. Lola gave Dorothy one last indecipherable look before turning away.

"Good evening, everyone," Irene said from the landing. "It's a pleasure to welcome you all to Driftmoor's Annual Silent Art Auction."

A beat of poised silence.

"Tonight is about more than art. It's about legacy. About investing in creativity, and ensuring that it lives on, untamed and unforgotten. Every bid placed tonight supports the Young Artists Foundation, and helps preserve the artistic spirit of our community, and the Academy's heritage." Her gaze swept across the room. "So enjoy the evening. Savor the art, the wonder, and, of course, the wine."

Applause rippled and movement resumed as guests flocked toward bid stations where clipboards exchanged hands with silent urgency.

Camille nudged Dorothy. "This way."

They slipped into a corridor veined with wallpaper the color of cherries and reached an alcove where guests had gathered around a display beneath a skylight. The painting showed a forest cloaked in mist and at the center a woman in white, her face eclipsed by shadow while one hand extended toward the viewer.

"Beautiful, isn't it?" a woman said.

Irene stood beside her, statuesque and severe in a maroon gown with black lace gloves. Up close, her presence felt magnified.

"Yes," Dorothy said. "It's...unreal."

"That's the idea." Irene stepped closer, her heels silent on marble. "She's called *The Seeker*. Some say the woman is searching for a lost lover. Others think she's being hunted." She looked at Dorothy. "What do you see?"

Dorothy glanced back at the woman's hand. It was full of longing, but also desperation.

"I think she looks scared," she said softly. "Lonely."

"Perhaps she is." Irene's voice dropped. "Art reflects us more than the artist. We see what we're afraid to name aloud."

A pause filled with nearby chatter.

"I don't believe we've formally met," Irene continued, offering her hand. "I'm Irene. My son, Aiden—you may have seen him skulking around. He tends to keep to himself."

Dorothy reached out. The moment their palms touched, pain stabbed her ribs. Her breath hitched and the gallery spun slightly.

Irene's brow lifted. "Are you alright?"

"Yeah, just a cramp." Dorothy smiled thinly. "Weird timing." The pain was piercing, as if a nerve in her chest had pinched.

Irene adjusted the lace at her wrist. "Well, I should be going. So many people to entertain," she said. "Enjoy the rest of your evening, Dorothy. Take your time with the collection. It was a pleasure."

She disappeared into the crowd, her silhouette vanishing. Dorothy turned back to the painting. Her chest still stung. *The Seeker* hadn't changed, and yet the woman's hand no longer seemed to be reaching for help. It looked like it was trying to hold Dorothy back. Urging her not to follow. Not to go any further. As if it already knew what waited for her in the future.

CHAPTER 19
Declan Albatross

HE SAT ON A TUFTED SETTEE, ONE LEG FOLDED BENEATH HIM, THE other stretched across a Persian rug. In one hand, he held a fan of playing cards. Across from him, Aiden grinned as he flicked a spade onto the table between them. Lola perched on the armrest beside him. Her dress spilled over one side, her eyes cataloging faces the way people appraised the auction pieces. He laid a card down without looking, tapping a rhythm against the table, a beat he didn't notice until Aiden raised a brow.

"You're not even paying attention," Aiden said. "That's four hands in a row."

Declan tipped the corner of his next card. "Just going easy on you. Remember last time?"

Lola reached for her drink, her heel brushing his shoulder. He barely registered it as he glanced toward the entrance. He shifted, collar suddenly stifling. The string quartet transitioned into a waltz as another wave of guests entered beneath the ballroom, though none of them were her.

Aiden clapped down a card. "And I win. Again."

Lola sighed. "Okay, let's move on," she said. "This party is boring me. And this year's bartender is being painfully uncooperative."

"Like what?" Aiden asked. "The auction's always the same.

Someone overbids on art that looks like a toddler made it, and the servers try not to cry on their uniforms."

Lola sipped her drink. "So we suffer through monotony, or we pretend to care about art. I'm willing to feign appreciation if it means a little chaos finds us."

Declan grinned. "But you hate art."

"I don't hate it. I just have a low tolerance for things that take themselves too seriously."

She wandered off toward a portrait of fruits arranged in the shape of a skull. Aiden followed, posture loose and smiling. Declan stayed back, searching for Ophelia. Her black hair. A glimpse of her silhouette. Anything.

"Declan," came a voice.

Irene stood beneath a sconce shaped like weeping lilacs. "What are you doing, sitting alone? Are you enjoying yourself tonight?"

"Of course," he said, standing. "You've outdone yourself as always, Ms. Oldwyck."

A laugh escaped her. "And you are always such a charmer." Her hand found his shoulder.

Across the room, Aiden and Lola examined a skewed landscape.

Irene followed his glance. "And Aiden? Does it seem like he's having fun?"

Aiden made some exaggerated gesture at the painting while Lola tried suppressing a grin. "I'd say so."

"And Doris?"

People didn't ask about his mother, unless they wanted gossip. But she, Irene, and Gwen had once been three names whispered like a spell in Driftmoor's golden years. They'd ruled the Academy's halls with matching bedazzled headbands, knowing glances, and secrets no one else was allowed to touch.

"She's good." The words tasted flimsy. "Busy with the company and the usual."

It was more like an omission wrapped in wishful thinking. On paper, his mother held an executive title with Albatross Shipping Lines, but she hadn't been involved in any meaningful way in years. The work had transferred to his grandfather, who ran the company from an office that smelled of brine and fading ambition, keeping the illusion intact for the sake of money.

"You know you're always welcome here," Irene said. "Don't you?"

Her words carried a weight that others rarely bothered to hold. Declan glanced up at her, and for a moment, the auction faded. She wasn't his mother. But somehow, she'd filled the spaces Doris had left hollow. It was in the way she remembered his birthday without needing a reminder. How she asked how he was and actually waited for an answer. In the steadiness of her voice now, low and certain, a pressure in his chest that he hadn't realized was there eased. He nodded, swallowing the words he couldn't say. *Thank you. I wish I belonged here. I wish she was like you.* Before he could question it any further, Aiden returned with Lola.

"Is my mother boring you with the history of brushstrokes and oils?" he asked.

"Never boring," Declan replied, forcing a smile.

Irene's rings flashed as she clasped her hands. "Don't forget to enjoy yourselves. These events can feel like pageantry, but you deserve joy, too. It's your final year, after all."

Then, with a glance toward Lola, she added, "Will you and your mother be attending the annual tea next week? Gwen always like to know ahead of time for the seating arrangements."

Lola's smile didn't falter, but there was a beat too long before she answered. "I'll be there."

Irene gave a small nod, gracious but unreadable. Then she patted Aiden's shoulder and walked off toward a group of guests who were betting on a painting of a floating dinner table.

The three of them moved toward a tucked-away display just off the main gallery. A velvet rope cordoned off the frame. Behind the glass, a painting revealed a forest blurred in fog. At its center, a woman in white extended one hand. Declan leaned in. In the lower corner, swallowed by pigment, someone had etched a compass. It wasn't identical to the one from the book, but it was close enough. His hand twitched toward the case.

"Declan?" Aiden asked. Declan pulled back like he'd touched a hot surface.

"Since when are you so into art?" Lola glanced between the painting and Declan.

"That symbol…I've seen it before," he said. "On a book, but it had no title, and its pages were blank."

Aiden squinted. "It kind of resembles a compass."

He shouldn't have brought it up. Out loud, it sounded ridiculous. "It's nothing. Forget it."

But Lola didn't look away. "That's a banshee," she said.

"A banshee?" Aiden asked. "How do you know?"

"I read about them once. Woman of the fairy mound. It's Irish mythology. They're death's messengers. Screaming, wailing, generally making a spectacle of things."

Declan stared into the painting. The mist seemed thicker and bruised, swallowed the path as though the canvas didn't want the woman found. And the compass pulsed like an omen. He leaned closer, heart knocking against his ribs. It didn't feel familiar. It felt predestined.

CHAPTER 20
Dorothy Hale

Dorothy had imagined fading into the background, admiring artwork while Camille dispersed into her natural element. Instead, Camille had taken the role of guide with the zeal of a campaign manager, ushering Dorothy through a blur of introductions to guests with surnames engraved on Driftmoor's gates and vowels polished by private tutors. Their smiles gleamed, their laughter chimed, and Dorothy nodded through each exchange like a foreign diplomat just learning the language.

Somewhere in the flurry of names and niceties, she caught mention that Camille had been crowned queen of the Founders' Ball, a title Lola had expected to win. It explained the chill beneath their politeness. The tension disguised as courtesy. Here in Driftmoor, Dorothy was beginning to understand that even crowns left casualties.

"Okay. I'm running to the ladies' room," Camille said after they had finished speaking to a former member of the Academy's board. "Would you mind waiting for me?"

Dorothy nodded. But the moment Camille walked off, she slipped away. She couldn't help it. Unlike Albatross House, which felt as barren and cold as the ocean floor, Oldwyck Manor pulsed with life. Lamps cast pools of amber over marble busts and velvet upholstery. Shadows stretched, but never felt vacant. For a while, she lingered in a side room filled with clawfoot furniture and frames of a girl who looked like Irene. A gramophone sat in the corner beside a statue of a weeping angel, its face tilted just enough to seem aware of her presence.

When she stepped back into the hall, she meant to return to Camille, but her feet moved the other way. Her heels slowed against the parquet, the quartet's music receding behind. At the far end of the narrow corridor, a pair of tall doors stood beneath a pediment carved with flames, their handles ornate as swords hilts. She paused and glanced over her shoulder.

Drawn forward, she crossed the threshold into the shadow. Her fingers had barely brushed the handle when one of the doors creaked open on its own. A fire crackled in an enormous hearth. Painted clouds churned across the ceiling, storm-drenched and violet, like a bruised sky nailed into place. A table ran the length of the room, flanked by high-backed chairs with lion feet. Beyond them, the hearth's stone floor was dusted in ash, trailing outward in streaks and whorls like pawprints leading into the fireplace.

She stepped forward, a chill knotting at her spine. The air felt brittle, charged. She dropped to a crouch, her fingers moving without permission toward the soot.

"Hello?"

Dorothy shot up, spinning toward the door. Aiden Oldwyck stood on the threshold, framed by candlelight, the tuxedo making him look younger than he was. "What are you doing?" he asked. "Guests aren't allowed in here."

"I—sorry." She stepped back from the hearth. "I didn't mean to barge in. I got lost. I didn't know."

His gaze dropped to the soot, then back to her. "You're Dorothy, right? The scholarship student?"

The way he said it—*scholarship student*—settled bitterly, as if that label alone defined her worth.

"That's me," she said, flatly.

He stepped inside, the fire catching on the warm undertones of his skin and the glint of cufflinks. "The locker next to mine used to be Elliot's. We weren't close, but we talked sometimes. He was a good guy."

Dorothy's gaze fell to her lap, fingers together like she could twist the grief down where it belonged. She hadn't spoken to anyone at Driftmoor about Elliot or Jack. She wasn't even sure what she was allowed to feel for two boys she'd only known for a night.

"Yeah," she said. "He was nice to me too."

Above them, the chandelier flickered. They both looked up. A gust passed through the dining room, and the fireplace stuttered in its grate. The floor tilted seconds before her knees buckled. Aiden caught her before she hit the marble. His grip was steady, one hand bracing her back, the other gripping her arm.

"Hey, whoa. Dorothy? What's going on?"

The fresco above them rippled like water and the carved lions along the chairs blurred, shifting between form and shadow. The ashes stirred. Then everything went dark.

She stood in a misty forest. It pressed against her lungs, thick and sour, every breath leaving her lips in a trembling plume. Her gown had vanished and in its place clung a linen nightdress. Her bare feet sank into moss that seemed to pulse. Ahead, paw prints burned through the undergrowth while smoke rose from their indentations. Whispers moved through the trees, slithering between twisted trunks, brushing her skin.

The forest opened to a clearing and at its center stood a wilting mansion, its once vibrant shutters sagged, beams bent at every angle. Windows wept smoke as a fire burned from within. And amidst it all was the woman from *The Seeker*. Chains bound her wrists and dragged to the ground, iron searing into her skin, glowing like coals. Her mouth hung open in silence while her eyes—seafoam green—locked onto Dorothy.

Recognition sent Dorothy stumbling back. That's when the woman screamed, splitting the clearing like lighting. Dorothy dropped to her knees, palms pressed to her ears, but the sound carved through her. Skin blistered from the woman's face as fire consumed her. She stared at Dorothy as if remembering while the house crumbled behind her. Smoke swallowed everything as a wave of ash and wind surged toward Dorothy. She closed her eyes, waiting for the impact.

Upon opening them, she found herself back in Oldwyck Manor. The carved dining table. The hearth. The chandelier casting broken halos across polished floors. It had all snapped into place. Except her hands trembled against Aiden and her cheeks were slick with tears she hadn't felt fall.

"Dorothy." His voice was gentle now. "What happened?"

The heat clung to her skin. The scream rang in her ears. Ash seemed to coat her tongue.

"I…I don't know," she said. "Did I pass out?"

Before he could answer, Heather appeared in the doorway in a lavender dress, an opened wine bottle in one hand. But her expression was cold. They landed on Dorothy. Then Aiden. And back to Dorothy.

"What's going on?" she asked.

Aiden stepped in front of Dorothy. "She had a dizzy spell. That's all. What are you doing in here?"

Heather didn't blink as she stared Dorothy down. "You think you can waltz into our town and be someone, don't you?"

Dorothy stiffened.

Heather's mouth curled "Like he'd choose you."

The words struck harder than Dorothy wanted to admit. Before she could find a reply, Heather turned, heels clicking once before exiting into the hallway.

Aiden's shoulders dropped. "I'm sorry about this, but I think maybe you head back."

Lightheaded, she walked toward the door. Her limbs felt disconnected. Noise floated through the manor's hall like a party happening in someone else's life. But all she felt was the warmth. And all she saw was the woman screaming through the fire.

CHAPTER 21
Aiden Oldwyck

HE'D BEEN THINKING ABOUT HEATHER. NOT ABOUT HOW SHE FELT about him—he was certain that part had long since unraveled—but about when she found him with Dorothy. He hadn't meant for her to become an afterthought. But Heather had always seemed invincible. She played her part, and he followed suit. They looked and sounded good together. But beneath that paragon, a disconnection he never found the words for existed.

Footsteps interrupted him as Aunt Maeve stepped into the dining room, her hair twisted into a bun that carved out every angle of her face. She looked past him like he was part of the furniture. When she crossed the hearth, the flames stirred and reached toward her.

"Leave," she said.

"Why should I?" he asked, the words out before he could stop them.

Maybe it stemmed from the afterglow of his moment with Noah. Maybe it ran deeper, a long-nursed defiance, shaped by years of being tolerated.

She turned, slowly, her footsteps striking the floor. "How dare you speak back? Have you learned nothing from living in this house?"

"Exactly, I live here," he said. "This hasn't been your home in decades. So why do you get decide what I do?

Her glare could've cut glass. "And that's why your mother should've gotten rid of you when she had the chance. Every man we let in tries to take what's ours."

"I don't know what other men have done," he said, "but what have I done to deserve your hate?"

And then, like an overture: "There you are, little brother."

Veronica's heels tapped as she stepped between them. "I've been looking everywhere for you. Declan and Lola are in the library," she said, eyes locked on Maeve. "They want to play a game of pool. You should go meet them."

Only she could lie like that and make it sound like gospel. Her gaze met him, urging him to move. He took a step forward, but Maeve struck first. Veronica shoved him aside just as a streak of fire lashed through the air. It came from Maeve's hand, a whip of flame coiling like a serpent, warping the air around it. Aiden staggered back, his heel snagging the edge of the rug. He hit the floor hard, eyes clamping shut as the fire roared toward him—

—and stopped.

It vanished inches away, dissipating in a hiss of smoke. Maeve laughed. It was the delighted sound of someone who hadn't missed. The chandelier blurred. Veronica's face hovered into view, painted with disbelief. Then the doors burst open, and Irene entered, the hearth flaring, flames leaping higher.

"How dare you?" She closed the distance between herself and Maeve. "My son is off-limits," she said. "Try this again, and I'll ensure the fire you worship becomes your undoing."

Maeve smirked. "Mother may have left the deed in your name," she murmured, circling Irene. "But don't forget who holds true power in this family."

"Out."

The two women stared at one another. One with restrained rage, the other cloaked in venom. Maeve inclined her head, the smallest concession. On her way out, she leaned close to Aiden, breath hot against his air.

"Next time," she whispered, "you won't have mommy dearest to protect you."

Her heels retreated down the hall.

Irene knelt beside him. "Are you hurt?"

"I'm fine," he said, though his hands trembled.

Veronica appeared beside him, sliding her arm across his shoulders.

Irene's gaze passed from him to her. "Take him upstairs. I need to make sure she's gone."

The hearth had simmered as Irene strode from the room.

Aiden felt where the fire might've struck him. His cheek, his chest, the insides of his arms. Every inch of him hummed with the memory of a pain that hadn't come. And it wasn't Maeve's magic that lingered. It was the look in her eyes. Not rage. Not heartless. But certainty. As if his death would've been nothing more than a course correction.

CHAPTER 22
Dorothy Hale

DOROTHY BARGED INTO THE NEAREST BATHROOM AND SLAMMED THE door. The lock clicked beneath a twist of her wrist. She caught herself against the sink, palms sweaty, knees threatening to fold. The scene replayed on a brutal loop: the woman's skin peeling away as flames devoured her. Dorothy squeezed her eyes shut, but it only worsened her headache. When she opened them, her reflection flickered. She leaned closer. Her eyes stared back, but not the way they should have. They were too still. And the glass rippled. That's when the others emerged from its depth. The other Dorothys. Their faces were hers, but their lips moved in protest, speaking works she couldn't hear. Some bled from eyes. Others grinned too wide.

"No," she whispered, backing away. "No, no, no—"

The scream tore from her before she realized it was happening. It rattled the walls. A lightbulb popped overhead. Cracks zipped across the mirror, splitting her reflection into broken selves. She dropped to the floor, arms curled over her head, while the tiles vibrated as though caught in some current.

Then it stopped. Warmth trailed along her jaw. She reached up with trembling fingers. Her eardrum stung. When she pulled her hand back, her fingertips were red.

"Dorothy?" Camille called through the door. "Are you okay in there?"

Dorothy forced herself up, staggering as she gripped the sink. She lunged for the faucet. Cold water gushed forth as she splashed it over her face, scrubbing away the blood, makeup, the panic.

"I'm—" She swallowed. "I'm fine."

Her reflection stared back. Pale. Dripping. Eyes ringed with red. She grabbed a towel and patted herself dry, willing herself to look normal. The door creaked open as she stepped out. Camille stood waiting, brows drawn tight. Guests had gathered in the hallway, whispers flowing among them.

"Did anyone feel that? Was that an earthquake?"

"Is she hurt?"

"It appears she's…bleeding."

"What happened?" Camille asked, stepping closer. "We all heard a scream."

Above them, the photographs had cracked. Several frames hung skew, their painted eyes staring.

Dorothy dabbed her cheek with the edge of her dress and managed a smile. "A scream?" she looked around. "I didn't hear anything."

Camille's brows drew together. "But the mirror?"

"Sorry, I need some air. Is there a backyard? Somewhere quiet?"

Camille hesitated, then nodded toward the end of the hall. "There's a garden through the door around the corner."

Dorothy nodded, already moving. She slipped away, her footsteps soft on the parquet floor. The moment she stepped outside, the cold air kissed her skin. The air smelled of ivy and damp brick. All around her, the word hushed. Only then did her breath escape in a shuddering exhale.

A moss-eaten stone bridge arched ahead, fog curling in the basin below. Beyond it, the entrance to a hedge maze loomed, flanked by gas lamps whose flames leaned sideways. A rusted gate stood between them, the Oldwyck crest gleaming at its center, greened with age. Dorothy lingered at its threshold, her hand brushing the iron. She had never set foot in a maze before, and tonight hardly seemed like the time to start. Still, the pull was there. The same one that had drawn her toward the paw prints in the dining room.

Gravel crunched underfoot. The hedges rose taller with each step, their leaves too glossy, their tangled vines studded with thorns that looked more like veins than flora. The party vanished behind her, cut off, like a needle yanked from a phonograph. In the hush, a rhythmic buzz snaked around her, rising and falling in sync with her breath.

Soon the path forked, revealing a lily pond ring by braziers, but the water refused to reflect the flames, not even her face. Headless statues knelt along the edge like mourners frozen mid-prayer, their hands outstretched, some pressed to where their eyes should have been. Stone arches loomed ahead, their keystones chipped and blackened with age. Cracks veined their columns, and beyond them, crumbling steps descended into shadow, where wooden doors stood half-ajar, weather-warped and streaked with what looked like claw marks.

She could turn back. She knew that. But a deeper instinct pulled her forward. Not with direction, but with certainty. As if whatever lay beyond those doors had already seen her coming.

One opened into a clearing where a stone gazebo stood, strangled by ivy. Foxgloves bloomed at its base, pale as bone. Heather sat on a bench, her dress dusted in leaves. She was turning a rose by the stem, watching as its petals fell one by one. Her gaze was turned inward, as if she too had lost herself in the maze. It felt wrong to intrude, so Dorothy retraced her steps. Only to find the hedges pressed closer than before and the air thinner. The vines above had sealed off the sky and braziers hissed, sputtering out one by one.

"Don't walk away from me when I'm speaking to you, Maeve," came a voice.

Dorothy's heart drummed in her ears.

"You're lucky walking away is all I'm doing," another replied. "Are you going to pretend we didn't hear the same thing?"

She crept forward, parting the branches. Through the leaves, two women stood beneath the gaslight. Irene. And a taller figure in black—Maeve.

"I don't care about that," Irene said. "Aiden is never to be touched again. You never should've revealed your magic to him."

"Of course you don't care," Maeve snapped. "You've never cared about the matriarchy the way you cared about him." Her voice sharpened. "You think you can spare him from the hounds? There are no loopholes. No mercy. No exemptions."

A flicker of pain crossed Irene's face. "I don't expect you to understand what it means to care for someone other than yourself."

"No," Maeve said. "You expect me to be like you. Sentimental."

"The sisters are whispering, Irene," she continued. "They sense your softness and question your claim. Even I question it."

Irene lifted her chin. "I want you gone."

Maeve inclined her head. "As you wish. This is your house, after all," she said. "I'll leave you to your delusions while I find the banshee."

Fire licked the hem of her dress and curled around her. In a blink, she was gone.

Before Dorothy could even process this, a snarl broke the hush behind her.

The scent of ash and iron reached her first. A shadow peeled itself from the hedge. A creature, black as coal, stalked into view with amber eyes. Saliva dripped from its fangs in glistening strands, each breath curling in the air.

A scream rose but never made it past her throat. She sprinted in the opposite direction. Braziers flared in stuttering bursts of light and heat. Thorns tore at her arms as she forced herself through a narrow passage. She stumbled into a dead end with a statue, arms raised toward a sky that no longer showed. A bench leaned crooked nearby, half-swallowed by moss, its clawfoot buried in dirt. Behind her, the creature's footsteps dragged. She crawled beneath the bench, cold mud soaking her dress, her knees and caking her fingers.

The creature stopped. She heard it breathe close by. Wet and ragged. Leaves rustled. Then came the snout, nosing through the green. She bit her fist and closed her eyes. And the maze held its breath with her.

CHAPTER 23
Lola Godfrey

LOLA STOOD BESIDE A LEMON TREE, ITS BRANCHES SAGGING UNDER overripe fruit. One hand held a glass of sparkling water; the other traced circles along the rim. From a distance, she might've appeared entranced by the sculpture before her—a winged, headless woman draped in marble. But her gaze had settled on Declan. He was nearby, facing a canvas rendered in rust and slate. His arms were crossed, head tilted, but he wasn't really seeing the art. Others saw the charisma of an Albatross. But she noticed his stiff shoul-ders and the way he kept turning toward the conservatory's entrance.

"She's not coming," Lola said.

His jaw shifted. "She might. You don't know that."

He tapped his sleeve, same spot, again and again. She remembered those hands in the hallway at Albatross House, the night his parents finalized the divorce. They'd been trembling so badly she'd reached for them without thinking. She'd been the one to sit beside him night after night, the one who'd dialed Theodore's number when he couldn't bring himself to speak. She'd stayed, while Ophelia hadn't even said goodbye.

"And if she does," Lola said, "what could you say that you haven't already?"

His green eyes met hers like he wanted to believe that something good could come out of tonight.

"You deserve someone who doesn't run," she said. "Someone who stays by your side."

That stayed between them, suspended in the lemon-scented air, until Aiden approached.

He moved with his usual reserved composure, eyes sweeping them before settling on Lola.

"Hey," he said. "Can I ask a favor?"

She raised a brow. "Depends. Am I going to regret saying yes?"

"It's Heather. Camille saw her go into the maze. She's upset, and I'm worried. Could you check on her? She's likely at the gazebo. I'd go myself, but I don't think she wants to see me."

The sarcasm softened before it could form. "Sure," she said. "I suppose I'll go."

Aiden nodded in thanks, his expression taut with worry, and turned to Declan. The two drifted into the conservatory's crowd, toward abstract works and champagne-slick conversation.

Lola lingered for a moment longer, then walked toward the garden path. The Oldwyck maze was designed by Irene's great-grandmother, twisting in ways that didn't make sense, responding less to logic than to emotion. Most visitors found it enchanting while others found it disorienting. Lola always had a feeling it was a bit of both.

When they were kids, the maze had been magic.

They'd chased each other through the hedgerows in wool coats and knee socks, breath fogging in the cold. The air had tasted of pine needles and mischief. Lola remembered the shrieks of laughter as they darted around corners, the thrill of vanishing just before someone turned the bend. Declan always hid near her, even when it meant losing. Heather clung to Lola's arm, whispering strategy like espionage.

Aiden was always the first to be found. Half because he didn't hide well, half because he'd preferred being referee. And Ophelia—Ophelia was the best at hiding, of course. She was always the last found. Only found when she wanted to be.

Now, the hedges towered over Lola and the stone path softened beneath her heels, moss creeping into the cracks. The air no longer smelled like childhood, and she didn't feel like the seeker or the hider anymore.

She squinted into the dark, a chill coiling beneath her sleeves. Her hand hovered near the clasp of her bracelet. The one Heather gave her in eighth grade, during one of their *let's promise to always stay close* moments. Heather had cried during the exchange while Lola had pretended not to notice, just to keep from crying too.

"Pull it together, Lola," she murmured.

She took the left fork without thinking. The braziers ahead burned, their flames bending backward. Vines crawled overhead and statues emerged. Some with cracked limbs, others eroded to eyeless anonymity. A few had crumbled altogether.

She found Heather sitting on the bench in the gazebo, her posture folded inward. Heather twirled a rose by its stem, petal by petal falling to the stone floor. Heather's sadness was never loud, but it clung to her in that way best friends recognized. Lola had seen it before—after the school play sophomore year, when Heather's stepmother left before she took the stage. After her mother's argument with Irene Oldwyck about *marriage expectations*, back when everyone assumed Heather and Aiden would be together forever. Heather had cried in Lola's lap, nose running, makeup ruined, and Lola had handed her tissues without a word.

She stepped forward carefully, the crunch of gravel underfoot announcing her arrival. She crossed the threshold and settled beside Heather.

"Okay." She brushed a petal from Heather's sleeve. "Spill before I start guessing and make it worse."

"Isn't it obvious?" Heather said. "I miss him. I miss the way things used to be."

Even crying, Heather was beautiful. Cheeks flushed, lashes damp, that same impossible symmetry in her face that always made people stare. And Lola hated how much it hurt to see her like this over a boy.

"I used to think," Heather said, "if I walked into every room on Aiden's arm, people would stop second-guessing me. Stop seeing me as just Gwen Croft's daughter. The one with no bite." Her laugh was short and joyless. "But I've bitten. And I'm still not enough."

"You know that isn't true," Lola said. "You bit back when Ms. Farley told you to smile more during cotillion and told her to adjust her wig before adjusting you. You snatched the mic from Declan during the Spring Fête and raised five grand in ten minutes. You even made Camille cry in mid-fencing finals. People remember that."

Heather's lips parted, whether in protest or disbelief, Lola couldn't tell.

"Not as much as everyone remembers you," Heather said. "And since Aiden and I broke up, everything's so different. I couldn't even find you tonight. You're always with Declan. And Aiden's always with Declan. And I'm…here. Waiting for someone to notice I'm not okay."

That stung more than Lola expected.

She exhaled dramatically. "You are such a nightmare when you're sad. Tragic, poetic, full of meaning. You know I hate that."

Heather's smile didn't reach her eyes, but at least it appeared.

"Look." Lola tucked her hair behind one ear. "You're going to be heartbreak personified until at least Valentine's. Then you'll rebound with someone infuriatingly good at golf, and I'll help you figure out how to dump him before graduation."

Heather laughed through tears.

"You'll go to Harvard. Marry a thoracic surgeon. I'll give the best maid of honor speech in couture Valentino. No pastels."

"Obviously."

"And whether you get back with Aiden before prom or fall for someone new, you don't get to disappear. Got it?"

"Got it."

Lola held out a hand. "Now let's bribe the bartender, sip an expensive bottle, and pretend none of this happened."

Heather looked up, hope resembling beneath the remnants of mascara. "You're insufferable."

"I'm your insufferable." Lola helped her stand. "And for the record? You've always had bite. People are just too busy choking on it to notice."

They stepped down from the gazebo. Behind them, the ivy-draped columns vanished into shadow just before a hedge rustled.

Heather latched onto Lola. "Did you hear that?"

"Of course," she said. "It must've been a stray or a racoon."

The sound came again. Then from the hedged gloom, a monstrous shape emerged. Two ember eyes burned, smoke curling from its silhouette, tendrils wrapping its four legs. The path shifted, gravel hissing as claws pressed down.

Heather's voice dropped. "Oh my God."

Lola grabbed Heather's wrist. "Run."

They sprinted, braziers flaring and sputtering as they passed. Lola risked a glance behind them. The beast followed, no faster than a loping nightmare, as though it enjoyed the chase. And then—Dorothy. They nearly collided. Her eyes were wide with a terror that said she already knew what was behind.

"There's some an animal in here!" she gasped.

"We're aware," Lola snapped. "It's behind us. Move!"

The three of them ran in a desperate panic of limbs and tulle. Shoes slipped on moss. Heather tripped, Lola yanked her up. Dorothy stumbled, Lola shoved her forward.

"Do you even know where we're going?" Dorothy yelled.

"Would I still be running if I did?" Lola shouted back.

They turned a corner and slammed into a dead end. The hedges gave way to a clearing, and in its center stood a statue, but erosion had stripped her of identity. Her face was gone, arms sheared at the elbows, vines curled around her throat.

Heather backed into a hedge. "This—this can't be happening."

The air grew warmer as the beast approached. Hedges bowed away, as if the maze feared it. It didn't snarl. Nor lunge. It approached them like death, slow and inevitable. The legends clung to memory. Half-whispers stolen from behind her father's locked office door, warnings buried between curses and bloodlines. But here, in the flesh, this wasn't some story. This was a living, breathing hellhound.

Lola placed herself in front of the others. She didn't think. She stepped in like she always had, because control felt safer than helplessness. Because it was better to face the monster than to wait to be saved.

"Leave us alone," she said, though she felt ridiculous for even negotiating.

The hellhounds' gaze held hers. Time seemed to have slowed. Then—a blinding flash. A scream. She didn't see the claws, only felt them. She hit the ground hard, her knee slamming into gravel. Blood ran hot down her face.

The hellhound stilled. Then it turned toward Dorothy. It looked like it was about to attack her next, but its shape rippled, fur drawing inward like smoke reversing. Its muscles contracted as limbs reformed. Until it no longer looked like a beast, but like a wolf. It glanced once more at Dorothy and Lola before it thinned into vapor and dissipated into the night.

Heather turned to Lola. "Your face…"

Lola reached up. Her fingers found blood, but no wound.

Heather stepped closer. "Lola?"

Behind them, the hedge shuddered and separated. Branches curled away to reveal a path back to Oldwyck Manor. No one questioned it. They simply walked.

Each step felt like stepping further from who she'd been. Before the eyes of two girls had settled on her like spotlights. There'd been no time to hide. No way to deny what her body had undone. Heather looked at her the way she'd looked at the hellhound. And now Lola was tied to Dorothy, a stranger. But more than anything, Dorothy was witness to a truth that was never meant to be discovered.

PART TWO

October

In October, the dead remembers their names.
Don't walk the beach after moonrise.
Be sure to leave salt at your door.
And if you hear footsteps behind you, don't turn around.
It's never someone you know.
—Old Driftmoor superstition

CHAPTER 24
Dorothy Hale

SHE MOVED THROUGH THE DINING HALL LIKE SOMEONE CAUGHT IN the residue of a dream she hadn't fully shaken. No one spoke as the three of them re-entered the auction, cheeks flushed, skin scratched (except for Lola's), sweat clinging to the silk and tulle of their gowns. Lola offered a half-truth in her effortless tone: a story about a wolf loose in the maze, chasing them beneath the hedges. It was just absurd enough to earn a few gasps. Plausible enough to deflect suspicion.

Students lounged beneath the vaulted ceiling, their uniforms layered beneath cardigans and scarves in Driftmoor colors. Lanterns flickered above monastic tables polished by a century of hands and spilled ink. Some read with surgical focus; others toyed with fountain pens, their laughter echoing against stone.

The tray in Dorothy's hands grounded her as the warmth of the food prickled. But still, her thoughts were stuck on fiery eyes and claws.

Near the hall's center, she spotted Lola, Declan, and Aiden. They sat with their heads bent close in conversation. Declan was angled away, tapping his knuckles against the table while Aiden leaned back in that effortless, ruined way of his. Lola caught Dorothy's gaze just as Aiden lifted a hand in greeting. Dorothy lifted hers in return, but

Lola leaned in, murmured, and pushed his wrist down. His attention returned to his plate.

Dorothy tightened her grip on the tray. She hadn't expected them to call her over, but they could've at least looked her way. A nod. A flicker of recognition to prove she hadn't imagined the moments they shared. She slipped into a seat along the far wall, where the windows didn't reach, and the stone held autumn's chill. The tray clattered softly as she set it down. From here, the dining hall felt blurred at the edges, like a world she'd been shut out of mid-sentence.

"Hey!"

Noah appeared beside her, his backpack slung over one shoulder, blazer wrinkled like he'd slept in it.

"Oh. Hey." She brushed a strand of hair behind her ear.

He nodded toward her tray. "How's your first week back treating you?"

"It's been okay." A patchwork sentence stretched thin over the holes left by a hellhound, magic, and a cracked mirror. "The food's better than St. Augustine's, so that's a plus."

"I'd hope so, considering what Driftmoor charges just to breathe their air."

She gave him a tired smile. She hadn't slept all weekend. But he didn't push or ask too much. And maybe that was why she didn't mind him sitting across from her. Why, despite the noise in her head, his presence didn't feel like a threat.

"So, about that job at The Salty Dog," Noah said. "I asked my boss. Turns out he's not hiring."

Disappointed flared, then receded. "It's okay." She smoothed her thumb over the tray's edge. Part of her had given up on expecting good news to happen. "Thanks for checking."

"It's nothing personal. He just doesn't hire after summer." His expression brightened. "But the catering company I work with? They've got some highbrow tea party this weekend. They might need extra hands. I can probably get you in."

"You really think so?"

"Yeah. It's hauling trays, clearing glasses, avoiding eye contact with the social elite." His grin crooked. "But tips aren't bad if you don't mind fake smiles and monograms."

A laugh escaped her before she could stop it. "I think I can manage that," she said. "That would be super helpful. I'll take anything I can get at this point."

"Cool. I'll drop the details tonight."

"Thank you."

She watched him go, then turned to her lunch. She picked at a fry, thoughts turning over. A job. A real one. A chance to move forward instead of treading in place. She smiled, but it vanished the moment she looked up. Across the dining hall, a familiar face stood near the hot food station, laughing at something someone said. Moving like he hadn't been in the car with her. Like he hadn't been the last face she saw before the world shattered.

Jack.

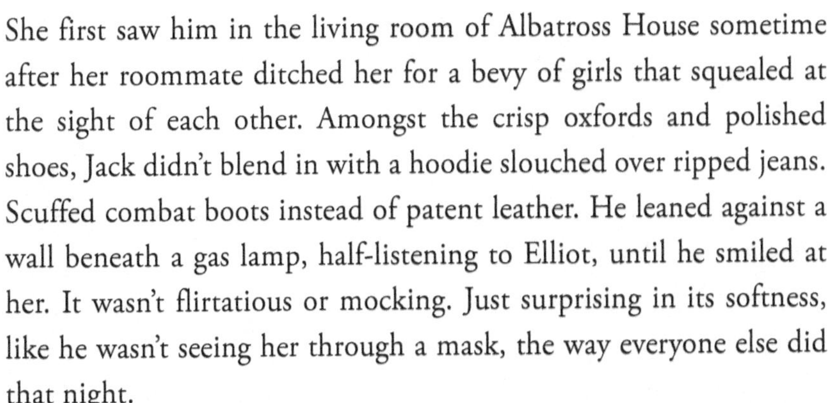

She first saw him in the living room of Albatross House sometime after her roommate ditched her for a bevy of girls that squealed at the sight of each other. Amongst the crisp oxfords and polished shoes, Jack didn't blend in with a hoodie slouched over ripped jeans. Scuffed combat boots instead of patent leather. He leaned against a wall beneath a gas lamp, half-listening to Elliot, until he smiled at her. It wasn't flirtatious or mocking. Just surprising in its softness, like he wasn't seeing her through a mask, the way everyone else did that night.

She turned too fast, collided into someone's drink, muttered an apology that tasted like embarrassment, and fled into the corridor. Her heart thudded hard. *Idiot. So stupid.* Music pulsed behind, dulled by thick wood paneling and faded maritime tapestries. When she reached the line for the bathroom, she pressed herself against the wallpaper, hoping to disappear.

A girl in a sequined dress strutted past without a glance, cutting to the front. She moved with a confidence that suggested rejection had never touched her. The kind of girl who had never waited for anything. Dorothy bit her lip and stupidly, she tapped her shoulder. The girl turned, hair bouncing in glossy curls. Her eyes swept over Dorothy like she was inspecting a smudge on glass.

"And you are?" she asked, tilting her head.

Dorothy leaned in over the blaring music. "Sorry?"

"I said, who are you?" Her perfume took up the whole hallway. "Why haven't I seen you around? Who do you know?" A lazy smile lifted her lips. "Because I doubt someone like you got an invitation to Albatross House."

Dorothy opened her mouth, but another voice jumped in.

"Piss off, Heather."

Jack stood at the end of the hall. "There's a dozen other bathrooms," he said. "Pick one of them and go puke in peace."

A few people in line snorted behind their hands.

Heather's eyes narrowed. "What are you doing here? I know for a fact you're not on the guest list."

Jack rested a boot against the wall. "If Declan's got a problem, he could come tell me himself," he said. "Which I doubt, since he's busy chasing Ophelia. I'm surprised you're not doing the same. Unless you already knew she'd be coming back."

Heather gave him a withering look. "Whatever." She turned, but not before delivering one final dagger toward Dorothy. "If I were you, I'd stay far away from him. You might think he's cute now but just wait till you see the ugly underneath."

Maybe she should've listened. But Jack had looked at her like she mattered. And in those few hours, that was all she'd wanted. To be seen. Not pitied. Not passed over. Just seen.

Her heart hammered as he moved through the dining hall. She waited for him to look up, for his honey brown eyes to find hers. She'd never wanted someone to look at her so badly. It felt ridiculous. But still, her fingers curled around her tray as anticipation knotted in her stomach.

He walked right past her without a glance.

Her grip whitened, the plastic tray biting into her palms. Her lungs forgot what to do. The clatter of forks, the scrape of chairs, the chatter blurred into a distant hum. She stared at her plate and tried to smooth her face into a portrait of restraint while heartbreak splintered inside her.

She sat there, pretending she wasn't bleeding from a wound no one else saw.

CHAPTER 25
Lola Godfrey

Lola traced the gouges on the wooden desk, worn smooth by decades of restless hands. The classroom buzzed with the rustle of pages, the drone of students murmuring about essays, quiz dates, and weekend plans. Curtains tamed the daylight, streaking the room in amber bands that sliced across the floor. The door opened enough to admit Heather and everything in Lola tensed. Heather's uniform was crisp, her curls tucked behind one ear, with lavender glasses balanced on her nose. She walked in and took the empty seat beside Lola.

The last time she saw Heather, they'd been running for their lives with the scholarship girl. Heather had clutched her arm until the skin whitened. Not only had they seen a hellhound, but Heather had seen the scratches on Lola's face disappear. But now, she opened her notebook, flipped to a fresh page, and copied notes like none of that had happened.

Professor Birch stepped to the front of the classroom and chalked quotes from a classic Greek poem:

The journey home is never simple.
Memory's cruel grasp.
Some forget, some are forgotten.

Lola's father used to say that true memory couldn't be trusted in

Driftmoor. That certain forces had a way of manipulating the truth, but she never believed him.

Lola leaned toward Heather. "Hey."

She didn't react. Someone near the back stifled a yawn.

Lola tried again, quieter. "Hello? Have you gone deaf over the weekend? Or are we not okay?"

Heather glanced over. "Why wouldn't we be?"

"For starters, the maze. That…wolf. The fact we nearly died?"

Heather's pen hovered above the page. There was a shift behind her eyes, like a flicker of confusion. Then she let out a soft, almost amused laugh. "What? I have no idea what you're talking about." She flipped a page. "Maybe I had too much tequila."

Lola's skin prickled. Too much to drink? No. She remembered how Heather cried, her voice breaking as she said she missed Aiden. How she'd flinched when the hellhound appeared. How she hadn't screamed, just whispered, *oh my god*. And now she didn't remember?

The bell rang an hour later. Chairs scraped back. The hush fractured into voices and motion.

Heather stretched, tucked her books into her bag, and stood. "I cannot wait for this day to be over."

Lola remained seated, staring at the blank page of her notebook. Heather walked away, curls bouncing against her back. If she hadn't known better, she'd think Heather was fine. She wasn't. Lola knew her. Had known her since they were five and shared a dance routine at Gwen Croft's summer solstice party. She knew how Heather covered sadness. Unlike Lola, who could handle the brutal pressures of Driftmoor, Heather folded herself beneath expectations even if she couldn't breathe. She'd rather rewrite her suffering than share it.

But this? This wasn't that. This was forgetting. And then there was the scholarship girl. Did she remember? Lola looked up from her notebook. The chalkboard bore the last line: *Some forget, some are forgotten.* And Lola wasn't sure which she feared more.

CHAPTER 26
Declan Albatross

THE AIR CARRIED CHIMNEY SMOKE FROM THE DORMITORIES. It threaded through colonnades and hung over the quad, the kind of smell that settled into your clothes and made you think of late autumns that had already come and gone. It gave the morning a sense that the Academy had woken before its students did. It reminded Declan of Sundays when Theodore lived at home and Doris would light every fireplace, as if it could make the house feel less empty.

He was always early, part of that handful who didn't live on campus but weren't considered the typical local either. Town students like Declan, Aiden, and Lola arrived by car, their rides quiet and separate. They didn't walk from dorm rooms or tumble out of bed and into the dining hall for breakfast. They entered through the gates each morning, dressed and absorbed in their own world.

Declan shot Aiden a glance as they moved along the flagstone path. Aiden walked beside him with his hands buried in the pockets of a charcoal overcoat, the hem brushing his knees. His tie hung slightly askew beneath a dark wool vest, collar starched but wrinkled, like he'd yanked it on in a hurry. His brows were drawn in that analytical way that meant he was already running through worst-case scenarios.

"Are you sure this is a good idea?" Aiden asked.

"Yes," Declan said. "It's just a book. Relax."

Their shoes crunched over fallen leaves and pine needles. Students passed in scattered clusters, jackets pulled tight, their laughter muffled by the cold.

Aiden's gaze drifted toward them, then lingered on a professor disappearing under the cloisters. "People don't risk detention for just a book," he said. "What's so special about this one?"

The compass hadn't left Declan's mind since the auction. It couldn't be a coincidence. Or maybe it was, and this was a theory doomed to lead nowhere. But either way, he wouldn't know until he tried.

"I think it has to do with my family," he said. "I've seen similar compasses in our library. In old star maps. Not exactly the same, but close."

"Okay. Since when do you care about symbols in dusty atlases?

"I don't. But this feels different."

Aiden's breath fogged as he studied him. "So I'm supposed to follow you into all this because of a feeling?"

"No," Declan said. "Because you trust me."

Nearby, the bell tower tolled the hour, echoing across the lawn.

Aiden looked away. "Yeah, I always do," he said. "That's the problem."

Declan could've asked him to jump off the cliff behind Albatross House (something they'd dared each other to do in middle school), and Aiden wouldn't blink. He'd just ask if they were holding hands on the way down.

Past the cloisters, the Athenaeum emerged with its spires. Statues of cloaked scholars with crumbling scrolls clutched to their chest lined the gables. Beneath them, the doors loomed tall and narrow, iron-braced and embossed with the school motto.

Declan slowed as they reached the steps. One hand hovered over the handle. "I wouldn't be asking for your help if it didn't feel important, you know that?"

Aiden watched him a moment longer, then pulled the door open. Their hands brushed, but neither acknowledged it. Warm air chased off the cold. Beyond the entrance, the circulation desk rose like an altar, where Ms. Alpine sat, cocooned in a fortress of unshelved books.

Declan approached the counter, wearing what he hoped passed for sincerity. "Good morning, Ms. Alpine. How are you?"

"Mr. Albatross," she replied without looking up. Her glasses perched on her nose, pen scratching steadily across a ledger. "Mr. Oldwyck. Shouldn't the two of you be on your way to class?"

Declan flashed a hall pass he'd stolen from a professor's desk. "Professor Gilbert sent me to retrieve a book from the Preserves. *The Alchemists of the Moors?*"

Her pen paused mid-stroke as she raised her eyes. "The Preserves?" she repeated. "He of all people should know that titles from that collection require a minimum twenty-four hours' notice for retrieval and handling."

"Yes. That's what I said," Declan replied, scratching the back of his neck. "But he said it was urgent. Adamant, actually. It's to be used for today's lesson on lunar distillations and origin mythologies." A pause. "He also mentioned you'd understand."

"Understand what?"

Declan hesitated long enough to seem reluctant. "He said you owed him from that symposium at The Barquentine last spring. Something about a misfiled manuscript and a favor he never cashed in."

Ms. Alpine's face flushed a pink. "That…was not meant for student ears."

Declan leaned in slightly. "He also said you'd be discreet. And generous."

She turned to Aiden. "And why is he here for this errand?"

"To keep me from knocking over anything priceless," Declan said before Aiden could respond.

Aiden cleared his throat. "Think of me as library insurance."

Ms. Alpine exhaled through her nose, shoulders tightening. Then she stepped out from behind the desk. "Wait here."

The click of her heels echoed as she disappeared into the back room.

As soon as she was out of sight, Aiden whispered, "What symposium?"

"There wasn't one," Declan said, already crouching behind the desk. "Gilbert once tried to ask Ms. Alpine to the Winter Ball. Got rejected. He's been awkward around her since. Seems Heather's flair for gossip has its uses."

Aiden's jaw tightened at the mention of her name.

"Sorry," Declan added, without looking up. "Didn't mean to bring her up."

"It's fine." Aiden flipped through a brochure on Driftmoor's academic honor code. "So what now?"

"Keep watch."

"And if she comes back?"

"Charm her."

Aiden gave him a flat look. "That's your specialty."

"Then I hope you've been taking notes."

Declan's fingers skimmed past catalog drawers, paperbacks, and unfiled returns. Somewhere in the clutter was the real prize. He sifted through forgotten notebooks, half-filled library cards, scarves, a magnifying lens—and then he felt it. Not just cool leather, but cold. Like stone pulled from the bottom of a winter river. His hand closed around it and shoved it under his jacket and stood, breath caught in his chest.

Aiden glanced over the counter. "Did you find it?"

"It was exactly where it should be."

Aiden folded the brochure. "So what now? We walk out and hope she doesn't notice the lump under your coat?"

Declan smirked, adjusting the fold of his jacket. "You've got a cute, innocent face," he said. "Smile like you believe in the honor code."

"We're screwed."

Declan was about to respond when heels echoed back toward them.

Ms. Alpine reappeared, carrying a tome wrapped in plastic. "Here's your book," she said, setting it on the counter. "Please be careful. This is over a hundred years old. Though Professor Gilbert shouldn't need reminding."

Her eyes flicked to the shape under Declan's coat, then to Aiden, who met her stare with a disarming nod.

Declan mustered a smile and took the decoy. "Thanks, Ms. Alpine. I'm sure he'll be grateful for your help."

They stepped back into the chill. The air was sharper now, laced with wet stone and wood smoke. Wind curled past the cloisters, scattering leaves across the flagstone path.

"Okay," Aiden said once they were clear. "Do you want to tell me what that was about?"

Declan pulled the book from inside his jacket, letting the decoy dangle at his side. The leather gleamed under the gray light, the compass on the cover catching a flicker of sun.

"I told you," he murmured. "It feels…familiar."

"Let's see it, then."

They slipped beneath the cloister's arches. Declan hesitated, then cracked the journal open. Still blank. Page after page of untouched parchment. No ink. No symbols. No notes in the margin. Just silence bound in leather.

"Great." Aiden stared. "We risked detention for an unused sketchbook. I thought you said this was important?"

"It is. It's not a sketchbook. I don't know what it is."

Declan closed the book, and they walked in silence. The leather felt warm. Not from his hands, but as if it held a memory. It felt like a summons that was long delayed and finally answered by him.

CHAPTER 27
Aiden Oldwyck

Rain fell in a wispy mist over Oldwyck Manor, beading along the balustrades of the loggia. The terrace stretched into a colonnade, each arch framing a silvered view of the hedge garden, its labyrinthine paths fading into fog. At the far end, wrought iron torches flickered, their flames shivering in the breeze.

The manor had belonged to the women in his family for generations. Grand enough to impress visitors. Cold enough to quiet a child. Irene had taught him to admire its beauty but never trust it. There were wings he wasn't allowed in. Portraits whose names he wasn't told. Doors that locked, not with keys, but with intention. No home was forever. But the manor didn't even pretend to be one.

Beneath the terrace, Aiden sat across from his mother. Between them, a chessboard rested on a slab of black marble, the onyx and maroon pieces gleaming in the dull light. Irene reclined, amulet at her throat, fingers grazing the stem of a half-finished wine glass. The glass in his lenses caught the torchlight as his gaze caught the way she watched the fog curl. She hadn't looked at him once since they sat.

"Can I ask you a question?" he said.

Her lips curved. "You can always ask." She set her glass down. "Whether I answer is another matter."

His leg bounced under the table. "At the auction. Aunt Maeve spoke to me," he started. "She said…she said you should've gotten rid of me when you had the chance. Why did she say that?"

The words hung in the air like a guillotine poised to drop.

Irene's fingers grazed her queen, then slipped to her lap. Her face became harder to read. "Oh, Maeve," she said to herself. "I'm sorry she said that. I wouldn't even know where to begin to explain."

"Try. Please. I think I deserve that much."

Her gaze softened like she saw him not as a nearly grown man, but the boy who used to wait on the stairs for her to come home.

"You're a special boy, you know?"

His shoulders tensed. He knew this script: a careful setup, followed by omission. "Mom, please."

"I mean it. You must've noticed that you have no male cousins. And that husbands don't stay, and the women never change their surnames."

He thought of his father Reginald, now little more than a voice on the phone and a signature on a birthday card. Aiden had been six when his parents split, and no one offered an explanation. At least with Declan's family, there had been signs. Fights. Theodore's affair. With his own, there were vague reassurances: *It's better this way. Trust us.* But better for who?

"It's not like we chose this," Irene said. "Maeve clings to tradition—power above all. But my children," her voice softened, "you and Veronica will always come first."

"Then don't hold back," he said. "Please."

She hesitated, then sighed. "I'm going to hate myself for telling you this. But you're right. It's time I tell you the truth."

Another truth, another thread unraveling enough to show how little he understood. At ten, it was the hellhounds. At fifteen, it was the fire. How it lived in their blood and the matriarchy passed it down like inheritance. Now, standing at the edge of seventeen, he braced for the next rupture.

"Long before Driftmoor, there was a woman named Selene Oldwyck," Irene said. "She lived in a time when our name belonged to a man. Her husband was brutal with brothers, just as barbaric. One night, she fled into the woods with her infant son. She walked barefoot for miles, hungry, paranoid she'd been followed. She was running toward a future she couldn't see. Only knew it had to be better than the one behind her."

The rain whispered against the balustrades as thick mist clung to the arches.

"She came here," Irene said. "To Driftmoor. And that's when it found her."

"What did?"

"The Entity. It emerged from the fog. Sometimes a shadow, a man, a woman. It spoke with her voice and knew her name, knew her pain. It knew what she would ask before she could form the words."

Aiden's skin prickled. "Have you seen it?"

"Not directly. But it lingers in this town. Sometimes I feel it watching. Most times, I tell myself it's my imagination."

She returned to the story.

"The Entity offered her what she sought: safety and power. A means to never be at a man's mercy again. But it warned her that while no Oldwyck would be powerless, no son would belong to her."

Aiden's heart twisted. "So Selene gave him up?"

"She begged for time. *Let me keep him until he's grown.* She offered her soul, everything she was. The Entity agreed, but it wanted a seal."

"What kind of seal?"

"A drop of blood in fire."

Her gaze dropped to the chessboard. "Her hand burned. She screamed. But the pain changed her as the flame rooted inside her. She didn't know it, but that was the beginning of the Oldwyck magic. The beginning of the matriarchy's power."

Aiden looked at the board, his king surrounded.

"Selene was the first to raise her son to adulthood," Irene said. "But after her, the magic grew stronger. The cost grew steeper. The women chose differently. Most handed over their sons at birth than to have to deal with the pain of surrendering their child."

"Surrendering to who? The Entity?"

"The hellhounds aren't just protectors. They're collectors. Enforcers of the bargain. They come when time runs out."

His stomach turned. "Are you saying?"

Irene reached for him, but he pulled away. His chest tightened, like everything he believed about himself had been carved out and hollowed. He pushed back from the table. The chair scraped hard against the stone.

"So I'm waiting for them to come for me."

"No," she said. "I'm trying to stop it."

He looked at her in disbelief.

"I don't know how," she said. "But I will. I don't care what it costs me."

The rain struck harder, rattling the torches. A single chess piece lay fallen. The queen.

Expectations had always been a part of his life, from grades and reputation. Burdens, he trained himself to shoulder without flinching. But this wasn't pressure.

It was a countdown.

CHAPTER 28
Declan Albatross

Vesper Lake stretched slate-gray, edged with reeds that bowed in the breeze. Beneath the maroon and black unisuit, Declan's muscles strained with each pull of the oars, slicing through Driftmoor Academy's most secluded corner. Out here, nothing mattered but the rhythm of his strokes and the burn in his arms. On the lake, there were no whispers about his mother. No sidelong glances filled with questions he didn't want to answer.

His breath misted with each pull of the oars—*Pull. Exhale. Recover.* The rhythm anchored him. Heavy rock thudded through his head-phones, muffling thoughts he couldn't outrun. He'd imagined Ophelia's return a hundred different ways. Reunions that burned or healed or unraveled. But she was back, and the version he'd carried all these years didn't match the girl who'd come home.

He'd held on to fragments like they were sacred. Her laugh echoing across the sand, the tilt of her head when she lied, and the way she kissed like she didn't believe in consequences. He'd memorized those details like verses in a favorite song, convinced they mattered because he needed them to. Now he wasn't sure what hurt more: the version he'd invented, or the one reality delivered. The ache he felt was for the years he'd spent building a story where they found their way back.

For the boy who believed in promises whispered beneath stars and the weight of a look.

He neared the kilometer marker and eased off, letting the boat drift. The book rested beside him, a curious presence he didn't understand. Two days had passed since he stole it. Each morning began with his fingers tracing the compass. Each night ended with him flipping through parchment, expecting words to appear. He couldn't leave it alone. Just like he couldn't stop thinking about her.

Then—a thud beneath the hull. Gentle enough to dismiss as a fish.

When he yanked his headphones, silence rushed in. No wind. No birdsong. Just the water lapping and the sound of his breath. The lake, which had reflected an overcast, now rippled with a green-black sheen while rings widened from beneath, distorting the boat's reflection.

The scull lurched and a jolt slammed through the hull, splashing water across the seat. Declan scrambled, hands slipping on wet fiberglass. His eyes snapped to the book as it slid toward the edge.

"No!"

It splashed into the water. Without thinking, Declan unbuckled and dove. The cold wrenched his breath as everything stilled. Only the roar of blood in his ears, the slow drift of his body, and the shimmer of light filtering from above. He blinked himself alert and squinted into the murk.

There, the book, suspended in a net of lakeweed, its compass glowing. Then, movement behind the lakeweed. A webbed hand with claws, nearly translucent slipped forward and closed around the book. Declan kicked hard and lunged. He gripped its wrist—slick and rubbery, like holding the belly of a fish. Light shimmered across the creature's arms. When their eyes locked, Declan's thoughts stuttered. Its eyes were opalescent and lidless. Gills flared at its neck while a crown of kelp—hair, maybe—floated around it. Then came a hum. A tune threaded into his mind, fragmented and familiar. A song he couldn't name but somehow knew.

He shook his head and tightened his grip. The book twisted between him and the creature in a desperate tug-of-war, as slit burst upward in clouds, shrouding everything in mud and shadow. Shapes spiraled around him, too fast to catch, too many to count. Pressure built behind his eyes. His lungs shrieked for air. Still, he held on, desperate to see it. The creature pulled with unnatural strength, but Declan fought back, muscles straining.

Finally, the book tore free. The creature hissed and vanished into the murk. He kicked toward the surface as a sudden brush skimmed his ankle. The creature? A root? He burst into air, gasping, limbs flailing until they found direction. The scull bobbed nearby. He swam, one burning stroke at a time, flung the book inside, and hauled himself after it. He collapsed against the seat, water streaming from his unisuit. Scrambling for the oars, he didn't row so much as thrash, strokes uneven and sloppy, but the boat lurched toward shore. He didn't stop. Not when the dock came into view. Not when the boathouse rose through the mist.

The moment the boat thudded against the dock, he stumbled out on his hands and knees. He stayed like that, shaking while trying to catch his breath. He didn't want to think about what he'd seen. And the way it clutched the book terrified him more than the silence that followed.

The book. He scrambled upright and snatched it from the scull. He backed away, not daring to look at the water. He looked around to see if anyone was nearby, but he was alone. He jogged up the slope toward the boathouse, leaned against its wall, dripping. The book was slick. His thumb rested on the edge of its cover before opening it. Still nothing but waterlogged parchment.

Then the page rippled. Subtly at first, like a breath exhaled beneath the surface. Lines bloomed in elegant sweeps. Letters unfurled one by one in a deep blue shimmer. Not ink. Blood, maybe. Or magic. The shapes curled into sentences, old and looping, until a full entry emerged, penned in an unfamiliar hand. The date in the corner read over a hundred years ago.

CHAPTER 29
Dorothy Hale

The tea party unfolded inside the country club's parlor. Sunlight filtered through ivory curtains and stained-glass transoms, casting the floors in honeyed gold and sapphire light. Gilt-framed landscapes adorned the damask-paneled walls, while a harp sat in the corner beneath a portrait of a woman in fox fur. The ceiling, coffered and frescoed with faded allegories, seemed to press down with expectation. Even the air smelled expensive—bergamot, beeswax, and the faintest trace of old roses.

Dorothy glimpsed men in cream suits smoking cigars between squash rounds, their laughter rising above the thud of rackets like boys who'd never been taught shame. Back inside, women in pearls and bias-cut silk shifted on carved walnut chairs, their voices like the clink of spoons against porcelain. They glanced at Dorothy in her black-and-white uniform, curious, then indifferent. Noah had insisted she'd be fine, but even his confidence couldn't change the truth: she was meant to be invisible. Tolerated when necessary. Vanished when not.

Balancing a silver tray with pastries and powdered scones, she moved between tables dressed in bone-white linen. The china bore gilt crests, the teaspoons monogrammed. Her hands trembled as she set down a new plate, trying not to let the teacups rattle.

Around her, conversations flitted like wind through drapes. Woman with inherited diamonds and lacquered fingernails discussed lives untouched by costs:

"My husband's taken up cigarette boat racing. I told him he'll crack his neck before the season's out. But alas, men love their diversions."

"Princeton or Columbia. She can't decide. Though her grandfather insists on Yale. It's tradition, after all."

Dorothy's eyes skimmed over their frosted smiles and powdered décolletage. Laughter as brittle as china. Every sound felt sharpened, every glance an inspection. She kept her head down, willing herself to stay invisible. But one conversation pierced the din.

A woman leaned in, whispering behind a gloved hand. "Did you hear?" she said to her neighbor. "Anne declined today."

"Can you blame her?" another replied, stirring her tea. "She and Joseph just buried their youngest. The funeral was what? Not even a month ago."

Dorothy froze.

"The Putnam boy was as much a victim as that scholarship girl," the blonde added. "But the real culprit? The Salisbury boy. His parents ought to be ashamed."

Nausea came fast. It wasn't their words. It was the ease and how they'd reduced it into a narrative. As if grief were another topic to be politely discussed over chamomile and dainty sandwiches.

"Do you think it's true? The bit about the drugs?"

Dorothy made for the kitchen. The tray suddenly felt like it was filled with stone. She pushed through the door as Noah glanced up from the sideboard, where he stood steeping a fresh pot.

"You okay?"

"I'm fine," she said. "I think we need more sugar."

He paused. "Top shelf in the pantry. Want me to—"

"No. I've got it."

She gripped the pantry shelf hard enough to turn her knuckles white. Spices and tea leaves filled her nose—cinnamon bark, crushed lavender, old cedar—but none of it dulled the echo of what she'd heard.

A victim as much as that scholarship girl…The real culprit…the Salisbury boy…

Elliot had met her that night, but he'd looked at her like he already knew who she was. Not in the way Jack had, but like she was some secret worth uncovering. Tucked in the kitchen while the music swelled, he'd leaned in and said, "*You don't belong here, but I don't think that's a bad thing.*"

She hadn't known how to respond. She still didn't. Now he was dead. And the girl who didn't belong was still here, serving tea to the people who'd buried him.

She found the sugar and carried it out like a soldier with an empty rifle. She had barely stepped through the doorway when Heather waved her over.

"Oh, excuse me, waitress. It looks like I dropped my fork," she said, a saccharine smile curling on her lips. "Would you mind fetching me another please?"

Dorothy stilled as a dozen heads turned in unison. "Of course." Her voice didn't waver, but her skin burned.

"You know, I'm impressed she's managing this," Heather mused to her companions. "It must be so hard keeping up after everything she's been through. I'm surprised she hasn't transferred home."

Dorothy held herself together as she pushed through the swinging door into the kitchen. Noah looked up, arms folded, one brow quirked in amusement.

"She's making you get a fork, isn't she?"

Dorothy reached for the cutlery drawer.

"I get it," he said, gently. "They thrive on making people like us feel small. But they don't see you." He placed a hand on her shoulder. "I know we hardly know each other, but you're stronger than they'll ever know because you're not like them."

The words passed over her like smoke. Thin and weightless.

Back in the parlor, civility smiled like a beast. Dorothy crossed the floor and set the fork on Heather's plate with perfect poise. "There," she said. "A fresh fork."

"Thank you," Heather said. "You're so good at following instructions."

Dorothy wanted to slam her face onto the table. Lola's eyes met hers just in time to distract her. There was a flicker of pity, maybe. Dorothy couldn't tell. They hadn't spoken since the maze. None of them had mentioned it—not that they would. Lola and Heather passed her at school like she didn't exist. Maybe they didn't want to remember, and Dorothy was the one who hadn't stopped replaying it.

The rest of the afternoon blurred. She moved on autopilot, refilling teacups, clearing plates, but she wasn't there.

Jack. Elliot. Heather. Lola. The glances.

She set a stack of plates down too hard. Noah looked over, offering a smile, but even he couldn't stop the doubts from creeping in. For all her efforts to start over, she couldn't shake the feeling she was destined to be an outsider in Driftmoor, trapped in the margins of a world that refused to open for her.

Dorothy straightened her spine, tightened her apron, and lifted her chin. Maybe belonging wasn't hers to claim. But she could at least deny Heather the satisfaction of seeing her break.

CHAPTER 30
Lola Godfrey

Lola sipped from her teacup, pretending the seat beside her wasn't empty. The porcelain was rimmed in gold and warm against her lips, its pattern a lattice of lilies and cranes, a custom design for the Driftmoor Women's Social Club. Or so they claimed. Around the parlor, mothers leaned into daughters, one adjusting a collar, while another reached over lattice gloves to tuck a curl behind an ear. Lola couldn't help but correct her posture against the chair.

"Welcome, ladies." Gwen Croft stood at the front of the parlor beneath a chandelier of teardrop crystals. One gloved hand rested on Heather's shoulder. "What a pleasure it is to gather on such a lovely day to celebrate the unique bond between mothers and daughters, and to honor a cherished tradition that unites generations."

Polite smiles bloomed across tables set with tiered cake stands and embroidered linen napkins. Faces spanned decades yet shared the same attentive glow. It was a learned elegance, passed down like heirlooms. Beside Gwen, Heather twinkled beneath her mother's spotlight.

"Today's tea is a special blend imported from India and Sri Lanka," Gwen continued. "For those with dietary restrictions, we have chocolate ganache cookies that are gluten free, as well as a variety of wonderful vegan options."

Lola's attention drifted.

A woman took her daughter's saucer with a fond grin. Another leaned to whisper, *elbows off the table, sweetheart,* her pearls catching the light as she adjusted her daughter's napkin. Lola's throat tightened. Not with envy, but with an ache she didn't want to name, unshapely and lodged behind her heart. It crept up from nowhere and made her want to scream into a pillow until her voice cracked, then sit back and reapply lipstick like nothing happened. Because that was the Godfrey way. You didn't spiral in public or admit the hollow. You blotted your lips and smiled prettier.

The parlor broke into gentle applause after Gwen's introduction. A few minutes later, Mrs. Hatchet—a long-standing committee member—attempted to make conversation with Lola.

"Your mother couldn't make it, Lola?" she said.

Lola instantly saw the curiosity disguised as sympathy. Her fingers curled around the teacup's gilt handle. "She's in Paris. A diplomatic conference, I believe." She waved a hand like she hadn't checked the RSVP list three times.

Mrs. Hatchett nodded, but the judgment clung to her expression like static.

Nearby, Ms. Farley, a divorcee with more ex-husbands than fingers, leaned toward her daughter and whispered, "Such a waste of potential, that one."

At first, Lola thought the comment was aimed at her. But Ms. Farley's gaze had settled on Ophelia. A satisfactory blip fluttered Lola's ego before she smothered it behind her teacup. Once, she might've defended Ophelia. Back when they'd stayed up late trading secrets beneath the silk canopy of Lola's bed. A time, when Ophelia had known every flaw in Lola's armor and guarded them like her own. But now, all Lola could do was watch.

Ophelia and her mother, Meredith—her mirror in silk and bone— were locked in conversation, their laughter soft and unbothered. Meredith wore a dove-gray hat with gray netting and mother-of-pearl buttons stitched into her sleeves, her gloved hand occasionally brushing Ophelia's in some automatic intimacy Lola had never once received from Esmeralda.

Meredith cleared her throat. "Gwen, I couldn't help but notice that Irene and Veronica aren't here," she said. "Is everything alright? I thought they'd be attending."

Gwen's smile tightened. "It seems the Oldwycks had more pressing matters to attend to," she said. "But I must say, Meredith, it's an absolute delight to have Ophelia back. She brings a special energy to our gatherings. Driftmoor hasn't felt the same without her."

Delight? Lola nearly scoffed into her cup.

"It is wonderful seeing the girls together again, isn't it?" Meredith's dark blue eyes swept between Lola, Heather, and Ophelia, as if they were still girls playing dress-up in the Lockhart's sunroom.

Heather laid a hand on Ophelia's. "It's been such a long time," she said. "I'm glad she's back."

Lola recognized that smile on Heather's face. It was the same one Heather had worn when she told Lola her mascara was smudged— right after the class photo. Now, it was like watching two ghosts pretend they hadn't once haunted each other. One had vanished without goodbye. The other had flinched whenever her name came up. And here they were, performing kindness in pastel nail polish.

Lola didn't trust the smile. Worse, she didn't trust how she felt. Because for a single, idiotic second, she wished Ophelia would look at her instead. The impulse made her want to gag. She forced her gaze down to the pastries, feigning interest while resisting the urge to roll her eyes. Driftmoor girls didn't make scenes. Not in daylight, not in silk. Success here meant self-control, a delicate veneer of grace, no matter how deep the blade of betrayal went.

Ms. Farley sliced a scone, her gaze sliding toward Ophelia again. "Between us ladies," she said, "ending your relationship with Declan Albatross was a wise decision."

Lola's teacup paused midair as Meredith and Ms. Farley exchanged a glance, heavy with shared understanding.

"It's no secret that family is troubled," Ms. Farley continued. A few women agreed, but Gwen seemed uninterested in the topic. "Theodore may have left, but let's not pretend the apple fell far from the tree. And Doris? Well, there's a reason she's holed up in that old house."

Beneath the table, Lola twisted her napkin. These were the same women who used to fawn over Doris's parties, who clinked champagne flutes on the Nantucket terrace, now talking like they'd never clawed for a seat at Albatross House.

"Lola." Mrs. Hatchett turned toward her. "You and Declan are still close, aren't you?"

The question was a trap.

"Of course," she said. "He's one of my oldest friends. Why do you ask?"

"Well, has he ever exhibited any troubling behavior?"

"I'm afraid I don't understand, Mrs. Hatchett."

"Oh, you know how people talk." Mrs. Hatchett leaned in. "Has he mentioned hearing voices? Music that's not there?"

Lola squeezed her napkin so tightly her nails might've torn through it.

"It's that sailor's curse," a woman said.

"Oh, hush, Martha," Gwen said. "There's no such thing as curses."

"What sailor's curse?" Heather looked toward her mother.

"It's a story," Ms. Farley answered before Gwen could. "A tale as old as Driftmoor."

Lola expected the conversation to return to mundane topics and gossip, but teacups stilled, and heads turned toward Ms. Farley.

"The Albatrosses story doesn't begin on land. It begins at sea," she said.

Their table quieted.

"Captain Albatross the First was determined to deliver cargo to a growing settlement along these shores. But days before landfall, his ship, *The Caulerpa*, sailed into a tempest. Waves rose like giants, winds howled like the damned, and lightning split the heavens."

Heather leaned forward, her skepticism slipping into fascination.

"The captain was thrown overboard," Ms. Farley continued, "and swallowed by the raging sea. He woke on the rocks, clutching nothing but an astrolabe. And there a figured emerged from the surf."

She glanced in her tea. "It was a siren. Her skin glistened. Her nails curved like talons. And her teeth were made for one thing: tearing flesh from bone."

A few women shifted in their seats. Some glanced toward the windows, as if expecting the harbor to come crashing through the glass.

"She promised him wealth and influence," Ms. Farley continued. "Riches from the deep. Influence far beyond the horizon. But at a price, of course."

"What was it?" Ophelia asked.

"The astrolabe he fell off board with."

"And what was so special about that astrolabe?"

"It was said to possess magic woven from the stars themselves. It revealed the fate's branching paths, whispering secrets of what could be. And for those bold enough to follow, it promised clarity. The key to the future they longed for.

"The captain refused. He vowed he'd give anything else, but he had lost everything in the storm." She let the words hang before continuing. "The siren smiled, for she had thought of a crueler bargain. She would grant him everything he desired, and in return, his descendants would belong to the ocean."

Lola remembered fragments of stories her father used to tell after a glass of scotch and always in a voice too grave for a child's bedroom. He spoke of days when power didn't come from inheritance, but from four bargains, struck beneath blood moons and eclipsed suns. Not born of greed, but of desperation. Each family made their choice. Each paid a price. But none of them understood the cost until it was too late.

Ms. Farley proceeded. "Desperate to cement his fortune, Albatross agreed. To seal the deal, the siren sank her claws into his arm and plunged it into the tide. Brine rushed into his veins, and from that moment on, he and every Albatross after him belonged to the sea."

Clatter from the kitchen startled a few women out of their trance.

"The Albatrosses would have their wealth and influence, but never true freedom," Ms. Farley said. "The siren's song would pull them to the sea and either claim them or force them to do their bidding on land."

"But what happened to the astrolabe?" Heather asked.

"Some say it was lost. Others claim the sirens still search for it. And there are those who believe it's in Albatross House where magic guards it from sirens."

Lola had always known the Godfrey's were one of Driftmoor's founding family. The other three faded into its lost history. All she'd been told was that there had been four. The rest vanished after some fallout, a dispute, her father had once admitted, over how to wield what they'd inherited. Whether to serve the town. Or rule it.

"What a preposterous tale," Gwen said. "If every curse were real, we'd all be holding séances." She sipped her tea. "And I'd have much better gossip to offer.

Laughter flickered around the parlor, but it couldn't thaw the chill the story left behind.

"So, Lola." Ms. Farley turned back to her. "Have you noticed any abnormal behavior in Declan? Anything that might allude to unwelcomed voices?"

Both Heather and Ophelia stared at Lola, waiting for her response.

If the Albatrosses were one of the founding families, Lola would've known. She'd spent years inside that house. She used to be close to Declan's mother before she withdrew from society and locked the doors. But maybe the signs had always been there, and Lola had mistaken them for the usual kind of aloofness money afforded.

She met Ms. Farley with a calm smile. "I can't say I have," she said. "But I suppose such gossip fills the void when one doesn't have a life of their own."

A few women stiffened. Gwen's mouth twitched into a shape that might've been a smirk if it weren't so composed. Across the table, Heather and Ophelia raised their hands to their lips, poorly masking the amusement that flickered there. Lola set her napkin beside her plate, the silk creased and crushed from how tightly she'd been holding it.

She stood, eyes watching her every movement. As she walked past the rows of tables, she caught a glimpse of a younger girl giggling while her mother brushed a crumb from her cheek. The intimacy twisted her heart. But she wouldn't cry over an empty seat. She didn't look back at Mrs. Farley and the others. Let them whisper. Let them speculate. She'd survived worse. And if she had to, she'd do it again.

CHAPTER 31
Dorothy Hale

Dorothy wiped her hands on her apron, exhaustion settling into her shoulders. That's when she saw Lola Godfrey standing by the marble counter, looking misplaced amid the steam and clang of trays. But this wasn't the same girl Dorothy had seen at Oldwyck Manor. The one who moved through rooms like they were hers by right. There was tension in her posture now, her arms crossed not out of defiance but restraint. And in her hazel eyes, something flickered. Not superiority or contempt, but guardedness.

Dorothy hesitated, the towel in her hand damp from her grip. "Um…are you okay?"

Lola looked up. "You again," she said, straightening. "You keep turning up like bad weather."

"Maybe it's because we go to the same school?"

"How insightful. Anything else you want to state that's obvious?"

Dorothy bit the inside of her cheek, immediately regretting saying anything. "No. Sorry."

Lola sighed. "It's not you. I'm—" She glanced at Dorothy's hair. "I shouldn't be taking out my frustrations on a complete stranger with split ends."

Dorothy reached for her pigtails, then let her hands fall. She should've gone back to wiping down counters or folding towels. Anything to look busy. But her chest tightened when she thought about the maze and the way Lola had stood between them and that creature.

Her voice came out quieter than she intended. "Can I ask you a question?"

Lola tilted her head, guarded.

Dorothy twisted her apron's hem. "What…what are you?"

"Excuse me?"

"I don't mean it in a bad way. I'm trying to figure out what's happening to me. I saw what you did in the maze after that wolf attacked us." She didn't want to call it the wrong name in case Lola remembered differently. "You healed. Are you some kind of witch?"

Lola studied Dorothy, suspicion softening into recognition. "Look, I don't know what you're going through, but I've got my own mess to deal with," she said. "You haven't been blabbing, have you?"

"No. Who would even believe me?"

Lola looked at the door. "You'd be surprised. People in this town have a knack for superstition." She paused. "I don't know what's going on with you, but I'd keep quiet. And just so you know, that wasn't a wolf."

"It wasn't?"

"Did you not see the size of that thing?" Lola stepped closer. "I promise you this: that was no wolf. It was a hellhound."

Hellhound?

"Are you messing with me?"

"You watched someone's skin stitch itself together in seconds and this is the part you don't believe?"

Dorothy's mouth tensed, gaze dropping to a crack in the floor tile. "Okay. But why are you telling me this?"

"You said you're trying to figure things out." Lola's gaze dropped, then lifted. "And I know what it feels like when you're coming apart at the seams."

The kitchen door creaked open.

Heather stepped in. "Oh. Sorry. I didn't realize you two were friendly."

Lola straightened so fast it looked rehearsed. Her face smoothed into impassiveness. "We're not. Godfreys don't make friends with the help."

The words landed like theatrics. Lola hadn't looked at her once while saying them. That somehow, hurt worse. Dorothy had let herself believe there was more to her, more than the smirk and the shine. That the girl who had bled beside her in the maze might've seen her and cared. But Driftmoor's social order had snapped back into place and Lola had chosen her side.

"What are you doing here?" Lola asked Heather. "Shouldn't you be strolling down memory lane with Ophelia?"

Heather shifted. "I—" she exhaled. "I'm sorry. I wanted to see if you were okay after that thing with Ms. Farley."

"I truly don't care."

The word hellhound curled in Dorothy's thoughts. She recalled Heather's scream. Lola's blood smeared across a hedge. The breath of the creature—hot, sulfur-bitten. She pretended the memory hadn't just stolen the air from her lungs. Trays. Teacups. Movements she could control. She busied herself with them, as if neatness might tether her. But the word echoed louder than the clatter of china. Hellhound. No matter how tightly she folded the napkins, how deeply she buried the memory, some part of her already knew nothing was going back to the way it was.

CHAPTER 32
Declan Albatross

UNDER THE HARSH BATHROOM LIGHT, DECLAN GRIPPED THE SINK, knuckles bleached. His breath hitched—stuttered—and broke apart in uneven intervals. Each inhale scraped through his throat, as if his lungs had forgotten what it meant to hold air. Water clung to his lashes, traced the cut of his jaw, and dripped into the porcelain basin. Steam curled along the mirror's edges, swallowing his reflection until all that remained was the blur of a boy unraveling.

He'd never feared monsters as a child. Not the ones in closets. Not the ones beneath the bed. But the lake had cleaved him open in a way he couldn't name. He couldn't tell where the panic ended, and the truth began. Only that both clawed at his head, demanding for escape. He shut his eyes tight, willing the sink to stop swaying, the walls to stop pressing in.

He stumbled back into his bedroom, breath ragged, robe clutched like he could hold himself together if he tied it tightly enough. Books stood in neat towers beside the bed. Silver pens aligned with surgical precision. The quill and ink set Lola had given him for Christmas resting in its stand, unopened. Above the shelves, a model ship leaned into imagined wind, its paper sails frozen mid-journey.

Everything in its place. Except the journal.

It sat at the center of his desk like it knew he'd return. Like it wanted him to. He hadn't touched it since the boathouse. Had tried to forget how the words had revealed themselves for him. But it pulsed in his vision, louder than the beat in his throat.

Behind him, a floorboard creaked.

He turned. "Mom?"

The dark hallway stared back.

His chest constricted even tighter. He crossed to the nightstand, fingers fumbling through essays, receipts, dog-eared paperbacks. A photograph slipped free. One of him, Ophelia, Lola, Aiden, and Heather, half-smiling in the sun at Silver Shoals. A distant life. He wondered if Ophelia had already decided to leave. If she'd known that would be the last summer before everything broke.

Beneath the photograph, the pill bottle waited. He'd started taking them after the divorce, when Doris stopped playing music and his father stopped coming home. The pills fixed nothing. But they made it easier to breathe without falling apart. He unscrewed the cap with trembling fingers and dry-swallowed one, counting backward as it lodged in his throat.

A breeze swept through the room. Pages rustled. The journal, closed minutes ago, now lay open. Every part of him screamed to leave it. To turn away and forget. But another pull, quieter and stronger, whispered: *You need to know.*

He stepped closer. The page was dense with signatures.

Homer S. Albatross

Homer S. Albatross II

Cecilia Albatross

Lineage written in ink, every name heavier than the last. His grandfather's booming laugh echoed in memory. A house full of portraits watching him grow up. And then a name that pulled the air from his lungs: *Doris Albatross.* His mother. He hadn't known she'd touched this book. Hadn't thought she'd even knew it existed. But here it was, written in the same looping strokes from his report cards and piano sheet music. He thought of her whispering nonsense to the sea. Her trembling hands above the keys. Maybe it hadn't been nonsense at all.

His fingers shook as he turned the page. A sketch stared back of a woman half-submerged, hair wild, mouth open in a scream. Arms ending in claws, face veiled in shadow.

Siren.

Someone had scrawled the word beneath the image. Cramped notes filled the margins:

Bound to water, drawn to blood.

They were not born of the sea but cursed to return to it.

Daughters of grief. Sons of silence. Carriers of longing made flesh.

A line had been scratched out:

Their voices do not soothe. They ruin.

And in the corner, barely visible:

The ocean remembers.

He turned another page. Another figure waited, this one shrieking. Mouth gaping, eyes vacant.

The banshee foretells the end.

Harbinger of death.

Her voice carries the weight of souls.

The pages snapped shut—then flared open again, right back to the signatures. The list ended with Doris, and beneath hers, a blank space. His gaze slid to the quill Lola had given him, resting on its stand. She'd joked when she gave it to him: *For when you want to be dramatic.*

He nearly laughed.

This is madness. You don't believe in any of this.

But he reached for it anyway. The quill felt carved from bone, not wood. He dipped it in ink.

Declan S. Albatross

The letters seeped into the parchment. As they did, pressure pinched his nose. He reached up—his fingers came away smeared with blood.

"Shit," he muttered, fumbling for tissues.

A drop splashed onto the page, then vanished. And then slowly, his name returned in red. Not ink. It was his blood.

He stumbled back as the journal shook. A guttural screech burst from its spine. The lamp flickered, plunging the space in wild flashes. Windows flew open, and a gust shrieked through his room. It was as if everything around him was screaming. He dropped to one knee, hands pressed to his ears. The screech grew unbearable, less a sound and more a presence, like grief given a voice. He lunged for the desk and slammed the journal shut. Silence fell. The light steadied. The wind stilled. And the air settled like nothing had happened. He backed away, chest rising and falling.

"What did I do?"

He bolted, the hallway spinning around him. Doors slammed open along the corridor, one after another. Sconces flickered in stuttering bursts, casting warped shadows that twisted and reformed. The wallpaper rippled like breath beneath plaster. He turned a corner—and tripped. His knees scraped against the runner. He groaned, tried to push himself up. And froze.

A figure stood over him, faint but unmistakable. A man in naval uniform, coat damp and frayed, seaweed clinging to his shoulders. His features were pale and ruined by time, but there was no mistaking the family resemblance. The same eyes. The same mouth. The same bone-deep sorrow. He reached out, palm open.

Declan scrambled back. "No—no, no, no—"

He ran the other way, arms brushing portraits that watched too closely as he barreled down a side hall. He didn't stop until he reached the far door, nearly wrenching it from the frame as he stumbled into his mother's bedroom.

It was dark. The only sound was her breath. Doris lay asleep, a lamp casting amber light across the sheets. She looked impossibly peaceful. Like nothing had ever changed with her. Declan stood there, panting, the silence louder than the chaos he'd left behind. His mind spiraled with what just happened before he finally slipped beneath the covers and wrapped an arm around her.

"Mom?" he whispered.

She stirred slightly. Her lips parted. "The ocean," she murmured, "it remembers."

Declan closed his eyes tight and held her closer, hoping the night would pass without calling him back.

CHAPTER 33

Aiden Oldwyck

AIDEN PEDALED THROUGH THE WOODS, THE ROAD UNFURLING beneath his tires. The wheel's rhythm and his breath were the only thing keeping his mind from spiraling as anger simmered within. Anger at his mother, for lying all these years. At himself, for ignoring the gaps and silences. She'd hidden the truth to spare him the weight of it, and he understood that. But understanding didn't dissolve the fury or distress that came with it because, he should've had time. Time to figure life out. To graduate and leave Driftmoor. To fall in love again and make stupid, beautiful mistakes. But the sands were running out.

The road curved downhill, and the patinaed gates of Albatross House rose with the family crest: an anchor tangled with rope, flanked by seaweed, and crowned with a seahorse. The gates revealed the drive beyond—cobblestone bordered by overgrown hedges, the kind trimmed less by gardeners and more by generations of neglect.

Just as Aiden reached them, the asphalt shimmered. Heat distorted the air, and fire split the road wide open. He swerved. Tires shrieked. The bike fishtailed and flipped. He slammed onto the pavement, pain shooting through his hip, gravel digging into his palms. Smoke drifted across the road, cloaking the night like fog after a battle. Maeve stepped from the haze, her cloak trailing behind her. Blood smeared Aiden's hands as he scrambled to his feet.

"Hmm," she said, eyeing him. "That was quite the fall."

His breath rasped. "What—what are you doing here?"

"Would you believe I was passing through?"

"I'd believe you almost set the road on fire."

Her smile thinned. "The world doesn't revolve around you, nephew. No matter what your mother may have led you to believe."

"Then what do you want?"

With a flick of her wrist, fire bloomed at her fingertips. She tossed a flame toward his bike and the frame went up in seconds, metal groaning, tires popping, paint blistering. Aiden's stomach clenched as useless, impotent rage surged. What good was it against someone who could set the world on fire with a gesture?

Maeve let out a soft hum. "Careful. Your mother should've taught you better manners when speaking to your elders." She stepped closer. "Since you already know your fate, perhaps you'll cooperate. Have you seen anyone at Driftmoor exhibiting banshee-like abilities?"

"What? I don't even know what that means."

She watched him for a moment, her russet eyes unreadable. Then her voice dropped. "At the auction, you asked me a question," she said. "You asked why I hate you so much."

His chest tightened. He hadn't expected her to ever bring that up.

"The truth is, I don't," she said. "I've barely bothered to know you. I'm not the villain you imagine." She crouched beside him. "What I hate is how weak you make my little sister."

His mouth opened before he could stop it. "She's far from weak."

"She used to be ruthless and devoted to the matriarchy. Until your father softened her and made her dream of mercy. And then you came along, finishing what he started. You made her believe there was another way. That we could keep our sons and still survive."

Aiden's fists balled at his sides, bloodied and shaking. "You're telling me you've never wanted a son of your own?"

A shadow of a bruise passed over her face.

"I did," she said, quieter now. "Julian. That would've been his name." Her voice didn't crack, but it carried an ache too old to mask. "He didn't make it past the first breath. Before the hounds came for him."

Aiden stepped forward. "Why didn't you keep him like my mother did with me?"

Maeve sighed, like he'd disappointed her with the question. "Because I would've loved him. And I'd lose him. Like my sister will lose you." She stared down the road. "And I don't believe in building a life around grief. That kind of hope—" her mouth twisted, "it makes fools of us."

Aiden had never imagined someone like Maeve could carry pain like this. One that was unspoken and buried beneath decades of control. "That doesn't make you a fool," he said. "It makes you human."

She looked at him like she wanted to correct him. Or agree. Then she turned away, moonlight catching in the folds of her cloak. "Enjoy your final months. And if you learn anything useful regarding a banshee, do pass it along."

She lifted her hands. Embers spiraled up her arm, catching the wind.

And she was gone.

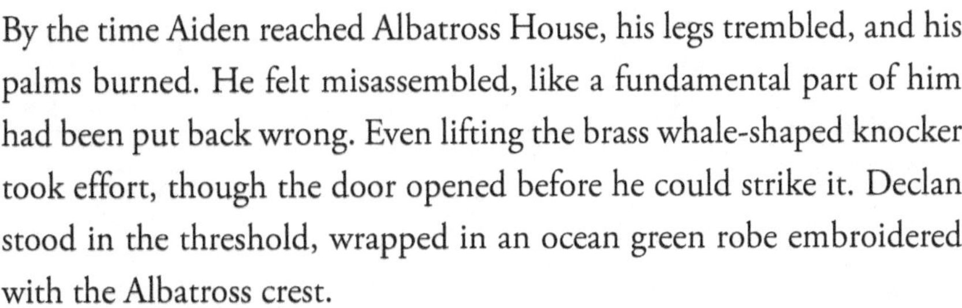

By the time Aiden reached Albatross House, his legs trembled, and his palms burned. He felt misassembled, like a fundamental part of him had been put back wrong. Even lifting the brass whale-shaped knocker took effort, though the door opened before he could strike it. Declan stood in the threshold, wrapped in an ocean green robe embroidered with the Albatross crest.

"Aiden?" Concern cracked across Declan's face. "What the hell happened to you?"

Aiden glanced at his sleeves, torn at the elbows, and his bloodied hands. Gravel clung to the knees of his jeans. "Nothing. I fell off my bike."

"Is that so?" Declan leaned against the doorframe, arms folding. "And where's your bike?"

He sighed. "Does it matter?"

"Fine." Declan's gaze sharpened but he stepped aside. "You can tell me later."

Albatross House's warmth met Aiden like a memory he hadn't known he missed. Light pooled from the chandelier, gilding the wallpaper etched with constellations and waves. As kids, they used to trace the stars with their fingers, arguing over horoscopes and making up ones of their own. His gaze landed on the seahorse statue nestled at the foot the stairs, once polished to a mirror finish, now dulled. Strange, how a house that didn't bear his name could feel like home.

Declan led him into the library, its arched windows draped in damask, the shelves filled with cracked spines and first editions. "Sit. Don't move."

Aiden dropped onto the leather couch and leaned back. His mind wouldn't stop. The hellhound, Maeve's fire, Heather's sidelong glance. Everything barreled toward him like a train he couldn't stop.

Declan returned with a glass of water and a first aid kit stamped with a tarnished family sigil. He crouched beside the couch, snapping the latch open.

"You look like shit," he said, dabbing a cotton ball against Aiden's scraped palms.

Aiden gave a breath of laughter. "I suppose that's an upgrade from looking like crap."

Declan's mouth quirked as he carefully moved his hands. Aiden found himself watching him more than the wounds. How his lashes threw shadows across his cheekbones, how his brows drew together in concentration, how the light caught in the dip above his collarbone. Even like this, even in a robe, there was gravity to him. And Aiden hated that he felt it.

Declan cleared his throat. "So are you gonna tell me what happened, or do I have to guess?"

Aiden rubbed the back of his neck, catching a fleck of gravel. "It's been a long night," he said. "My mother and I had a fight. It's not really something I want to unpack right now."

Declan studied him for a beat, then nodded. "You want to crash here then?"

He should've said no. But the thought of returning to Oldwyck Manor and facing his mother again after Maeve and everything she'd hidden—he couldn't.

"Yeah. That'd be nice," he said. "Thanks."

Silence settled. The kind that asked for nothing. It reminded Aiden of the nights spent half-studying, Declan buried in a novel while Aiden pretended to do homework, more attuned to the sound of pages turning than his textbook. With anyone else, the quiet might've been unbearable. But with Declan, it felt like rest.

Aiden's eyes drifted to the coffee table where the leather-bound book with the compass pressed into its cover rested. "How's the empty sketchbook going along?" he asked, the hint of a smile tugging at the corner of his mouth.

But Declan didn't smile back. "It's not a sketchbook," he said. "It's more like a journal."

"Weren't the pages all blank?" Aiden asked. "Did you find something we missed?"

Declan lifted the journal, tracing the design with his thumb. "I was rowing on the lake to release some steam. Just a regular afternoon, you know. I had the journal with me, and it fell in the water."

"You dropped it?"

"By accident, of course," Declan said. "But here's the thing. When I opened it, the pages weren't blank anymore."

Aiden sat forward. "What do you mean?"

Declan opened the journal to a page filled with a list of names—everyone one of them an Albatross. And at the bottom, the final name looked fresher than the ones before:

Declan S. Albatross

"Wait a minute. What's your name doing in this?" Aiden asked.

"Don't know. It was already there. All of them."

"Did you show your mother?"

"What? No." His laugh was humorless. "Why aren't you more freaked out? These pages were blank and now they're not. It doesn't make any sense."

"I mean, it's strange. But maybe it's a trick of the water like a chemical reaction."

Declan looked up at him. "There's no way you truly believe that."

Aiden didn't respond. Not with words. The pause was enough.

"Okay, well what else is in there?" He reached toward the next page.

Before his fingers touched the parchment, Declan snapped the book shut and stood.

"Sorry," Declan said. "I think that's enough for tonight."

He crossed to the door. "You're staying, right? We should get ready. We have that study session with Lola." His voice steadied. "She'll murder us if we're late."

Aiden followed him into the hallway, his steps cautious and uncertain. The journal clung from Declan's hand like it had grafted to his skin. Aiden's pulse hadn't slowed since the moment he caught it—that glimpse of inked fur and fangs, the unmistakable form a hellhound sketched across the parchment.

They reached the landing where Doris's door was slightly ajar. Her voice drifted out, soft and frayed at the edges.

"Sea glass can be deadly," she murmured.

Declan froze. Aiden met his eyes, but neither spoke. He'd heard stories about Declan's mother. Her forgetfulness, the strange things she muttered. But they never talked about it. It hovered between them, something they'd agreed not to name. Now, hearing her voice like that, Aiden felt it settle. Fragile. Off. And somehow worse for how ordinary Declan made it seem.

Still, Declan walked. So Aiden did too.

"The usual guest room's out, by the way," Declan said, as they walked the corridor. "The ceiling collapsed about a month ago. Been meaning to get someone to come in fix it but haven't had the time."

"Oh."

"You can take the one down the hall."

Aiden hesitated. "Would it be weird if I stayed in your room?"

Declan turned, surprise flickering through the mask he wore. "You okay?"

"I'm not sure. I…I don't want to be alone tonight."

They used to share a bed all the time when they were younger. Sleepovers that blurred into early morning whispers and shared blankets. But that was before.

Declan didn't answer right away. Then, just barely, he nodded. "Sure."

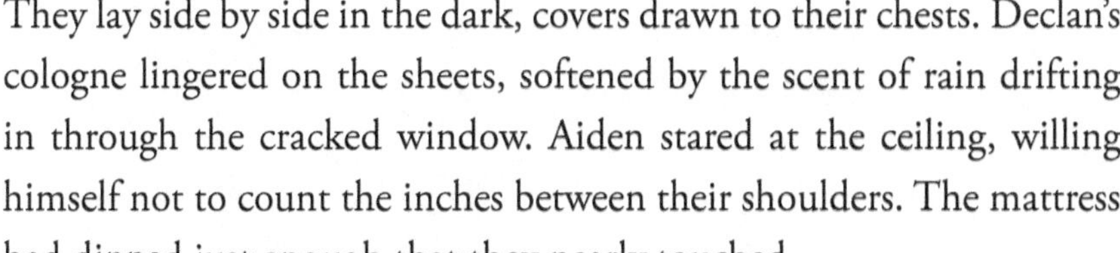

They lay side by side in the dark, covers drawn to their chests. Declan's cologne lingered on the sheets, softened by the scent of rain drifting in through the cracked window. Aiden stared at the ceiling, willing himself not to count the inches between their shoulders. The mattress had dipped just enough that they nearly touched.

He didn't dare turn to him.

"Declan," Aiden whispered. "Are you awake?"

A pause. Then, groggily. "Barely…"

"Sorry. Just…do you mind if I ask you a question?"

Declan gave a vague hum of permission.

"If I the world were ending…what would you say to me, if you had the chance?"

The question hung in the dark like a live wire.

Declan sat up a little, curls sticking to his forehead, the blanket slipping from his chest. "What kind of question is that?" He glanced at the clock. "It's almost midnight."

Aiden flinched. "Sorry, you're right."

But Declan looked at him like he saw through the smirk Aiden tried to hide behind. Then he reached over and brushed an eyelash from Aiden's cheek. "You idiot," he murmured.

He could've stopped there.

"I'd tell you that the world ending wouldn't change the fact that I see you. Even when you try to disappear."

He fell back against the pillow, eyes closing, the mattress shifting with him. His arm grazed Aiden's and stayed. Neither moved. They stayed there, shoulder to shoulder, breath to breath, while Aiden's mind continued spinning with his imminent doom, and now this journal. But it all faded out beneath this small, impossible closeness.

CHAPTER 34
Dorothy Hale

The town's church was nothing like the chapel at St. Augustine. The incense hit her first—sweet and smoky, clinging to her throat. Stepping into the church felt like intruding in someone else's dream. Shadowed arches loomed above, their lines catching the votive candles burning along the altar. Light fractured through stained-glass, spilling across the pews in restless color. She didn't know what had drawn her here. Maybe loneliness or the fear of not understanding what her life had become.

Near the back, the confessional waited, half-swallowed by darkness, its wood grain glowing in candlelight. She hesitated. Did non-Catholics confess? Was she even allowed here? Before uncertainty could take hold, she slipped inside. The booth was smaller than she'd imagined. She knelt, folding her hands less out of faith than instinct, as her knees sank into the frayed velvet.

"Hello?" she whispered. "Forgive me, uh Father. This is my first time."

A gentle voice answered through the partition. "Then I'm glad you're here," he said. "What's on your heart today?"

"I'm not sure." Her throat tightened. "I guess I feel lost. Confused about life."

"That's more common than you think. Many people come looking for direction. What's weighing on you?"

She thought of the last few weeks, and the memories came like a puzzle she couldn't finish, afraid of what picture it might reveal.

"I've seen things," she said. "Things that shouldn't be possible."

Silence stretched. She wondered if he thought she was crazy. But his reply came softly.

"Sometimes the world shows us what we're not ready to understand," he said. "But that doesn't mean you're alone."

She stared at the partition's carved lattice. "I don't know if I believe in any of this. God. The Devil. Not even the things that I've seen."

"That's okay." His tone didn't shift. "Doubt doesn't mean you're incapable of faith. It means you're still reaching for it. The questions—they're part of the journey forward."

She scraped a splinter on the kneeler, her thumb worrying it loose. "What if the truth is scarier than not knowing?"

He paused again, and this time, it felt intentional.

"Truth can be frightening," he said. "But it brings light. And light always wins over darkness."

She wasn't sure she believed that. But a part of her wanted to.

"Have you ever seen the Devil?" she asked, surprised at herself for even asking.

The quiet stretched for a moment.

"Not in the way you're picturing," he said. "The Devil doesn't need horns or fire. They're quieter. They're the voice that creeps in when everything else goes still. The one that says you're nothing. That no one's coming. That this—what you're feeling—is all there is. That's the voice I try not to listen to."

She took a deep breath, and said, "I think the Devil has cursed me, and I don't know why."

A sound slipped through the partition, sliding against the wood. A rosary.

"Keep this close," he said. "Hold it when the Devil feels louder than your thoughts, even if you don't pray, even if you don't believe. Let it remind you that you are not facing the dark alone."

She thanked him for his time and took the rosary. Outside the booth, the church's hush folded around her. She stood with the rosary clutched, as if it might tether her to what was left of her sanity. But nothing felt sane anymore. Everything strange had started in Driftmoor. Before this place, shadows didn't move on their own. Mirrors didn't crack when she screamed. Girls didn't bleed and heal in seconds. No one vanished in fires.

She passed the crucifix where Christ hung. But as she walked, she could've sworn his eyes shifted. Not accusing. Not even pitying. Just watching. And somehow, that was worse.

Dorothy sat cross-legged on her bed with the rosary in hand. She didn't know if it would protect her or if it did anything at all but letting go felt like bad luck. Relief stirred when she realized the beads didn't burn and her skin remained untouched. No divine flame seared her fingers. No ash clung to her. Maybe whatever had awakened inside wasn't born of darkness.

A knock shattered her thoughts. She hesitated, then walked over to the door. Noah stood in the hall, framed by the corridor light. His coat hung open over a threadbare button-down and faded corduroys. He glanced at the rosary lying on the sheets.

"Didn't take you for a Bible thumper."

Dorothy retreated without answering, sinking back into her bed as he let himself in.

"That doesn't seem like a nice thing to say," she said. "But I'm not."

Noah plopped into the desk chair, turned it around to face her, and slung one leg over the armrest. "Then what's with the holy beads?"

"I don't know. Guess I wanted to see what it could do."

"No judgment. We all need a reason to hold on to—religion, hope, whatever gets us through. Or so I've heard."

She picked up the rosary. "What about you? What do you believe in?"

He leaned back, the chair squeaking. "Oh, you know. The usual… capitalism, deep state conspiracies, and the sacred ritual of a well-timed nap."

"So, nothing."

"I didn't say that." He tapped against the chair. "I think there's some kind of force out there. Some cosmic whatever. But religion? Nah. Too many rules. Too many men playing God."

Laughter drifted through the cracked window, tangling with the rustling leaves. Some of the tension in her shoulders loosened. There was something disarming about him. How he moved through life like it didn't faze him. She envied how simple life must feel when you didn't carry the same shadows every day.

"Oh, almost forgot." Noah dug into his pocket and tossed an envelope on her lap. "Your paycheck. Welcome to the ranks of the underpaid."

It wasn't much, but it was hers. A small claim in the chaotic unknown. Proof she was carving purpose for herself, even if it wasn't grand.

"Wow. Thank you," she said. "You have no idea how much this means."

He waved her off, but pride softened his usual mischief. "You're one of us."

"Us?"

"A certified Driftmoor survivor." He leaned forward. "And in honor of your initiation, there's this birthday party this weekend. Yacht party."

"A yacht?"

"Yeah. Friend of mine. His family's, like, disgustingly rich. It won't be that bad. Some music, drinks, possibly a human sacrifice to the ocean gods. Standard weekend ritual." He paused. "Thought it might be good for you. You know. As friends."

Dorothy flushed. The word friends left a trace of shame.

"Not that you're not attractive or anything," Noah added. "I kinda got my eye on someone."

Dorothy smiled. "Lucky girl."

He laughed, quieter. "Yeah, you can say that."

She chewed her lip. Parties hadn't been kind to her. But his ease was disarming. The invitation extended without pressure, just an open door and the promise that she didn't have to walk in alone.

"You think it's a good idea?" She glanced at the window. The evening sun washed Driftmoor Academy's spires in copper and gold, making the idea of normalcy believable.

"I think," Noah said, "it's exactly what you need. Especially after serving people like Heather Croft."

Color bloomed in her cheeks. "I'll think about it."

"Cool." He stood, stretching as he made for the door. "Don't worry about fitting in, Dorothy. Most of us never do."

With a salute, he disappeared down the corridor. Dorothy stared at the door long after he'd gone. Maybe he was right. Maybe she did need a night away from the strangeness—before it swallowed her whole.

CHAPTER 35
Lola Godfrey

Lola leaned against the marble island, swirling a wineglass. The kitchen gleamed like a showroom—spotless, curated, more performance than comfort. At the stove, Miriam moved quietly, sleeves rolled up, stirring with the grace of someone long resigned to being invisible. Even the comforting scent of her garlic aioli couldn't disguise the artifice. Beyond the towering windows, the gardens unspooled in clusters of pink and lilac hydrangeas that bowed under their own weight. At the far edge of the grounds, were limestone gates inlaid with brass filigree and iron vines in bloom, their edges kissed gold by the sunset. It was all so beautiful, so meticulously arranged, and yet it felt like standing in a dollhouse someone else had furnished.

Lola sipped, letting the bitterness settle on her tongue as footsteps echoed behind her.

Frederic entered in a tuxedo, adjusting his cufflinks, their silver glint catching the light. His salt-and-pepper hair was slicked back, his presence composed and rehearsed as a monologue. He looked every bit the man he'd chosen to become, dripping in refinement, utterly unbothered, as if he hadn't come from a long line of healers he now pretended didn't exist. Lola could still remember the way he flinched when her grandmother mentioned *the gift* like it was a stain he could scrub off their name.

He kissed Lola's forehead in passing. "Are you sure you don't want to join us tonight?"

She smirked behind her glass. "And miss an evening of wealthy people pretending to enjoy the opera?"

"It's Wagner, so you're not wrong."

Esmeralda appeared behind him, her silk gown hugging her frame like it had been poured on. She moved like a statue that had learned to glide—impeccable, untouchable, and exhausting. Lola sometimes wondered if her mother had been born that way, or if Driftmoor had carved her from something softer. Either way, there was no trace of softness left.

"Lola." Her eyes swept over her. "I trust you're not drinking the good wine."

Lola raised the glass with an icy smile. "Wouldn't dream of it, Mother."

Esmeralda didn't return the smile. She never did. Not when she looked at her.

"I heard about the tea party," she continued. "Ms. Farley is a valued donor to the Academy. Next time, perhaps remember that before telling her to—what was it?—*mind her own business.*"

Lola's smile sharpened. "Next time, perhaps she will."

"Perhaps." Esmeralda brushed a speck from her sleeve. "But try not to alienate every woman with a social circle larger than yours. It's not a good look."

Faustino entered the kitchen, sweat slicking his brow, tank top clinging to his muscles. He strode to the fridge and downed a bottle of water. "Smells good, Miriam," he said, wiping his mouth with his hand.

Miriam smiled at him over her shoulder in a way Esmeralda never smiled at either of them.

"And now your sweat's in the sauce," Lola said, wrinkling her nose. "Charming."

He smirked. "And you're half a glass away from drunk before dinner. We all have our vices."

Their father adjusted his cufflinks with that compulsive elegance of his. "Try not to burn the house down while we're gone."

Lola tilted her head. "No promises. But I'll wait until dessert this time."

Frederic kissed her forehead once more, and with Esmeralda's heels clicking behind him, they swept toward the front hall without so much as a glance at Faustino.

"Miriam," Lola called, "be a dear and give my brother and I a moment?"

Miriam arched a brow and grabbed a rag before disappearing into the pantry.

Lola's sweetness dissolved. "If I tell you a secret," she said to Faustino, "you have to swear not to tell Dad."

He leaned on the counter, arms crossed. "Depends."

"Tino."

A long sigh. "Fine. I swear. Now talk."

She set her glass down and braced her palms on the marble. "Okay. So…Ophelia may or may not know about my healing."

Faustino's posture straightened. "What?"

"It gets worse." She held up a hand before he could launch in. "I was attacked by a hellhound in the Oldwyck maze. Can you believe it? A real hellhound."

He went still, like the words hadn't landed yet.

"And," she continued, "Heather and the new girl also saw me heal."

The color drained from his freckled face. "Wait. Are you okay?"

She lifted her arm and gave a sarcastic little twirl. "Do I look dead?"

"That's not funny, Lo." He stepped closer, the sarcasm falling flat. "You're lucky it wasn't a full moon."

A full moon. The one night their blood didn't obey. No mending. No stitching. No rewinding what had been broken.

"Oh, please," Lola said. "You think I'm going to cry into a silk handkerchief? We're healers. Or did you forget, since you and Dad like to pretend we're all just charmingly normal?"

"Lo." His voice lowered. "Has Dad not drilled it into you enough?"

She raised her wineglass in a mock toast. "*If the wrong people find out, we'll be hunted, drained, sold*—yes, yes. The bedtime horror stories. I could write them in calligraphy."

"They're not stories." He rubbed the back of his neck, fingers snagging in the waves at his nape. "You know that."

She swirled the wine. "Here's the twist: Heather doesn't remember. Like, at all. She saw everything. Front row. And now? Poof. It's like it never happened."

He frowned. "Okay, that's not normal. The only explanation is she's suffering from amnesia or magic."

"Right. But if it was magic, someone did it on purpose. Who on earth would even bother erasing her memory?"

"I don't know," he said. "But it sounds like the bigger problem is Ophelia. And this new girl."

Lola tapped her nail on the marble. "Interesting."

"Interesting? That's your takeaway?"

"Oh, relax. Ophelia won't say a word. And I handled the new girl."

"What does handled mean?"

Lola sipped, cool as ever. "Let's just say I'm resourceful when the need arises."

Silence stretched between them. He looked at her like he wanted to believe her. Needed to.

"I'm trusting you," Faustino said finally. "But if anything else happens, I'm telling Dad. You know how careful he is. We've stayed under the radar for over two decades. He'd lose it."

"And our lovely mother?"

Faustino snorted. "Esmeralda? She doesn't count. She's just bitter she doesn't have our genes."

Outside, Galleon's Wharf glittered faintly, the masts of fishing boats rising from the harbor.

"Don't worry your pretty little head, Tino," Lola said. "Everything's under control."

But even as she said it, the words tasted hollow. She'd built her silence out of instinct. Scraped knees vanished before teachers could send her to the nurse. Paper cuts sealed in seconds. Fever never dared linger. Her body had made a lie of fragility, and she'd learned how to sell it. Silk. Smile. Straight A's. Never sick. Never weak.

But now?

Three people knew.

Three too many.

CHAPTER 36
Declan Albatross

THE LIBRARY AT ALBATROSS HOUSE WAS ENCASED IN DARK OAK-PANELing. A spiral staircase climbed toward the upper gallery with copper railings etched with swirls that resembled waves. Above the fireplace, an astrolabe hung like a relic of celestial ambitions, its brass limbs reaching outward. Below it, a trunk gaped open, spilling yellowed maps and ink-blotted scrolls, remnants of past voyages and ancestors half-remembered. At the center of it all, Declan hunched over the reading table. The lamp illuminated family albums, maritime logs, Latin dictionaries, each more cryptic than the last. He had been chasing answers for hours, only to wander deeper into uncertainty.

He traced a line in the journal, the ink smudged from too many nights spent searching.

The firstborn shall hear the call of the deep, bound by blood, unable to resist when the tide turns.

He rubbed the knot forming between his shoulder blades, as if pressure might coax clarity from bone. *The call of the deep* surfaced again and again throughout the journal, scattered across entries decades apart, always written in the same jagged desperation. Paragraphs were scratched out, while entire sections obliterated, as though the writer had tried to erase the past.

He turned the page.

The sirens wait.

Their songs are not meant for mortals, but for us. We are marked. Chosen.

His mother's voice echoed, not in words, but in fragments. How she'd stare out at the harbor at dinner, lips moving as if listening to a melody only she could hear. Had she heard the same call their ancestors wrote about? His thumb skimmed the edge of the page. In the margin, a ringed device had been sketched, mechanical in design, gears nested within arcs.

It wasn't a compass.

He tilted the journal beneath the lamplight. His fingers slid across the engraving he'd memorized by touch but never truly seen. It was the same shape as the device, with the same interlocking gears.

Above the hearth, brass caught the light. He rose, heart thudding, and crossed the floor.

It stood taller than he remembered. Rings in interlocking loops across its core. Cosmic markings etched along the bands. His reflection distorted in its surface as he drew closer. The engraving hadn't been a compass. It was an astrolabe.

The phone on the wall rang.

He jumped before glancing at the grandfather clock. Nearly dinnertime. Had to be Lola. She always seemed to know when he lost track of time.

He picked up the receiver. "Hello?"

A pause.

"Lola?"

"Um. Hi."

His fingers curled around the receiver. He hadn't heard that voice over the phone in years.

"Sorry to call out of the blue," Ophelia said. "I didn't know if you'd still have this number. Or if you'd even answer my call."

"No, it's—I mean, I still have it." His mouth went dry. "Is everything alright?"

Theories swarmed his mind of what this meant. He tried to stay calm, but his hands had already begun to get clammy.

"I was wondering if you had time to meet," she said. "If you're not busy."

"Meet? Like tonight?"

He almost heard her laugh. Was he imagining this?

"Yes," she said. "I think it's time. Don't you?"

His eyes flicked over to the journal, then to the scattered family albums, each spine cracked, each photo yellowed and curling at the corners. The pages were full of people with his eyes and none of their answers. He thought of all the nights he'd stared at the phone, waiting for a call like this. Imagining what he'd say. What she might say. Hoping—stupidly—that hearing her voice might patch the silence she left behind.

"I—sure," he said. "Where?"

"Our old spot."

The memory clicked into place. A booth at a restaurant on Galleon's Wharf.

He leaned back against the wall and closed his eyes. The answer hovered on his lips. No. He should remember that she'd left without a word. But this was what he'd wanted. A chance to understand. To ask if leaving had anything to do with something he'd said or hadn't had the courage to say. Maybe this was his only chance to make it right. Even if only as friends. If that was even possible anymore.

"I can be there in fifteen," he said. "Does that work?"

"Perfect." She hesitated. "And Declan?"

"Yes?"

"It's best you don't mention this to Lola. Or Aiden."

He nodded before he even thought to question it. "Of course. See you soon."

"I'll see you soon."

The line clicked dead. He stood motionless, the receiver warm in his hand. He was on the verge of discovery, but it would have to wait. He needed to shower. Fix his hair. Choose the right shirt. His hands were shaking, but he didn't care. This was Ophelia.

He didn't notice the draft as he left the library or saw the journal flutter open behind him, its pages rustling until they settled on a sketch of a banshee, mouth open in a scream.

CHAPTER 37
Dorothy Hale

As a child, Dorothy had stood on the boardwalk, watching boats drift across the bay. She'd point them out to her parents, her voice rising each time a motorboat zipped past. But it was the yachts that fascinated her. Glimmering and towering, with decks stacked like a staircase to another life. They weren't just boats. They were floating kingdoms behind mirrored glass. She used to imagine the lives unfolding onboard: candlelit dinners, lovers dancing barefoot beneath velvet skies, confessions exchanged over the sea.

Now, years later, standing at the base of a yacht's gangway, her chest tightened. The vessel rose in three tiers, its chrome railings catching the last light of day. Tinted windows reflected the harbor, breaking the horizon into a shattered mosaic. Guests wandered across each level in slip dresses and shawls and tailored jackets over turtlenecks.

Dorothy tugged at her denim jacket. She didn't shine like silk or sharpen a room like tailoring. She wore a thrifted white dress and frayed sneakers, a pesky smudge against all this glamour.

"You're positive it's okay we're here?" she asked Noah, stepping onto the sun-warmed teak.

Around them, eyes briefly flicked over them before gravitating back to cocktails and curated laughter.

Noah's confidence was as effortless as the oversized sportscoat he'd thrown over his shoulders. "Yes," he said, glancing at the rooftop crowd. "Rowan's the kind of guy who throws a party and doesn't notice who shows up, as long as the champagne doesn't run out."

He flashed a grin that was equal parts mischief and reassurance. It wasn't fair, the way it landed. Something fluttered in her chest, sharp and quick, before she could chase it off.

"You're with me," he added. "You're fine."

The deck gleamed beneath strings of suspended bulbs, their amber light casting soft halos that flickered across the party's glass enclosure. Plush white lounges curled around lacquered cocktail tables, each one crowned with orchids and gardenias that looked too pristine to be real.

Beside her, Noah practically vibrated with anticipation. His eyes swept the rooftop like he'd already mapped out the night's opportunities. Like he couldn't wait to be anywhere but standing still. And before she could ask where he was going, he was splitting off the opposite direction.

Dorothy's stomach lurched. "Wait." She caught his sleeve. "Where are you going?"

A grin tugged at his mouth. "Just a minute," he said with a wink. "You're the shiny new toy tonight. Go mingle."

Her breath caught, confused by the sudden abandonment. "No, wait!"

But he was already gone, swallowed by movement, vanishing into a blur of suits and sequins. Left in his wake, she hovered at the edge of a world she still wasn't sure would let her in. Sea salt clung to the breeze, tangled with expensive cologne and the sweetness of something burn-ing. Silver trays floated past, bearing foods she couldn't name. Above her, a hot tub pulsed with turquoise light, throwing silhouettes against the canopy like shadows caught mid-laugh.

Her hand drifted toward the rosary. Fingertips brushed the beads tucked beneath her collarbone. Tonight, it felt like a superstition at a masquerade. Holy things didn't belong here. Not among the glittering strangers and bottomless glasses. Not in a place where names were currency and masks were worn like second skin.

"Dorothy?"

She barely heard it above the music, but she was certain it was her name. When she turned to see who it was, the lights, the noise, the faces, it all slipped from focus like a film reel burning between scenes.

She found herself in the billiard room at Albatross House. Sconces cast honeyed shadows across the velvet pool table, where half-drunk glasses sweated beside scattered cues. Jack stood across from her. His brown eyes flickered while a crooked smile curved his lips. Distant chatter floated in from the hallway, a reminder the world beyond their corner still spun.

"The moon and the Pleiades have set," he said. "It is midnight, and the time is passing, but I sleep alone."

Dorothy tilted toward him, swayed by the words and alcohol. "You wrote that?"

"I wish. It's Sappho. Ancient Greek poet. He's like a gazillion years old."

She moved closer until their shoulders touched. "Can I tell you something?"

Jack raised a brow, his grin tugging wider. "Wait, let me guess. You're a spy from another universe, sent to kidnap a debatably handsome boy. And you chose me?"

"What? No!" Her cheeks flushed. "How did you even come up with that?"

"It's a gift."

She laughed again. The kind of laugh that claimed space. What she wanted to tell him was that she wished they'd met sooner. That she'd never felt more seen. But the words caught, too honest for two people who had only met hours ago. So instead, she took his hand, and they danced. If it could be called that. Spinning through the room, their shadows tumbling across the walls as music pulsed faintly from another wing. She stepped on his toes once, but he didn't seem to mind. Their movements blurred into chaos and giggles, but he steadied her, gaze locked on hers like she was the only person who'd ever made sense.

"I see you, Dorothy!" he shouted as he spun her, her scarlet hair fanning out.

She let herself believe that nothing else mattered. That her life could be this: his hand at her waist, the light catching his grin, the echo of Sappho hanging in the room like a benediction.

Jack leaned in, eyes soft. "Is it cool if I kiss you?"

She had wanted nothing more. When he kissed her, it felt like the turning of a season, like the first leaf loosed from a branch, golden and weightless. Everything slowed as the air thickened with meaning. It wasn't a kiss she would tuck away and forget. It rooted itself inside her, like the kind of memory that lingers like smoke on flannel or the warmth of a late October sun.

The billiard room vanished and in its place was the harbor breeze, the lights swaying above, and the yacht's rhythmic roll beneath her. The bulbs softened the edges of Jack's face, but they couldn't reach the emptiness in his eyes.

"This is the last place I expected to see you," he said, voice low, like the words had surprised even him.

Dorothy managed a breath of a smile. "Yeah, same. My friend Noah kind of dragged me along."

Up on the upper deck, the crash of shattering glass cut through the music. Jack didn't flinch, but his gaze drifted in its direction, then back to her.

She stepped forward. "Jack…I'm sorry. About Elliot—"

"Don't." His voice cracked more than he probably meant it to. "Don't do that. Please."

"I just need you to know—"

"We were drunk," he said, cutting her off. "And high. And Elliot… he always thought he was invincible."

His eyes met hers, then dropped. "It wasn't your fault. I know that. But I still wake up thinking he's going to be at our table in the dining hall. And when I see you…"

She nodded, even though it stung.

"I don't regret meeting you." He exhaled, shaking his head. "But that night was a mess. And I never should've let you get in that car. It was just a kiss, but everything after—"

Her voice softened. "When you say it like that, it almost sounds like I mattered."

"You did," he said. "That's the problem."

He glanced at the crowd, backlit in gold and movement. "Right now, I don't think we're good for each other."

Dorothy swallowed the lump rising in her throat. "Then I guess this is goodbye."

He hesitated, then nodded. "I'm so sorry, Dorothy."

She turned away before the tears could spill. Her pulse pounded as she shoved through the blur of glittering dresses and strobing light, past bodies swaying and cackling as though she weren't about to break down. The yacht's engine rumbled to life, a low and final sound. Wind slapped her face as she stumbled toward the stern, the chill catching the tears carving tracks down her cheeks. Her hand closed around the gangway door handle.

Locked.

"Wait. No."

Beyond the glass, the dock had begun to drift. Noah stood there, framed in the distance, frustration etched across his face as a security guard gestured him back.

"Noah!" She slammed her palm against the plexiglass. "Noah, don't leave me!"

Their eyes met across the widening gap. He mouthed words she couldn't hear. An apology, maybe.

"Please wait!" she cried, voice cracking.

But he was already receding, growing smaller by the second, swallowed by the dark. She pressed her forehead to the glass and squeezed her eyes shut. Behind her, conversations swelled at an all-time high, and glasses clinked. The party continued as if she didn't exist. Because she really didn't. Not here.

CHAPTER 38
Dorothy Hale

She drank until she liked herself.

The bartender served her without question, refilling her glass with a smirk, as though she'd crossed some forbidden threshold into adulthood. Each sip of whiskey helped subdue her emotions and chase the heartbreak away. Back home, alcohol had always been a line she never dared cross. Not because she feared the consequences, but because she feared who she might become because of it.

By the third glass, the night felt a little less harsh. The music blurred, and the sting of her conversation with Jack dulled to a faint ache. Even the image of Noah on the dock began to dissolve, tucked away like a page she didn't want to reread. At first the questions came from eyes—curious, narrowed, knowing. They flitted toward her like locusts, impossible to pin down and harder to ignore. Why was she here? Who had she come with? Had anyone invited her?

But then they started to approach her. One by one, like she was some story they weren't finished telling.

A girl with glossy hair leaned in, voice syrupy with fake concern. "You're the one from the crash right? With the boy who died?"

Another chimed in before she could answer. "Was it true you weren't wearing a seatbelt? My cousin heard you were thrown from the car."

"Did your life flash before your eyes?"

A boy leaned against the railing, curious in the careless, privileged way. "Is it true Jack and Elliot roofied you?"

Dorothy's knuckles whitened around her glass. Condensation slid down the sides, numbing her fingers, a mercy against the heat of so many stares. She was cornered, but she denied the drug rumors. The truth was simpler. Jack had offered her weed after they left Albatross House. She'd taken a few hits, laughed, felt light. And her life hadn't flashed before her eyes. There was no montage. No slow-motion farewell. Just Jack in the back seat, screaming before death swooped in for her and Elliot.

She tightened her grip on the glass. She didn't want their pity or their hunger for details. Her father would tell her that she needed to refuse becoming the story whispered between classes, the headline in someone else's cautionary tale. This week's tragedy, eclipsed by next week's scandal. She just wanted to feel normal and safe. Anything but the dread that had stalked her since the night she came back to life.

"I appreciate the concern," she said, forcing a smile. "But I'm okay. Really."

Except she wasn't. She knew what okay felt like once. And it wasn't this.

An hour later, she met Rowan, the birthday boy. He was propped against the bar, blond hair tousled, spinning some story for a half-listening crowd. He looked like someone from another life—sun-kissed, self-assured, untouched by darkness. When his gaze met hers, his smile softened. Less performative, more real. He didn't ask about the crash or mention Jack or Elliot. He pulled her into conversations about boats and Seattle—anywhere but the wreckage. And for a while, she let herself to forget. She laughed at his jokes and listened as he spoke of cities she'd never seen and places she couldn't point to on a map.

He led her into the galley, its counters gleaming, every appliance shining like something expensive and meant to impress. He grinned as he opened a refrigerator that looked more like a vault.

"You've saying you've never been on a yacht before tonight?" he asked, pulling out a beer.

Dorothy brushed her fingers along the stainless-steel fridge. "Wow. I can see myself," she murmured, awe brushing against the pleasant haze of alcohol.

"You're funny, you know that?"

She giggled more than she meant to. "And you smell *rich*."

"Thanks?" He laughed. "It's Italian cologne, I think. My grandmother bought it for me."

"Fancy." She swayed closer, fingertips grazing his shirt. She gasped. "Is this what real silk feels like?"

But the mood slipped away, replaced by an unsettling awareness. Her heart ticked faster as it traveled into her ears. A melody drifted through the room, light at first, almost imagined.

Sweet and mournful.

"Do you hear that?" she asked.

Rowan tilted his head. "Hear what?"

The melody wove deeper into her.

"You really don't hear it?"

Rowan's brows tightened. "Do you mean the music from upstairs?"

The glass slipped from her hand and shattered. His voice became a muffled echo as she turned toward the deck doors. A breeze swept through the galley, carrying the melody with it. It sounded like grief trapped in the ocean's throat. Everything else—voices, lights, Rowan calling her back—blanched into white noise.

She moved through the crowd like a sleepwalker, their faces warping at the edge of her periphery. Somewhere, she spotted Jack and the worry tightening his brow, but he felt irrelevant.

Her body moved without her. Until the railing met her waist.

Below, the ocean shimmered. It sang louder, pulling, promising.

It asked nothing, but offered everything. She climbed the railing, toes on the edge, wind rushing past her face. The sea was calling for her. It promised her peace. An ending to the strangeness. A return to normalcy.

"Dorothy!"

Arms seized her, yanking her from the edge. Her body collided with a chest, or at least she thought it was, while a voice cracked in her ear.

"What the hell are you doing?" Jack asked.

The world came rushing back. She turned, dizzy, and looked up at him. His honeyed brown eyes were wide with fear, as if he'd almost lost her.

"I—I don't know," she whispered. "One minute I was in the kitchen. With Rowan. And now I'm here."

His grip loosened, but he didn't let go. She stared at him as her knees shook. She'd nearly jumped. Not because she wanted to. But because the song demanded it.

CHAPTER 39
Declan Albatross

The Drowned Pearl perched at the edge of Galleon's Wharf, its weathered beams resilient against the harbor wind. It blended into Driftmoor's stubborn charm with its slate-gray roof and swaying lanterns. Declan brushed his peacoat's lapel as he stepped through the doors. The ceiling arched in undulating navy bands designed to mimic the ocean's current. Fixtures cast shifting light across the floor to create the illusion of being submerged. Along the far wall, dark reflective glass shimmered like an abyss, interrupted by pulses from bioluminescent orbs drifting beneath the surface. His coat pressed against him in a way that made him acutely aware of his body. Somewhere near the bar, a pianist played, the notes mingling with conversation and the waves sloshing against the pier.

He wasn't supposed to be here. The thought repeated. And yet his boots tapped forward, past tables and curved velvet booths. Deep emerald and indigo cushions disappeared into shadows, each nook designed for privacy, for confession. The bar gleamed ahead, a black marble slab streaked with gold, like tide lines drawn by moonlight. He should've been on his way to Lola's for a simple dinner with someone who could put back the broken pieces of him without pressing them deeper. But Ophelia had called, and despite every warning, ever scar she left behind, he came.

She sat in a booth nestled against the reflective wall, her black hair falling over one shoulder. Her eyes—those impossible oceanic blues—swept the restaurant. One finger traced the glass in slow, absent circle. He hesitated before slipping into the seat across from her. Neither of them spoke. Her hair was shorter, curled at the ends, and the candlelight played beneath her in a way that almost convinced him none of it had happened. That they hadn't ruined each other. That this was another night where they still loved each other.

"You're quiet," she said, not looking at him.

Declan grabbed his drink. "And whose fault is that?" Guilt flickered across her face. "I deserved that."

"You think?" He drank the sparkling water, hoping it might keep his voice from splintering.

She pulled an envelope from her coat and slid it across the table. The paper was creased by too many second thoughts. He didn't need to open it to know what it held. The money. What remained. Proof that betrayal hadn't just happened, it had been counted.

He pushed it back. "I don't want it."

"Declan—"

"That's not how this works." His jaw clenched. "You don't get to leave town, hand me some guilt-stained apology cash, and pretend that fixes everything."

Her eyes didn't waver. "You think that's why I asked you here?"

"I don't know why you asked me."

Behind them, the piano whispered a melody while glasses clinked like wind chimes.

"Why did you even take it?" he asked. "You know I would've helped you. If you needed anything, I would've given it to you."

Her fingers curled around her glass. "It wasn't about money. It was about making it easier. For both of us."

"How the hell does stealing my savings make anything easier?"

"Because I knew how long you'd been saving for that boat. Because for once, you wanted to choose yourself." She took a deep breath. "So I ruined it and gave you a reason to hate me. Because I knew hate would be easier to carry than heartbreak."

He stared at her. "That's the dumbest thing I've ever heard. You thought I'd hate you over a few thousand dollars? What part of I'm infatuated with you did you never understand?"

She shook her head, softly. "Infatuation isn't love. It's your heart sprinting ahead of reason." She gave a sad smile. "For God's sake, we were fourteen."

"And I still haven't figured out how to forget you."

A couple at a table nearby glanced over, but neither of them noticed. The restaurant had vanished. It was the two of them again, in a different wreck.

"I thought you wanted to talk," Declan said.

"I do. Just…not about the past. Not like this."

His gaze hardened. "So that's it?"

She sighed before asking, "How's Doris?"

He blinked. "Seriously?"

"What?" Her tone stayed even. "It's a genuine question. I know the divorce was hard on her. My mother mentioned it."

He started to rise, shoulders coiled. But before he could stand, she reached across the table, fingers brushing his hand. The contact was light, but the memory was powerful.

"You want to know why I left?" she said.

Her hand rested there. But it was enough to make him stay.

"I couldn't breathe," she said. "You. Lola. Heather. Driftmoor. I loved it all. God, I loved you. But it felt like I was staring down the rest of my life and seeing one version of me mapped out, before I had the chance to choose."

The world beyond the window shimmered, warped by candlelight and dark glass. Her reflection beside his looked like it someone he used to know.

"So that's it?" he said. "You felt boxed in, so you vanish?"

"I had to leave," she said, more to herself than to him. "I don't expect you to understand."

He lowered his eyes, thumb tracing condensation down the glass. "You could've called."

She reached into her bag, pulled out a braided twine bracelet with seashells knotted in like promises. The kind of thing you make barefoot on the shore, when your skin smells like salt and sunscreen and you still believe the summer will never end.

"I made this," she said. "For good luck."

"You don't believe in luck."

"You're right. I don't." Her smile was faint. "But you always did. So…"

She set it down beside the envelope. Two things neither of them wanted to touch.

"I know I can't fix what I broke," she said. "I'm not here to ask for anything. I just needed to see you. To know you were still…you."

He didn't answer. Couldn't. Because he wasn't sure he was—not since she left. He'd waited for her longer than he should've.

She stood. But before walking, she looked back one last time. Then she was gone through doors like a ghost retreating to sea.

The bracelet and the envelope sat between his hands. Pieces of a goodbye she'd started long before tonight. He ran his fingers over the twine and the little sun-bleached shells. It was just like her to leave a token that clung to memory, one that made forgetting feel like betrayal.

Ophelia had never belonged to Driftmoor. Not to him. Maybe not even to herself.

CHAPTER 40
Lola Godfrey

THE TOWN CAR HUMMED. LEATHER COOLED HER PALMS, BUT A SLOW heat had gathered just beneath her collarbone. Outside, streetlights dragged past in amber smears, washing the tinted window in streaks of gold and dusk. Her fingernails tapped an even rhythm against the armrest. One thing about friendships: you shouldn't expect everything from them. She wasn't angry. What had unset-tled her was the silence. The absence of even a lie to fill the void.

"Xavier," she said, eyes fixed ahead. "Take Osprey Road."

He nodded. No questions. That's what she liked about him.

Driftmoor's storefronts leaned into the fog, windows aglow with the last bits of evening commerce. Lanterns swung from wrought-iron hooks. Galleon's Wharf flickered into view, cobblestones slick from the tide. On the sidewalks: couples lingering after dinner, men smok-ing beneath awnings, the occasional tourist tracing spirits through the mist.

And then she spotted her. Ophelia. Alone. Hollow-eyed beneath a charcoal coat, walking away from The Drowned Pearl. Lola lowered the window, the glass sighing as it slipped down.

"Running away again?" she called.

No reaction.

She leaned out farther, the breeze tugging loose strands of her hair. "Go ahead. It's what you do best."

Ophelia didn't turn. But her posture shifted, chin lifting, back straightening. A final refusal to give in to the taunting. The restaurant door opened behind her, and Declan stepped out. When his gaze flicked from Ophelia to Lola, it didn't surprise her. She'd already known where she'd find him. It was only a matter of time.

She didn't raise her voice. Just said, "Get in."

He had one foot toward the curb. One facing her. But he moved. Slipped into the seat beside her and shut the door.

Lola rolled the window up. "Albatross House, Xavier."

The car eased back into motion, gliding along the harbor road. Declan's jaw clenched as he stared ahead, like he could outrun the moment if he just looked far enough.

"What did she want?" Lola asked.

His hands flexed, fingers tightening against his knee.

"You were supposed to be at my house for dinner. Remember that?"

He turned to her. "Why are you here, Lola?"

Heat crept up her neck. She had no answer he wouldn't see through.

"That's what I thought," he muttered.

She pursed her lips, swallowing the humiliation. She could let it go. Should. But Ophelia's tear-streaked face lingered.

"You haven't answered my question," she said. "What did she say to you?"

Her thought spiraled to Silver Shoals, to that terrible fall, to the moment Ophelia looked down at her like she was already dead. If Declan knew, if Ophelia had told him, wouldn't he say something? Or would he just sit there and let her in drown in it?

She crossed her legs and smoothed her skirt. Her voice came softer than she intended. "She was crying."

He didn't look at her. But his posture faltered.

"She still has power over you," Lola said. "That's the part that ruins you, isn't it? That she could hurt you and still leave you hoping she won't do it again."

He looked at her then, sharply. "You don't know anything."

She smiled. Not smug. Just tired. "You forget. She was my best friend first. I know what it feels like to wait for someone who's already gone."

The car filled with silence. The kind that wasn't awkward, but final.

She glanced at his hands as they fidgeted. "I had Miriam make your favorite. You said you'd be there."

The car curved past the cliffs, the sea below black as ink.

Lola looked out at the dark horizon. A pressure built in her ribs. Not the anger she expected, not even jealousy. Just the ache of having too much tenderness and nowhere to put it.

She turned back to him one last time. "I wanted a night where you chose me. Just once."

He didn't speak. And maybe that was her answer.

CHAPTER 41
Dorothy Hale

The fog blurred the partygoers ahead into silhouettes as they stepped into taxis and sleek cars. None of them looked at Dorothy. Not even Rowan, who pretended as if they hadn't had a thirty-minute conversation about their lives. Even Jack had slipped away, despite being the one who pulled her back from the railing. There was no sign of Noah, and the trolley had stopped for the night. She hadn't brought any of the cash she'd earn from the tea party. That left her with no choice but to walk to campus, though she wasn't sure how far that was or which way to begin.

Her footsteps echoed through the narrow lanes as she passed shuttered taverns and boarded-up bait shops on Galleon's Wharf. The mist seemed to move with her, rising in swirls beneath the lamplight. Her shoes slipped on the slick cobblestones, and she quickened her pace, the silence gnawing at her paranoia.

A blur darted from the shadows.

She stumbled back as a black cat streaked across her path, vanishing into the fog with a hiss and yellow eyes. Her hand flew to her chest. *Just a cat*, she told herself. Only a cat.

She hadn't made it more than a few steps when footsteps echoed behind her.

When she stopped, so did they.

A lantern hanging from a rusted hook groaned as it swung. Every sound seemed amplified. From the creaking moored boats to the toll of a buoy. Her eyes strained through her surroundings. Nothing. Just the pier's outline and boats swaddled in mist.

"Well, well, if it ain't the fairy girl."

The voice curled around her like cold iron.

Dorothy spun. Three men were walking toward her. They were broad-shouldered and wore raincoats slick with seawater. Their faces stayed half hidden beneath the brims of their hats, but she recognized them. The fishermen from her first visit to the Wharf. The ones who wouldn't stop looking at her and who'd called her names. Like fairy girl.

The leader stepped forward, coat flaring open. His beard was grizzled, his eyes like tarnished steel—eyes that no longer expected the word to be kind. His mouth pulled into a crooked yellow smile.

Dorothy's pulse quickened. "Please stop calling me that."

"Why?" he sneered. "Ashamed of what ya are? Or scared of what'll happen if the ocean gets its hand on ya?"

Her hands tensed at her side. "I—I don't know what you're talking about. I'm just trying to get back to my dorm."

They kept advancing. A gust rattled the dock sign to her left.

"Oh, but I think ya do." His boots echoed, eyes never leaving hers.

Dorothy stepped back. The pier's edge was behind her now.

"Why're ya here, huh?" he asked. "In Driftmoor. These waters. Who sent ya?"

"No one—no one sent me. I go to school here. That's all."

The grin dropped from his face. Wind tore through the alley, whistling between hulls and masts.

"Ya don't belong," he said. "The ocean don't like yer kind."

A rough hand seized her arm. She tried pulling away, but another hand clamped her free arm. Panic surged. Her shoes skidded across the boards as they dragged her toward the pier's edge.

"Stop, please!"

In a flash, the leader revealed a fishhook, its tip catching a lantern's light.

"Why are you doing this?" Dorothy cried. "I'm not this fairy girl you think I am. I'm just a seventeen-year-old girl who goes to school here."

"Let's see if the ocean claims ya," he said, and slashed her palm. "We'll let it decide."

Pain split through her hand as blood swelled. He yanked her wrist over the edge and held it there as blood dripped into the dark water below.

"If yer as normal as ya claim," he murmured, "ya got nothin' to fear."

"But I don't know what you're talking about. Please—"

With a nod, the others shoved her. For a heartbeat, she hovered—suspended between air and sea—as the world tipped sideways. The cold struck her like a thousand cuts. Her breath locked in her throat. Limbs seized. Her dress tangled around her legs, dragging her down as the surface receded above her.

Terror bloomed bright and hot, snapping her back into herself. She kicked through the dark, fighting the fabric and temperatures that turned her limbs to stone.

She gasped through the surface, coughing salt and bile as her arms clambered for balance. Her eyes stung and her muscles screamed while laughter spilled from above. She didn't see them through the fog, but she heard them loud and clear.

"Good luck, fairy girl!" one called. "Guess yer normal, after all."

She opened her mouth, ready to curse them, to scream, to beg, but a ripple in the water stopped her. She froze. The harbor stretched like darkened glass. Mesmerizing. But beneath the surface, a fish brushed her leg.

Once.

Then twice.

And before she could react, it yanked her under.

Water crushed her lungs as she fought against it. She couldn't see, but claws pressed in her shoulder as it dragged her down. Part of her wanted to give up. She had cheated death once already and maybe this was God coming back to finish the job. Or the universe. Or whatever.

But power flared within her. It cracked open behind her ribs and tore out in a scream too massive for her body to contain. A shockwave erupted from her and hurled the creature into the abyss. She hung there, suspended in the dark, lungs starved of air. With what little strength she had, she kicked upward. Stroke after stroke, she clawed her way up until she broke the surface, choking on light and oxygen.

The ladder loomed nearby, barely above the waterline. She reached for the rungs, fingers slipping before finally catching. She let out a strained groan as she hauled herself out the harbor, water sheeting from her body, limbs trembling. The climb felt like it would never end, and she kept turning back, thinking the creature would jump out and pull her back under.

At last, she collapsed onto the pier, wood scraping her cheek as she tried to catch her breath at the same time a buoy tolled in the distance. Dazed and confused, she blinked at the fog and salt and stars.

She rolled onto her side.

Eyes. Vacant and unblinking. Staring into hers.

A strangled cry tore from her throat. She scrambled back, heels scraping, and collided with a solid surface. Slowly, she turned around. Another body. A fisherman. His head bent at an angle, blood leaking from his ears in ribbons. Vomit singed her esophagus as she fell forward, choking on sobs that wouldn't stop.

She barely heard the wet, rasping sound approaching through her coughing and gagging.

She raised her head up. It was the leader. He was crawling toward her, blood streaking his raincoat, one eye bloodshot and bulging as his mouth trembled. "I—I didn't mean—" he gasped, hand reaching. "P-Please…have mercy. I beg ya."

Gone was the menace. The sneers. He was on his knees. Pleading. Dying. They'd called her a fairy woman. And while she didn't know what it meant, she knew one thing. They'd could've drowned her. Treated her like she was less than human. They spoke of her as if she were a curse. If she was a curse, then they had summoned her.

She stared at the trail of bodies behind her, their blood soaking into the wood. She didn't feel sorry. Only a rising, mystifying quiet inside her. Like a broken part of her had settled into place. They'd deserved it. And the worst part? She believed it. The horror wasn't what she'd done, but how easy it had been. Their eyes might haunt her forever. But tonight, they were the ones who screamed.

Colonial homes stretched ahead, as Dorothy trudged along the sidewalk. Her wet hair clung to her cheeks in tangled strands. Salt covered her tongue while her dress dragged against her legs. Jack-o'-lanterns grinned from porches. Cobwebs sagged from railings, and skeletons leered from windows. October pressed close, thick with the scent of autumn, but all she could smell was brine and blood.

Tonight was the first time she'd seen a dead body—unless Elliot counted. And still, she felt calm. Not because they deserved it. Not even because she survived. But because death felt like it had always been waiting to meet her.

By morning, the shops along Galleon's Wharf would open. Windows scrubbed clean, doors propped to catch the sea breeze. And somewhere between the florists and fishmongers, an innocent soul would stumble onto three locals sprawled beneath a lantern with blood seeping from their ears. Would it be tracked back to her?

Behind her, headlights sliced through the mist. Tires hissed as a car slowed to a stop.

She squinted as the beam blurred. In the rear seat, Lola Godfrey leaned forward. From the opposite door, Declan Albatross stepped out, his gaze sweeping her drenched dress and the blood crusted along her palm. Without a word, he slipped off his coat and draped it over her shoulders.

"What happened to you?" he asked. "Are you okay?"

She clutched his coat close, grateful for its warmth. "I'd rather not talk about it. It's a long story, but I'm okay now. I think."

"Do you need me to call someone? Campus security? Or maybe—"

"No!"

Declan flinched. From inside the car, Lola observed as if calculating every second.

Dorothy softened her voice. "I just want a shower. And sleep."

Declan glanced at Lola, who folded her arms, gazed fixed ahead.

"Alright. You shouldn't be out here alone. We'll take you back," he said.

Lola eased over as Dorothy slid in, her dress clinging to warm leather. Lola's perfume lingered—rich and floral, the same as she'd been wearing when the hellhound had chased them. Declan slid in and pulled the door shut. The car eased forward, gliding into the mist-veiled street.

Lola clicked her tongue. "Well, isn't this grim." She leaned toward Dorothy, curiosity brightening her eyes. "You're dripping all over the upholstery, by the way. And you reek like a fish market."

Dorothy's fingers tightened on the coat's hem.

"Not an insult," Lola continued, inspecting her nails. "Merely an observation. And before you get defensive, I'm providing transportation, so technically, this makes me charitable."

"Lola," Declan warned.

She raised an eyebrow. "I'm acknowledging the situation." Her gaze shifted back to Dorothy. "So, are you going to tell us what happened, or do we need to guess?"

Dorothy's breath shook more than she wanted. "I fell into the water. And…I think something pulled me under."

Declan angled himself toward her. "Pulled you under?"

"What does that even mean?" Lola asked. "Did you trip over a dock rope? Had too much vodka?"

"No. None of that," Dorothy said. "I don't know what it was. But it couldn't be human."

Lola scoffed.

Dorothy turned to her. "You don't believe me? After everything we saw in the maze?"

"You mean the Oldwyck's maze?" Declan asked. "What happened there?"

"Nothing happened," Lola said. "Right, Dorothy?" Dorothy's mouth parted, but the words crumbled. Her fingers curled into the coat and pulled it closer. The fear was fresh. But it didn't matter whether they believed her. She knew what had happened.

The car stopped in front of Winthrop Hall, its brick draped in ivy, its arched windows glinting. At night, the façade looked older, watchful, as if it had been waiting for Dorothy to come home. Lola's chauffeur, Xavier, reached for the door, but Declan stepped out first. He offered Dorothy his hand. She took it, hesitantly, sliding out and pulling his coat tighter around her. She was relieved that nothing had happened like the last time she shook his hand.

"Want me to walk you in?" he asked.

"I think I'll be fine, but thanks."

His green eyes lingered with unspoken words.

From the backseat, Lola sighed. "Alright, this is getting too emotional." She leaned forward, chin in palm. "New girl, you're fine. Get some rest. And for God's sake, dry your hair before bed or you'll catch pneumonia."

Dorothy raised a brow. "Thanks. I guess?"

Lola waved a hand. "You're welcome."

Declan stepped closer. "Look, I believe you," he said. "Whatever you think you saw tonight in the harbor, I believe you."

Warmth flared under her skin. "You do?"

"I can't explain it yet. But you're not imagining it." He glanced toward the car. "Take care, Dorothy. And stay away from the ocean. We'll talk again."

He slipped back into the car. Lola turned toward the window, face unreadable as the taillights vanished into the fog. Winthrop Hall loomed like it knew more than it let on. She pushed through the doors. Warm air closed around her, but it didn't shake the cold.

In her dorm, she peeled off Declan's coat and draped it over the desk chair. Lamplight pooled across the hardwood floor. She caught her reflection mid-step. Her hair clung to her skin in damp strands, eyes rimmed red. But it wasn't her face that held her. She pulled the dress strap back. Red marks clawed across her shoulders. When she brushed them, pain lanced sharp and immediate. She staggered, a wave rising in her chest before she bolted.

She barely reached the end of the hall. The bathroom door creaked as she shoved it open, stumbling to the nearest sink. Her knees hit cold tile as vomit scorched her throat again, retching until she was left gasping for air.

A stall door groaned open.

"Dorothy?" Amani, her old roommate. "Are you okay?"

Dorothy wiped her mouth. "I'm fine."

A pause. Then Amani left, the door closing behind her.

Dorothy gripped the sink and stared at her reflection.

She wasn't a stranger in Driftmoor anymore.

She was prey.

CHAPTER 42
Dorothy Hale

She woke to rain.

Torrents slammed the earth, drenching her before she could rise. Dorothy's eyes opened, lashes clumped with water. Mud sucked at her fingers as she pushed herself upright. Around her, headstones jutted from the ground while crypts slouched into the soil, half-swallowed. Time had eaten the names once etched in reverence. Angels with chipped wings stood watch, their glassy eyes catching lightning.

Cracked brick columns loomed ahead. Ivy twisted through them, binding what little remained. Steps led nowhere. Broken stone and a path cleaved in two. At the top stood a single archway, its keystone bearing a moss-eaten crest.

Her pulse pounded, syncing with the storm that split the sky. She couldn't remember leaving her dorm. But here she was, barefoot, her nightgown clinging, her feet bleeding at the edges. She searched through her thoughts for a reason, a memory, but all she found was a block of missing time.

Rain stung the scratches on her shoulders. But the pain was minimal compared to what slithered beneath her. What she'd taken for mud shifted—slick and alive. A cold, fleshy shape grazed her ankles and slid between her toes.

She looked down.

Worms.

Dozens. Maybe hundreds. Glinting and writhing in the storm light, a slow, relentless mass coiling over itself. They pushed against her skin, sliding between her toes. A strangled sound slipped from her throat. She stumbled back, shaking her legs, clawing at her calves. Her fingers scraped skin. The ground vanished, and she hit a tombstone, pain cracking up her spine.

Rain filled her mouth, her nose, her eyes. She gasped, crawling back up, as her hands grabbed on a headstone for support. Through the blur, letters bloomed beneath her hands.

MAREK.

The name meant nothing and yet she recoiled. As if her body remembered what her mind didn't.

Through the rain, the groundskeeper emerged. He stood crooked in the downpour, holding a dim lantern. Water streamed from his hat, his windbreaker sagging with the storm.

"What are you doing out here, miss?" His voice barely cut through the thunder.

Dorothy opened her mouth, but before she could speak, the scream rose from her. It ripped free like it had been waiting for this man. His lantern exploded, flame and glass scattering in a burst. He dropped the handle and clutched his ears, as blood poured from his ears, thick and unstoppable.

He dropped with a muddy splash. His body twitched. Then went still. Dorothy sank to her knees. The storm howled, wind and rain battering her skin like punishment. The cemetery tilted, blurred, and vanished altogether.

Flashlights jittered through the dark, their beams slicing over tombstones and catching her face in stuttering burst. Fingers moved through the light, boots sinking into wet grass, radios crackling with clipped commands. Hands seized her arms—firm, slick with rain.

"Juvenile located at Driftmoor Cemetery," a man said to his walkie-talkie. "No visible injuries. Returning to station."

An officer loomed into view, rain streaming off his hat as his eyes searched hers. Cold threaded through her as he lifted her. Red and blue strobes ricocheted off the headstones, painting the graveyard in dizzying lights. She opened her mouth to speak but no sound came.

◄

Buzzing fluorescent lights bleached the interrogation room.

Dorothy sat on a metal chair, squinting up at them. The oversized sweatshirt they'd given her sagged against her frame, steeped in the scent of industrial laundry. The blanket around her shoulders did little to block the chill that came from the cinderblock walls. She stared at the faint scratches etched into tabletop, grounding herself in their randomness, trying to keep herself from slipping back to the cemetery.

Across from her, two officers sat, unmoving. The man studied her with patience that edged toward expectation. The woman, Officer Cortes, scribbled on a notepad, her eyes flicking up between strokes.

"Just to confirm, you weren't under the influence? Drugs? Alcohol?" Cortes's tone was flat but edged with courtesy.

Dorothy shook her head.

Their questions struck one after the next. How did she get to the cemetery? Had she taken anything? Who else had been there? Her voice broke apart, each answer thinner than the last. But her thoughts looped back to the groundskeeper and the way his limbs spasmed before crumpling. The image flickered like a nightmare. And still, the mud on her feet and packed beneath her nails said otherwise.

"Dorothy?" Officer Cortes's attention dropped to the gauze wrapped around her palm. "What happened to your hand?"

"Papercut," she mumbled. The lie landed flat. But it was easier than trying to explain the claw marks that stung beneath the borrowed sweater.

Cortes set her pen down. "Look, I promise we're not here to scare you. We just need the facts. A minor waking up in a cemetery in the middle of the night with no idea how she got there—we have to take that seriously."

She glanced at her partner, whose jaw had hardened.

"That being said." Cortes leaned back. "We're going to hold off. It's best we wait for Colonel Godfrey."

The name took a moment to register.

The officers stood, chairs scraping against the floor. They left without another word. She had barely begun to collect herself when the door opened again and a man stepped in, uniform crisp, posture straight. He was younger than she expected and handsome. He looked like Lola, but at the same time, he didn't.

"Hello, Dorothy." He pulled out the chair and sat across from her. His badge glinted under the overhead glare. "I'm Colonel Godfrey. But Faustino's fine, if that's easier."

Dorothy shifted under his hazel gaze. "Hi."

"How are you feeling?"

She adjusted the blanket, her fingers clenching its seam. "Tired. Confused."

"I get that. It's been a rough night." He flipped open a notepad and clicked his pen. "You're a senior at Driftmoor Academy, right?" A pause. "Bit unusual to transfer in your last year."

She hadn't thought of it that way. "I couldn't turn down the scholarship."

"Fair enough. Didn't mean anything by it." He jotted a note, then added, "My sister goes to Driftmoor. Lola Godfrey. Maybe you know her. I'd be surprised if you didn't."

He laughed, but Dorothy's gaze lingered on him, searching for traces of Lola in his expression. Maybe he knew more than he let on.

Or maybe he was just a man watching from the shore of something too deep to see.

"We're just trying to understand how you ended up at the cemetery," Faustino said. "Have you ever sleepwalked before?"

"No." The word came too fast. She thought of St. Augustine, how security had found her alone in the chapel.

He let the silence stretch to the point it made her squirm in her seat.

"Any reason you were near the Marek property?" he asked.

"I don't know who that is." Her voice faltered. "I didn't even know anyone lived out there."

"They don't. Haven't in decades. The land's abandoned, but we try to keep kids away. With the state it's in, it's not exactly safe for wandering."

He watched her close, pen hovering above the page.

"I know tonight's been difficult," he said. "But I have to ask. When we found you, the groundskeeper, Mr. Tenebris, was nearby. Unresponsive. Did anything happen between you two? A disagreement, maybe? Anything physical?"

Blood spilling from the man's ears flashed behind her eyes. Nausea rose again, but she swallowed it.

"No," she said. "I didn't see anyone."

Faustino marked a note on his pad.

"Did this man...has he said anything?" she asked.

The pen stilled. "Unfortunately, he passed on the way to St. Augustine's. Some kind of brain aneurism."

The blanket bunched in her fists. She'd tried to deny it, but the truth had caught up. Four people were dead because of her. And at least one hadn't deserved it.

A few moments later, Officer Cortes returned with a phone in hand.

"We got in touch with the parents," she said.

No.

Faustino took the phone and handed it to Dorothy.

"I'll give you some privacy," he said. "I'll be out in the hall if you need anything."

Once the door shut, she slowly lifted the receiver.

"Dorothy?" her mother said, breath catching. "Oh, my goodness. Are you okay?"

"I think so." Dorothy's voice felt small. "I don't really know."

Her father cut in, the edge unmistakable. "Are you drinking again?"

The accusation hit like a slap amid everything.

"What? No—I wasn't drinking." Though that wasn't true. She'd been tipsy on the yacht, but that felt like another lifetime.

"We're just trying make sense of this," her mother said. "First the accident, and now this? Barefoot? In a cemetery?"

Tears welled, but she blinked them back. She didn't need a reminder. Sympathy might have opened her up. Courage might have convinced her to tell them more. But nothing stirred. No truth surfaced. And help, however close it may have seemed to be out of reach.

Her father's voice tightened. "We didn't send you there to spiral. Do you understand how serious this is?"

She pressed the phone tighter. *I understand. But you wouldn't. I didn't choose this.*

"I promise it isn't what you think."

"Then help us understand," her mother said. "Do you miss home? Maybe you should come back for a weekend. We'll figure out the flight."

A spider descended from the ceiling, legs twitching as it spun into view. She could go. She could disappear into old routines and soft lights and the illusion of safety. But would it matter? Or would this darkness still find her?

"Dorothy?"

Her gaze stayed locked on the spider as it crept along its web—suspended, delicate, and calm.

"Hello? Are you there?"

Her mother's voice belonged to another life. One of casseroles, curfews, and a girl who hadn't yet been remade by death. What could she possibly say? That she'd nearly drowned? That she'd screamed people to death? That there was a darkness inside her awakening, and she wasn't sure she feared it or welcomed it?

Her grip tightened. Then she hung up. The dial tone hummed, similar to the emptiness inside her.

The door opened again a few minutes later. Faustino returned, his footsteps measured.

"We've been in contact with Headmistress Mortimer," he said. "She'll be waiting to help you get settled."

As if normalcy were an option.

"I'm sorry you went through this," he said. His eyes flicked toward the phone before returning to her. "If it were my sister, I don't know how I'd react. Doesn't make it easier, I know. But maybe cut them a little slack."

Dorothy's fingers curled around the blanket. "I've met her," she said. "Earlier, you asked if I might've known her. I've met her. She's... pretty special."

She hadn't meant to say them aloud, but once the words left her, she eased on the inside. As if admitting it gave shape to the strange, magnetic presence Lola Godfrey carried. Sharp edges and all.

Faustino's smile was soft, but proud. "Yeah. She's something, isn't she."

He gave her a moment before adding, "Whenever you're ready, there's a car waiting to take you back."

Officer Cortes appeared at the doorway. She smiled, warm but restrained, and stepped aside. Dorothy stood on unsteady legs, afraid the world might tilt open if she moved too quickly. Their footsteps echoed down the hall. She didn't look back, but she felt Faustino watching, his gaze full of questions he hadn't voiced.

Wind whipped through the front of the police station, tugging at the corners of the blanket draped around her shoulders. She clutched pulled it tighter, not for warmth, but to hold herself together. The fabric felt like it could split in her hands if she breathed too hard. As if she were stitched together by nothing more than will, and the seams were starting to fray.

CHAPTER 43
Declan Albatross

DECLAN STEPPED INSIDE THE ATRIUM BESIDE AIDEN, THE JOURNAL pressed tight beneath his arm. Morning light poured through the dome, sharpening every edge. Across the hall, Ophelia stood at the center of a cluster of girls. She laughed a moment late, smiled when she was supposed to. She looked like she belonged there. But her eyes kept drifting toward the exits. He hadn't told Aiden about seeing her at The Drowned Pearl. Aiden had always been wary of her. Never a fan, never an enemy. The only thing the two of them had in common was Declan. And when she left, Aiden had almost seemed relieved. Declan never questioned it. He of all people understood how tangled things got between friends who'd known each other since kindergarten.

They stopped at their lockers. Elliot Putnam's was next to Aiden's. Declan didn't look at it anymore. It was empty now. Someone had cleared out the photographs and notes over the weekend. As if grief had an expiration date.

"I think Professor Chau hates me," Aiden muttered, yanking open his locker. "I studied for hours for that test. Actually studied. Still for-got how to do derivatives halfway through."

"I'm sure you passed." Declan didn't bother to lift his gaze from the journal in his hands.

"You don't know that."

Declan stared at an illustration of a figure half-submerged in water, mouth parted mid-song, hair fanning like kelp. The author had left the face unfinished. He thought about the journal falling in Vesper Lake and the thing tugging as he fought to get it back. And now Dorothy had said she had a similar experience. He hadn't wanted to believe her, but if she was telling the truth, it meant he wasn't losing his mind. Unless they were both were. Still, deep down, he knew what he saw in the lake hadn't been a hallucination. It was a siren.

Aiden nudged his locker. "Are you even listening, or communing with your creepy diary again?"

Declan didn't look up. "Of course I'm listening," he said. "I'm the only one who ever listens to you."

"Well, it doesn't seem like it," Aiden said. "I'm telling you, that journal is cursed. I'm convinced its demonic."

Declan laughed bitterly. "What would you know? You can't even pass first semester math."

The words landed sharper than he meant. Aiden's shoulder stiffened and his faced dropped. They both knew how hard school had been for him, especially since the diagnosis in the sixth grade. Declan reached out, but Aiden stepped back. "I didn't it mean it like that," he said.

Lola swept toward them, casting a glance toward Heather, who stood by her locker, pretending to read physics, but kept peeking over. "Important announcement." Lola tossed her hair over one shoulder. "You two will be at my field hockey game tonight. Front row. No excuses."

"We were already planning to go," Declan said, flatly.

"Were you?" Her brow lifted. "Because I haven't seen an ounce of school spirit from either of you." Her gaze dropped to the journal, lips curling. "Since when do you journal?"

He shut it with a snap. "It's for a research paper."

"Good. Wouldn't want you pouring your heart out in a leather-bound tragedy." She turned to Aiden. "And you. She still talks about you, you know."

Aiden's eyes dropped to the floor.

"You could at least pretend that doesn't devastate you," she said, mock pouting, before adjusting her cuff. "Seven o'clock sharp. If you're late, I'll ensure you regret it." With that, she disappeared into the crowd.

Declan looked over. "You alright?"

Aiden shoved a notebook deeper into the locker. "It depends. Are you done being a jerk?"

"I said I'm sorry. I just haven't been sleeping."

"Because of the demonic journal?"

Before he could answer, the intercom crackled to life.

"Will Declan Albatross and Aiden Oldwyck report to Headmistress Mortimer's office. Declan Albatross and Aiden Oldwyck, to the Headmistress's office."

The hallway quieted as heads turned. Lola paused mid-step, her brows furrowing. Heather froze. Even Ophelia, half-hidden behind her admirers, stole a glance at them.

"So much for not getting caught," Aiden muttered.

Declan slid the journal into his messenger bag and shut his locker. "Maybe it's not what we think."

They headed for the front doors without another word, every gaze trailing behind.

The Administration Building's corridors were dim, sconces humming as their amber light flickered across wallpaper. Sepia-toned photographs lined the hall with Driftmoor Academy's history captured in still faces and stiff collars. In one, Eldridge Hall rose mid-construction, stone blocks suspended by ropes. In another, a boy in a tailcoat stood beneath the newly christened bell tower, his eyes blank beneath the plate bearing his name.

The staircase creaked as Declan and Aiden climbed in silence. Declan kept his eyes on the steps, searching for the right words to undo what he'd said. He wanted to stitch the moment shut before it festered. But his thoughts came jagged, slipping just out of reach. At the top, they stopped before a door marked by a dull nameplate: *Headmistress T. Mortimer.*

Aiden exhaled. "You first. It's your fault we're here anyway."

Declan gave him a sidelong look before knocking twice.

"Come in," Headmistress Mortimer called.

Firelight flickered across mahogany bookshelves lined with leather-bound yearbooks and tarnished trophies. A hearth crackled beneath a portrait of the Academy's founding class—their gazes rigid, as if disturbed by the living. Behind a desk, Mortimer sat with composed elegance, her high-backed chair exaggerating her height.

"Mr. Albatross. Mr. Oldwyck." She gestured to two leather armchairs. "Please."

Declan dropped his messenger bag and sat. Aiden followed. Declan had only been here once, when she summoned him to congratulate him on his early acceptance to Dartmouth. It should've been a milestone worth celebrating. But his family overshadowed the achievement. The divorce had hollowed the parts of his life that once felt certain, and sitting across from Mortimer that day, all he'd felt was the aftermath of everything falling apart.

Mortimer steepled her fingers. "Has anyone told you that you have your mother's eyes, Mr. Albatross?"

Declan's hands tightened on the armrests. "People used to. When I was younger."

"She was a remarkable woman. Charismatic. Difficult. Ambitious. We were roommates once."

"You lived in the dorms together?"

"She avoided Albatross House when she could. For personal reasons." A faint smile tugged at her lips, though it didn't reach her eyes. "But that's not why you're here."

Aiden leaned forward. "To clarify, are we in trouble?"

Mortimer slid a folder across the desk toward Declan. "Ms. Alpine filed an incident report. Security footage shows you removing an item from the lost and found with Mr. Oldwyck as your accomplice. Care to explain?"

Declan's mouth went dry. "It wasn't theft. The journal's mine. I just didn't want to draw attention."

"Why not go through the proper channels?"

"It's personal," he said, more defensively than he intended.

Her gaze sharpened. "I'll need to verify it belongs to you," she said. "Do you have it?"

Aiden cleared his throat. "Headmistress, that's a bit dramatic, wouldn't you agree? It's just a journal after all, not state secrets."

Mortimer didn't look at him. "Mr. Albatross?"

Reluctantly, Declan retrieved the journal from his bag and placed it on the desk. When Mortimer reached for it, she recoiled. Her chair scraped back as she stood, one hand pressed to her chest.

Aiden jumped to his feet. "Headmistress?"

She stared at the journal, lips parted without sound. "Forget what I said. Take it."

Declan hesitated, before he grabbed the journal. As it left the desk, Mortimer collapsed back into her chair. Her skin had gone bloodless, and her eyes remained fix on the space where it had been.

"Headmistress—" Declan started.

"I've seen enough."

Aiden hovered near her desk. "Are you okay? Should we call someone—"

"Take that thing away from here!" Her voice cracked under the strain.

Declan shoved the journal under his arm. He and Aiden left her office, the door closing behind them. The fog had thinned, but the morning held a damp chill. They crossed the quad in silence, their shoes whispering over wet stone. The journal stayed tucked beneath Declan's arm.

Aiden slowed, letting a few steps fall between them. "Why won't you show it to me?"

Declan didn't break stride. "I'm not ready to."

Aiden stepped in front of him. "You've been off ever since you found that thing. Obsessed, secretive. I've watched you lose sleep, zone out mid-sentence. I feel like you're pushing me away."

Declan's fingers curled around the journal. "Don't be ridiculous. I'm not pushing anyone away."

Aiden shook his head. "You don't trust me. Why?"

"That's not true," Declan said.

"Then prove me wrong." Aiden reached for the journal. "Let me see it."

Declan yanked it away. "No."

Aiden's patience snapped. He lunged. They collided, both trying to wrestle the journal from the other. Their feet slipped on wet grass, limbs tangling, curses muffled. The journal flew and landed with a thud near the edge of the quad. They hit the ground hard, mud streaking their uniforms.

Aiden rolled off him. "What the hell is wrong with you?"

Declan sat up, chest heaving. "You won't get it."

"Because you won't let me."

A voice rang out, sharp and dry. "Should I be jealous, or just concerned?"

Lola stood several feet away, arms folded, boots damp from the lawn. Her eyes flicked from one to the other, then to the journal in the grass.

"I thought I was the dramatic one," she said, striding over. She plucked the journal and handed it to Declan. "Whatever this is, maybe don't do it on the front lawn next time." She glanced at them both. "Seven o'clock. I'm not above bribing faculty to check attendance."

She walked away without another word. Declan stared after her, mud streaking the journal's cover. Aiden stood, brushing off his blazer, but didn't say anything more. They didn't speak again as they walked to class, but the distance between them stayed—cold and unspoken.

CHAPTER 44
Aiden Oldwyck

THE BOY'S LOCKER ROOM REEKED OF MUSK, DAMP TILE, AND THE sharp bite of deodorant—a cocktail of odors that clung to the air long after practice ended. Overhead, buzzing lights cast a pallid glow that flattened every surface. Aiden twisted the dial on his locker while behind him, the usual towel slaps, bragging, and half-serious dares echoed down the rows. Practice had been a disaster. Every swing, every step had felt too late. He'd wanted to prove himself to Coach Adams, to the team, to himself. To show he could step up next season. But today, he might as well have been invisible. Worse, he'd been a letdown.

He stripped down and stepped into the showers, hoping the hot water would melt the frustration from his skin. Jets pounded his shoulders as he closed his eyes and let the hissing drown out the failure on the court.

Clang.

His eyes snapped open, droplets clinging to his lashes. He twisted the knob, and the spray cut off with a screech. The room stilled. He wrapped a towel around his waist and scanned the locker room.

"Hello?" His voice bounced off tile and metal.

Some lockers hung ajar. Others were stuffed with uniforms and tennis gear. The aisle was empty, but footsteps echoed from the opposite side. Aiden knew who it was by the tousled curls, the slope of his shoulders, the scar peeking over one blade. Noah stood by his locker, stuffing clothes into a worn duffel.

He glanced up, lips curling into a smirk. "Look who it is. Trust fund baby himself."

Aiden clutched his towel. "Picasso, right?"

Noah raised an eyebrow as he tugged on a T-shirt. "Didn't think I made that much of an impression under all that paint."

"You were kind of hard to miss."

Noah's green eyes lingered. Whatever look he gave, Aiden couldn't read it, but it didn't stop the butterflies.

"You're underdressed compared to last time," Noah said, nodding to the towel.

Aiden let out a breathless scoff. "Well, it's not exactly black tie around here."

Noah laughed, zipping his bag. "Touché."

The room shrunk. Aiden shifted, unsure of what to say or do next.

"You played well today," Noah said.

"What are you talking about? I flubbed two returns and tripped on the baseline."

"So?" Noah leaned against the lockers. "You've got presence. People notice that. Doesn't have to be perfect to turn heads."

Aiden had grown up in the shadows of people who shone too brightly to ignore. Declan with his popularity and impossible charm, Lola with her radiance and calculated poise. Even his sister, Veronica, whose every move commanded a room like their mother. He learned to shrink himself without realizing it. To listen more than speak. To excel quietly, knowing it would never echo the same way.

Noah clapped him on the shoulder, fingers warm, resting a second too long. "See you around, Captain," he said, already halfway to the exit. He tossed a two-finger salute over his shoulder.

"Captain," Aiden repeated under his breath, a smile tugging at his lips.

A showerhead behind him erupted.

Then another. And another. Jets roared to life. Steam curled toward the ceiling as heat thickened the air. Aiden frozen, towel dampening against his skin. His gaze swept the stalls, which were all empty. Moisture clung to his skin. Lights flickered overhead. His mind scrambled for logic, from a plumbing issue to a timer to a stupid prank. Anything that made sense.

He swallowed and crept toward to a shower stall. The second his fingers touched the knob, pain bit into his palm—hot and sharp. He yanked back and cradled his hand, but before he could process it, a shadow moved behind him.

He whipped around, breath caught in his chest. Steam curled across the benches. His skin was glistening with sweat now. He blinked against the air, every breath heavier than the last. He scanned each row, expecting someone to step forward. But the space remained empty except for the rushing water and buzzing lights. He turned toward the sinks where the mirrors were fogged.

He wiped a line through the condensation, revealing two red eyes behind him.

A hellhound hunched in the steam, its ribs rising and falling with measured breaths.

Aiden spun too fast, feet sliding. His knees cracked against tile as he caught himself on the sink's edge. He looked up. The mirror showed only the locker room. No creature. No eyes. He stared into his reflection, shaking. Water dripped from his hair in uneven rivulets, streaking down his cheeks like tears. His chest heaved, but it felt like the room had been emptied of oxygen.

But in his mind, those eyes were burning as if watching him from within. Like it had recognized him. The hellhounds weren't coming. They were already waiting for him. Patient and certain. And maybe this was how it started. Not with fire and fangs, but with something calmer. A presence in the dark corners of himself, until he couldn't tell where fear ended and the curse began.

CHAPTER 45
Lola Godfrey

Driftmoor Academy's field hockey had stood poised to defend their championship title in the season's first game. Floodlights cut through the fog curling along the turf's edge, their harsh glow spilling across the sidelines. The bleachers shook beneath the marching band, blaring under cheering students wrapped in Driftmoor scarves. The scoreboard glowed, waiting for its first tally.

Lola stood near midfield, one gloved hand tightening around her stick. Her breath fogged in the cold, nerves fluttering low in her stomach, but not from the game. Her gaze drifted toward the stands. Declan and Aiden sat shoulder to shoulder, their heads bent close in conversation. So they'd made up, then. Funny how boys could bruise each other one day and laugh the next. Several rows above, Ophelia reclined, legs crossed, chin lifted, a near-smile brushing her lips. Even from this far, her presence pulled at Lola's heartstrings.

"Hey." Heather appeared, stick slung over one shoulder. "Forget about her. Focus on what matters: kicking Hawthorne's ass."

Lola bent forward, touching her toes, the hem of her skirt brushing the tops of her cleats. When she rose, she rolled her shoulders back. "Does it look like I'm thinking about her?"

Heather gave her a sideways smile. "I mean, I just saw you looking."

Lola turned, all polish and chill. "You'd be amazed at how many things I can do at once." Her eyes flicked over Heather's uniform. "Like focus on the game. And remember who spent an afternoon giggling with the enemy over scones."

"This again? I told you, it wasn't like that."

"Of course not. You just have low standards for company."

The umpire's whistle cracked through the air, signaling both teams to gather.

"Positions, ladies!" the umpire said. "I want a clean match. No foot-to-ball contact. No hands. And no high back swinging. That means you, Godfrey."

Lola crouched, breath curling in the cold, muscles coiled tight. Her eyes flicked toward Hawthorne. She remembered freshman year, when an elbow caught her eye. The bruise never surfaced, of course. But that year, Ophelia had been on the team. Their plays seamless. Their victories routine. They'd shared pregame rituals and exchanged glances before the whistle. But that lifetime had ended the night Ophelia vanished.

The whistle blew, and a Hawthorne midfielder broke from the circle, snatching the ball and slicing across the field. Lola sprinted after her, cleats biting into the turf. The girl was fast, but Lola closed the space between them. She angled her stick low, reaching for the intercept, and missed. The ball flicked away to a second player, past Heather.

Lola's jaw clenched. She charged after the Hawthorne forward with renewed force. The girl moved to pass, but Lola clipped her foot just enough to send her sprawling onto the turf. Gasps rippled from the stands. A whistle cracked the air.

"Godfrey!" the umpire shouted, striding over. "You know better."

Lola held her arms out, feigning surprise. "Oh, please. If that counts as contact, I should be arrested."

The girl groaned while clutching her knee.

The umpire reached into his pocket and held up a yellow card. "Next time, you're out."

Lola nodded with practiced compliance, but her heart rattled.

Heather jogged up beside her as play resumed. "What was that? Are you—?"

"I'm fine." Lola shouldered past Heather and moved back into position, eyes scanning the crowd. But her pulse wasn't coming down. Her palms slicked with sweat inside her gloves. She rolled her shoulders, trying to shake the pressure building behind her eyes.

The crowd's cheers blurred into a murmur while fog pooled at the field's edge. The air tasted wrong—like burned hair and old matches. Her tongue pressed to the roof of her mouth. Static tingled along her arms. The lights above the bleachers shimmered, and for a split second, she thought they flickered. A breeze swept across the field. Not cold, but hot, acrid, the way a curling iron smells after being left on too long. She squinted toward the sideline, toward the edge of the bleachers where shadows gathered beneath the metal.

Lola halted mid-stride.

Under the bleachers, two red eyes burned through the gloom. Smoke curled from the grass where it stepped. The hellhound unfurled from the dark, its fur shimmering with embers. Each paw seared the earth, leaving behind smoldering prints. Yet the crowd roared. The band played. Her teammates dashed past. In that liminal moment, Lola planted her feet and clenched her stick so tightly her knuckles paled.

"Godfrey!" Coach shouted from the sideline. "What the hell are you doing?"

The hellhound didn't move. Neither did she. Confusion rippled through the bleachers—whispers, a pointed hand, then finally a scream. Cheers turned into shouts. The stands quaked as students and parents surged upward. Horns fell silent as the band members fled.

"Lola! Run!" Heather's voice tore across the field.

The hellhound barreled into Lola, knocking her to the ground. She crashed onto the turf, air deflating from her lungs. The world spun into light and noise in a dizzy blur. She gagged on blood and twisted her head as the hellhound prowled a few feet away.

She rolled onto her knees and scrambled for her stick, swung up and caught the beast mid-charge, wood slamming into its fang. Hot breath washed over her face as its mouth snapped inches from her skin.

"No!" she gritted out. "I didn't get into Yale for this to happen!"

The hellhound shoved harder right before its jaws clamped around her arm. It was like fire igniting in her veins. She screamed, driving her hand into the beast, pushing with everything she had until it momentarily backed off. Quickly, she scrambled back. The hellhound's eyes shifted toward the trees edging the field. It growled, almost reluctant, then prowled and vanished into the darkness.

The turf trembled with footsteps as people scattered in every direction. Her teammates, Coach, Declan, Heather—even Aiden—closed in, their faces blurred by panic, mouths moving too quickly to follow. Her blood had stained the field. She staggered upright, one hand pressed to her arm, while beneath it, torn skin pulled together as cells stitched themselves back.

Declan reached her first, gripping her shoulders. "Are you okay?"

She forced a smirk, despite the tremor in her limbs. "Don't be so dramatic," she said. "It's barely a scratch."

His eyes dropped to the blood on her arm.

Heather stopped beside them. "Was that a wolf?"

"Back up! All of you!" Coach forced through the crowd. "Give her space!"

"I'm fine, Coach," Lola said, even as her knees wobbled. "It's a scratch, not a tragedy."

"Let me see."

She gave a breezy laugh. "Coach, that's really not necessary." But there'd be no getting out of this. Reluctantly, she moved her hand away from the bite.

Heather's brows drew in. "There's…nothing there?"

"Have I not been saying that?" Lola said, brushing at the blood-stained jersey.

Coach stared. "Then where'd all this blood come from?"

Aiden stepped forward. "The wolf." Both Lola and Declan shot him a look. "It—it was bleeding. From the leg. I saw it."

Declan squinted. The lie dangled, but Aiden delivered it with just enough weight.

"Yes, the wolf," Lola said, eyes narrowing at Aiden. Her voice held, but her mind reeled. He had never stood up for her. Especially when the lie was so obvious.

Coach looked from Aiden to the blood, and then back to Lola. "I still want the nurse to check you out."

She dusted turf off her knee, ensuring every motion was calm. "Coach," she said, meeting his eyes, "How many times do I need to say it? I am fine."

She snatched her stick from the grass and walked off the field without a backward glance.

Behind her, the lights gleamed over the turf where her blood shimmered.

The locker room was silent.

Lola sat on a bench, hands braced at her sides, elbows locked. Her stick lay across her lap, blood streaking the grip while her jersey clung to her back, damp with sweat. Turf and mud stained her legs. No one had followed her. They were giving her space—or maybe avoiding her. Her arm ached where the hellhound had bitten, even though no wound remained.

She unwrapped the athletic tape at her wrist in mechanical motions, the strips falling like old skin. She hadn't even meant to fight the hell-hound. Not at first. She'd frozen. And then she snapped. A part of her that refused to bleed again. But she had. She looked down at her arm again. Smooth. Untouched.

Liar, she thought. Her own body, lying for her.

She dropped her head to her hands. Not to break, just to breathe. But the silence didn't soothe her. It watched her. In the mirror's reflection—half-fogged with steam—she swore she saw movement behind her.

When she looked again, it was gone.

CHAPTER 46
Aiden Oldwyck

The ball thudded against the racket.

Aiden adjusted the hem of his maroon polo—crisp but slightly untucked—and tugged the waistband of his tennis shorts, damp from the morning dew. The towering hedges swallowed the sound, muffling even the rustling oaks. Sunlight filtered through their branches, casting shadows in bars of gold and brown that moved with the wind. He tossed the ball up and swung. It veered wide, clattering against the fence. He muttered a curse and jogged after it. How was he supposed to focus when Lola had been mauled by a hellhound and walked away with nothing but blood on her jersey and that infuriating smile?

He served again and missed.

"You've gotten sloppy."

He didn't turn. "Maybe I've grown tired of trying to be impressive."

Irene stepped to the court's edge, a bowl of sliced fruit in her hands. Her shawl trailed like smoke, shadows parting. A silk blouse buttoned high at the neck disappeared into a wool skirt, hem skimming her boots with each step.

"If Coach Adams doesn't name you captain, perhaps I ought to remind the athletic board who funded the new scoreboard.

Aiden caught the rebound and tossed the ball aside. "You already did. Last spring."

"And yet, you're still not captain."

"Is that supposed to be encouragement?"

"Eat." She offered the bowl. "It's important to refuel."

He accepted it, knowing better than to refuse. He chewed on a strawberry—his favorite.

An owl hooted in the distance. Beyond the court, the maze rustled. Then: "Why would a hellhound go after Lola?"

Irene turned toward the trees, as if the flaming foliage might whisper a better answer.

"That's preposterous."

"It happened. The whole Academy saw it. Most of them are calling it a wolf, but it wasn't. It was a hellhound, and it attacked her. Why?"

"You must be mistaken," she said. "You see, the hounds never act freely. They're summoned. With purpose."

"Well, maybe Aunt Maeve did. Or someone else in the matriarchy. I don't know. But I saw it." He paused. "And it wasn't the first time that night."

Irene's eyes found his.

"There was one in the locker room," he said. "Before the game. It didn't attack. It just stood there. Like it knew me."

The breeze picked up, pulling the scent of pine through the court.

"Stress can manifest all sorts of monsters," she said. "Especially ones we were never meant to see. You're under a lot of pressure. Your match. Your studies."

"Do you think I'm making this up? For—for attention or pity?"

Her reply came too quickly. "Don't be ridiculous."

"Then why are you acting like I'm crazy?" His voice cracked, edged with hurt more than anger.

She studied him. "Perhaps for the same reason you and Declan lied to Headmistress Mortimer about the journal."

Aiden's fist curled. "We didn't lie. Not really. It's Declan's. It's—" He hesitated. "Some kind of family heirloom."

"You and I both know it's more than that."

He shifted his weight, avoiding her gaze. He didn't want to talk about the journal, or the way Declan had started to change since finding it. In seventeen years of friendship, they'd never come close to a real fight. No punches were thrown, but it was close enough. And that, more than anything, hurt in a way Declan would never fully understand.

"What is it?" he asked. "What's in it?"

She looked to the sky, where clouds were gathering. "It's not my place to say. But you'd do well to keep your distance from the Albatrosses. Especially now."

Aiden laughed, sharp and bitter. "Do you mean Declan? My best friend? You want me to cut him off?"

"I want you safe," she said softly. "And sometimes safety means knowing when to let go of the ones we love."

He shook his head, gripping the racket tighter. "These secrets. They're poison, you know?"

"Oh, button." She lifted a hand to his cheek, brushing it like she used to when he was small and sick, and the world was simple. "Of course they are."

But it wasn't comforting. Or an apology. It was resignation.

Aiden stared at her. "You've known this whole time, haven't you? About Declan. About his family?" His voice wavered. "Is that why you stopped being friends with Ms. Albatross?"

When she didn't answer, his voice dropped. "Is there something about Lola you're hiding? Is she the banshee? Is she the one you've been looking for?"

Irene reached his hand. He didn't stop her, but he didn't hold on, either.

"It hurts me to hear these questions from you," she said. "But I can't give you answers. What I can do is protect you. Your sister and I—we've been working on a solution. A way out of the hunt. To save you."

His brows drew together. "How? How is that even possible?"

She hesitated, fingers tightening around his. "Believe it or not, it was your Aunt Maeve's idea. There's a record. Buried deep in the family archive. An Oldwyck woman who bartered with the Entity. She spared her son."

He leaned in. "What kind of trade?"

"A banshee," she said, "in exchange for the boy's life."

"Why would it want a banshee?"

"Because the banshee was its first creation. The first voice it shaped. A harbinger of grief, tethered to death and prophecy. The Entity made them to serve, but they resisted. They wept warnings instead carrying out orders. And it never forgot the disobedience. To reclaim a banshee is to silence a threat. To remind them who they belong to."

He wanted to believe her. To fall into the comfort of her voice like he had when he was five, when monsters hid in closet shadows and her lullabies were enough to keep them at bay. But he wasn't five anymore. And this time, the monster wasn't in his head. Her eyes didn't match her words. They held something else.

The wind tore through the branches, clawing at the windows like it knew what she wasn't saying. Like the manor itself had overheard and understood exactly what she was willing to sacrifice.

CHAPTER 47
Lola Godfrey

At first, it was nothing more than an itch beneath her skin, persistent, but ignorable. A memory masquerading as sensation. But then it tightened, anchoring itself to muscle and bone with merciless pressure. Lola jolted upright, sheets tangled around her legs. She fumbled for the lamp, fingers slipping over the switch. Light flared—too fast, too sharp. She shoved up her sleeve. Her skin looked smooth. But the pain still clung, as vivid as the hellhound's teeth sinking in. Pain wasn't supposed to last this long for a Godfrey.

She squeezed her eyes shut, willing it to pass. But no matter how tightly she clenched her fists, no matter how hard she tried to shove the memory aside, the sensation burrowed deeper.

It ebbed, only for a few seconds, then surged again.

A cry tore loose as she buried her face into the pillow, the sound muffled against fabric. She curled inward. It flared again, blazing through her veins. Her nails dragged across her forearm, desperate to claw it out. But it only climbed higher, up through her shoulder, down to her fingertips.

Hot tears streaked the pillow. *Make it stop. Please—make it stop!*

She would've torn her arm off if it meant relief. Anything to sever the tether to the bite had left behind. The pain had no edge, no shape. Just pressure. Just fire.

The room blurred. Muscles shaking, she curled tighter. The pillow soaked against her cheek, as her sobs frayed into whimpers. Sleep didn't come. It dragged her under, as the pain settled like a parasite just beneath her skin.

When she opened her eyes, sunlight seeped through the sheer curtains, soft and indifferent, while the chandelier scattered fractured rainbows across the ceiling. The lamp still glowed beside her—she hadn't turned it off. She sagged with exhaustion. Her limbs felt waterlogged, every breath thick with the weight of something unshaken. She couldn't remember falling asleep. If not for the damp pillow beneath her, she might've convinced herself it had all been a nightmare.

Moving was an effort. Every shift dragged like she was wading through water. She pushed upright, her body lagged behind the command. Her stomach flipped as she looked down. A mark stretched across her arm—raised and ridged. The bite had returned, scabbed in purples and blacks. She pressed her fingertips to it, bracing for pain, but none came.

A knock jolted her.

"Lo, can I come in?" Faustino called through the door. "I brought coffee. How you like it."

She yanked the silk sheets to her chin, hiding her arm beneath them. "One minute!"

A glance at the vanity confirmed she looked like death warmed over. Nothing to be done now. She raked a hand through her bed hair. "Okay. You can come in now."

The door creaked open as Faustino stepped in with two steaming mugs. He wore a navy tracksuit, and a white tank showed a dusting of chest hair. Auburn hair combed. Clean-shaven. Irritatingly fresh.

He paused by her bedside. "Wow. You actually look awful."

Lola grabbed the mug with her good arm. The ceramic warmed her hand. "That's no way to speak to a lady, Tino."

He dropped into the blush velvet wingback chair by the window. "Right. Because you're so delicate."

"Glad we're on the same page."

He hummed into his coffee. "Heard about last night." His gaze lingered over the rim. "Some wolf tried to take your face off?"

Lola kept her hand steady around the mug, though the ripple on the surface betrayed her. "That's the rumor."

"And what's the truth?"

"It barely touched me. Everyone overreacted. Especially Coach."

"That's because most people don't walk away from a wolf attack without a mark."

"Well, I'm not most people." Another sip. Another twitch in her fingers.

His eyes flicked toward the arm she'd hidden. She caught the glance, the almost question, but he let it drop.

"Listen, I've been thinking about what you said. Heather not remembering the attack? That doesn't track. But something else is bothering me. Something stranger."

Lola quirked a brow. "Stranger than a hellhound in suburbia? This I've got to hear."

He hesitated, then sighed. "Dad is gonna lose it if he finds out we're keeping things from him."

"Oh please," she said, adjusting the blanket with a sharp tug. "Father prefers not knowing. Makes it easier to keep sipping scotch and quoting Voltaire."

"Still. Listen. You know what a banshee is?"

"The supernatural drama queen who screams whenever someone's about to die?"

Faustino's lips twitched. "Their scream isn't just a warning. It's a weapon. Used wrong, it can hurt people. Kill them."

"What does that have to do with me almost getting turned into hellhound kibble?"

"I'm not sure." He leaned forward. "But hellhounds react to banshees. Some say the scream disorients them. Fries their senses. Make them lose focus."

Her grip tightened on the mug.

"You know that old estate near the cemetery?"

"Vaguely. I try not to spend weekends lurking around haunted properties, thanks."

"Lo, this is serious. It used to belong to a founding family. The Mareks."

Her gut twisted. She blew on her coffee.

"They were forced out years ago," he continued. "Supposedly over hellhound control. If there's a banshee in Driftmoor, it means things are shifting."

Lola sighed dramatically. "Tino, you're acting like we're in some gothic horror novel. We're Godfreys. We are the status quo."

"Maybe," he said. "But it's getting messy."

"How messy?"

He dragged a hand down his face. "We found three bodies by Galleon's Wharf. Same cause. Hemorrhaging. Eyes, ears, lungs. Like something ruptured them from the inside out."

She went quiet.

"And a fourth," he added. "The cemetery groundskeeper."

Lola froze.

"But here's the thing," he said. "He wasn't alone when it happened. A girl from the Academy was there."

"Who?"

"Dorothy Hale."

The drenched girl. The server from the country club. The girl who'd seen her heal.

"When did you say this was?" Lola asked.

"Saturday night. Why?"

"No reason."

His gaze lingered. "You'll keep this between us, right? I kept your secret about the Oldwyck's maze. I expect the same."

Lola smirked, flipping her hair. "Dear brother, I practically trademarked discretion."

"Yeah, yeah. Try not to spend the whole day in bed."

The door shut behind him.

Lola listened for his footsteps to fade before peeling back the sheets. The bite mark rose stark against her skin. One banshee. Two attacks. Four bodies. Her brother was right. Driftmoor was shifting, and she didn't know if she was meant to rise with it or be pulled under.

CHAPTER 48
Declan Albatross

THE SENIOR BONFIRE BLAZED ON CRAFT'S BEACH, FLAMES CLAWING at the sky as embers spun into the dark. Smoke tangled with the breeze, and the sand anchored Declan, even as the firelight fractured faces into surreal blurs. He stayed to the edges, where laughter dulled and popping wood filled the pauses between waves. He should've been blending into the current of high school revelry and celebrating survival. Instead, his gaze drifted past the sparks and music, past the silhouettes dancing in firelight, to where Ophelia and Heather sat.

Seeing them without Lola snagged like a splinter under his skin. There was a time the three of them had been inseparable. Lola, Ophelia, Heather. Driftmoor royalty. They used to claim the corners of every party, heads bowed in conspiratorial whispers, speaking in half-sentences only they understood. Heather was the grounded one, Lola the radiant one, and Ophelia the storm you didn't see until it was too late. But when Ophelia left, she hadn't just disappeared from his life. She'd left all of them. And it had been Lola and Heather who stayed behind, who leaned on each other in the silence that followed. Declan had watched them grow closer. Surviving the void Ophelia left was something they had done together. And now, seeing Heather at Ophelia's side—as if those years hadn't happened, as if Lola hadn't been the one who stayed—felt like watching a wound reopen.

Not far off, Camille sat on a driftwood log, arms curled around her knees, eye on the ocean. A cream wool coat draped over her shoulders, the collar turned up against the breeze. Beneath it, her dress—royal blue velvet—caught glints of firelight. Her boots were polished, laced to the ankle, elegant even in sand.

Declan walked over. "Hey. Mind if I sit?"

She looked up, flames catching in her blue eyes. "Not at all," she said. "Seems like you could use an escape."

He dropped beside her. Moonlight stretched across the water's surface.

"You've been pacing since you got here," Camille said. "Is this about Ophelia?"

His fingers tightened around the strap of his messenger bag. The journal pulled at his thoughts—Mortimer's reaction, that look of pure terror. And the pages that hadn't smudged, even after they'd been soaked.

"No, I think I'm past that." He tried a laugh, but it stuck. "Just AP coursework. It's eating me alive."

Camille looked at him, half amused, half unconvinced. "Declan, you're a terrible liar." But she didn't press. Unlike Lola, she never demanded answers or reached past where no invitation lay. She waited, holding space, in case he offered the truth.

He slipped the bag off his shoulder and unlatched it. "Remember that book I found in the library? The one we gave to Ms. Alpine?"

"The one with the compass?" she asked. "Of course. Why?"

He pulled it free. "I went back for it."

Camille's gaze sharpened. "Why would you do that? I thought you said it wasn't yours?"

"I know, but I couldn't stop thinking about it. It's like…" He exhaled. "Like it was calling me."

Her brows pulled together as she looked from the journal to him. "Calling you?"

He flipped it open, and the yellowed parchment and ink caught the firelight. When Camille reached for it, he tensed—Mortimer's panic flashing back. But her fingers brushed the leather without consequence.

"What is all this?" she said, flipping slowly. She paused on a sketch of jagged cliffs beneath an inscription: *The voices of the sea are the gates.* "I swore the pages were blank when you showed me."

A sound rose above the fire's crackle and the chatter. Soft at first. Almost like singing.

"Did you hear that?" Declan asked.

Camille turned toward the waves. "Hear what?"

"A song." He stood slowly. "I think—I think it's coming from the water."

She followed his gaze, confusion knitting her features. "I don't hear anything. Maybe it's a choir student trying to—"

But he was already walking toward the shallows, the journal clutched tightly. The music grew clearer with each step, eerie and beautiful, like it had been written for him. He stepped into the surf without hesitation. Cold water climbed his ankles and to his calves.

"Declan, stop!" Camille grabbed his arm. "What are you doing?"

"Something's out there." His eyes were glued on the horizon.

A splash broke the surface that was too sharp for a fish and too precise for a wave. Ripples widened, disturbed by a shape just below. Moonlight struck the glint of scales before they vanished.

Camille stiffened beside him. "We should go. Now."

But the song enveloped him, drowning out the bonfire, Camille's voice. It pulled at his mind, and he was more than happy to allow it. Eyes waited beneath the surface. He knew what they belonged to. Even before the journal had shown him, he'd seen it. A siren.

Before he could venture any further, a green light flared behind him.

Camille's brooch—the mistletoe one she always wore—blazed with emerald light.

The siren recoiled, body writhing as its scales reflected the mistletoe's glow. An inhuman shriek erupted from it and the ocean surged forward. Declan lost his footing and plunged into the surf, arms wrapped around the journal as a wave crashed over him.

When he resurfaced from shallows, the water had begun to still and the siren was gone.

He staggered upright, coughing. Camille stood beyond the tide with her hand over the brooch as its glow faded. He stumbled onto shore, sand clinging to his clothes, journal in hand.

"What was that?" Camille asked with a slight tremble in her voice.

He forced the word out. "A siren."

Behind them, the bonfire raged on. Students laughed. Sang. Roasted marshmallows. Nothing had changed for them.

Camille hugged her arms. "No...I think I need to go. Sorry."

"Camille, wait!"

But she was already walking, disappearing into firelight and bodies.

Water dripped from his sleeves, pooling at his feet, seeping into the sand. His hands sook as he opened the journal, the soaked leather slick in his grip. Its damp pages curled slightly, but the ink remained untouched. A line near the center of the parchment stared back:

The sirens call not to the heart but to the depths of the soul, their song a gate, their waters a prison.

His gaze lingered on the final word. *Prison.* The echo of it tightened something him. Behind, lively sounds crackled through the firelight. But here, at the water's edge, the night felt hollowed out. The waves rolled in gently, reaching for his feet with soft insistence. He took a step away. Because now, even the ocean felt like a lie. And he didn't trust it anymore.

CHAPTER 49
Aiden Oldwyck

AROUND THE BONFIRE, STUDENTS GATHERED IN CLUSTERS. THEIR laughter and conversations rose and fell between bursts of flame. The glow caught on linked arms and closeness from the casual press of shoulders to fingers tracing patterns in the sand and jokes exchanged in tipsy voices. Aiden remembered what that felt like with Heather, once. She stood near the grills, Ophelia beside her. Heather's posture seemed relaxed, but her voice was too casual, like someone so used to power she no longer needed to perform it. She tilted her head toward Ophelia, a smile playing on her lips.

She looked intense. Meaner. Not in passing moments or offhand remarks, but in the way her persona settled beside Ophelia. He'd caught glimpses of this before in cutting comments embellished as jokes, that glint in her eye when she wanted an underclassman to fear her. But standing there, laughing with Ophelia, it wasn't a glimpse. It was the whole picture of a colder person who had taken root where his ex-girlfriend used to be.

"It's ridiculous, don't you think?" Lola's voice floated over from the quilt, where she was propped on one elbow, swirling her drink.

Lola could be ruthless, but she never pulled Heather into cruelty the way Ophelia did. With Lola, Heather's mean girl streaks had limits, whether or not she wanted them.

With Ophelia, it could be endless. And Aiden couldn't tell where one of them ended and the other began.

Aiden turned toward her. "What is?"

"How easily she forgave Ophelia," she said, tilting her chin toward the grills. "After all that time she spent crying in my room, pretending it didn't matter. And now they're laughing over skewers like none of it ever happened."

Heather's laugh rang out across the sand as if she wanted them to hear her.

Aiden watched her. "Have you ever thought about doing the same?"

Lola scoffed. "You sound like my mother," she said. "I rather set myself on fire than hand out second chances like party favors."

She took a defiant sip and stood. Her heel slipped in the sand, throwing her off balance, long enough for Aiden to reach out. "Are you okay?" he asked, steadying her.

"Can everyone please stop acting like I'm made of porcelain?" She shook him off and brushed the sand from her dress in brisk, agitated swipes. Then, without hesitation, she tossed her drink into the fire. The flames hissed as sparks snapped upward. "See? Crisis averted."

She walked off, shoulders tense, leaving no room for questions.

A few seconds later, Declan sank onto the quilt without a word. His pants clung wet to his ankles and damp hair curled at the ends like it had been caught in rain. Aiden glanced at him, about to ask, but stopped himself. The strap of his messenger bag dug into one shoulder, half-zipped, essays and notes threatening to spill out.

"Where's she going now?" Declan asked.

Lola's retreat dissolved into the shadows. "I have no idea," Aiden said, the words edged with a tired fondness. "She's been like this since we were kids. I can't tell if she likes me or wants to punch me in the face."

"It's Lola. Both are true." Declan held out a hand. "Pass the bottle."

Aiden handed over the bottle of vodka Lola brought from home. "Did you go for a swim?"

Declan tipped the bottle back, wiped his mouth, and pulled the journal from his bag. The compass caught the firelight, casting a glint.

"Got any ideas on how to make this thing disappear?" he asked. Aiden arched a brow. "I thought you didn't want to get rid of it?"

Declan traced the journal's edges. "I don't know what I want to do."

Aiden had seen the way Declan looked at that thing like it was telling him secrets. It reminded him of how Doris Albatross spoke to the air. This was an obsession. And it scared him, the way Declan sank deeper into it. He could hear his mother's voice: *You'd do well to stay away from the Albatrosses. Especially now.* He'd thought she was being dramatic, now he wasn't sure.

"Are you still mad at me?" Declan asked.

"I was," Aiden said. "But as much as I want to stay mad at you, I can't."

Declan fumbled with the journal. "I really am sorry," he said. "For what I said. I didn't mean it."

Noah pulled Aiden's gaze across the bonfire. He stood by the drink table, talking to a group of lacrosse players. Firelight gilded the copper in his hair and played along the line of his jaw. His blazer—a dark, frayed tweed—hung open over a button-down that looked like it had survived more than a few hand-me-down cycles. He leaned into a girl, their shoulders brushing.

Noah caught his eye. Then peeled away from the group and crossed the sand toward them.

"Room for one more?" he said, raising a beer. His gaze flicked from Declan to Aiden but settled on Aiden.

Declan didn't glance up. "Do we know you?"

"Aiden and I are on the same team."

"Plenty of people are. Doesn't mean they get to crash the party." Declan's voice was dry, tight. "There's this thing called personal space. Try it sometime."

Noah just smiled, unbothered. "Relax, man. I come in peace. Ask your friend. He knows I'm not the worst."

Aiden hesitated, then said, "It's fine. He's cool."

Noah raised his beer in a mock toast. "See? A ringing endorsement."

Declan pushed to his feet without a word. He shoved the journal beneath his arm, muttered words Aiden didn't catch and stalked off into the night. That left just him and Noah.

Noah's smirk softened. "Come on." He nodded toward the stretch of beach leading to Silver Shoals. "You look like you could use a break."

Aiden looked toward the bonfire, toward Heather and Ophelia, toward the classmates who had once been familiar. Then he followed Noah into the dark, leaving the noise behind.

Silver Shoals' walls muted the crash of the tide below.

Aiden followed Noah up the spiraling iron staircase. The metal sighed with age, like the lighthouse might give in at any moment. Sounds from the bonfire faded with every turn, replaced by their echoing footsteps and the wind squeezing through streaked portholes.

At the top, Noah shoved open the lantern room door. Moonlight spilled through jagged panes, slicing the dust-choked air with silver. The rusted machinery stood like skeletal remains beneath the dome. The space reeked of brine and abandonment. Aiden couldn't remember the last time he'd stood in this room, only that it hadn't felt this empty.

"Creepy," Noah muttered, trailing his fingers along the corroded lantern base. "My buddy Rowan said this place is haunted. Supposedly, a group of students held a séance to reach the old lighthouse keeper. Legend goes he used to lock kids in the tower and bleed them dry. Said it kept the light burning longer."

Aiden smirked. Silver Shoals had a dozen stories. From ghosts and demon possessions to poisonous moss that made you lose your mind. But the version adults told, the one said with a shrug over brandy, was simpler: they never found another lighthouse keeper. So brick by brick, the place became unloved until it became what it is.

He stepped further inside, gaze sweeping the fractured glass walls and the warped floorboards. "Honestly, I'd be more surprised if it wasn't haunted."

Noah pulled a joint from his jacket. "You good with this?"

Aiden hadn't touched weed since freshman year, when Declan and Lola dared him to try. That night had ended with him on a bench behind the tennis courts, staring at stars that weren't there. But Noah watched him like he already knew what'd he'd say.

"Yeah," Aiden said. "Sure."

Noah struck the lighter, shielding the flame with his hand. The spark briefly lit his face, highlighting the dip of his upper lip and the fair stubble along his jaw. He inhaled, turned the joint, then offered it. Their fingers brushed warm where their skin met. Aiden took a breath too deep and coughed immediately, his stomach turning over.

Noah laughed, low and patient. "Not a pro, huh?"

Aiden grimaced, his throat tender. "Is it that obvious?" He handed it back, already regretting it.

Noah took another drag. The ember glowed. "Second try's always better."

Aiden narrowed his eyes but took the joint again. "I'm not convinced that's true."

A few minutes passed before they stepped onto the balcony. The wind hit hard, salted and sharp, pulling at their clothes and hair. They lingered where the rusted railing curled around the lighthouse in a crooked, precarious loop. One section bent outward as if someone had struck it before falling through.

Aiden stared at the misshapen metal. He didn't know why, but the sight unsettled him.

"Maybe we should stay inside," Noah said, eyes fixed on the same spot.

"Yeah. That's probably not a bad idea."

The lantern room hung in the quiet haze, thick with the curl of smoke drifting from Noah's finger. They sat in old beach chairs, close enough that their knees nearly brushed, backs turned to the cracked glass behind them. Far below, the bonfire flickered like an ember inside a snow globe—muted, distant, while the wind tapped at the windows like it was trying to get in.

"You don't really seem like the party type," Noah said, flicking ash into the mouth of dented soda can.

Aiden glanced sideways, lips tugging into a half-smile. "Neither do you."

"Fair. But I fake it pretty well."

Aiden gave a small shrug, leaned forward on his knees. "I don't. Never learned how."

Noah bumped his shoulder, just enough to register. "That's what I like about you."

"I'm not sure that's a compliment."

"It is." Noah's voice softened. "You don't try to be someone else."

Aiden's smile faded a little. "Declan's says that's part of the problem."

"Declan Albatross, right. He seems…complicated."

"He is." Aiden paused. "But he's always been there for me."

"Even complicated people can be constants." Noah's tone was gentle, not pushing. "Still. Doesn't mean they always get you."

He rubbed his palm across his knee, debating how far to go. "I've got stuff that makes school harder. I take twice as long to get through assignments. Reading comprehension, essays—none of it comes easy. I wouldn't have passed middle school without him. He used to come over after crew practice, rewrite half my work in ways I could understand. Sit with me until I finished. Even when he had his own stuff going on."

Smoke unraveled between them, a ribbon twisting in shadow.

"So yes," Aiden said. "He can be complicated. But he's also the reason I made it to the end of high school."

Noah was quiet. "Most people wouldn't do that. Not in the way you described. That's not loyalty. That's love. Whether or not he knew it."

The words hit a nerve Aiden didn't want to acknowledge.

Noah glanced sideways. "And for what it's worth…you made it. That's yours too."

The glass rattled in the wind. Below, waves dragged rock against rock.

"That was a good answer," Aiden said. "Do you say stuff like that a lot?"

Noah gave a lopsided grin. "Only when I mean it."

Aiden hadn't meant to say so much. But Noah hadn't flinched. He didn't prod or reframe it into something delicate. He didn't treat Aiden like his mother did, like every vulnerability was a crack she had to plaster over. He'd listened as if the mess wasn't a flaw to correct, but a part of him that deserved to exist.

They let the quiet settle. The night wrapped close, and the space between them shrank.

"What about you?" Aiden asked. "You don't scream party guy either."

Noah stretched his legs, flicking the last bit of ash. "I enjoy people watching. Seeing how they act when they think no one's looking."

"You're observant?"

"Pays off. Like now. You've got that look like your head's somewhere else."

Aiden followed his gaze to the floor, then out to the sea. "Do you ever think about how fast it goes?"

"Existential thoughts already?" Noah said, grinning. "Didn't think I rolled that strong."

Aiden almost laughed. "I'm serious. One minute you feel like you have time, and the next it's slipping through your fingers."

"Sounds like you're carrying more than school stress."

"I don't know," Aiden said. "There's so much I want to do. And I don't know if I'll get the chance. I feel like I'm already behind. Like the clock's running out before I've even started."

Noah leaned in, elbows on his thighs. "You're here though. Still standing. That counts for more than you think."

Aiden met his gaze. "What if doing what I want isn't enough?"

Noah's gaze dropped to his lips and back. "Maybe it's not about enough. Maybe it's about now."

The air thickened with smoke and salt. Aiden didn't move. Didn't look away. Noah shifted closer, his knee brushing Aiden's. He reached out, fingers grazing along Aiden's wrist—gentle, tentative. A test of what could be. Aiden tilted his chin. Their breath mingled in the space between them, and for a moment, it felt like the world had folded in around this small, quiet corner. Just the two of them, suspended between a thought and a decision.

Then came a splash—loud and sudden—echoing from the water below.

Aiden jerked back. They both turned toward the window, where the glow of the bonfire flickered in the distance.

"I—" Aiden's voice caught. "I'm sorry. I thought…"

Noah didn't flinch. He just exhaled, steady. "It's okay."

But he didn't look at him. Not fully. Aiden's hand curled in has lap. The warmth that had started to bloom now twisted into something quieter.

"We should probably head back," Noah said, rising to his feet, brushing ash from his sleeve. "Before Declan comes stomping with a torch."

"Yeah," Aiden murmured. "Yeah, okay."

Noah's footsteps faded down the stairs, leaving only the wind rattling through the broken panes and the distant hush of waves below. He stayed a moment longer, as if the room might return to what almost was. Eventually, he followed, the soles of his shoes grating against rusted metal. Each step felt slower than the last, reluctant, like his body was moving forward while something else remained behind.

CHAPTER 50
Lola Godfrey

THE TIDE WHISPERED AT HER SIDE UP AHEAD, THE BONFIRE BURNED high, its glow reaching toward the dunes that unraveled in the direction of the Academy. Firelight grazed her shoulders but never touched her face. Her arm throbbed. The hellhound's bite had darkened over the day. The skin mottling into a sickly gray violet with swollen edges. The pain had crept in, persistent and intentional, like it knew what it was doing to her. She shook it off. Or she tried to. And kept moving.

Her gaze found Ophelia near the waterline. A cup dangled from her fingers, her head tilted while moonlight caught her new haircut. It made her look colder. Or maybe she'd always looked like that, and Lola was only now willing to see it. She wore a charcoal duster with a high collar, its hem trailing over lace-up boots. Beneath, layers of black—matte satin, sheer gauze—shifted in the wind. She looked like she'd been dress for a funeral no one else had been invited to.

Still, Lola couldn't see what Declan saw in her. Not when it came to personality. Ophelia Lockhart was one of the most beautiful girls she'd ever seen. That wasn't in question. But the rest? The aloofness, the guarded glances, the way she held herself like nothing and no one could touch her. It baffled her. And it wasn't because Lola was secretly in love with Declan like some clichéd schoolgirl crush. She used to think she was, back when they were younger, before the world sharpened its edges. What she wanted was his attention. The kind he gave to people like Aiden and Camille. The kind that made you feel chosen. She craved it in the way someone craves sunlight after too many wintry days.

Lola approached Ophelia, spine straight. She wouldn't appear weak. Not in front of her.

"You look like awful." Ophelia's eyes swept over her, drifted toward her arm, where Lola had tugged her sleeve high.

"And yet, you can't stop looking at me."

"Do you need something, or are you just here to linger?"

Lola glanced toward the bonfire. "Why did you ask Declan to meet you at the Drowned Pearl?"

Ophelia sighed. "I needed to talk to him."

"About what?"

"Why do you care?" Ophelia turned back toward the sea.

Lola stepped closer, the surf curling near her heels. "Did you tell him what happened at Silver Shoals?"

Ophelia's hand tensed around her cup. "No. I haven't."

"You saw me fall. You thought I was dead. And you've told no one."

Ophelia didn't answer right away. When she did, "You should be grateful I haven't."

Lola let out an incredulous laugh. "Oh, grateful, is it? Should I send you a thank-you note? Maybe flowers? A tasteful arrangement, obviously."

Ophelia's face had shifted. Not coldness. Not distance. Just exhaustion. Like whatever she'd been holding onto had clawed at her from inside, scraping everything it touched.

"I didn't push you," she said. "The railing broke. I thought we established that."

"And you haven't told Declan. Or Heather. Which is odd, considering how close the two of you seem. Where is Heather, by the way?"

"If you have to know, she wasn't feeling well. But please, what would me telling anyone do? Make you feel better? Make me look worse?"

The fall didn't matter. Not compared to the look on Ophelia's face when she saw her alive at the Founders' Ball. She had thought Lola was dead and done nothing. If the roles were reversed, Lola would've searched until her lungs gave out. She would've scaled the rocks herself, screaming Ophelia's name into the dark, refusing to leave without proof. Not out obligation or show. But because love, once felt, didn't vanish just because it hurt.

"I don't understand what happened that night," Ophelia said. "But since you keep asking why I haven't told anyone."

"I'm listening," Lola said. "Go on. Let's hear the noble speech."

"You would've told everyone. If it had been me who fell, if you'd walk away from it." Her gaze narrowed. "You would've ruined me. You would've spun the story until you came out the martyr. Because that's what you do. You strike first."

Lola's breath hitched.

"You turn everything into strategy. It's how you've always survived. I don't blame you for being that way. But I'm not playing anymore."

Lola held her stare. "And here I thought you liked that about me."

"I did, and I think that was the problem. We enabled each other like fire and gasoline." Her voice softened. "You don't change. You adapt. You twist yourself into whatever shape the world rewards most. I may have left without saying goodbye, but at least I came back different."

She turned and walked toward the bonfire.

Lola stepped forward. "Who said I was done talking?"

Ophelia glanced over her shoulder, eyes tired beneath the moonlight. "But I am."

She kept walking. The flame swallowed her. Lola stayed where she was, arms crossed, wind catching her hair.

You would've ruined me. You would've spun the story until you came out the martyr.

The thought burrowed in, even though she should've let it roll off her. She should've laughed and ripped her apart with words. But Ophelia's words pricked like a thorn, catching at a part of her she didn't want to acknowledge. Being around Ophelia had always been like staring into a mirror that showed you everything you wanted to believe and everything you tried to hide.

Lola pressed the bite. It pulsed, warm and watchful, like it had heard every word. The dizziness swelled again, blurring sound and sight. She turned from the waves, each step heavier than the last.

Past the dunes, beyond the firelight, the gravel lot came into view. Xavier waited in the front seat, headlights dimmed, engine purring like he knew not to ask questions. He stepped out as she approached, his hand already on the door handle. His eyes scanned the lack in her posture and the way she held her arm.

"Miss Godfrey," he said gently "You look unwell. Shall I call someone?"

Her throat burned. She steadied herself on the doorframe. "No. I need to go home. Now."

"Are you certain? Perhaps St. Augustine would be best," he said. "I can call your brother."

"I said home."

Without another word, Xavier helped her in the car and closed the door behind her.

They eased into motion, leaving the bonfire behind in shimmering orange and smoke.

CHAPTER 51
Declan Albatross

Fog clung to Albatross House, smothering the estate in a veil of damp gray. It slithered over the gables and spires, swallowing stone and shadow. Salt-stained vines clutched the façade, their brittle tendrils worming into every crack, every weathered carving. Declan stood at the threshold. The journal tugged at his shoulder from inside the messenger bag. Even here, away from the ocean, he swore he could still hear the siren's song echoing through him.

The doors opened beneath his hand, heavy and silent. The memory clung to him like sea-slicked cloth—what he'd seen in the surf. A real siren. Not a fever dream or a sketch from the journal. His ancestors had drawn creatures like it, but seeing one—hearing its music—had torn myth into flesh. He needed answers. Now more than ever.

He walked past the music room and slowed. Doris sat at the piano, hunched, her cardigan slipping from one shoulder, sleeves puddled around her wrists. Her hands hovered over the keys like a ghost trying to remember how to haunt.

"I didn't know you were playing again," Declan said, voice low. Seeing her there, almost as she once was, felt too delicate to disturb.

Tears shimmered in her eyes, but she wiped them away with her hand. "Oh, I–I'm not." She pulled herself straight, conjuring a brittle smile. "I didn't hear you come in. How was the race? Did you win?"

"It was a bonfire, Mom."

"Right." Her voice faltered. "Of course. Silly me." She pressed two fingers to her temple and closed her eyes. "I'm sorry."

Her hands dropped back to the keys and pressed one. The note came out off-key. "I used to hear music in everything. Wind through the trees, waves hitting the shore. But now, when I sit here…" Her words unraveled. She closed the lid softly.

Declan stepped into the room but kept his distance. "What do you hear instead?"

She drifted toward the stained-glass window. The design bloomed outward like a compass rose, framed in kelp and rolling waves rendered in green and gold. Her fingers brushed the glass, and the dull light spilled across her skin in shifting shades of ocean and sunlight.

"It's not all bad," she murmured. "Not if you see it that way. The water…" Her voice trailed, lost to some memory.

Declan stiffened. The siren stirred in his mind. He reached for the journal from his bag and laid it on the piano.

"There's a humming—" Doris's eyes landed on the cover and her face tightened. "Headmistress Mortimer called. You brought it to the Academy."

"You knew. All this time."

"I hoped it wasn't real. That maybe it skipped you." She stepped forward but not close enough to touch him. "I didn't keep it from you to hurt you. I kept it because I love you. Because I remember what it did."

She swallowed. "Your grandfather had a chance to destroy it. He didn't. Instead, he charted tides and moons and dreams, convinced it was speaking to him. He said only we could understand it—us, the Albatross line. I begged him to stop. But he said it was tradition. And it was mine now."

For once, her words didn't twist or dodge.

"What did he make you do?" Declan asked.

She opened her mouth, then closed it again. "I'd rather you didn't make me say."

He looked at the grief swimming in her eyes. At the way her body moved as if underwater. Whatever his grandfather had forced on her hadn't just scarred her. It had hollowed her out. She had once been a scared girl dealing with a force she didn't understand.

"So, this," he said, brushing the journal's spine, "this is what broke you."

Familiarity passed over her expression, one he hadn't seen in years. The mother who hummed through storms and who kissed his forehead goodnight. The one who once existed before the ocean took her.

"Don't worry about me," she said. "What matters now is how you carry it."

"Carry what?" Frustration clawed at his throat. "What is this even about? What happens now that I've signed my name?"

She lowered her gaze. "You were always going to. The journal would've driven you to it, eventually."

"Then why fight it?"

A faint laugh slipped out. "Maybe it's how the ocean keeps its debts. Maybe it's how it remembers who took more than they gave."

"Is this why Dad left? Did he find out?"

Her face stilled. "I told him. Once," she said. "He couldn't accept it. Not what it meant for me. Or for you. That's why he never wanted another child."

The questions rose fast and sharp, but her eyes were already going distant.

"Mom…" His voice cracked. "Should I be afraid?"

An old glimmer flashed behind her eyes, but then she turned to the window, whispering to the air.

"The deep is terrifying, yes." Her gaze drifted toward the journal. "You showed Aiden, didn't you? Good."

She smiled, clouded, as if speaking through a haze. "Irene called today. Will you tell her it was lovely to hear her voice?" She traced patterns across her sleeve. "No, I don't go too far in. They bite."

Declan gripped the journal tighter. His vision blurred, not from fatigue, but from tears he couldn't stop. He didn't cry for the version of her standing in front of him. That grief was old. This was worse. It was knowing that no matter how much he needed her, no matter how many times he begged the universe for guidance, he was alone.

He opened his mouth to call her back, to ask more questions, but the words wouldn't come. What could he ask that hadn't already withered between them? What answer would change what she'd become? She spoke again, caught in a conversation only she could hear. She turned slightly, smiling like he hadn't been standing there the whole time.

And Declan, with the journal pressed to his chest and salt clinging to his skin, stood in a house that had never felt emptier.

CHAPTER 52
Lola Godfrey

THE CHANDELIER BURNED TOO BRIGHT, EACH BULB A SHARP BLADE driving straight through her skull. The marble floor swayed beneath her, and the walls seemed to breathe—stretching and contracting in a taunting rhythm. She caught the doorframe, fingers clenching into the molding hard enough to leave impressions. From a distance, she might've looked like a girl sneaking in after one too many drinks. That would've been easier to explain. Simpler than admitting her own body was turning into a traitor.

"You're home earlier than I expected." The voice floated in from the kitchen. "How was the bonfire? Did Declan get plastered as usual?"

Her mouth opened, but her tongue felt heavy as she pushed forward, legs wobbling. Her hip struck the edge of console table, hard enough to send a tremor through the wood. Decorations rattled. A vase tipped, then shattered against the floor in a burst of glass and water.

"What the hell is going on?" Faustino's voice sharpened as he rounded the corner, his face swimming in and out of focus. "Are you drunk?"

"Faust…" She reached for him, her other hand trembling as she dragged back her sleeve.

The bite had become an ink-like stain that branched like veins across her arm.

Her knees folded, and she crumpled at his feet, the light above her spinning.

When Faustino lifted her, the movement barely registered. Cold air raised goosebumps along her skin. Behind them, the chandelier's glow was swallowed by the hush over the estate. Only the driveway lights remained, pale and harsh, casting shadows that blurred at the edges of her vision.

Her head spun. Nausea boiled up. A garbled sound escaped her throat.

Maybe she'd tried to speak. Maybe it was the pain breaking loose. The world rocked as Faustino eased her into the car's back seat. Cold leather pressed against her spine. The engine rumbled to life, vibrating through her. Tires whispered across pavement. The night dissolved into motion. And then darkness again.

When she surfaced, her cheek was pressed to Faustino's jacket, his scent cutting through the haze. Cool air licked at her fevered skin, and gravel crunched beneath them. Some part of her expected to be at St. Augustine. But even through the depths of her confusion, she knew that no doctor could diagnose whatever was happening to her. She tried to lift her head, to ask where he was taking her, but the effort sank through her limbs.

His arms tightened around Lola's limp body.

"You shouldn't have come here," a woman said. "If your father finds out, he'll never forgive you."

Faustino stepped forward, breath ragged. "I didn't know where else to go. Please. I think she's dying."

Dying.

The word snagged in Lola's mind, a hook pulling her up from the dark. Her eyes parted, lashes fluttering as light bled into her vision. The air carried the scent of damp earth, herbs, and smoke. A figure stood before them, her silhouette backlit by a porch lantern that glowed behind a curtain of ivy. Her hair shimmered in the light, but the rest of her remained shadowed.

A drawn-out sigh broke the stillness.

"Come inside. I'll see what I can do."

A plush surface met her back. Fire crackled nearby. Lola forced her eyes open.

Faustino leaned into view, his face lined with a fear she'd never seen in him. He had always been unshakable. The older brother who teased her, protected her, taught her how to lie with a straight face. But that steadiness was gone. A woman stood behind him, her features haloed and indistinct in firelight.

"Faust…" Lola's voice cracked.

"I'm right here." His fingers wrapped around hers. "This is going to work, right?"

The woman's hand settled on Lola's forehead, a jarring contrast to the heat radiating from within her. "I haven't done this since I was a teenager," she said. "But it should remove the bite."

That voice. It was familiar.

Lola's brow twitched. "What's…what's happening?"

"Shhh." The woman brushed the damp hair clinging to her temples. "I'm sure you're scared, sweetheart. You have every right to be."

There was an edge in her voice that Lola had grown up around. She blinked hard, trying to decipher the silhouette. Slowly, the woman's face emerged from the blur, features sharpening like a photograph in solution.

"This never should have happened to you," Irene Oldwyck murmured.

The ache in Lola's arm surged, sharpening everything. She clung to her words, tried to grasp their meaning, but it was like trying to hold water.

"I need you to trust me." Irene said, eyes fixed on the bite. Her touch hovered, light as air, but it still made Lola flinch. "Your brother is here. You're not alone." She paused, gaze flicking between them. "But I must warn you both, this will hurt."

Faustino hesitated. His voice came low and ready. "Do whatever you need to do. Just help her. Please."

Irene lifted Lola's arm into the firelight. The bite glared back at them, blackened and swollen, its edges branching out like poisoned veins. Irene studied the mark, her brow furrowed.

Footsteps padded into the room.

"Mom?"

Through the haze, Aiden appeared. His maroon pajama shirt clung to his frame, hair sleep-mussed, but his eyes—sharpened behind tortoiseshell glasses—were wide awake. He looked from Irene to Lola, the connection settling across his face. "This is about the hellhound, isn't it?"

Irene exhaled. "We don't have time for this, button. Please give the Godfrey's their privacy."

Lola met Aiden's eyes, and she seemed to have calmed. Seventeen years she'd carried the truth alone. The Godfrey's gift. The pain. The secrecy.

"Let him stay," she rasped.

Faustino tensed. "Lola, no. We can't—"

"I understand this isn't my place," Irene said, calmly. "But perhaps they'll make wiser choices than those before them."

Lola didn't understand. It didn't matter. If she was dying, if this was her only chance, let them see.

Irene's hand returned to her arm. "This will be quite painful. Stay as still as you can."

A blue ember sparked in her palm. Quiet at first, steady as a heartbeat. The light bathed Lola's face, casting blue shadows over her sweat-drenched skin.

The flame dropped, and Lola screamed.

The pain was immediate, electric. It tore through her like lightning. She arched, but Faustino and Aiden held her down, bracing her shoulders and arms as her body convulsed. Her thoughts shattered. She clawed into Faustino's wrist, her scream torn by ragged sobs. Aiden said words meant to smooth, but they couldn't find her.

She bit her tongue. Blood flooded her mouth.

The fire sank into her veins, purging whatever poison had rooted there. Irene remained focused, even as the smell of scorched flesh filled the air. Lola's sobs thinned into shallow gasps. Her limbs trembled, muscles unraveling one by one. The pain didn't fade. It just snapped. And then it was gone. She crumpled against the cushions, chest heaving, her mind blank. The ember in Irene's palm flickered once more, and extinguished. Darkness edged in again. But this time, it was peaceful.

CHAPTER 53
Aiden Oldwyck

AIDEN SAT BY THE FIREPLACE, THE WOODEN CHAIR PRESSING INTO HIS back. Across from him, Lola lay curled beneath a quilt, one arm tucked beneath her head. She looked strange like this. Unguarded. Stripped of glamour and razor-edged confidence. For as long as he'd known her, she had never let herself unravel. Not in public. Maybe not even in private. But in the fire's glow, she seemed smaller, less invincible.

It reminded him of the fourth grade, when a group of boys tried to corner him during recess for wearing Ophelia's nail polish. Before he'd said a word, Lola had stepped between them—tiny and terrifying, in a velvet headband and penny loafers—daring them to try.

They never did.

She stirred on the couch, brow furrowing. A murmur slipped from her before she shot upright, eyes panicked.

"Hey." Aiden leaned forward, gently touching her wrist. "You're okay."

She pressed a hand to her chest. When her gaze landed on him, hazel eyes heavy with sleep, the alarm in them ebbed and folded back to her usual indifference. "Where's my brother?"

"He's speaking to your father about what happened."

Lola's fingers brushed the spot where the bite had been. She shifted but winced before she smoothed it away. "Guess this means I survived."

Aiden huffed a laugh, leaning back into the chair. "I'd say barely."

Her lips curled. "Barely still counts." A beat passed. "Thanks for sticking around. I'm sure there's a whole list of people you'd rather be babysitting."

Such a simple acknowledgment. So flippant. But Aiden had seen her break—venom in her veins, her body seizing beneath his mother's hands. He'd watch Irene burn it out, scorched flesh thickening the air, Lola's screams echoing through the manor. Without her, she might've—he shoved the thought aside.

"So, you're some kind of healer?" he asked. "My mother let that slip. But even that, it's not supposed to work on hellhound bites." He hesitated, then added. "You shouldn't have survived. But you did. Because you're you."

Lola flexed her fingers, rotating her arm. "Good to know I have an Achilles' heel, I guess."

The fire crackled, casting patterns across the damask wallpaper, flickering in Aiden's glasses.

"How are you holding up?" he asked.

Lola blinked, caught off guard. "What?"

"You know. Tonight. Everything." He gestured vaguely. "My mother turned into a flamethrower. Figured that might be…a lot."

She let out a breath—half a laugh. "Please. That barely cracks my top ten strangest things this year."

"You're ridiculous."

"And yet you keep me around." Her smirk softened as she pulled the blanket tighter. "But really, I should ask you that. This must be emotionally taxing. Have you always known?"

He ran a hand through his hair. "In a way, yes. But me and her never talked about it. She preferred pretending things were normal."

Lola studied him for a moment, then nodded. "Well, pretending's overrated. You don't have to do this alone anymore."

She traced a loose thread at the hem of the blanket, hesitated, then looked up. "And for what it's worth…I know Declan and I kind of left you to deal with Heather."

"It's fine," he said quickly. "Honestly, I think I've moved on."

Her brows lifted, interest sparking. "Oh? Do tell. Who's the lucky girl?"

He shifted in his seat, gaze drifting toward the fire.

Lola tilted her head. A smirk formed. "Lucky guy, then?"

His pulse quickened. Not from fear exactly, but from exposure. She'd said it so casually, like it was nothing. Like it didn't matter. And maybe it was only a flicker of curiosity, a tease. But something in him still braced, a tension born from years of uncertainty. He hadn't said it aloud to anyone. Not even to himself, not completely. There was safety in ambiguity, in letting people assume. But Lola didn't assume. She saw. And somehow, that terrified him more than if she'd laughed.

She eased back into the cushions. "We'll unpack that once I'm not fresh off the brink of death."

Aiden shook his head, but a small smile crept in anyway.

Silence settled again, filled only by the crackle of burning logs.

"So you know about me now," Lola said. "The healing thing… What does that make you?"

A bitter smile tugged at his lips. "Nothing. Magic runs through the women in my family. I'm just…me."

He didn't say the rest: that sometimes he wondered what it would feel like to have power like his mother or sister. To move through the world with a secret hidden beneath the skin. But if that was the trade—magic in exchange for not being hunted—he'd give it up in a heartbeat.

Lola watched him with a strange tenderness. "At least you get to be normal."

He rubbed his hands together. "Does Declan know?"

"Not yet," she admitted. "Now that you do, I feel like I should tell him. I just don't know how."

"He might understand. He found this journal—some creepy thing tied to his ancestors."

Her eyes narrowed. "Let me guess. He won't let anyone near it?"

"Pretty much. I've been thinking it might actually be evil."

"That sounds about right. Declan finds one cursed object and suddenly he's the main character."

He laughed, briefly. Then she added, more quietly, "It's wild, isn't it? All this time, our families kept everything from us like some treasured family recipe."

"What do you mean?"

"The founding families," she said. "There was a split. A fallout. Whatever it was, it was big. Big enough that they thought it was better to keep us apart than to tell the truth."

Aiden's brows furrowed as he leaned forward, elbows braced on his knees. "There's six, right?"

Lola shook her head, brushing hair from her face. "Four. Godfrey. Looks like we can count Albatross and Oldwyck."

He sat back. "Gotcha. So the fourth is the banshee."

"You do know more than you've let on."

"Not really." He shrugged. "I've just overheard my mother and aunt whispering. They think there's a banshee in Driftmoor. And that it's connected to the hellhound attacks."

"My brother thinks so too," Lola murmured, rubbing her arms. "And I think I know who it is."

"Who?"

She raised her eyebrows. "Miss-Not-In-Kansas-Anymore herself."

He stared at her.

"The scholarship girl," she clarified. "Dorothy Gale. Or Hale.

Whatever. My brother thinks she's a banshee." She paused, then added, "Which would make her a Marek."

"Marek?"

"The exiled family." She searched his face. "Your mother never told you about them?"

"There's a lot she hasn't told me."

She grabbed his hand and gave it a small, steady squeeze. She didn't need to say anything else. The look in her eyes said it clearly enough: *You're not alone anymore.*

Aiden stared into the fire, its flicker catching the edges of his thoughts.

If Dorothy was a Marek—if she was the banshee—maybe there was a way to use that. A way for him to survive his birthday. But if he used her, if he exploited her the way the matriarchy had used his curse, what would that make him? Even thinking about it made him feel sick. Would that make him any better than Aunt Maeve?

CHAPTER 54
Dorothy Hale

THE TROLLEY RATTLED OVER THE TRACKS, ITS WHEELS GROANING against the metal.

Dorothy clutched the leather strap overhead, her grip tightening with each shuddering jolt. A headache pinched behind her eyes, pulsing in sync with the lurching carriage. Streetlights blurred past in streaks. Halloween decorations clung to iron fences and lampposts—bats cut from paper, scarecrows with waterlogged faces, and skeletons that twisted in chains. A witch dangled crookedly from a storefront awning, her painted grin dripping in the drizzle.

Across from her, the only other passenger sat beneath a wide black hat, her face obscured. Dorothy tried not to look, but the woman's stillness felt more statue than person.

Up ahead, St. Augustine rose from the fog, a monolith of stone and archways. Rain glazed its façade, turning the building into a glistening sentinel. Even from inside the trolley, the place radiated a pressure that curled in her stomach. She could already smell the antiseptic and feel the cold fluorescent lights.

This was Headmistress Mortimer's idea. A sleep study, courtesy of the Academy. *Just precautionary, given your episode at the cemetery.* Dorothy had agreed, though she hated the idea of being treated like a problem.

The trolley hissed as it came to a stop, steam curling from it like breath in the cold. As she stepped toward the exit, she glanced back at the woman beneath the black hat. She hadn't moved. Not even to look up.

Dorothy hesitated.

"Good luck, kid," Neil said from the conductor's seat.

She nodded without turning, more to acknowledge the moment than him. The doors opened with a groan. The rain hit her face like pinpricks. She pulled her backpack closer and looked up toward the entrance. Lanterns flickered at the base of the steps. The doors gleamed like ice, concealing the sterile world beyond. The last time she'd left this place, she hadn't looked back. After the crash, after the wreckage of her life had been stitched together with IVs and morphine, she'd fled toward whatever scraps of normal she could salvage. But now, standing here again, her feet refused to move.

St. Augustine wasn't just a hospital. It was a witness.

One that had seen her come back to life and remembered.

Dorothy hugged herself after changing into a hospital gown. The fabric clung against her, thin and institutional, and vaguely damp, as if it had absorbed the unease of everyone who'd worn it before. Slipping into it felt like stepping back into a memory of fluorescent rooms and muffled cries. The walls were different, but the air smelled the same sterile dread.

The sleep study room resembled a motel room more than a medical suite, with beige walls, a warped dresser, a bed, and a nightstand chipped at the corners. A chemical tang lingered beneath the surface, faint but inescapable, mixing with the hum of hidden machinery. *To make patients feel at home*, the technician had said, as if home was somewhere you were wired so someone else could measure what was wrong inside your head.

"Ready for me to hook you up?" the technician asked, gesturing toward the sagging bed.

Dorothy sat on the edge. She flinched when the first adhesive electrode touched her scalp. Cold. Sticky. Intimate in a clinical way.

"These record your brain activity." The woman pressed leads to Dorothy's temples. "This will monitor your breathing," she continued, wrapping a strap snugly around her waist. "And this," she added, clipping a device to Dorothy's finger, "tracks your oxygen levels."

Dorothy's gaze slid toward the observation window. At first glance, it looked like a mirror. But she knew better. Someone sat behind that glass, watching. Listening. Pen tapping against a clipboard.

"What happens if I can't fall asleep?" she asked.

The technician grinned. "Most people don't. That's normal. Just try to relax."

Relax. In a hospital gown. With wires trailing from her skin. Watched like an insect pinned to a card.

The door shut behind the technician with a soft click.

Dorothy reached for her sketchbook, careful not to pull at the wires. She hadn't drawn since coming to Driftmoor. Every time she tried, the pencil felt like it belonged to someone she used to be. But tonight, her fingers moved on their own. No plan. No thought. Just graphite on paper. The room blurred. The scrape of pencil against the page melded with the mechanical buzz and the tightening pulse of the electrode pads. The mirrored glass faded to black. She forgot she was being watched.

She surfaced like a diver breaking through water.

A hellhound stared up from the page. Crouched, limbs too long, its body coiled and bristling with fur. Its claws dragged through a heap of human bones she hadn't meant to draw. The snarl on its face revealed fangs, but it was the hollow and burning eyes that tightened her stomach. She dropped the pencil just as a knock snapped through the silence.

The door opened, and Alma stepped in, draped in her habit. Her hands folded at her waist, rosary beads clinking with each step. Dorothy hadn't seen her since discharge. The woman looked unchanged, her presence was as grave as a prayer whispered in the dark.

"I was told you'd returned for the night," Alma said. "I thought I might look in on you. Just for a moment."

Dorothy nodded, uncertain. "That's kind of you."

Alma's eyes dropped to the sketchbook. "I see you're finally drawing again."

"I didn't mean to." Dorothy hesitated. "It just…happened."

Alma approached, eyes settling on the page. Her mouth thinned. "I know this shape."

"You do?"

"There are stories older than this hospital. Some say such creatures walk between the veil and the earth. Hounds of judgment. Called when the balance tips too far."

Dorothy swallowed. "Have you seen one?"

Alma's fingers tightened on the rosary. "Once. I was a child—too young to lie well. It stood outside our chapel after my sister died. I thought it an omen. The priest told me I was mistaken." She looked at Dorothy. "But I have not mistaken it since."

A long silence passed between them.

"They're not always sent to destroy," Alma murmured, more to herself than to Dorothy. "But they are never sent without purpose."

The observation door opened. The technician stepped in, clipboard tucked against her hip. "Lights out in five."

Alma inclined her head. "Then I'll take my leave." She turned to Dorothy with sorrow in her eyes. "Do not be afraid of what you are, child. But do not take it lightly, either."

And then she was gone, the soft clatter of rosary beads trailing her as the door closed again. Dorothy looked down. The hellhound stared, etched in graphite, eyes smoldering.

The adhesive sensors tugged at her skin as she shifted. Wires tethered her to the bed. It reminded her where she was, but the deeper discomfort came from an itch. Not physical but in her nerves like static. A pressure in the air. The sense of being watched.

Her eye swept across the dim room. The armchair was no longer empty. A woman sat in it, her hands folded in her lap, her face obscured by a curtain of dark red hair. Dorothy couldn't tell if she was breathing. Fear prickled at her spine, but so did recognition. Not of the woman, but of the hush that came with her. Slowly, she sat up. The wires brushed across her skin as she moved across the cold linoleum.

The woman stood to meet her. "You shouldn't have come here," she said. "They can smell you."

Dorothy kept walking toward her.

"They made monsters of us," the woman murmured. "Not with claws or teeth, but with lullabies that soured in our mouths. They sang over our cradles and bonded us before we had a name for it. And when we got older, they carved the future from our palms with hands that claimed it was love."

Her voice sounded as if Dorothy had once heard it in a dream.

"I don't understand," Dorothy whispered. "Who are you talking about?"

The woman's skin looked normal. But then Dorothy saw the cracks spidering across her face and throat. A strange shimmer pulsed in the crevices. Dorothy didn't know why, but she raised her hand, fingers hovering above the woman's cheek. Trembling, she brushed the flesh—and whatever lived inside wriggled.

It crawled out, antennae twitching, and crept across Dorothy's hand. A beetle. Jet-black and glistening. Its legs ticked as it climbed her wrist. Shortly, another followed. Then another. They emerged in droves, from the woman's mouth, her eyes, her throat, until Dorothy's arm was covered in a living, writhing sleeve.

Dorothy swayed. "What's happening to me?"

The woman's smile was soft. Almost maternal. "You're waking up."

Dorothy's head jerked back. Her spine arched. Her eyes rolled white, milky and sightless. A tremor passed through her body, but she didn't speak. The beetles slid from her arm in waves, as if her skin were a road they remembered.

"You were never meant for silence," the woman said. "They tried to quiet you—smother the sound before it could take shape. But the truth always survives. You were born to split the veil. To let the dead speak and the living tremble." She paused. "That is your inheritance."

It sounded like there was a heartbeat buried in the walls, syncing with the thudding in Dorothy's chest. The corners warped and shadows stretched inward. Her body stayed frozen, but her mind screamed, a fragile voice trapped inside bone. Every instinct told her to run, but there was nowhere to go.

The door burst open.

Light flooded in from the observation room and washed over Dorothy's face.

"Dorothy?" The technician's voice cut through the hum.

Dorothy looked around, blinking hard. The woman was gone. No beetles. She stood alone in the middle of the room, wires slack around her arms, her chest rising too fast.

The technician stepped closer. "Hey, are you alright? You're not supposed to be out of bed."

"I…I don't know."

The technician glanced at the monitor by the bed, her brows knitting. "Huh. Nothing unusual on the readings." She paused. "You must've been sleepwalking."

Dorothy's eyes dropped to the floor. A single beetle lay on its back, legs twitching.

"There!" she said, pointed. "Do you see it?"

The technician looked, grimaced, and stepped on it. "Gross. Old building. Happens sometimes. I'll call someone to clean it up."

Dorothy stared at the crushed shell, at the legs that refused to die. Her skin buzzed—not with fear, but as if her soul remembered that woman, but her mind couldn't recall from where. Like waking with a word on your tongue and no voice to speak it.

CHAPTER 55
Declan Albatross

HE THREW OFF THE COMFORTER. HIS FEET SANK INTO THE RUG before meeting the cold bite of hardwood. Moving on instinct, he drifted through the hushed corridors of Albatross House. He passed through the hall, down the grand staircase where shadows pooled beneath oil portraits and crossed the foyer's checkered tile. Another corridor stretched ahead. The back doors loomed at the end, tall and glass-paned, his unmoored reflection waiting in them.

The doors opened without resistance. Wind swept through his hair and across his bare chest. His pajama pants fluttered at his legs as he stepped barefoot onto the stone patio. Beyond the railing, the sea whispered like it knew his name.

The salt-stained staircase had appeared. He didn't remember deciding to move, but his feet carried him down. The wood groaned beneath each step as the beach greeted him in silence. Moonlight glazed the sand in silver and the tide reached for him. Somewhere in the back of his mind, a voice begged him to turn around. The water climbed around his calves, then his waist.

His breath hitched, not from the temperature, but from the shape shimmering beneath the surface. He knew how he had gotten there. He just didn't know why. He should've been terrified. Should've ran home. But his soaked pajamas clung to him, and he couldn't move. The world had narrowed to that fixed point ahead where the water stirred.

She rose from the depths. First her forehead, hair slicked across it like seaweed. Then eyes—blue and as wide as the moon. A nose. A mouth. Shoulders breached the surface, her skin luminous beneath the waves.

"You have your mother's eyes," she said.

Declan's mouth went dry. Every instinct screamed for him to back away, but his body refused, like being caught mid-step in a dream.

"Hers were clearer once," the woman said. "Before the sea got inside her."

He found himself unable to look away. It was like watching a star fall or a car crash, beautiful in a way that felt wrong. "You're not real," he whispered, more to himself than her.

"You Albatross men," her gaze swept over him, "always so easy to summon. So easy to frighten. Though getting you to cooperate has always been the challenge. Your grandfather came of his own will. And your mother, Doris…" She smiled faintly. "Sweet, foolish Doris. She thought I was something holy."

Her name made his stomach drop. The woman just smiled.

"Are you going to kill me?" His voice cracked, and he hated how it sounded.

Her head tilted, water slicking off her arms. "If I'd come for blood, you'd already be beneath the waves."

"Then…what do you want?"

One webbed finger brushed his collarbone. "A favor."

He flinched and stepped back. "What kind of favor?"

"I suppose you could call it a debt."

"Debt? I don't even know who you are."

"I'm Nerida," she said, as though that should mean something.

Her face was serene, almost human, but like a mask holding still for too long. He searched it for emotion, a tell, anything. But her eyes were as deep as the ocean and offered nothing. He forced himself not to let the fear show through his voice or on his face.

"You should be grateful," she added.

"Grateful? For what?"

"If not for me, you'd still be fumbling in the dark with that book of yours."

His mind leapt to Lake Vesper. The way the ink had revealed itself only after the pages were wet. "That was you? But the lake—how?"

She laughed mirthlessly. "You haven't read far enough, little heir. I took another form. Waited in that sour water until sundown," she said. "It tasted of rot. But it served its purpose."

A line from the journal surfaced—*They wear what the dead leave behind.* He hadn't understood it then. He wished he didn't. But now the meaning slid into place.

"What is it that you want from me?" he asked.

"It's simple. I want the astrolabe."

Declan's mouth opened. He tried to buy a second of clarity. "I—I've seen it in the journal, but that's it."

He could see it in her eyes that she didn't believe him.

"You lie poorly." She dipped her hand into the water. "Do you think I haven't been watching?"

"I'm not lying. I swear. I—I don't know where it is."

In a flash, her talon slashed across his chest.

He staggered, pain blooming as blood trickled down his skin. "What the—"

She raised the crimson-stained claw to her mouth and tasted it. Her eyelids fluttered. "You Albatrosses always taste of sorrow."

He gritted his teeth. "Why do you want it?"

"Do you truly wish to know?" Her voice dropped. "Because once, I loved a human. He sang to me like I was sacred—a god. He made a promise beneath a bleeding sky, and I have waited lifetimes for him to keep it." Her lips thinned. "You, of all people, should understand what it means to chase someone you've already lost."

The words struck deeper than they should have. He dropped his gaze.

"Find it for me," she said.

"But I wouldn't even know where to start."

"Begin with the journal. Dig through the waste your ancestors left behind. Or…ask Doris, if there's anything left of her to remember."

The journal hadn't mentioned the astrolabe. But it had warned of sirens and their hunger for control. How they bended thoughts, twisted truths, and sank commands beneath the surface of the mind.

Nerida's gaze fell to his wrist. "Drowned Man's Luck?"

He glanced down at the bracelet Ophelia made. "What? It's just a good luck bracelet."

"A girl gave it to you, didn't she?" she asked. "And you wore it like it mattered?"

She snapped the twine in one brisk motion. The shells scattered into the tide, vanishing beneath the waves. He stared at his bare wrist, the skin already feeling colder without it.

"I'll ask one final time," she said. "Will you find the astrolabe for me?"

He didn't understand what the astrolabe truly meant. But the way she said it sent a chill through him, like she was asking him to hand over the deed to Albatross House. Or something worse.

His voice came quiet. "No."

Her face didn't change. "Would you rather I take what you can't afford to lose?"

His heart skipped a beat.

"Perhaps the boy you keep beside you. The one with the tender voice and loyal brown eyes. Or the girl with all that shine and fury in her mouth. Perhaps—"

"Fine," he snapped. "I'll look. But leave them out of this. Please." He took a deep breath. "How long do I have?"

"Until the end of the month. I believe that's when you all wear your masks and pretend to be braver, stranger, better." She glanced at her webbed hand. "I never needed to pretend."

Halloween. That was less than five days away.

"Alright," he said. "I'll do it. But I want something in return."

She gave a soft sound—half sigh, half amusement. "You wish to bargain with me?"

"Yes. In exchange for the astrolabe, you help my mother."

Her expression shifted. "What's wrong with her?"

"She's—"

"Her spirit broke, didn't it? Madness, grief, the sea. It doesn't matter. I can stitch a semblance of her back together."

"We have a deal then?" he asked.

She reached toward his chest, traced the smear of blood, and brought it to her lips.

After savoring it, she murmured, "We have a deal, little heir."

Then her face changed. Her lips parted, revealing needle-pointed teeth. In a blink, she lunged. He stumbled back and water surged over, burning his nostrils, crushing his eardrums. He flailed through the current. When he surfaced, gasping, she was gone. Only the waves remained, lapping softly.

PART THREE

Halloween

In Driftmoor, Halloween is not a holiday. It is a warning. The one beneath the earth—the one who was promised things—listens for footsteps, for voices, for names spoken. They say if you feel watched, you are. And if you hear a knock with no one at the door, you've already let it in.
— From *The Driftmoor Almanac, 1899 Edition*

CHAPTER 56
Aiden Oldwyck

THE ORANGE JUMPSUIT WRINKLED AT THE SHOULDERS, HALF-ZIPPED over a t-shirt, a handcuff swinging from one wrist in the breeze. Albatross House loomed ahead, its lancet windows glowing while music throbbed faintly through stone. Normally, Camille hosted the Halloween party. This year, Declan had insisted. No one asked why. Aiden suspected it had to do with Ophelia.

The onyx-beaded chandelier warped the silhouette of every guest. More than a hundred jack-o'-lanterns lined the main staircase and sideboards—each carved not with smiles, but with sinister gaping mouths that glowed violet in the dark.

Aiden moved through the crowd. Cloaks brushed past, and glittered horns. Laughter distorted by fog machines and strobe lights. Teammates slapped his shoulder in passing. Every face wore a mask. Some literal, some not. He spotted Lola leaning against the upper banister. She raised a hand in a casual wave, but a gentleness he wasn't used to lingered in her eyes. Ever since his mother scorched the infection from the hellhound's bite, the space between them had thinned. She'd seen the fear behind his calm, and he'd seen the grief she'd masked in glamour.

He offered her the smallest before slipping deeper into the party.

Declan wore a billowy linen shirt, and a tricorn perched on his head, with a glass tilting carelessly in his hand. He looked the part: charming, handsome. But Aiden saw the tension in his jaw and the lags in his replies. He saw the way his gaze flitted toward the entrance like he was expecting someone.

Aiden pushed through a tangle of plague doctors and bloodied angels, the silk of a trailing wing brushing his arm as he cut across the foyer. The air smelled of candle wax and spilled champagne, and the chandelier pulsed in time with the music.

"Hey," he said.

Declan blinked like he'd just stepped out of a dark room. His collar was rumpled, shadows sunk deep beneath his eyes. "Hey," he said, voice scratchy at the edges. "You made it."

"It's your party." Aiden managed a smile. "I figured someone should be here to make sure you don't set yourself on fire."

Declan laughed, but the sound was brittle. "Wouldn't be the worst thing."

Aiden's gaze dropped to the drink, then back to Declan's face. "How are things with the journal?"

The smirk faded. "Not this again." His shoulders stiffened. "Why do you care so much?"

"Because I see what it's doing to you. And you're not the only one dealing with things."

Declan looked toward the blur of dancers beneath the lights. "There's nothing wrong with it. You're just making this into a bigger deal than it is."

"Sure."

Cold air crept in from the open patio doors. Somewhere nearby, someone screamed before it turned to laughter.

"If I told you the truth," Declan muttered, "you'd think I'd gone crazy."

Aiden stepped closer. Close enough to smell salt and vodka on Declan's breath. "No, I wouldn't. Trust me when I say that."

Declan met his eyes, and for a moment, they were boys again, dueling with play swords on the cliffs behind Albatross House, building kingdoms from driftwood and hiding from things they didn't yet have names for.

"Just stop," Declan said.

"Stop what?"

"Stop looking at me like that." He backed up a step. "Like I'm…like I'm someone for you to save."

"Okay. Now you're not making any sense. I'm trying to help you."

"You know exactly what I'm talking about," Declan said. A flush crept into his cheeks. "Stop looking at me like…you're in love with me."

Aiden flinched.

"I'm…not…in love with you," he said, but it sounded small, even to him.

Declan turned, jaw set, and downed the rest of his drink. "Just—leave me alone tonight, okay?" he said. "I can't deal with this. I can't deal with you."

He disappeared into the crowd before Aiden could think of a reason to follow.

Near the ballroom, Aiden spotted Dorothy beneath the chandelier, her red hair braided through with a blue ribbon that echoed her gingham dress. It swayed just above her knees as she hovered beside Noah. They were mid-conversation, Noah gesturing with his drink while she nodded quickly, her arms folded across her middle like she wanted to shrink into the wallpaper. Aiden's gaze lingered, guilt flaring inside him, but he shoved it down before it could take hold.

He considered turning back. Instead, he stopped at the drink station, grabbed a cup, and poured a *very* generous measure of vodka.

"Careful," someone whispered behind him. "They spiked the punch twice."

A portrait flickered in the shifting light—a bearded man who seemed to tilt his head toward Aiden before settling back into stillness. Aiden stared into his drink, watching the ice spin, then he stepped away, glass in hand.

Noah's eyes found him first. He smiled like he'd been waiting. The scent of his cologne met him halfway—tobacco leaf and citrus peel, grounded by a woody undertone like cedar left out in the rain.

"Trust fund baby," he said, raising his glass in a toast.

Dorothy gave a small, unsure wave.

"I didn't know you two knew each other," Aiden said.

"Oh, me and Dorothy go way back," Noah said, tossing her a teasing look. "Right, Dorothy?"

She looked at Aiden like she wished the floor would open beneath her. The last time they'd spoken, she'd collapsed in his dining room, and he'd caught her just before Heather walked in.

"Noah helped me get some money at that mother-daughter tea," she said.

Aiden nodded. "I'm sure that was…a good time."

Dorothy smiled faintly but didn't add anything. She excused herself and slipped into the crowd, leaving them alone.

Aiden's mind spun back to Silver Shoals, to the unspoken thing hanging between them. What this was. What it wasn't. What it almost became. He didn't know if Noah simply filed it away, like a harmless memory.

"Are you always this charming at haunted house parties?" Aiden asked, tilting his glass toward him.

Noah raised a brow. "Only when I'm trying to impress someone." He leaned in, the gold in his green eyes catching the candlelight. "Is it working?"

Aiden didn't answer. But the look he gave said enough. And maybe for tonight, that was all it needed to be. Even with the echo of Declan's words clinging to him. Even with the guilt gathering in the back of his throat.

CHAPTER 57
Lola Godfrey

LOLA SAW EVERYTHING: THE CONGREGATION OF BODIES NEAR THE DRINK station, monogrammed flasks exchanged like secrets, flirtations in alcoves. The whole night shimmered with curated chaos, a spectacle put together in less than a week. But she recognized the look in Declan's eyes when he asked to host it. How empty he'd sounded. He didn't throw parties like this unless he needed the noise to drown out something deeper. And maybe she should've stopped him. Asked him what was wrong. But she hadn't, because some unravelings, she knew too well.

Crimson velvet molded to her, corseted at the waist with a collar flaring at her throat. Lace fluttered at her wrists, her cape cascading down the stairs like spilled wine. Heads turned. They always did. Halfway down, Heather emerged carrying two drinks in hand. Her lilac dress shimmered like a silken bruise, the hem floating as she approached.

"Wow," Heather said, offering a glass. "You look like you stepped out of an oil painting."

Lola accepted it without breaking stride. "So do you," she said. "If the painting was titled *Girl Regretting Her Life Choices in Gossamer*."

Heather laughed, quick and sheepish, and they slipped beside the banister, half-shield by carved wood and faux cobwebs strung with orange lights.

"Look. I'm sorry I've been distant," Heather said. "And for you know. Letting her back in. I clearly didn't think how it would affect you."

Lola said nothing. Her eyes didn't even blink. From the corner of the room, she spotted her teammates taking shots of some neon green liquid. Part of her felt like she was missing out.

"It's over," Heather rushed on. "For real this time. I caught her trying to put some kind of herb in my juice. When I asked, she acted like I was the crazy one."

Lola took a sip, her gaze cool. "That girl's a walking hex. Don't give her the power of a second thought."

Heather looked toward the foyer glowing with jack-o'-lanterns, where laughter bled through fog and the music rattled through the house. "Do you really think he did all this for her?"

Lola found Declan near the seahorse fountain with Camille. "It's Declan. He'd cross the Seven Seas for Ophelia if it meant she'd take him back."

Heather's expression shifted, caught somewhere between understanding and exhaustion. "She doesn't deserve it," she muttered.

Lola's lips curled, but her eyes stayed flat. "No one ever does."

They clinked glasses. And drank the night away.

Lola spotted Aiden by the windows, deep in conversation with a boy she didn't recognize—tan skin, dark curls, a confidence that didn't beg for attention but held it anyway. She drifted toward them, her cape whispering behind her.

Aiden turned at her approach, straightening. "Lola, this is Noah. Noah, Lola."

She tilted her head, assessing him with a faint smile. "Ah. So you're the lucky guy."

Noah returned it, enough to seem amused but not flattered. "Guess that depends on who you ask."

She faced Aiden. "Mind if I borrow you? I promise to return you in one piece."

He followed her a few steps toward the hallway's edge, half-sheltered from the noise of the party.

"It's time," she said.

They'd agreed days ago, if Declan refused to share what was inside the journal, they'd take it. Not to betray him, but because it seemed like they were running out of time. The more Declan sank into whatever he'd uncovered, the more distant he became. Lola hadn't even noticed until Aiden mentioned it. The journal wasn't just consuming his attention. It was changing him.

She studied Aiden's face in the shifting light, searching for any second thoughts.

"Can you keep him distracted?" she asked.

Aiden huffed. "All he is is distracted," he said. "But I'll try. We're not really speaking right now."

"Well, find a way to change that. This is for his own good."

"I know."

Declan stood near the music room in a conversation he clearly wasn't listening to. Lola moved through the crowd, offering fleeting smirks, touches that meant nothing except presence. With each step, the music thinned. The rear staircase rose ahead, quieter and less traveled. Albatross House had always been full of silences that hummed behind wallpaper and echoed in your ribs. Sconces flickered against gilded frames and threadbare tapestries, the faces in oil paintings seeming to turn as she passed. She'd grown up wandering these halls. Memorized every turn, every nook. Every place to hide when his parents argued, or the housekeepers muttered warnings. She and Declan used to play here like spies with their backs pressed to the wall, sneaking into rooms that had started to fall apart.

Even now, as nearly an adult, the nostalgia curled around her.

Her hand hovered over the brass handle to his bedroom. A line waited here. And once she crossed it, there was no stepping back. If he wanted her to know about the journal, he would've told her. But if what Aiden said was true, if this thing was dangerous—evil—she had to know for herself.

The bed was made, the desk aligned with precision. The quill and ink set she'd given him two Christmases ago sat untouched. Even the bookshelf looked curated to the millimeter. It was all so quintessentially Declan she nearly rolled her eyes. If anything was out of place, he'd know. She skimmed the desk before trying the shelves where textbooks had been arranged by subject, fiction alphabetized, spines aligned.

She checked the lower shelves. Nothing. Tried the higher ones, her fingertips brushed a ship model and undisturbed dust. Still nothing. She turned to scan the room. Not for what stood out, but for what had always been there.

In the corner was a globe on a clawfoot stand, the kind that cracked open to reveal a bar. It had always felt like a prop from some adventure novel. Declan had used it to stash Aiden's birthday gift—an autographed racquet she'd helped find. Back when they gave each other gifts.

The continents were faded, their borders in crumbling ink. She pressed along the equator until the latch opened. There were no bottles or glasses. Though one object rested in the center. The journal. Its design seemed to pulse. She reached for it, fingers trembling.

The first pages recorded generations of Albatrosses. Her eyes landed on Doris's name, and Declan's. His looked freshly inked. Illustrations filled the spreads of other pages, of banshees, and sirens. Even hell-hounds. She kept flipping, faster now, until she reached a page with an image she'd never seen before: a serpent eating its tail. Below it: *The blood of the healer is held to possess virtue to cure others.*

Her fingers clenched around the leather spine. No names were listed. But she didn't need them. Even if the Godfreys weren't men-tioned, the page might as well have been signed by them.

A floorboard creaked behind her.

Declan stood in the doorway, his eyes dropping to the journal. "What are you doing?"

She tucked it behind her back.

"Lola. I said, what are you doing?" he asked, stepping toward her.

She considered playing dumb and say that she was looking for him. But she saw the way he squared his shoulders and how trust dissolved. She sighed, like it was his fault for making her go through all this trou-ble, rolled her eyes and held the journal up.

"Why do you have that?"

She met his stare, chin lifted. "So this is what you meant by research? I thought you were writing a paper, not unraveling a prophecy."

"You have no idea what you're talking about," he said. "Whatever Aiden said to you is not true. I haven't even shown him."

His hands curled into fists at his sides. She thought he might lunge at her. But he just stood there looking at her with that look. The one where he chose his words so carefully, it almost hurt to watch. Not lashing out. Not giving in. Just holding it in.

CHAPTER 58
Declan Albatross

Bass thudded beneath the floorboards, reminding him that one floor below, classmates were losing themselves in the illusion of another Halloween. He'd asked Camille to throw this party for two reasons. To lure Ophelia here and ask about the bracelet she'd made for him. And to surround himself with enough people that Nerida might at least keep her distance. He knew it was foolish to think so. And despite everything, he hadn't decided whether he would give her the astrolabe. His ancestors had held on to it for a reason. And her promise to help his mother felt more like a threat disguised as mercy. Lola stood across from him in the glow of the desk lamp. Her costume looked theatrical for the room that had become his sanctuary. The lace cuffs at her wrist trembled as she adjusted her grip on the journal.

"What did you hope to accomplish?" His voice was sharper than intended.

"Does it matter?"

"It does to me." His gaze dropped to the journal—his journal. She held it so carelessly, like it hadn't consumed him for weeks. A needle of pressure slid behind his eyes. He clenched his jaw harder. A voice inside him said to rip it away from her fingers, consequences be damned. He didn't even think she'd scream. She'd blink, stunned, as he pried it and shoved her back hard enough for her heels to skid.

He crept forward. "Can I have it back?" he asked. "Please." She tucked it against her side. "Not until you tell me why it matters so much." A pause. "Why didn't you tell me? I thought we were supposed to be best friends."

He hated the way she touched it. Hated that she'd found it.

Hated how badly he wanted to shake her.

"Tell you?" He laughed dryly. "And say what? That my family's cursed? That some mythological creature bled into our bloodline and I get to be the next Albatross to lose their mind?"

From the adjoining bathroom, a sound stirred. At first, he thought it was the pipes. But then came the hiss, like a faucet. Darkness cloaked the room beyond, the light stretching only so far.

"Do you hear that?" he asked.

The hissing grew louder. And within the darkness, there was movement.

Water slithered in the shape of a serpent. It hovered above the carpet, coiling midair. It shimmered in the lamplight, translucent and veined with awareness.

Lola stepped back. "Declan?"

He reached for her, but the water serpent struck first.

The impact knocked her against the bookshelf. Hardcovers rained down as she hit the floor, the journal slipping from her grasp. Her hands flew to her throat, where the water had wrapped around her throat like a noose. She staggered, choking, heels skidding over the rug.

A second tendril split from the serpent's body and shoved its way between her lips.

Declan froze. "No, no—"

She convulsed as water forced its way down her throat. Her pupils dilated. She dropped to her knees, cape tangling, one hand clawing the floor, the other reaching blindly toward him.

He dropped beside her. "Stop. Please. Please, stop!"

Ink bloomed across the journal's open page in dark branches, pulsing outward from a sketched serpent. He looked from it to her face—gray now, lips parted, limbs twitching weakly.

"You've made your point!" he yelled to whatever force had possessed the thing. "Stop!"

Nothing.

He grabbed the journal and slammed it against the floor. "Let her go!"

The serpent held its shape before collapsing into a splash. Lola fell with it, water gushing from her mouth. Her arms shook as she tried to rise, gasping, her entire body shivering.

Declan knelt beside her. His hands hovered, useless. "I—I had no idea that would happen," he whispered. "I don't even know what that was."

She coughed harder, braced on the floor. "I don't know…what the hell that journal is," she rasped, "but you need to get rid of it."

"No," he said. "You should've never touched it."

Her head snapped up. "So it's my fault?"

"Yes! You and Aiden keep pushing. Snooping. Just leave me alone!"

She wiped her mouth with the back of her hand. "That thing tried to drown me and you're defending it like it's more important than me."

"I'm sorry, Lola, but I don't expect you to understand," he said. "Not this."

She stared at him like he was curdling before her eyes. "This is a new low. Even for you."

She staggered up and, in one swift motion, snatched the journal.

He seized her wrist. "Don't," he said through clenched teeth, "you dare."

"Are you serious?" she tried to break free. "You're hurting me!"

His eyes dropped to where his fingers dug into her skin. Pale blotches already appeared.

"Give it back and I'll let go."

"Declan—" She struggled, twisting. "Let me go now!"

But he couldn't. Not with everything unraveling. Not with the one person who'd always known him was looking at him like a stranger. He didn't want to lose her like this. So he did the one thing he hadn't meant to do. He kissed her. It wasn't soft. It wasn't kind. His mouth crashed into hers, like he could stop time. Like if he could remind her he was there, she'd forgive him and let him keep the one thing that gave him purpose.

For one breath, she froze. Then slapped him. The sound cracked through the room.

Her cape whipped around the corner as she fled. He stood there, hand outstretched, the slap burning on his face. And still, all he could think about was the journal was no longer in his hands.

CHAPTER 59
Aiden Oldwyck

THE BALCONY CURVED IN A CRESCENT, CARVED WITH ORNATE FLOUR-ishes. Below, the garden and fountain unspooled into mist, overgrown hedges smudged at their edges while the sea whispered in the dark. The cold worked its way through Aiden's shirt, though he didn't mind. The chill anchored him in a body that felt like it might drift off into the night.

"There you are."

Noah stepped onto the balcony, the light from the hallway halo-ing him before shadows folded in again. Beneath the red puffer vest, his shirt clung to him. Aiden's gaze lingered—long enough to notice his shape beneath the fabric—before he turned back to the horizon, heat rising to his ears.

"Sorry," he said. "I needed some air."

Noah came to stand beside him, their shoulders nearly touching. He was quiet, but his gaze lingered on Aiden. "Thought you didn't drink."

"Doesn't mean I can't."

"How many?"

Aiden hesitated. "Enough."

Noah tilted his head. "And now you're acting different."

Aiden wanted to say he'd done something he couldn't take back.

But he stared ahead, afraid he'd come undone if he met Noah's eyes. The memory rose like a splinter: the cold of the solarium, Veronica's voice low and tense, Aunt Maeve's even colder. He had told them that Dorothy might be the banshee. Maeve had smiled without warmth. He'd ask if that meant he could bargain out of the hunt. If there was a way to be spared on his eighteenth birthday.

Maeve only said, "I'll see what we can do."

But Aiden hadn't believed her. Still, it was worth a try.

He swallowed the guilt and forced a smirk. "I'm fine, really."

"You're not."

The wind pushed Noah's scent toward him. It electrified his senses. Noah rested his hand beside Aiden's.

"You're staring," he murmured.

"I know." Aiden's breath caught, embarrassment flaring. "I'm sorry." He was unsure what to do with his hands, as if apology alone couldn't disguise the truth.

"Don't be."

Warmth radiated across the space between their knuckles. Aiden's mind screamed at him to close the gap, but his body refused. Fear, tangled with longing, had trapped him between want and retreat. Noah looked at his lips before rising to meet his eyes again. He leaned in, eyes flicking to Aiden's lips. Aiden's fingers curled against the railing. He leaned in, heart pounding. His breath hitched as their mouths drew closer.

The balcony doors slammed open behind them.

"Aiden?"

They sprang apart.

Heather stood in the doorway, her eyes uncertain about what she had walked in on.

"Oh." She raised a hand to her mouth. "I—I didn't mean to—" She turned back inside.

The afterglow of what might've happened hovered between them.

"Wait!" he blurted, glancing once at Noah before following her.

The hallway narrowed while music echoed. Heather's heels clicked across the marble as she descended the grand staircase, weaving through the crowd.

"Heather, please wait!" he called.

Aiden pushed through costumes and masks, dodging laughter and flashes of light, his breath catching as he burst through the front doors. The wind tugged at her curls and turned the estate into a mythical scene. She stood beneath the porte-cochère with her back to him.

She exhaled, slow and controlled, but it shook anyway. "Is that why you broke up with me? Because of him?"

"I…" Aiden swallowed hard. "I didn't know. Not until tonight."

A breathy laugh slipped from her. "God, I feel so—" Her voice cracked, but when she looked at him again, she wore that composure she'd learn from Lola and Ophelia. "I'm not angry."

"You're not?"

"Of course not. No one should have to hide who they are. I'm just…confused."

He hated seeing her like this, trying so hard to stay intact. But he knew her well enough to see the cracks beneath the surface.

She let out another short laugh. "But you know what's funny?" Her lips tugged into a shape that wanted to be a smirk but couldn't hold. "I used to think I had it all mapped out. Like, I really thought I knew where we were going. Thought I knew who we were."

Her voice cracked. "I thought we'd be forever. Not in the fairytale way. Just…the kind of forever where you don't have to keep looking over your shoulder. Where someone stays. And then one day I woke up, and everything I'd been holding onto—" She broke off, blinking hard. "It wasn't even mine anymore."

Aiden stepped closer.

She held up a hand, not in rejection, but in request. "I'm not blaming you. I just need to know. Was it real? The dates. The late nights.

Our inside jokes. The way you looked at me. All of it."

They weren't the best love story. Not the kind people envied or tried to write songs about. They'd never been perfect—too many sharp edges, too many silence that last too long. But still, what they had was real. Messy and flawed, yes, but it mattered. There were moments where the world had felt a little softer just because they were in it together. And whatever had unraveled between them, she deserved to know that. To hear, at least once, that it hadn't all been a mistake.

He reached for her, and to his relief, she didn't pull away. "Every day with you meant the world to me. I never doubted how much I loved you. I thought we'd grow up, get out of Driftmoor, get married someday." He steadied himself. "I held onto that for a long time. Maybe longer than I should have."

He drew a slow breath, eyes meeting hers.

"But something started shifting in me, and I didn't know how to name it. I kept thinking it was fear. Or guilt. Or pressure. But tonight…" His voice dropped. "Tonight made it clear. I wasn't just changing. I was becoming someone else. Someone I needed to be. And I deep down, I knew that person wasn't going to be yours in the same way anymore."

He pulled her into a hug, and she didn't hesitate—just folded into him, her face pressed to his shoulder. They both held on like it was the last time, even if no one said it aloud.

"No matter what anyone calls it," Aiden whispered, "it was always love, okay?"

"Okay."

They stepped apart, both looking more at peace than they had in months. Aiden tilted his head to the sky. Stars blinked through the mist, and the ocean rumbled in the distance. He rubbed a hand down his face.

Heather sniffled. "I probably look ridiculous."

"You?" Aiden smirked. "Never."

She nudged him with her shoulder. "Liar." She wiped at her cheeks, schooling in her composure. "He's likely wondering where you are."

Before Aiden could respond, the front door creaked open behind them.

Noah stepped out, his jacket slung over one shoulder. "Hey," he said, eyes flicking between them. "Just wanted to check if everything's okay."

Heather offered him a faint smile. "You've got good timing. We were just wrapping up."

She turned to Aiden. "Let's talk more tomorrow," she said. "Maybe get some taffy from Winchester's?"

"Yeah," he said, grateful for the out but meaning it. "I'd like that."

"Thanks. I'm calling for a ride home," she added, stepping past him toward the driveway. "I think I hit my limit on haunted parties and exes."

She gave Noah a nod in passing and disappeared into the darkness.

The breeze cut through the heat clinging to Aiden's skin.

Noah moved closer. "You alright?"

"Actually. Yeah, I think I am."

They both looked toward the drive's edge where the overgrown hedges gave way to trees. A figure walked barefoot across the gravel. Her skin shimmered wet under the light posts. Her dress—if it could be called that—clung to her like seafoam.

"Now that's a bold costume," Noah said.

A chill unfurled in Aiden, but he ignored it. "I suppose it is."

The figure slipped through the doors without hesitation.

Aiden's voice came quieter. "I think I'm ready to go home too."

"I can take you."

"You drove?"

Noah smiled and gestured his chin toward the end of the driveway. Aiden followed his gaze and sure enough, tucked near the trees was a gleaming motorcycle.

He raised an eyebrow. "Of course."

Noah's smile widened. "Come on, trust fund baby."

And together, they disappeared into the night.

CHAPTER 60
Dorothy Hale

DOROTHY STOOD INSIDE AN ALCOVE, HALF-SWATHED IN SHADOW, HER costume catching in the candlelight. Pale blue gingham clung to her—*too perfect to pass up*, Camille had said, already zipping the dress before Dorothy could protest. She didn't usually dress up for Halloween. And the last time she'd stepped foot in this house, she'd almost died minutes later. But tonight felt different. Maybe it was the sleep study results. No apnea. No neurological irregularities. No answers. The doctor had said it was the stress with being away from home. Called the cemetery incident a *one-time thing*. She'd nodded and pretended to believe him.

In the foyer's center, a marble seahorse reared from a fountain filled with dark liquid, lit from within like oil catching fire. Students gathered around it, plucking tiny flasks from between metal lily blossoms. At the top of the staircase loomed a mannequin in Victorian funeral apparel—one gloved hand extended in like it had been waiting for her. The scene teetered between dream and hallucination. Too extravagant to be real. Too beautiful to trust.

Dorothy stirred her soda with a straw. All around her, faces blurred in sequins and false teeth, masks shifting in and out of form. But behind the blur, a man in a raincoat stood still. The fabric was streaked with blood while seaweed curled from his shoulders, and a fishhook hung from his belt. His eyes, when they met hers, looked scooped out.

She held her breath as another figure stepped out behind him. Overalls. A windbreaker torn at the sleeves. Blood dripped from his ears as worms writhed at his collarbone. Dirt was packed so deep beneath his nails it split the skin.

The fisherman.

The groundskeeper.

Her grip tightened on the cup. They didn't move. Didn't blink. They just watched her as if judging her for being alive. She shut her eyes. One breath. Two. When she opened them, they were gone.

A blur of crimson caught the light halfway down the stairs. Lola. In one hand, she clutched a leather-bound book. Her steps were pur-poseful, shouldering past a couple as she descended. Dorothy stepped forward, but Declan appeared. He scanned the room, frantic. Then moved quick, clipped steps, almost stumbling. Whatever steadiness he carried had cracked. He didn't look like the boy she'd met weeks ago. There was something unmoored in his eyes now. Something desperate.

Dorothy walked into his path. "Hey. Do you have a second? It's about that thing I saw in the harbor—"

His eyes barely met hers. "I—I can't. Sorry."

He brushed past her. The music surged in the background, but it felt distant.

"Always drama with those two," came a drawl at her side.

Camille's tiara gleamed in her blonde curls, and glitter dusted her lashes like frost. The mistletoe brooch she always wore shimmered where it pinned to her gown. She cast a glance after Declan and Lola, then back to Dorothy.

"It's like they're allergic to peace," she said.

"They look really upset," Dorothy said softly.

"They always do. Anyway. Want to dance?"

Her mind flashed to the billiard room with Jack, to the last time music filled this house. "I don't think you'd want to see that."

"You haven't seen me on the dance floor," Camille grinned, spinning herself into a playful twirl.

She grabbed Dorothy's hand and led her into the ballroom. The parquet floor pulsed beneath their feet, the bass trembling through the walls. Jack-o'-lanterns lined the baseboards, their mouths carved in spirals and slashes, glowing with violet light. One leered wide, its teeth serrated. Camille pulled her away from it.

"Dance with me!" she shouted.

Her hair flashed beneath strobes, her laughter rising above the beat. A few students turned to watch her, their stares trailing her. Dorothy didn't care. Not with Camille's hands twining with hers, not with the music dragging her deeper into a rhythm that felt almost like freedom.

She twirled and caught Jack lingering at the ballroom's edge. Wearing his usual hoodie and jeans, looking out place in the decadence, but his crooked grin hit her like sunlight through cloud. She let herself forget what he'd said on Rowan's yacht. Forget the tension, the unraveling, the way his words had lingered. Tonight, she just wanted music and movement and to have fun for once.

"I didn't think you'd be here!" she called, the joy in her voice catching her off guard.

"Dorothy." Jack leaned close over the music. "We really need to have a talk. About what I said."

"One song," she said, grabbing his hand. "Then talk all you want."

"All right, all right," he laughed. "Show me what you've got."

"Oh, you already know what I'm capable of," she said. "Or did you forget me stepping on your shoes?"

He smiled at her. "How could I ever forget?"

They danced, and Dorothy believed that maybe life could be simple again. That life could be good. Camille spun beside them, her laughter bubbling over the beat. Dorothy smiled and the night shimmered. But when she turned to Jack, he was gone.

Her stomach dropped. She scanned the crowd. He stood by the arched windows now.

"What are you doing?" she said, reaching for him. "Come on!"

He appeared beside her. Too fast. She startled, blinking. And when she looked again, he was across the room, pressed against the far wall.

"What?" She slowed down.

He reappeared at her elbow, smiling. A chill passed through her. She tried to hold on to the moment, but it felt like she'd wandered into a dream seconds before it soured. She turned toward the jack-o'-lanterns, their grins twitching. Then their carvings split open and from within, beetles poured out, skittering across the floor in a black tide that went under costumes and shoes.

Dorothy stumbled back. But no one screamed. No flinches.

"Dorothy?" Camille gently touched her shoulder. "What are you doing?"

A woman appeared in the doorway. Water ran down her arms and pooled at her feet, her skin slick with sheen. Her eyes scanned the crowd as she stepped inside. Some kept dancing in their own bubbles while others noticed her and began to stare.

"Smokin' costume!" a boy dressed as a Roman soldier yelled.

The woman turned toward him. Water lashed from her hand and splashed into his face.

He stumbled back against a column, coughing.

Dorothy's eyes dropped to the woman's webbed hands. Nails curved like talons. A hush rippled through the ballroom as more heads were drawn to her without knowing why. She strolled unbothered through the crowd, water trailing behind her, until she reached the room's rear doors and slipped inside without a glance back.

Beside Dorothy, Camille's mistletoe brooch glowed.

CHAPTER 61
Declan Albatross

The kiss still burned his lips.

Lola's heels struck the floorboards as she crossed the library toward the hearth. Her hands trembled as she opened a brass tin of matches. The strike cracked through the silence. Flame burst from the matchhead, mirrored in her eyes, and she tossed it to the logs.

A hiss. A low roar. The fireplace came to life.

She straightened, the journal clutched to her chest. "Don't come any closer."

Flames flickered across her face, dancing over her cheekbones. Mascara had smudged beneath her eyes, but she held her chin high and her grip even fiercer.

"Lola," he said, halting. "Please don't. I need that more than you know."

"You kissed me," she snapped. "After all these years, why would you risk our friendship just to pull some twisted stunt like that?"

The slap still burned on his cheek. "I–I wasn't thinking. I just wanted you to let it go."

"So that's all it was? A distraction?" Her voice cracked with disbelief.

"Yes," he said. "And I'm so, so sorry."

She stepped closer to the fire, the journal pressed to her ribs. "Tell me the truth. Why did you throw this party? Was it for her?"

Declan's mouth went dry. He didn't need her to say Ophelia's name. Firelight licked at the journal's edges. One flick of her wrist and it would catch. He couldn't bear to think of that.

"Were you even going to tell me about this?" she asked. "And don't lie, or I swear I'll burn it."

Music drifted in, bass-heavy and pulsing. Then came the water. It slid in streams across the floor, curling like tendrils toward the hearth. Nerida stepped through the doorway, framed in shadow and candle-light. The door slammed behind her. She bypassed Declan entirely and locked onto Lola.

"You won't manage it," she said. "Not with fire."

Nerida approached, her eyes narrowing like she was assembling a face from memory. "You look so much like him," she murmured, cir-cling Lola with the grace of a predator. "Even your lips are the same."

She leaned in. For a breath, it seemed like she might kiss Lola. But then she tilted her head in amusement and back away.

Lola's voice barely carried. "And who are you?"

"Nerida," she said. "Feel free to toss it. But I promise, it won't burn."

Lola stared at Nerida like something reached into her lungs and stolen the air. Then, without flinching, she flung the journal into the flames.

"No!" he shouted, lunging forward.

Orange curled around it, but it didn't burn. The pages didn't blacken. It sat whole and untouched, like it had been expecting this.

Lola's breath caught. "It was worth a try."

"It's older than that," Nerida said.

She stepped toward the hearth and looked up. A shift passed over her expression. Her voice, when it came, was lower. "The astrolabe."

It had always been there, part of the décor, Declan had thought. Another relic passed down through generations of Albatrosses.

"So this is where it ended up," she said. "And you knew."

He didn't meet her eyes. "They always say never trust a sailor."

"And yet here we are." She turned to face him. "Do you want her to stay like that?"

Upstairs, his mother remained in whatever held her captive, unaware of the party. Or she simply didn't care.

Lola cut in. "What is she talking about?"

Declan reached above the mantel and unhooked the astrolabe. It was heavy, cold and softly whirring.

"Here," he said, holding it out to Nerida.

Lola curled her fingers into her sleeve. "I have no idea what's happening," she said, "but this feels like one of those choices you'll regret forever."

Declan's gaze didn't leave Nerida. "You can't take it, can you?" he said. "Not unless I willingly hand it over."

"We had a deal," she said, her voice pulsing with restraint.

"That's true, but how do I know you'll actually help my mother?" he asked. "The journal doesn't exactly make your kind look noble. My ancestors wrote enough to make me weary."

Her jaw tightened. "Those words were written by men and women unraveling at the edges. They saw only what fear let them see."

"And what should I see instead?" he asked. "You say you loved this man. That you've crossed centuries for a reunion. But how do you even know he's alive? What if he's not? What if he forgot you?"

He stepped forward looking down at the astrolabe. "What if the man you loved is gone, and the only thing waiting for you is disappointment?" He looked up to meet her eyes. "Do you really think he'd love a monster like you back?"

For a heartbeat, Nerida didn't move. Then her face cracked. Not visibly. But perceptibly, like a hairline fracture in glass. She looked at him with an ache so ancient it made the air colder.

"You are a child," she whispered, "You know nothing."

Her hand rose to her hair. When it dropped, she held a blade of sea glass, gleaming in shades of blue and green.

She didn't hesitate. She threw it. It cut through the firelight like a sliver of lightning.

Lola slammed into Declan. He hit the hearth's edge as the blade buried itself into her ribs with a sickening, muffled crack. She didn't scream. She barely staggered. Her eyes dropped to the wound, lips parted. Blood spread across her corset, vivid against the fabric like an opening flower. Declan caught her as she faltered, his arms circling her, steadying her.

"Lola!" His voice broke.

Her lashes fluttered. She managed a grimace. "Okay," she said. "That sucked."

"You—you're—" His fingers came away slick and red.

No. This wasn't real. It couldn't be. Was this his punishment for kissing her? For thinking about hurting her?

Music spilled in again. Dorothy appeared, her face blanching at the scene. Camille followed close behind. Her hand flew to her mouth, stifling a cry. Then a light burst from her chest. Her mistletoe brooch flared— emerald— casting a spectral glow across the library. Nerida hissed, spinning toward the light, and for the first time, her mask cracked. Rage contorted her features as the water at her feet boiled. Her form shuddered, revealing a grotesque winged creature beneath the human skin.

Camille took a step forward and the brooch glowed brighter as Nerida recoiled, shielding her face with her webbed hands.

"You shouldn't have that," she snarled at Camille. "You have no idea what it's tied to."

Her eyes flicked to the astrolabe, now lying on the rug where Declan had dropped it. She reached for it, but the moment her fingers grazed the metal, a sharp hiss split the air. She jerked her hand away, steam rising from her palm. Her face contorted, not just in pain, but in betrayal.

She looked at Declan like she'd expected him to offer it freely. Without another word, she fled, seawater trailing in her wake. The doors slammed shut behind her, sealing the room in stunned silence. Within seconds, the glow dimmed. Camille stared at the brooch, confused and breathless, her hand pressed against it.

"I'm calling an ambulance," she said, rushing to the wall phone.

"No." Lola's hand shot up and latched around Declan's wrist. Her grip was shockingly strong. "Just pull it out. It's okay."

His gaze dropped to the dagger. "If I do that, you'll bleed out," he said. "You can't ask me to do that."

"I won't." A smile touched her lips. Not out of bravado, but certainty. "Trust me."

"Declan, you're not seriously considering this?" Camille said. "She needs a doctor."

Lola's eyes met his. There was no alarm. No hysteria.

"No," he finally said. "Camille's right. You need medical attention."

"I really don't," she whispered. "Watch. We'll do it together."

Her trembling fingers guided his hand toward the hilt. She wrapped hers over his, and together they grasped it. The sea glass was cold. Everything in Declan told him no. But with a breathless curse, he yanked, and the blade slid free. He braced for more blood, the collapse, for the finality of it.

But the skin knitted itself back together. The tear in her corset remained, but the wound had vanished. Her chest rose—shallow, then steadier as color returned to her cheeks and the light in her eyes brightened.

She rolled her shoulder. "See? Easy."

The sea glass slipped from his hand and hit the floor with a metallic clink.

He'd seen the page in the journal once. A symbol of a serpent eating its tail beside a passage scrawled with words about a bloodline that never bruised, whose wounds stitched closed without aid. He'd barely paused on it—too consumed by Nerida, by the lure of the ocean's curse. He'd thought it was myth. Someone else's legacy. He'd never imagined it could be Lola.

CHAPTER 62
Dorothy Hale

Dorothy had seen the impossible healing before. But this time, there was no chaos to hide behind. No hellhound or adrenaline. Just firelight and Declan whispering Lola's name like a prayer. One moment she was bleeding and the next she wasn't. And the most disturbing part wasn't the wound vanishing. It was how expected it felt. Dorothy couldn't pretend anymore that this town was normal. Not when the darkness inside her, whatever had cracked mirrors and howled from her throat, was stirring again.

Declan's hands trembled, bloodied. He stared at Lola not like a person, but a puzzle—one he'd just realized was missing a piece. And Camille stood nearby, arms crossed tightly over her chest, like she might come undone if she didn't.

"What the hell, Lola?" Declan looked from the wound to her eyes.

"You're welcome," she said, glancing at the sea glass on the floor. "I did save your life, by the way."

"How?" His voice pitched. "How were you able to do that? What are you?"

Camille came forward. "She's a healer," she said. Then, more cautiously: "Aren't you?"

Lola raised a brow. "And what are you?"

Camille touched her brooch. "I'm…nothing. But my grandmother used to tell stories. About people with blood that closed wounds. People whose healing caused death."

Lola winced as she rose to her feet. Declan rushed to help her, but she waved him off. "No offense, but it sounds like your grandmother was a bit of a pessimist. The Godfreys didn't cause death. We kept our heads down. That's what my father always said."

She sank onto the leather couch, crossing one leg over the other. "And let's not pretend I'm the only supernatural bitch at this party."

Declan and Camille exchanged a look.

"Are you two that oblivious?" Lola gestured toward Dorothy. "The red hair? The whole haunted orphan thing? She's a banshee."

All eyes turned to Dorothy. Lola had said it like it explained everything. Like it was a label everyone else had been too polite to assign. But Dorothy didn't know what it meant. Just that it sounded like a name pulled from a myth. She thought of the shattered mirror. The scream. Was that what she was? Some kind of an omen?

Camille's hand slipped into hers. "We should go," she whispered, already pulling away.

"Wait? Why?" Dorothy asked, but she noticed the shift in Camille—the guarded shoulders, the edge in her voice.

"I'll explain later," Camille said. "But if what she said is true, you shouldn't be near her. Or him."

Dorothy glanced at Declan. He looked just as confused as she was.

"What are you even talking about?" he asked.

Camille's grip tightened. "I'm sorry, Declan. I love you. You know that. Like a brother. But this isn't the first time my brooch reacted like this. I've ignored it before. I wanted the stories to be just that. Stories. But tonight confirmed what my grandmother always warned me." She hesitated, her eyes full of regret. "Albatrosses are born like hurricanes. Beautiful, but destructive. And I won't let myself be swept in it."

"Camille, hold on. I don't even know what half of this means," Declan said.

Dorothy looked from him to Lola. He looked like the ground had shifted and he hadn't found his footing. And Lola sat still, like none of this surprised her.

Camille turned to Dorothy. "Do you trust me?"

Camille had been kind since day one. But behind her stood two people who didn't just have stories to tell. They knew something.

"I do," she said.

"Then we have to go."

"Wait." Dorothy's voice cut through the space between them. She looked at Lola. "What does it mean? To be a banshee?"

Lola didn't blink. "You really want to know?"

Dorothy nodded, slowly.

"You're the first to know when someone's about to die," Lola said. "It'll always follow you. Death."

The words sank into her like a stone into dark water.

"Dorothy, now," Camille said again, firmer.

She pulled her toward the doors, and Dorothy let herself be led. As they reached the threshold and the music spilled in, Dorothy turned one last time. Declan and Lola watched her go, while a thousand questions raced through her mind.

CHAPTER 63
Dorothy Hale

DOROTHY LEANED HER FOREHEAD AGAINST THE CAR WINDOW, BREATH fogging the glass as trees streaked past in black and silver. Rain blended with the classical music playing from speakers. Camille had kept quiet since they left Albatross House, and Dorothy was grateful. She tucked her hands between her thighs and the seat cushion, hoping Camille wouldn't notice them tremble.

Banshee.

She tried to track it back, before the scream, before the mirror cracked, before the shadows began to move. Back to the crash. But nothing about that night had felt like a beginning. More like a reveal. Had it always been there? Had her parents known? A chill passed through her that had nothing to do with the temperature. She turned toward the glass, but her reflection blurred, like it no longer belonged to her.

"Dorothy?" Camille said.

"Yeah?" Dorothy didn't lift her head from the window.

"I didn't ask where you wanted to be dropped off. You're welcome to come with me, if you'd like. Some company might help. But I'll understand if you'd rather be alone."

The thought of being in her dorm with her thoughts made Dorothy's skin crawl.

"Can I come with you?" she asked.

"Of course." Camille smiled, before tapping the plexiglass divider. "Phillip, straight to Chateau Beaumont, please."

"Yes, Miss Beaumont."

As the car pulled forward, Camille gave Dorothy's hand a reassuring squeeze. Her voice was almost a murmur: "Don't worry. I'm going to take care of you now."

It was meant to be comforting. But something in her tone lingered, like she was too calm. Dorothy couldn't shake the feeling that Camille hadn't been surprised about tonight.

Headlights flickered through the mist, slicing across the drenched road. Shadows jumped between the trees, shapes that vanished too quickly to be real. The car's interior flooded with a white glare as the vehicle behind them surged closer.

Dorothy squinted. "What's their rush?"

Camille glance over her shoulder. "Phillip?"

A deafening crunch split the air, and the car jolted forward. Dorothy snapped against the seatbelt. Her vision blurred—noise, motion, and disorientation, like the world had tipped off its axis.

"What was that?" she gasped, her voice thin against the roar in her ears.

"Are you two alright?" Phillip called.

"I–I think so." Camille turned to Dorothy. "Dorothy?"

"I'm fine," she said, though her fingers were digging into the seat's edge.

Camille peered out the back window. "Do you think that was intentional?"

"I can't say," Phillip replied, already shifting gears. "But I suggest you hold on. I'm going to try to lose them."

The engine snarled. Tires shrieked as they surged forward. Dorothy gripped the armrest, each bump on the road rattling through her. Her breath came fast and shallow, and in the mirror, the headlights behind them swerved while keeping pace.

"It's going to be alright," Camille said, her voice strained but composed. "Believe it or not, this isn't the first time this has happened to a Beaumont."

A second impact rammed the car. Dorothy's head snapped sideways and collided with the window. Stars burst behind her eyes. Camille cried out while Phillip fought the steering wheel.

"Get us off this road!" Camille shouted.

"I'm trying, Miss Beaumont!" Phillip snapped.

The tires skidded, narrowly avoiding a guardrail. Rain battered the windshield in waves as the wipers fought to clear it. Dorothy squeezed her eyes shut, her mind yanked to the car crash. The squeal of tires. Jack's hand slipping from hers. Elliot's scream.

The pursuing car had slammed into them again.

Dorothy's heart seized as Phillip lost control. The Beaumont's car careened off the road, its frame scraping against a tree trunk. She whipped forward against the seatbelt as the collision rattled through her. The shattering of glass and grinding of metal drowned everything else out.

Rain leaked through a fracture in the windshield.

Steam rose from the crumpled hood and swirled into the air as the stench of gasoline thickened around her. Dorothy's vision swam, motion igniting a wave of pain at the base of her skull. The car's interior blurred into shifting shadows.

"Camille?" she croaked.

Camille was slumped against the passenger door. Blood carved thin rivers down her cheek and pooled at her temple while glass glittered in her hair like ornaments.

Dorothy reached for her. "Camille…" Her voice cracked as tears welled. "Please…please wake up."

Her plea met a void that expanded with every passing second. She hovered over Camille, panic clawing up her throat. She stared, hoping for the rise of her chest. She saw movement, or maybe she imagined it.

Footsteps broke through the silence. Her pulse hammered as she turned toward the front seat. The driver's door hung open, swinging with each gust of wind, creaking like a swing in a forgotten yard.

"Phillip?" she called.

No answer.

The footsteps drew closer.

She squinted through the dark. Shapes drifted through the mist—cloaked figures, their boots sinking into the soaked earth. The car's lone headlight flickered against their slick hoods, casting shifting patterns of light across the fog. Her breath caught as she shrank against the seat.

The figure at the front stopped at the edge of the wreck. Water stream down from their hood as they raised a hand and pulled it back.

"Hello, Dorothy Hale," Maeve Oldwyck said.

A smile curled her lips.

"Or should I say, Dorothy *Marek*."

CHAPTER 64
Lola Godfrey

The party was over, though traces of it lingered on glit-ter-stick floors and toppled champagne flutes. Someone had abandoned a fox mask on the stairwell, its sequins catching the chandelier. Lola stepped over a wilted rose and exhaled. The house felt haunted in its own right, as if holding its breath after what had unfolded in the library. She paused beside a shattered picture frame of Doris—she wasn't sure if the crack had been there before tonight—and pressed her fingers to her temple. This wasn't how she'd planned to reveal anything. Not with her blood on the floor and Camille playing crypt keeper. Somewhere between the kiss and that siren and Dorothy, her secret had unraveled. Declan had said little after. He'd ask for space. She wasn't sure if that was better or worse than him freaking out.

And Camille, what was that performance? Her whole I-love-you-like-a-brother monologue before dragging Dorothy away. The mis-tletoe brooch lighting up was one thing. But the *hurricane* speech? Dramatic, even by Lola's standards. She rolled her eyes and headed down one of the hallways usually roped off from guests. In her hands, she turned over the piece of sea glass. Its edges had dulled from the rinse in the bathroom sink, but it still held a green sheen.

A thump echoed from ahead. Carefully, she slipped the sea glass into her corset.

Another noise, closer. Squeak. Creak. A sort of rustle.

"Hello?" Her heels clicked as she followed the sound into a parlor. The door was cracked open, shadows spilling through the gap. She nudged it wider. "Unbelievable."

Rowan flinched. Parvati gasped and yanked her dress up, her lipstick smudged.

"Out." Lola stepped aside. "Scram. And maybe try drinking water before you decide to get handsy next time."

They scurried past her, giggling like idiots. Lola stared after them and leaned against the doorframe. She looked back at the room. Pillows were disheveled, a vase had been knocked off center, and a painting hung crookedly.

"Neanderthals," she muttered, while straightening a portrait of Declan as an infant.

A creak echoed from the foyer.

She headed for the hallway. "What part of party's over don't you—" She stepped into the foyer and stopped.

Ophelia stood beneath the chandelier.

"Oh, it's you." Lola leaned against the banister, one heel tapping against the checkered floor. "What are you doing here? You missed one of hell of a party, if you haven't noticed."

"I owe him the truth," Ophelia said. "And if I don't say it…I might never get the chance."

"Not a great time. He's already unraveling without you adding to it."

"Please, Lola. Let me talk to him."

"Whatever it is," Lola said, turning away, "I'm sure it's no different from the last thing you said that broke him. Go home."

But Ophelia's face made her pause. Not desperation. Ophelia wasn't the type to beg. It was borderline resignation.

Lola exhaled. "He's in the library."

They crossed through the hall, heels clicking against marble and wood. Lola pushed open the doors to the library. The fireplace had gone cold. Shadows pooled in the corners, books askew on the table. But the couch where Declan had been on was vacant. And the journal was gone with him.

Her eyes narrowed. "He was here," she murmured, stepping inside.

Ophelia hovered in the doorway. "Are you sure?"

Lola ignored her and scanned the aisles between shelves. A faint shimmer caught her eye. A pill, half-dissolved against the rug. Before she could say anything, a slam echoed through the house. Both girls were startled. A door, somewhere further within Albatross House, had closed.

"I swear, if one more door slams…" Lola's gaze snapped toward the windows. "That sounded like it came from the servant exit."

Wind picked up from the hallway in the rear corridor, billowing curtains beside the open rear door. An object lay beyond it. Lola rushed forward. It was Declan's tricorn Beyond the doorway, the garden sloped into mist and a figure moved through it.

"Where's he going?" Ophelia asked.

"I have no idea," Lola said. "Declan?"

He didn't stop.

Lola dropped the hat. "What is this boy doing?"

Ophelia followed, heels crunching over grass as they jogged after him.

The wind shrieked across the cliffs.

Lola's heels were gone, and she discarded her cape along the way. She ran barefoot along the sloping lawn, heart beating against her ribs. Declan's silhouette flickered in and out of sight like a ghost she was already too late to save.

"Declan!" she screamed. "Where on Earth are you going?"

He walked at a sluggish and aimless pace.

When she and Ophelia reached him, he stood on the cliff's edge with the journal dangling from his fingertips. In his other hand, a bottle of vodka glinted. His hair was slicked to his forehead and his eyes were vacant.

"We made a deal…I told her I'd do it," he mumbled. "I said I'd give her it to her…and I didn't. And—and now she's going to kill me…or Aiden…or my mother…or you."

He was so calm it made Lola sick.

"Don't say that like it's already decided." She stepped forward. "Yes, she's after you. But you're still here." Her voice caught. "And as long as you are, there's time to figure this out."

He tilted his head. "You don't know what she's capable of," he whispered. "She can get inside your head, and you won't even realize it's happening. What if she's in mine? What if one day she tells me to hurt one of you?"

Ophelia's gaze dropped to the ground near his feet. A small orange bottle lay on its side, empty. Her lips parted, but no words came.

"Declan." Her voice was gentler than Lola had ever heard. "Whatever's happening right now, I need you to come back to us."

"All you've done is make things worse," he snapped. "Everything was fine until you left. And then you came back and ruined it all over again."

Ophelia absorbed it, her face tightening, but she didn't argue. She nodded, like she'd been expecting it. And that hurt Lola more than she thought.

His hands shook, the journal bouncing against his thigh. "Do you know why my mother doesn't leave the house anymore? Why she's holed up in her bedroom while this is happening?"

He held up the journal. "Because of this godforsaken thing. And Nerida." He paused. "And me."

Lola's throat closed. "Declan, listen to me." She took another step forward, arms stiff at her sides. "You're not the reason she shut down. That thing—" she nodded toward the journal, "—is twisting everything. But it's not stronger than you. You can let it go."

He stared past her, eyes glassy. "They used to fight about it, you know. My parents. My dad thought she was having episodes. She said he was in denial about what was happening."

He was crying. It shook her because Declan never cried. Not when his father left. Not when Ophelia left. But in front of them, he wept like his heart had shattered, and it made Lola want to scream.

"Please. I know I ruined everything," Ophelia said. "I had good reasoning to. I'm sorry. Please just get away from the edge."

His knees buckled.

"No!" Lola reached for him.

But he was already gone. The journal slipped from his grip and spiraled after him.

"DECLAN!"

Lola ran and dove off the cliff.

Within seconds, salt ripped into her lungs as cold water pierced through her. The current tossed her like a rag doll, dragging her under, spinning her in all directions. Darkness pressed from every side. But she clawed through it, lungs strangled, legs thrashing against the pull. With a final kick, she broke the surface, gasping and coughing as the night split open around her.

"Declan!" she screamed. "Where are—"

A wave crashed over her and swallowed her words. She spun in chaotic circles, choking on brine and panic. A flash of lightning tore the sky, and the ocean lit up for a moment.

No sign of him.

Then another flash. She spotted a shape bobbing about twenty feet away.

"Oh my god. Declan!"

She swam, her arms slicing through the water that held her from reaching him. He drifted like a puppet without strings, arms floating aimlessly. She kicked toward him, eyes and nostrils stinging with salt-water. Her fingers were inches from grabbing his sleeve when a hand grabbed her ankle and yanked her.

Water flooded her esophagus. She kicked, but the grip persisted, as nails dug into her, inches from penetrating bone.

Lightning struck again, and in the stutter of light, she saw Nerida's face.

Lola thrashed, kicking hard with her free leg. Her heel struck Nerida's cheek, but it did nothing. She tried again, harder, and landed below Nerida's eye. Her grip loosened. Lola swam upward, fighting the water, until she burst through the surface.

The waves tossed her, coughing, hair plastered to her face. Each one felt like a hand trying to drag her back under. She blinked salt, desperate to find Declan again, but it so dark.

Then she felt it—claws raking down her back.

She cried out, the sound muffled by the sea. Pain flared, sharp and immediate, before another strike sliced across her face. Nerida moved fast. Too fast. Lola couldn't keep up. Salt stung her wounds. Tears blurred her vision. She was losing blood.

"What do you want from me?" she shouted.

It seemed like Nerida might've swum away. Lola searched for Declan until she spotted him a few feet away.

"Declan!"

Saltwater burned her wounds as they knit themselves shut. She was nearly to him when Nerida rose, sea-slick and snarling, her glare fixed on Lola like a promise. A hunger.

"He's a liar. Just like all the Albatrosses before," Nerida snarled, as another flash of lightning lit the sky. "He belongs to the ocean now."

"He belongs to no one," Lola said.

She fumbled with the torn fabric of her corset until her fingers closed around the sea glass. She pulled it up, arm swinging. Nerida dodged again and again, fluid as a ripple, until the edge caught her. A burst of dark blood spilled down her eyeball. The siren shrieked, a sound too sharp for human ears, and recoiled beneath the surface.

Lola lunged for Declan, hooking an arm beneath his and hauled him through the churning dark. The ocean dragged them back with every wave. When she risked a glance back, Nerida was gone, but Lola didn't stop to wonder. Eventually, through the mist, she spotted Ophelia, her coat flapping behind her as she waded into the shallows.

"Bring him in!" she called out.

Every stroke burned, but Lola didn't stop. Ophelia rushed in and seized Declan's arm. Together, they hauled him onto the sand. He collapsed onto his back, seawater spilling from his lips. Beneath Lola's trembling fingers, his pulse fluctuated.

"Declan." Her voice cracked as she gathered his head in her arms. "Please—" She brushed the soaked hair from his forehead. "Please wake up. You have to. Just open your eyes. Say something. Anything."

Then he jerked. A spasm tore through him, arching his back.

"I think he's seizing!" Lola cried. "Help me turn him!"

Together, they rolled him on his side and as his body convulsed, helpless to do anything more than make sure he didn't swallow his tongue or snap his limbs against the sand. Lola's hair dripped over his face. Her arms trembled. She couldn't stop crying.

"Come on," she whispered. "Please. You can't leave me."

Ophelia knelt in the sand, mascara bleeding into the hollows beneath her eyes. She didn't speak or reach out. She just looked at Lola. And for the first time, Lola didn't see the girl who had abandoned her. She saw someone just as wrecked and frightened. Someone who had once loved him enough to be here too, drenched and trembling, beside a boy they both refused to lose.

Author's Note

If you or someone you love is struggling with depression, self-harm, or thoughts of suicide, please know you are not alone.

Declan's story explores moments of isolation and despair, but in real life, there is always hope and help. You are not meant to face this alone. There are people who care deeply and want to support you through whatever you're feeling.

If you need immediate support, please reach out to a trusted resource:

For readers in the United States:

988 Suicide & Crisis Lifeline – Dial or text 988

Available 24/7, confidential, and free.

More information at 988lifeline.org

For international readers:

Visit findahelpline.com for a comprehensive list of mental health helplines and services in your country, available in many languages.

Asking for help is a strength—not a weakness.

You are not a burden. You are not alone.

Your story is not over yet.

CHAPTER 65
Aiden Oldwyck

AIDEN STOOD AT THE EDGE OF THE DRIVEWAY, NOAH'S HELMET clutched tight. The cold bit through his sleeves, numbing his fingers. Behind them, Oldwyck Manor watched in stillness, its windows like shuttered eyes. He could feel the house waiting. But he couldn't go inside yet. Noah shifted beside his motorcycle, shoulders hunched beneath a coat that looked like it had lived too many seasons. His boots crunched the gravel while his hair curled across his brow. He just stared down at the ground, lips pressed in a tight line.

Then: "I shouldn't have tried to kiss you."

Aiden looked over. The words felt like a stone dropped in a pond. Small, but it rippled everything.

Noah rubbed the back of his neck in that way Aiden found endearing. "And I shouldn't have done it right before she walked in. That was shitty timing. I…wasn't thinking."

Aiden opened his mouth, but nothing came. He didn't know how to shape the tangle of everything he felt about Noah, about Heather, about himself.

Noah kept his gaze low. "I know you've got feelings about her. About everything." His voice stayed low, but trembled at the edges, like he hated the sound of it coming out. "And maybe you're still figuring things out. About what you want. Or who you are. And that's fine."

He looked up at Aiden. "I'm not in a rush. I'm not going anywhere."

Aiden gripped the helmet tighter. His lungs hurt. Like he'd been holding his breath since Albatross House and didn't know how to let go. Noah reached forward, gently, and their fingers brushed as he took the helmet back. That one brief contact lit a spark beneath Aiden's skin.

Noah slung a leg over his bike. The engine shuddered, headlights slicing the mist. His hands settled on the handlebars. He still didn't look back.

This is your moment. Say something.

But the words didn't come. Not the right ones. Not fast enough.

He's leaving.

You're going to let him leave.

He told you he'd wait and you're letting him go?

"Noah."

His name cracked out louder than he meant. It carried across the drive, through the trees.

Noah froze.

Gravel scattered beneath Aiden's shoes as wind tore past his ears. Everything in him screamed, don't let him go. Noah barely turned when he reached him, breathless and burning, and before the panic could take hold, he kissed him.

No hesitation this time. Just want.

Noah inhaled sharply. His lips were soft, cool from the air, but Aiden kissed him like he needed warmth, like he was trying to climb out of his own skin to get closer. Noah's hands curled into Aiden's coat, anchoring him like he'd been waiting for this too. It wasn't delicate nor perfect, but it was the kind of kiss that made the world stop and made every doubt fall away, even as their teeth knocked once. Aiden's hand gripped Noah's shoulder, and he didn't care how hard he was shaking or that his heart felt like it might punch through his ribs. Because this felt like coming home.

When they finally pulled apart, their lips were swollen, foreheads pressed together. Their exhales mingled in the night, visible between them like proof of what had just happened.

Noah's lips parted. "So we're doing this?"

Aiden nodded. He couldn't speak. He could barely feel the ground.

"I meant it," Noah said. "I'll wait. But…I'm glad you didn't make me."

Aiden managed a laugh. "I'm not good at this."

"You're better than you think, trust fund baby."

Aiden looked at him. Not just the soft curve of his mouth or the reckless curl of his hair, but the steadiness in his eyes. The warmth he never asked for but couldn't stop offering. Aiden wasn't ready for this. But he wanted it.

"See you tomorrow?" he asked, voice low.

Noah nodded, his smiling breaking like sunrise. "Tomorrow."

He climbed onto his bike again, slower, as if the night didn't want to let them go. The taillight faded into the mist as the engine's roar vanished. Aiden stood in the silence he left behind, lips tingling, pulse out of sync. Somewhere behind him, the manor flickered with light—one window, one room, and then darkness again.

"Mom?" His voice carried through the foyer, swallowed by the high ceilings.

The house's usual warmth was gone.

He tried again, louder. "Mom?"

His footsteps carried him past the staircase and down the east wing hall. His mother's sitting room was empty, the fire reduced to a dull stain in the hearth. The curtains moved, though no windows were open. He checked the dining room next. The table gleamed with its chairs tucked in like soldiers. There was no trace of his mother or the matriarchy, just a vague scent of extinguished candles.

He glanced down each hallway, calling for his mother, but no reply came. When he turned the corner toward the west corridor, he stopped. At the far end of the hallway, beneath the row of arched windows, stood a hellhound. It stared, red eyes glinting, but there was no snarl or tension it its stance.

Aiden's body screamed at him to run. But the way it held him in its gaze was different. There was no malice. Only a strange pull, like a summons he didn't fully understand. It turned and padded down the hallway. Aiden hesitated a second before following.

The hellhound moved without sound, its movements fluid and ghostlike. It led him through a back passage and into the conservatory, where vines sprawled across the glass, and the scent of soil pressed in. Doors that should've been bolted creaked open and let the cold air sweep in as the hound slipped through.

The gas lanterns flanked at the maze's entrance caught on dew-slick leaves, and somewhere, a raven called once, then fell silent. The hellhound entered, disappearing between the hedges. Aiden trailed behind, each turn tightening his chest while the walls closed in. It didn't feel like he was walking a path. It felt like he was being drawn in. The twists grew fewer, and the temperature shifted. A hum echoed in the silence, almost like wind. It was chanting. Soft and rhythmic, traveling through him, raising the hairs on his arms.

Then came the smell of smoke. Not wood smoke, but earthier and older, like burning herbs and singed air. His steps slowed, the unease thickening into dread. Light flickered ahead, low and golden. The hedge walls fell away, and he stepped into a clearing.

At its center stood the gazebo, overgrown with moss and time. Dorothy hovered between the pillars, suspended in the air. Her eyes were open, but her limbs were limp as her hair haloed around her. At the edge, cloaked figures chanted in unison. He scanned the circle—one face, then—another. Maeve, Veronica, Irene, the entire matriarchy.

The hellhound padded forward and vanished into smoke.

Irene stepped forward with a dagger in her hands.

"And part of her will forever live within," the matriarchy chanted in unison.

The firelight flickered as Irene took Dorothy's arm.

Dorothy strained against the invisible restraints. "Please, don't do this," she cried.

A flicker of regret crossed Irene's face. "I truly wish there was another way."

Aiden's heart pounded as he stepped forward. "Mom, stop!"

The chanting cut off as every head snapped toward him.

The dagger in Irene's hand faltered. "You shouldn't be here." Her voice was strained. "Aiden, what are you doing?"

He stepped into the clearing. "You don't need to do this. I've changed my mind."

Maeve laughed. "Too late for second thoughts, dear nephew."

"I'll take her place," Aiden said. "Let her go. She's here because of me."

Maeve snorted. "And I thought you had a backbone."

Irene turned to Veronica. "Take your brother inside. Now."

But Veronica hesitated. Her mask of indifference cracked. When she reached for Aiden, he tore away.

"No," he said. "If killing her is the way to save me, then let me die. I'd rather be taken than let you do this."

A ripple of murmurs passed through the matriarchy.

Maeve stepped closer. "That girl is a Marek. Death runs in her blood. They don't foretell it. They bring it. Just ask her yourself. She's already killed a few innocent people. And that hellhound attack was no coincidence. The banshee's presence spreads like disease, and Driftmoor will rot if she stays."

Aiden's voice rose. "And I'm supposed to believe you?"

"She tells the truth," Irene said. "It's the same reason the Mareks were exiled from Driftmoor." She looked at Dorothy now. "It's why your mother—your *real* mother—perished."

Dorothy's eyes fluttered. "My…real mother?"

"The fire should've killed you. But someone saved you and took you far enough that the Entity lost its hold. You were gone before we could finish what had been started."

Dorothy trembled, lips parted.

"Aiden, we should go. This isn't your place." Veronica's grip tightened around his arm, but he tore free.

Dorothy strained against the restraints.

"Please, just let her go," Aiden said. "There has to be another way."

The matriarchy didn't flinch. Maeve smirked. Without thinking, he barreled past them, ignoring the gasps and bewildered whispers. Shouts rang from his mother and from Veronica.

Heat surged. It reflected in Dorothy's eyes locked behind him.

A fireball twisted toward him. Aiden braced for the impact. But Irene threw herself in front of him. Flames showered outward as she deflected the spell, embers spitting across the ground. Blood trickled from her nose and her knees buckled for half a second, but she kept her arm raised.

"This," Irene said to Maeve, "was not part of the agreement."

"No, it was your fantasy," Maeve said. The firelight caught the curve of her mouth. "You think the Entity trades in sentiment? Sacrificing the banshee wouldn't have spared him."

Irene stared at her. "You said there was precedent."

"I said what you needed to hear. There is no record. No reprieve. Just your softness deteriorating the spine of this matriarchy."

His mother's face cracked with betrayal.

"You manipulative, power-starved bitch," Irene hissed.

She hurled a fireball. Maeve blocked it with a crackling shield that buckled under the fiery impact. The ground split as a fissure tore through the clearing. Aunts screamed. Robes snapped in the wind. Magic shimmered like heat off stone. Aiden shielded his face as a wave of heat seared past him. His mother raised her hand again, magic trembling at her fingertips. Maeve flung her arm, summoning a fire that roared outward in a ring. Aiden whirled and ran to the gazebo where Dorothy was still floating, her back arching,

"I'm getting you out," he said to her.

Veronica appeared beside him. "Aiden!"

"Please don't stop me."

"I'm not." She stepped forward. "I want to help."

She murmured an incantation. Magic stirred, threadlike and shimmering. The invisible force around Dorothy loosened and her body sagged downward. Aiden rushed to catch her before she hit the stone.

Veronica bent beside them. "I'm so sorry," she said to Dorothy. "Our mother only wanted to protect him. I wanted to protect him."

A wave of heat roared behind them as Irene and Maeve went at it.

"Go," Veronica shoved them toward the hedges. "Take the shortcut. It'll get you to the conservatory faster."

Dorothy's eyes locked on Veronica.

Veronica's face hardened. "Go!"

Aiden grabbed Dorothy's hand. Together, they ran.

"She's getting away!" Maeve shrieked.

But Aiden didn't turn. Not even when the fire lit the sky behind them. Not even when the matriarchy screamed.

CHAPTER 66
Dorothy Hale

Smoke and fear filled her chest.

Aiden yanked Dorothy forward as they tore through the maze. Branches clawed at her dress, thorns nicking her arms. Every step cracked over dead leaves. The hedges twisted tighter around them, growing taller, more gnarled, as if trying to trap them inside. Behind them, the sky burned. Flames roared upward, casting flickering shadows that danced across the foliage. Smoke lit the fog in violent oranges and reds, and for a moment, it didn't look like magic at all. It looked like war.

Dorothy skidded to a halt, breath ragged, flames glinting off her eyes.

"What are you doing?" Aiden shouted, tugging her arm. "We have to keep going!"

The smoke thickened, illuminating the narrow path ahead in a molten glow. They ducked into a bend, shoulders brushing leaves, until the corridor widened just enough for their strides to fall into sync again.

Then a snap.

They froze.

A voice slithered out of the haze, smooth and taunting, curling around them.

"Run, little banshee."

She knew that voice. Maeve. Hearing it felt like splinters beneath the skin.

Aiden yanked her down a new path, his grip tightening. "I think we're close," he said, but even he didn't sound convinced.

Heat surged behind them. A fireball tore through the hedges with a hiss and a crack like splitting bone. Flames devoured the path ahead in an instant, sealing it off in a wall of fire. Dorothy stumbled forward, landing hard on her knees. Smoke poured through the corridor, turning the air into a smothering cage.

"Run if you must," Maeve hissed through the haze. "It makes the ending more satisfying."

Aiden dropped beside Dorothy pulling her close. His skin was slick with sweat, firelight trembling in his eyes.

"Dorothy, listen to me—"

She flinched before she could stop herself. "What did you mean this was your fault?"

He faltered. "This—this isn't the time," he said, voice tight. "All I can say is I'm sorry. And I'm trying to make up for it now."

The smoke blurred his face. And in that heartbeat, it struck her how little she really knew him. How little he knew her. Whatever guilt he carried, whatever secrets led them here, she didn't have time to demand them now.

"I think I can keep her distracted." His hands landed on her shoulders. "But you have to keep going."

The maze groaned behind them.

She nodded once and ran. Leaves slashed her cheeks, shadows lurching around every corner. Embers blinked through the smoke, casting abstract shapes across the hedges. She had no idea where she was going. The only thing she knew was that her survival hinged on running.

"Still running?" Maeve's voice curled around her. "Your mother did the same."

A shrill cry tore from Dorothy's throat as fire sliced across the path, a blinding, horizontal torrent. She dropped, arms shield her head as heat slammed into her. Cinders singed the back of her neck, the air filled with the choking taste of scorched leaves and smoke. Before she could move, hands clamped around her waist. She screamed, flailing—her heel collided hard with a shin. A grunt. The grip loosened. A hooded aunt stumbled back, and Dorothy bolted.

She didn't look back. She didn't know how far she was from the manor. The maze twisted tighter around her with every step, hedges blurring into walls, each turn indistinguishable from the last. Panic beat in her chest. Her lungs scraped for air. Everything smelled like smoke.

She skidded to a stop. A statue loomed where the path ended. Cracked and weatherworn, the woman stared through the leaves, her face half-sunk into moss, her arms broken off. Dorothy remembered this place from the auction. And last time a hidden path had appeared.

She rushed toward it. "Please." She pressed the hedge. "Please let me through."

She shoved her hands into the hedge. Leaves shredded beneath her nails, and blood slicked her palms. Thorns raked her cheeks, vines snagging in her hair as she ducked low, forcing her body into the tangled green. Branches snapped against her ribs. She clawed forward, blind and breathless—until a hand closed around her ankle. It yanked her back through the thicket and slammed her into the dirt. The impact knocked the wind from her. Gasping, she looked up.

Maeve loomed over her, framed by smoke and flame, her eyes burning brighter than the fires eating through the maze.

"I told you," she said. "There's no running from this."

Dorothy scrambled backward, colliding with the statue behind her—but Maeve caught her by the wrist. Agony ripped through her arm. Maeve's grip burned like molten iron, her hand glowing with a sick, searing light. Dorothy cried out, twisting, struggling to wrench free, but the pain only deepened, radiating up her shoulder, flooding her nerves like wildfire. The scent of scorched flesh filled her nose. She clawed at Maeve's fingers, but they held fast, branding her like a mark meant to last.

"Please, please stop!" she sobbed, as her body shook. "STOP!"

Maeve leaned in. "This is what happens when you run."

Maeve yanked her upright, and Dorothy stumbled, her feet dragging through mud and ash. Smoke curled into her eyes, her mouth, searing the inside of her lungs. The maze twisted around them—walls of bramble flashing past in a blur of green and flame. Everything narrowed to the crack of burning leaves, the hiss of fire, and the brutal grip on her arm. Her breath hitched in ragged sobs. She didn't have the strength to scream anymore.

The path gave way to the clearing with the gazebo. Aiden stood inside a ring of fire, his eyes locking onto hers the moment Maeve threw her to the scorched earth. Around them, the matriarchy emerged from the shadows as if they'd been waiting. On the far side of the clearing, Irene lay crumpled, her gown singed and clinging in blackened shreds. The dark brown hair she always kept perfectly pinned had fallen loose, streaked with ash and tangled in soot.

Veronica knelt beside her, her hands hovering, uncertain where to land. "Mother," she whispered. "Please…say you're still here."

But Irene didn't move.

CHAPTER 67
Declan Albatross

WHEN IT HAPPENED, THERE WAS NO LIGHT WAITING AT THE END OF A tunnel. No gateway to Heaven. No descent into Hell. The cosmos remained silent, offering neither answers nor revelations, no divine epiphany to soothe the ache of mortality. Even the mythic ferryman, was absent. No boat, no river, no coins to pay for the passage. Declan floated in the void, untethered and weightless, where time had unraveled into meaningless fragments. Thoughts once tainted with guilt, despair, and hope dissolved into a stillness that was neither peaceful nor terrifying. It simply was.

From this, a sound emerged.

A melody.

It came like a whisper across an endless sea.

The siren's call.

It held no cruelty, nor mercy.

Only age, existing beyond mortal notions of comfort or forlornness. It pulled at him, subtle yet inescapable, dragging him toward a horizon that defied shape or meaning.

He saw nothing. But he felt it.

Cold, vast, infinite.

The void wasn't empty.

It waited.
Waited for him.

CHAPTER 68
Dorothy Hale

SHE HAD ALWAYS IMAGINED DEATH AS AN ACHE ARRIVING AFTER A LIFE full of memories. After love, after growing old in the arms of someone who knew her name by heart. She had never imagined it in a burning cradle of earth, with smoke in her lungs and strangers waiting for her end. Not while the night held stars she hadn't seen, and moments of her life were still unwritten.

Tears burned her vision, heat swelling in her as she forced herself to lift her head. Aiden looked ready to fight the world, though there wasn't much he could do from where he stood. Beyond him, Irene lay, her once-imposing figure slack and lost to soot and burns. Veronica knelt beside her, whispering words Dorothy couldn't hear. Maybe her name. Maybe a spell. Or maybe goodbye.

The matriarchy waited like soldiers in front of Maeve, their cloaks billowing in the heat.

A sob choked in Dorothy's throat but never made it past her lips. It sat there as her thoughts cracked open with flashes of tender things. Her parents the day she left for Driftmoor, her mother's coat flaring in the wind, her father pretending not to cry. Camille twirling under the chandelier and Jack leaning, eyes crinkled in the way they did when he looked at her. There'd be no future birthdays. No first apartment.

No falling asleep to someone who made her feel safe. Would anyone know? Or would she become a cautionary tale, a missing girl folded into town gossip until even her name lost meaning?

Her fingers found the rosary tangled beneath the shredded neckline of her dress, the beads cool against her scorched skin.

Maeve stepped through the smoke, her silhouette blurred by the haze. "You look like her," she said, almost to herself. "The same way she looked at me, just before it all unraveled."

Dorothy crawled backward, every movement scraping fresh pain across her shredded arms. Blood mixed with dirt, and the skin at her wrist throbbed where Maeve's grip had scorched her.

"She begged, too."

The rosary beads dug into Dorothy's skin, but she didn't pray. She didn't even look at Maeve. The life she was about to lose kindled inside her—faint at first, like the strike of a match. Then it caught. Not with grief. She was done grieving. Not with fear. She'd spent too long cowering in its shadow. It was anger. Rising, blistering, absolute. Anger at the world. At herself. At every turn that had led her here. For the choices ripped from her hands. For a life shaped by others without her consent. For the girl they tried to silence before she could speak.

Maeve raised her hand, flame pooling in her palm like molten gold.

A fracture split open inside Dorothy. Not clean, but slow and splintering. Darkness bled through the fracture. It coiled around her heart, climbed up her throat. The rosary slipped from her hands. Her fingers dug into dirt. And she screamed.

The air buckled. Then came the scream's aftermath—a concussive wave that slammed outward. Fire vanished on contact. Smoke shot upward in a spiraling column, sucked by the vacuum of pressure, while leaves and ash pulled toward her. Aunts fell to their knees, veils torn from their hair, hands clutching their skulls as if the sound had torn straight through bone. Nearby, Veronica hunched over Irene, shielding her body. Maeve was thrown backward, striking the ground with a sickening crack, rolling once before going still.

The scream raked through the trees, snapping branches. Hedges lining the clearing howled and leaned away. Far beyond, windows at Oldwyck Manor burst in a glittering shatter.

Aiden stood at the heart of it, arms raised. His eyes shone with awe and dread.

Dorothy collapsed. Her lungs scraped for air, her throat shredded raw. Ash clouded her vision. Blackened leaves drifted through the haze like dying stars. Women lay scattered across the clearing, bloodied, stunned, some weeping into the earth. Their cries were fractured pleas, caught in throats too raw to release them.

"Run!" Aiden's voice tore through the smoke. He stood amid the flames, embers licking at his boots.

Dorothy forced herself upright. Every limb screamed. Her body felt like glass held together by breath alone. Through the smoke, she saw Maeve sprawled near the gazebo's wreckage, cloak tangled in soot, hair clumped with ash. But she was moving. Rising. Some of the aunts were stirring now too, blinking through debris, helping one another up with stunned silence clinging to their movements.

And beneath it all, came a sound that wasn't human.

Three hellhounds stepped through the ruined hedges. They moved like smoke made flesh, muscle and bone draped in seething black fur. Their eyes burned red, molten with purpose as every step scorched the ground beneath them. Sulfur curled off their breath. One snarled, lips back to reveal fangs.

"Kill her!" Maeve shrieked. "Protect your mothers. Kill the girl!"

The hounds snapped forward.

Dorothy was thrown back against a charred hedge, bark burning into her skin. Her hands flew up, but there was nothing to protect her.

"Please." Her voice sounded unfamiliar to her. It was so small.

They halted mid-pounce, muscles tight, fangs inches away from her face. Their glowing eyes locked on hers, unblinking. Not wild. Not rabid. But focused. One by one, their heads bowed. Dorothy blinked once. Twice. But they stayed. Kneeling. A breath caught in her chest.

Across the clearing, silence fell.

"What are they doing?" Maeve's voice cracked through the smoke. "Obey me!"

But the hounds did not move. The matriarchy stood in stunned stillness. No one reached for a weapon. No magic stirred the air. Maeve took a single step back, hand fumbling for the arm of the woman beside her. A veil drifted loose in the wind. Veronica remained hunched over Irene, but her gaze was also fixed on the hellhounds.

Maeve looked at them. Then at Dorothy. Her laugh was dry and brittle. "They serve us," she muttered, not to anyone in particular. "Our blood. Our command." Her ash-rimmed eyes narrowed. "And now they kneel for a banshee."

No one answered. The wind had picked up, rustling through scorched branches and curling smoke into shapes. Dorothy hadn't moved. She couldn't. A force was slithering inside her, alive and ancient and terrible. Not rage, not fear, but power, deep in her like the scream's aftershock.

The hellhounds were waiting for her.

CHAPTER 69
Aiden Oldwyck

THE FLAMES FROM THE RING OF FIRE LICKED AT HIS SKIN.

Aiden didn't understand what was happening, but he could read the stillness in the matriarchy's face, the flicker of fear in Meave's eyes. Whatever this was, it wasn't in their favor. Maybe that's why the hellhound had led him here. Because it knew Dorothy would need help. She looked wrecked. Her breath came in shallow bursts, her face streaked with soot, blood, and sweat. And yet she stood. And the hellhounds stood with her.

Across the clearing, his eyes snapped to his mother. She hadn't moved. Her body lay crumpled in the dirt, limbs twisted, hair matted with ash and streaks of red.

"Mom!" he shouted, voice breaking. "Get up, please! I need you!"

Maeve's head snapped toward him. "Hush!" she barked, then turned back toward Dorothy and the kneeling hounds. "This…this won't do."

She stepped forward through the smoke. Around her, the other aunts lingered in a loose uncertain ring, their gazes darting between Maeve and the hellhounds, unsure who was in control anymore.

Maeve lifted her hand. Fire swelled to life in her palm and coiled into a long, snaking whip. She cracked it through the air. The flame met the nearest hound, only to collapse into smoke on contact. A paw slashed out and four deep gashes bloomed across Maeve's cheek

She staggered back with a guttural cry. Several aunts recoiled.

And then rustling.

Irene rose, slowly. Her dress clung to her in tatters, arms blackened with burns, blood trailing down her temple. Veronica reached to steady her, but Irene pushed her off, eyes locked on the hellhounds.

"By nature," she rasped, "banshees are heralds of death."

The clearing fell silent.

"Hellhounds may serve the matriarchy," she went on, "but above all, they are guardians. They protect death when death is righteous. They are not our beasts. They are not mindless. They remember what we tried to forget."

She turned toward Dorothy. "In a sense…they are a pair. A balance."

Maeve let out a brittle laugh. "Do you hear her?" she spat. "Irene's lost her mind. The hounds have been ours for centuries."

A few aunts clung to the thought. But others faltered. Doubt moved through them as they processed what was unfolding.

Irene straightened. "You should read your history, sister. Yes, the hounds came to us after Selene's bargain. But banshees were here long before that. We silenced them. We buried them. But they never left."

Maeve's eyes narrowed to slits. Fire built in her hands. She hurled it.

Irene moved like lightning. She stepped in front of Dorothy and swept her arm up—deflecting the fireball with a sharp motion. It shat-tered against her hand, embers skittering into the dirt.

Maeve's face twisted. "You'd turn against your own?"

"I'm not turning," Irene said. "I'm remembering. The matriarchy was built for survival. Not domination. We were meant to live a better life, not rule through fear."

Maeve's eyes cut to Aiden.

"It doesn't matter," she said. "None of this will save him."

Her stare settled over him, the pleasure in her eyes making his stomach turn.

"That much, you're right about," Irene said. "The hellhounds will come for him. That has not changed."

Aiden felt it then. A throb a panic, low and cold.

Maeve tilted her head. "And you—" she sneered at Irene. "You knew this. And you still hesitated. You thought you could fight fate?"

"No," Irene said, calmly. "I knew you'd twist the truth. You always have. So I made a choice."

Maeve's smirk faltered. "What choice?"

"You can't undo a deal," Irene whispered. "But a mother's love created this curse. And only a mother's love can end it."

Her hand slipped beneath her cloak.

A glint of silver.

"No," Aiden breathed.

"Mother, stop!" Veronica cried.

But Irene had already turned the blade.

With a single breath, she drove it into her chest.

Gasps broke through the clearing. Time seemed to fracture.

Blood spilled down the front of Irene's dress, crimson on gray. She didn't cry. She didn't fall. Instead, her eyes searched through the haze of the fire and smoke until they landed on Aiden. Her lips parted. Not in agony, but in peace. She reached for him, fingers trembling, painting the air red. And even as her knees gave out, her gaze never left him.

"Aiden," she whispered.

He read her lips before he heard the word.

"I love you."

The world tilted. Something sparked in him, like an ember catching flame, flaring through his blood. The ring of fire collapsed inward. Smoke turned white-hot, blinding. A wave of light burst outward from him. Braziers exploded skyward in geysers of fire. Screams erupted around the clearing as aunts stumbled, shielding their faces. Some ran away. Maeve's smug mask shattered.

And through it all, Irene smiled. Bloodied. Dying. But proud.

CHAPTER 70
Dorothy Hale

BLOOD SEEPED INTO THE SOIL, SPREADING IN JAGGED VEINS THAT darkened the dirt. The hellhounds encircled around Irene, silent and watchful beneath the flickering firelight. Dorothy stood frozen, her breath shallow. Her gaze moved between Irene and Aiden, who had fallen to his knees. She opened her mouth, then closed it. There was too much grief in the air. Too much heat. Too many things that couldn't be undone.

Veronica dropped to the ground beside her mother with a strangled gasp. "No, no, no—" Her hands hovered helplessly, unsure where to press, what to hold, how to stop the blood from spreading. "You weren't supposed to—" she choked out, but Irene's fingers gave the faintest gesture like a hush.

"You should've let me help," Veronica whispered, her voice cracking. "We could've done this together."

Across the clearing, Maeve's voice rang out, cracked with urgency. "Veronica! We need to go. Now."

But Veronica didn't move. "No," she said, barely more than a breath. "I won't leave her."

Maeve was already moving, her cloak whispering through the scorched air. She slowed as she reached Irene's side and stood there for a moment, gaze unreadable. She murmured words too soft to catch, then straightened. Her eyes found Aiden's.

"I knew," she said, voice low. "I knew you'd always ruin her."

Then she grabbed Veronica's arm, yanking her away from the goodbye she didn't get to finish.

"Mother!" Veronica's voice cracked, part sob, part scream.

In a rush of fire, they vanished. One by one, the rest of the matriarchy followed. Some left without hesitation. Others paused at the edge of the clearing, casting final, uncertain glances toward Irene. Regret shimmered in a few expressions, but none stayed. The flames swallowed them all, until the only ones left were Dorothy, Aiden, the hellhounds, and the woman who tried to end a curse with love.

Aiden crawled to his mother, crumpling beside her. He reached for her hand and folded it gently in both of his. "Why?" His voice cracked. "Why did you do this?"

Her fingers stirred against his. Her lips barely moved. "Please, button…don't be angry."

He dropped his head. Tears cut through the soot on his cheeks. "How can you say that? You're—you're dying."

A faint smile touched her mouth. "Yes," she whispered. "I had gathered as much. But you—you'll be fine. You always were."

Dorothy took a step forward, then stopped. This moment didn't belong to her. Not to interrupt. Not to fix. Ash drifted around her like black snow. The clearing smelled of blood and smoke, and something older than both, like power.

Aiden looked up at her, his eyes red-rimmed and glassy. "Go," he said. "You don't need to stay. I nearly got you killed."

Her lips parted. "I—I can stay, if you want."

"You're hurt," he said quietly. "You should go."

"But—"

"It's fine." His voice wavered, but the meaning held.

This wasn't her burden to carry. Her battle was elsewhere, just beginning. She swallowed the knot in her throat and stepped back. The hellhounds moved aside to let her pass. One turned its head as she walked by, watching her with eyes like burning coal. At the clearing's edge, she paused. Behind her, Aiden remained kneeling, his head bowed over his mother's hand. Holding on to whatever time was left. A child cradling the one person who had tried to hold his world together.

CHAPTER 71
Aiden Oldwyck

HIS MOTHER'S BLOOD SOAKED HIS HANDS, SEEPING INTO THE CREASES of his palms like permanent ink. He cradled her in his lap, arms wrapped around her as if he could shield her from death. But the weight he held wasn't just her body. It was every bedtime story she told to keep the monsters at bay. Every warning she didn't give, every truth she swallowed. She had been a mother. His knight in shining armor. The architect of his safety. And now she felt like none of that as stillness crept into her limbs.

"I don't understand," he said. "Why? Was this your plan all along?"

Irene's eyelids fluttered. "A mother's love," she whispered, "is stronger than any bargain." Her breath hitched. "No curse. No entity. Nothing could keep me from giving you a future." She exhaled, a breath so shallow it nearly vanished into the air. "That's all I ever wanted."

"A future doesn't matter," he choked. "Not if you're not in it."

Her fingers twitched like she meant to reach for him but no longer had the strength.

"Even when the world forgets my name," she said, eyes unfocused, "you'll find me…in the hush between heartbeats…in the warmth that lingers, even after the light is gone." Her lips curved into the smallest smile. "I'll be there. Still loving you."

He buried his face into her shoulder, trying to hold on to the warmth that tethered him to anything real. "Why didn't you just tell me?" he said. "Why didn't you say this was the plan?"

"Because," she said. "I needed you to live."

"I can't—" His voice broke. "I can't lose you. Please."

A cough shook her ribs. Her breath rattled.

"Under a marked floorboard," she whispered. "In my bedroom…a letter."

Confusion flashed across his face. He shook his head, brows creased. "What? What letter?"

But her eyes were already drifting. Her gaze searched his face, as if stitching him into memory one final time. "Show them," she murmured, "what I already know…" A faint tremor passed through her fingers. "You were never meant to be small."

Her hand slipped from his cheek.

"No." The word fractured on his lips. "Mom…"

The scream that tore from him reverberated through the scorched maze and the silence. The hellhounds lifted their heads and howled a broken hymn of mourning. Their voices rose in unison as if answering his pain with their own.

Her soul had already gone where he couldn't follow.

CHAPTER 72
Dorothy Hale

The woods stretched ahead, each tree a sentinel against a sky drained of stars. Dorothy ran, legs burning, her entire body screaming for stillness, but the instinct to stop never came. A root snagged at her ankle and sent her tumbling forward. She caught herself, but not without scraping her palms. Maeve's grip throbbed on her arm. The matriarchy's chanting echoed in her skull. She blinked her tears, trying to force her mind back to rationality.

A twig cracked.

Dorothy whipped around, eyes darting through the dark.

"Dorothy…"

The sound was soft.

"Dorothy…"

Closer. And when she turned again, Jack stepped through the mist. Relief crashed into her so hard she nearly wept.

"Jack?" she cried, stumbling forward, arms outstretched.

But he stepped back. She stopped short, confusion rooting in her. He wasn't smiling or moving. And in the light, his face looked off.

"What's wrong?" she whispered.

Behind her, the forest rustled. Twigs snapped, footsteps pounded through the brush.

"Dorothy!"

Camille burst into the clearing, costume torn and hair wild. Blood crusted her shoulder. She looked like a disaster and a miracle all at once.

Dorothy gasped, stumbling to her. "Camille, oh my god!"

She threw her arms around her, clutching tight. Her body shook with sobs.

"I thought you were dead," she said. "I thought—I thought—"

"I'm okay." Camille held her. "I'm here. I've got you."

Dorothy pulled back. "Wait. You should be in the hospital. Your driver—"

"We can talk later. We need to get you out of here."

Dorothy swallowed the quake in her chest. She looked back at Jack and made a face. "Jack, what were you doing out here?"

"Who are you talking to?" Camille asked.

"What do you mean?" She gestured to him. "Jack."

Camille followed her gaze, her brows knitting. "Dorothy. There's no one there."

Dorothy laughed weakly. "Okay, very funny."

But Jack wasn't smiling. He wasn't reacting at all.

She forced a smile, though her flingers clenched at her dress. "Jack, why aren't you saying anything?"

He shifted, meeting her gaze. "I don't think she can see me."

Dorothy stared at him, unblinking. She turned to Camille, who looked at her like she was breaking. Or had already broken.

"What?" Dorothy shook her head. "How don't you see him? He's right there." She turned to Jack again. "You're right here."

Hesitantly, she lifted her hand toward him. Jack's hand twitched, rising to meet hers, but her fingers passed through empty space. No warmth. No pressure. No life. Dread slammed into her. She trembled as she reached again, but still, nothing.

"I..." Dorothy stuttered. "I don't understand."

Jack hesitated before his expression fractured. "I died, Dorothy. During surgery. I didn't make it."

"No," she said. "No, that's not—You were—you were fine. We talked. We danced. You—"

Her thoughts scrambled, looping images on a reel:

Jack in the hospital before anyone knew she was there.

Jack at the Halloween party, appearing and vanishing without reason.

Jack, who never spoke to anyone else. Only her.

"No. No, no, no…"

She hit the earth hard, her palms sinking into the dirt, tears carving paths through the grime on her cheeks. Jack reached for her like he could help. But he couldn't.

"I'm so sorry," he said. "I wanted to tell you…but I didn't know how."

Camille stayed beside her, looking at Dorothy with a mixture of pity and empathy. She wasn't even sure who she mourned anymore. Jack. Herself. Or the life she knew.

EPILOGUE
November

When the harvest is done and the veil has thinned, the old bargains stir in the roots of the land. What was promised must be answered. What was buried must rise.
—*Words scratched into the walls of the chapel, author unknown*

CHAPTER 73
Lola Godfrey

She hadn't slept in days.

The armchair beside Declan's hospital bed had shaped itself to her, threadbare upholstery pressing into her knees, the wooden arms bruising her elbows. A novel lay open across her lap, but the words dissolved into meaningless ink. She hadn't turned a page in hours. Declan looked almost peaceful, but he lacked color. His mouth was too slack. And the rise and fall of his chest had become her entire world. Each breath was proof he hadn't vanished. Each time his eyelashes fluttered, she braced herself. For what, she didn't know. Maybe for the moment when he didn't wake up.

The doctor had explained that hydration would help flush the sero-tonin from his system. He said it in way people talk when they've been trained to soften tragedy. He mentioned heart rates, reflexes, blood oxygen. She'd nodded through it, pretending she understood. But all that mattered was that Declan had taken nearly sixty pills. Pills she hadn't even known he was on.

Three days passed since they pulled him from the ocean.

Three days of watching that jug of water sit untouched on the table, the supposed solution to a crisis she hadn't seen coming. The signs were there, in the disinterest behind his laugh, in the way his hands trembled when he thought no one noticed. In the distance between them, that had nothing to do with Ophelia. She'd been too busy performing. Layering on lipstick, holding her chin high, insisting she'd moved on. Waging battles in ballrooms, trying to prove she could win. She tried to win arguments that didn't matter while he was losing a battle she never thought to ask about.

Declan stirred, his brows pulling together before he blinked against the light. "What time is it?"

"Noon." She grabbed the water, poured a glass and pressed it into his hands. "Take it slow."

He lifted it with shaking fingers and drank in careful sips, then placed it down.

"Where's Aiden?"

"He left a few hours ago. The funeral's today."

A shadow passed over his face. "I forgot about that. I should be there," he said. "Ugh…I said something shitty to him on Halloween."

"You can't. He knows that," she said gently, worried that if she spoke any louder, it might break him. "And whatever you said, I'm sure he'll forgive you. He always does."

She could've stopped there and let him drift back to sleep. But the question had been pressing at her chest for days, and if she didn't ask, she never would.

"Declan." She folded back the novel's edge. "Why didn't you tell me about the pills?"

His fingers tensed against the blanket, then loosened. "Because… it wasn't a thing I wanted anyone to know about."

"Did you think I'd judge you?"

"No," he said. "I just wanted to pretend I was healthy, and not falling apart. But I guess that wasn't the best approach."

Lola blinked against a sting. "I should've known you were hurting. And this journal, I—"

His gaze sharpened in a way that twisted her stomach. "Please don't. You couldn't have known. Not even Aiden. Maybe my mother would've seen it. If she were…there."

"Still. I wish I'd ask how you were doing once in a while instead of obsessing over things that won't even matter a year from now, like queen of the Founders' Ball."

"It's fine, really." He turned toward the ceiling. "It's not your job to catch me falling."

Lola's fingers curled into the chair. "I know. But I want to be the person you could come to about these things. That's all."

He leaned back against the pillows and closed his eyes.

"Your mother was around," she added after a pause. "I think she's deciding whether to go to the funeral. It was nice seeing her out of Albatross House for once."

He nodded faintly.

"Are you hungry?"

He shook his head, hands resting on his lap like he didn't know what to do with them.

Lola stood, her joints stiff. She stepped into the hallway, the light feeling too bright after the hush of his room. As soon as the door clicked shut, she leaned against the wall. She brought a hand to her mouth to muffle whatever sound tried to escape. Crying wouldn't change a thing.

A few breaths. One hand to smooth her dress. Shoulders back.

By the time she entered the lobby, she looked composed. Ophelia sat alone near a sun-washed window, a scarf around her neck, her hand clenched in her lap. She looked like a statue an artist had forgotten to finish, elegant but cracked. Lola crossed the room and sat beside her.

"How is he?" Ophelia's voice was quiet, eyes beyond the glass.

"Stable."

Between them, a neglected snake plant sat on the table.

"You can go see him," Lola said, crossing one leg over the other. "He's awake."

A dry laugh escaped Ophelia. "I'm not so sure he wants to see me. Ever."

"Maybe. Maybe not."

She turned, eyebrows raised. "You're impossible, you know that?"

"And you're still dramatic," Lola murmured, dragging a finger along the seam of the chair cushion. "Some things don't change."

Ophelia huffed out a breath but didn't argue. For a moment, the silence was unsteady. "Heather told me what happened," she said finally. "In the maze."

Lola's hand stilled. "Did she now?"

"She told me how that thing attacked you. How you healed." A pause. "Like you did when you fell from Silver Shoals."

"You mean after you pushed me off?"

Their eyes locked. The moment held, taut and wordless.

"How did Heather remember anything?" Lola asked. "She told me she didn't."

"She remembered," Ophelia said, her voice softer now. "At first."

"You did something to her. Didn't you?" Lola's voice dropped. "You made her forget."

Ophelia's fingers found a loose thread on her scarf. She wound it tight. "I didn't leave Driftmoor because I wanted to go to ballet school," she said. "I left because…things were changing. With me."

Lola couldn't tell if what rose in her chest was fear or fury. "What kind of things?"

Silence.

"Ophelia," she said, low. "What the hell are you?"

No answer. Just the faint sound of footsteps down the hall. The receptionist on a phone call.

"And why now?" Lola asked. "Why tell me this?"

"I figured," Ophelia said, barely looking at her, "if I know your secret, you should know mine. Best friends forever, right?"

Lola started to speak, but movement caught her eye. The snake plant stirred. Its withered leaves unfurled, a new green bleeding into the brittle edges. Life returning where there had been none. By the time she turned back, the chair across from her was empty.

CHAPTER 74
Aiden Oldwyck

His fingertips hovered over the envelope. The paper felt like petals left in the sun. The silence in Irene's bedroom pressed at his skin like a hand on the shoulder. She remained everywhere. The pillows remained fluffed. Her reading glasses, perched beside a romance novel she'd never finish. The air held traces of her perfume—orange blossom and clove, the scent of evenings spent in her sitting room and chess games on the loggia. The past few days twisted into surreal and unbearable memory. Declan at St. Augustine. Fire devouring the maze, turning his backyard to smoke and screams. Magic awak-ening within him. And Irene, unyielding even in her final moments. And now this. A boy too young for this much grief and too old to hide from it.

A portrait hung above the fireplace: Irene, holding him as an infant, her eyes shining with a devotion he'd taken for granted. It hurt to look, the image another reminder of all he'd lost. He knelt before the hearth, fingers brushing over the engraved floorboard. Carefully, he unfolded the letter, heart aching at her handwriting.

My dearest Guinevere,

Twenty-three years later, and your art still leaves me breathless.

This wasn't for him.

Isn't it strange how swiftly life passes, how choices we make with abso-lute certainty come to haunt us when we're left alone with our thoughts? If you're reading this, I'm no longer here, and for that, I'm sorry. Not for my absence, but for every way I failed you before it came to this. My greatest regret was never the power I chased or the legacy I upheld. It was turning away from you when I had the chance to choose differently. And I wonder, in my weakest moments, if things would have been different. If I would have been different.

I hope our children choose more wisely than we did.

Love always,

—I

Her words sliced through him. This wasn't a confession. It was a truth she had tucked away where no one could judge her for it. He reached into the compartment and discovered a bundle of photo-graphs—photos of Irene in a Driftmoor uniform, her hair longer, her smile freer. In one, she stood beside another girl, their arms wrapped around each other like a secret they hadn't learned how to hide.

Gwen Croft. Heather's mother.

His mother had carried a love she had hidden from everyone, including him. He traced the photograph, absorbing every detail of her smile, the way she leaned into Gwen. He tried to imagine that version of her. Hopeful and believing she had time. A time before she chose duty over happiness, before life had carved her into some-one who guarded every secret. Tears blurred the picture. Not just for her death, but for the pieces of herself she had surrendered. For every moment she'd never shared with him. For the love she'd hidden under a floorboard.

The letter crumpled in his grasp as he pulled it closer. He sank to the floor, her voice echoing around him. The voice that once said: *stand straight, articulate, and never let them see you afraid.*

If he had known this part of her—this softness, this sorrow—would he have understood her more? Would he have saved her?

In the quiet, he let himself crumble. Not because of weakness, but because she had trusted him with some truth. And even though she was gone, she had left behind everything she could. The rest was his to carry.

The Driftmoor Cemetery lay beneath a gray sky. Leaves skittered across the dull grass, catching on the edges of gravestones and statues. Aiden stood at the edge of the funeral. It unfolded in murmurs, words spoken like fragile offerings, but none of them reached him. It felt like someone had knocked him loose from his body and left him watching from the sidelines. Most believed Irene died in some sudden tragedy, but only the matriarchy, along with him and Veronica knew the truth.

His mother's coffin rested above the earth, swathed in maroon, too regal for a moment so absolute. He stared until the velvet disappeared, and he saw her standing in the gloom with her shoulders squared, eyes lit with that fierce, unwavering certainty. He had thought there would be more time to understand her. To prove he was strong enough to deserve her sacrifices. She used to say heartbreak was the price of love, but he hadn't known it would hurt like this.

Across the gathering, Heather stood beside her mother. Gwen clung to her wife Abigail, her grief uncontained. Her love for Irene seemed to carve into her from within. Heather stood motionless. Though the slight tremble of her fingers betrayed the depth of her confusion. Like Aiden, she'd been blind to the truth binding their mothers.

Further off, Veronica stood apart. She didn't look at the coffin. Nor at Aiden. She hadn't returned home since the fire, and she hadn't responded to his calls. He sensed Maeve's hold on her, an invisible chain pulling tighter by the day.

Beyond a statue of a weeping angel, a man in black emerged, his face obscured by the brim of his hat. Without thinking, Aiden moved toward him, cutting through bowed heads and sobs. When he reached him, they fell into an embrace that was desperate and trembling with apology.

"Please," Reginald said. "Please don't hate me. I'm so sorry I wasn't here sooner."

Anger and longing warred within Aiden. He wanted to demand answers to every question he'd been denied. But grief dulled his bitterness as he replied, "I could never hate you."

Reginald gripped his shoulders. "I wanted to keep you safe. Your mother protected me from Maeve, from all of them. Without her..." He faltered. "Listen. You can leave this behind. Come with me. Start over somewhere far from Driftmoor."

Aiden imagined a life far away. A place untouched by curses or shadows. Somewhere his ancestors couldn't reach. But his mother's final words echoed. She hadn't died so he could run. She'd given him a chance to stand firm and to choose differently than she had. Even if it meant facing the darkness head on.

"I can't," he said. "I owe it to her."

Reginald's face softened. They embraced again, and Aiden held on. Determination ignited within him. Irene had faced her fate without flinching. He couldn't dishonor her by running away.

When he returned to the graveside, the prayers had ended. Across the coffin, Maeve stood beside Veronica, lips close to her ears. His stomach twisted. He had already lost his mother. Had he lost his sister too? He searched her face the girl he'd grown up with, but her expression remained unreadable.

A hand brushed against his before fingers intertwined with his.

"Hey," Noah said.

Aiden turned. "You came."

"How could I not?" Noah's gaze met his. He tightened his grip, anchoring Aiden to the moment.

Heather's attention drifted toward them, gaze landing on their hands. Her eyes widened, then softened into a grief that belonged only to her. She drew her arms in, as if bracing against a feeling no one else saw. A pang of guilt tightened inside him. She had lost something too. Him.

But in Noah's touch was warmth. Tentative. Steady. Hope.

And for the first time in days, Aiden let himself feel it.

CHAPTER 75
Dorothy Hale

Dorothy's fingers tightened around the bouquet of daisies she'd picked from a florist on Galleon's Wharf. The simple cross bearing Jack and Elliot's names loomed stark against the sky. It was more than a marker for the deaths it commemorated. It marked a fracture, a night she'd spent weeks running from. Her knees pressed into the dirt as she placed the daisies down. How many times had she passed this road, pretending it wasn't there, that it had nothing to do with her? She'd spent every waking moment running from Elliot's death, from what she was, from the truth she didn't dare speak. She'd fought so hard to reclaim a version of herself that no longer existed. Maybe that was the point. Maybe Dorothy Hale had died that night, and Dorothy Marek had taken her place.

A gust stirred the fallen leaves, whispering through the trees.

"Dorothy."

Jack stood a few feet away, hair catching the last light of the day. He looked the same. Almost. But he cast no shadow.

She lifted a hand halfway. "Hey."

He smiled. "Took you long enough."

"I meant to come sooner, but I just couldn't do it."

"It's okay. I understand."

Dorothy glanced toward the parked car. Through the windshield, Camille watched her. To anyone, Dorothy looked like a girl who was talking to the wind.

"It's not okay," she said. "I should've—"

Jack's brows drew together. "Don't. None of this was your fault."

But how could she believe that? Jack was dead. Elliot, dead. And she was suffering through every undeserved moment of survival.

"Why can I see you?" she asked. "Why me?"

Jack watched her, compassion etched in his gaze. "I don't know. I think you need to be the one to figure that out."

She hated that answer. Hated its vague truth and the fear it brought.

A noise in the underbrush pulled her attention. Elliot stepped out from the trees. The fading light rimmed his hair in gold. He looked as she remembered. Vibrant, glowing with quiet energy. But like Jack, he cast no shadow.

"Elliot?" she said.

He regarded her, his lips curving into a smile. Dorothy's knees weakened, tears blurring her vision as her mind struggled to accept what she saw.

Jack and Elliot exchanged a look before Elliot stepped closer. "Dorothy," he began, "there's something you deserve to know."

Anxiety closed tight around her. "What is it?"

Elliot's eyes clouded with a remembered pain. "The night of the crash…" He paused, choosing his words carefully. "It wasn't just an accident."

Dorothy's breath left her lungs. "What do you mean?"

His gaze lowered. "There was a sound. Right before I lost control. Like a high pitch scream. It came out of nowhere. And then…it hit me. My ears were ringing. I tried to steady the wheel, but it was like brain my just shut off."

Her mind reeled to the scream. Her scream. It had always been her.

She didn't need him to spell it out, the truth was carved in his gaze as guilt pooled inside her.

"Elliot, I—"

He shook his head. "It's not what you think. The scream didn't come from you."

"Then whose was it?"

He didn't answer. He didn't have to. Because the truth was already unraveling. It hadn't been hers. That scream had come from someone else. Someone like her. Another banshee.

CHAPTER 76
Declan Albatross

Declan couldn't remember the ambulance or the moment Lola pulled him back from the edge of death. What lingered were fragments. Hands gripping his shoulders. A needle sliding into his arm. Nurses restraining him as he tried to remove the IV. Voices calling his name, but always too far away. Reality and hallucination had blurred, and he'd lost track of which was which.

He remembered signing the form. The pen had slipped in his fingers. His signature bled across the paper in a shaky smudge. *Voluntary admission.* That was the phrase they used. A neat, clinical lie. Sign the form, they'd said, or we will. Signing only gave him the illusion of control.

Lola had stayed until the end. She hadn't cried or begged him to reconsider. But she'd looked at him like she was afraid if she blinked, he might disappear. Before leaving, she said one thing: *I'll be here.*

The wheelchair groaned as the nurse pushed him down a series of badged-locked corridors. Each buzz of a door unlocking sent panic down his spine. He should've felt emotions about this. Relief. Fear. Anger. But emptiness consumed him opening a void where a part of him had been.

The final doors read *Bishop Five Wing.* The name flaked off the plate. Declan wondered if Bishop had been a patient or a doctor. Maybe someone wealthy enough to be remembered in paint. The doors opened on a ward with low ceilings and linoleum floors that glowed under the lights. Two nurses held the doors open. They exchanged a snarky look with the nurse pushing him. A prickle of unease crept his spine. *They always look at you like that. Like you're broken.*

A counter sat at the center where nurses typed on computers and scribbled on charts, their faces lit by pale blue monitors. Beyond them, a common room lay empty. A muted nature documentary played on the television. A lion prowled through tall grass, silent and slow.

The nurse wheeled him to a room halfway down the hall. She opened the door and nodded toward the far bed. "This is you."

A twin bed. A dresser. A nightstand too small to hold anything meaningful. The other half was already lived in. Sheets were unmade, a paperback face-down on the nightstand. Declan didn't speak. He moved to the bed and sat. Everyone had said this was his decision. That he'd chosen to get help. But it didn't feel like help. It felt like being buried alive in fluorescent light.

The nurse left without another word. The door shut behind her.

Declan leaned back on the bed and folded the pillow beneath his head. It was thin and rough, the fabric itchy against his cheek. The room's faint hum pressed in.

A hard object jabbed into his palm.

He flinched and reached. His fingers closing around leather that was worn and familiar.

The journal.

His heart stuttered.

He'd thought it was gone. Thought the sea had swallowed it when he fell in. He sat up and set it on his lap. The leather was warm in contrast to the room's cold air. He opened the cover. A new page waited with his name. Scrawled again and again in wet bloodred ink.

Declan. Declan. Declan.

Footsteps echoed in the hall. He looked up, clutching the journal against his chest.

The nurse appeared in the doorway. She stared, her eyes too knowing.

And then she raised a finger to her lips.